THE U
IN F

From magical tales of distant worlds to stories of those with abilities beyond the ordinary, Ace and Roc have everything you need to stretch your imagination to its limits.

Marion Zimmer Bradley/Diana L. Paxson

Guy Gavriel Kay

Dennis L. McKiernan

Patricia A. McKillip

Robin McKinley

Sharon Shinn

Katherine Kurtz

Barb and J. C. Hendee

Elizabeth Bear

T. A. Barron

Brian Jacques

Robert Asprin

M12G1107

Ace Books by Dawn Cook

The Truth Series

FIRST TRUTH
HIDDEN TRUTH
FORGOTTEN TRUTH
LOST TRUTH

The Princess Series

THE DECOY PRINCESS
PRINCESS AT SEA

hidden truth

Dawn Cook

ACE BOOKS, NEW YORK

THE BERKLEY PUBLISHING GROUP
Published by the Penguin Group
Penguin Group (USA) Inc.
375 Hudson Street, New York, New York 10014, USA
Penguin Group (Canada), 90 Eglinton Avenue East, Suite 700, Toronto, Ontario M4P 2Y3, Canada
(a division of Pearson Penguin Canada Inc.)
Penguin Books Ltd., 80 Strand, London WC2R 0RL, England
Penguin Group Ireland, 25 St. Stephen's Green, Dublin 2, Ireland (a division of Penguin Books Ltd.)
Penguin Group (Australia), 250 Camberwell Road, Camberwell, Victoria 3124, Australia
(a division of Pearson Australia Group Pty. Ltd.)
Penguin Books India Pvt. Ltd., 11 Community Centre, Panchsheel Park, New Delhi—110 017, India
Penguin Group (NZ), 67 Apollo Drive, Rosedale, North Shore 0632, New Zealand
(a division of Pearson New Zealand Ltd.)
Penguin Books (South Africa) (Pty.) Ltd., 24 Sturdee Avenue, Rosebank, Johannesburg 2196,
South Africa

Penguin Books Ltd., Registered Offices: 80 Strand, London WC2R 0RL, England

This is a work of fiction. Names, characters, places, and incidents either are the product of the author's imagination or are used fictitiously, and any resemblance to actual persons, living or dead, business establishments, events, or locales is entirely coincidental. The publisher does not have any control over and does not assume any responsibility for author or third-party websites or their content.

HIDDEN TRUTH

An Ace Book / published by arrangement with Cold Toast Writings, LLC.

PRINTING HISTORY
Ace mass-market edition / December 2002

ISBN: 978-0-441-01003-5

ACE
Ace Books are published by The Berkley Publishing Group,
a division of Penguin Group (USA) Inc.,
375 Hudson Street, New York, New York 10014.
ACE and the "A" design are trademarks of Penguin Group (USA) Inc.

PRINTED IN THE UNITED STATES OF AMERICA

15 14 13 12 11 10 9 8 7 6

For Tim

acknowledgments

I'd like to thank the core members of my writer's group, Nat for her above and beyond the call of duty critiques, my husband Tim for seeing it before I did, and of course, Richard Curtis and Anne Sowards.

Dawn Cook

I

Alissa crept up the stairway, her skirts gripped tightly in her fists. Gaze fixed upon the landing, she felt for the next step, easing herself up in what she hoped looked like casual disinterest. This was not a good idea, she thought. She had been making Bailic's meals all winter and knew risking his attention was asking for trouble. Taking a slow breath, she hesitated, the opposing feelings of curiosity and common sense teetering in her. Pulse quickening, she resumed her upward motion. Curiosity won. Not that that was a surprise, she admitted.

She had woken as usual before dawn, pulled from her warm covers by a feeling of discontent. There was nothing different she could see about today than yesterday. The sparrows still pecked on the rooftops of the Hold, the ice mist rose as the sky brightened in a false dawn, the fires needed tending, and the mice ran when she turned corners.

But an unexplained restlessness, an itching to do something, had filled her. Even worse, she was unable to tell what needed doing. It almost seemed she should have done it already, and the feeling of having been remiss tugged at her. This morning, as her feet touched the floor, a strange need to find out what Bailic wanted for breakfast filled her. It pulled her up the tower stairs when a healthy measure of caution urged her to go the other way, back down to the kitchen. Up until today, she hadn't cared if the madman liked what she made for his breakfast or not. And she said mad, for anyone who claimed ownership of the Hold, when it clearly wasn't his, had to be mad. The only reason she made Bailic's meals was to keep him out of her kitchen. But now it seemed as if knowing what he wanted might end her discontent.

Alissa drew to a stop as she realized her fingertips were tingling. She dropped her gathered skirts and stared at her hands, her disquiet growing. "By the Hounds of the Navigator," she whispered, opening and closing her hands. Her fingers only tingled when she was near a dangerous ward, and then it was painful, not this warm sensation. This felt more like . . .

"When I held my book of *First Truth*," she whispered in dismay, leaning back against the stone of the stairwell. A sound of self-disgust slipped from her. "Burn it to ash," she muttered. "Strell is going to have to pen me up like a nanny goat."

It was her book that had been filling her with this intolerable restlessness, enticing her to come and steal it back, not caring that if she were caught, Bailic would kill her. Last fall she had unknowingly followed its silent pull from her foothills farm across the mountains to the legendary Hold. Never would she have believed her papa's stories about the Hold were true and that her papa, Keeper Meson, had been anything other than the foothills farmer he had pretended to be.

Though she had found the Hold empty but for Bailic, a fallen Keeper, it had once been the home of the Masters, a race of winged scholars skilled in magic, posing as savage beasts called rakus. In return for small services and loyalty, the Masters taught a select group of people they called Keepers how to use their comparitively stunted magical abilities. The book of *First Truth* held the Masters' most powerful secrets. Now that all but one Master had been lured to their deaths by Bailic, the *First Truth* was possibly the only way to become a Keeper. And Bailic had taken it the moment she found it in the Hold's well, where her papa hid it fourteen years past.

She would sooner die than let Bailic keep it, but she wasn't going to steal it back today, and not under the guise of finding out what Bailic wanted for breakfast. That the fallen Keeper was going to use her book to put the foothills and plains at war seemed far away and distant next to her simple desire to possess its knowledge for herself. Her book was now resting in Bailic's chambers, as inaccessible as if it were at the bottom of the sea. But having touched it once, its pull upon her seemed all the stronger.

Alissa impatiently pushed her hair out of her eyes as she looked up the stairway, torn between being angry for not realizing why she was restless and being upset that she was so vulnerable to its call. "Maybe," she breathed, clenching her hands to try to drown out the tingling, "I'll ask Bailic what he wants for breakfast anyway, just to look at my book." She gathered her skirts and took a step, unable to help herself. "I won't go in. Just look at it through the doorway." The *First Truth* was rightfully hers. How dare Bailic, Keeper or not, claim it for himself. He couldn't even open it.

A muffled twittering came from the stairway below her. Heart pounding, she spun, embarrassed for having fallen victim to the book's call again so easily. Her kestrel, Talon, landed against the rough wall, gripping it awkwardly as the tight turn was too much to make in flight. Alissa's resolve faltered. Talon hated Bailic, often hissing and threatening violence when he was within earshot. Carrying on a conversation with Bailic, however stilted and contrived, would be impossible with her tiny defender near.

Her shoulders shifted, and she resolutely headed back to the kitchen. "Get off that wall," she said sourly as she passed the robin-sized bird, still hanging by her claws. "You look silly like that." The kestrel twittered and, as if understanding, half jumped to Alissa's shoulder. Alissa ran a finger over the bird's markings, now faded with age. Together they wound their silent way down to the first floor and the Hold's great hall. The room stretched high to make a cavernous space overlooked by the open balconies on the second, third, and fourth floors. Alissa's steps echoed against the barren walls. Passing through the empty, unused dining hall, she entered the Hold's smallest of two kitchens. It was still larger than her entire home in the foothills.

As she leaned to tend the long-burning fire, Talon jumped from her shoulder to land neatly on the chandelier. The metal and chain swung slightly, and the bird's head shifted to keep Alissa in focus. Alissa went back to the sweet-roll dough she had started earlier. She pushed the dough down with a growing feeling of discouragement. Knowing her book had lured her into risking her life to try to take it did nothing for her confidence. Even now, that same jittery feeling had begun to nag at her, urging her to rise back up the stairs again.

Alissa tucked a stray strand of hair back behind her ear as she glanced up at the kitchen's one narrow window high overhead. Closing her eyes, she took three slow breaths as taught by her papa, willing her restless emotions away. Her eyes opened. The gray patch of light was noticeably brighter. The sun would be up soon. She was going to be late to the practice room with Bailic's breakfast. Even worse, Strell hadn't come down for his meal yet and was going to be late as well.

Perhaps, she wondered, she ought to wake him? Flushing, she dusted the counter with flour and began coaxing the dough into a rectangle. Going to wake Strell wasn't prudent. The one time she had, she caught a glimpse of his uncovered feet. Bone and ash, she would have thought a well-bred plainsman would have the grace to sleep with his feet decently covered. She may as well have caught him naked in the rain. Perhaps it came from being a wandering piper for the last six years. But if he didn't come down soon, he was going to miss breakfast.

Deciding she couldn't wait any longer for Strell, she cut a slice of bread and set it over the fire to toast for her own breakfast. Talon shifted her feathers in an almost inaudible swish. "Why don't you go wake Strell?" she whispered, half serious, and the bird jumped to the rafters.

Thoughts of Strell pulled Alissa's eyes to the mirror. There was flour on her nose, and knowing Strell would tease her if he saw it, she hurriedly brushed it off. He had found the reflection glass weeks ago, propping it up in the kitchen with the claim it added to the light. She hadn't noticed any difference, but it did give her a good view of the dining hall when she was standing by the hearth with her back to the archway. The tall plainsman seemed to have taken it upon himself to see to her safety, something she insisted she could see to herself.

Squinting at her reflection, fuzzy in the predawn gloom, she gathered her straight, fair hair and retied the ribbon holding it back. Her hair was driving her to distraction as Strell refused to cut it, holding a true lady had hair she could sit on. It was a plains tradition, one she didn't subscribe to. She preferred it short, as her foothills papa had liked it. Her mother, though, would be pleased with its length. It was brushing the tops of her shoulders.

The small pouch hanging about her neck peeped from behind her shirt, and she nervously tucked it back, glancing behind her at the dining hall. She wasn't sure, but she thought the dust the sack held was her source, the sphere of power she found in her thoughts somewhere between her reality and imagination. One day she would use it and the silvery web she saw with her mind's eye to make wards. If Bailic knew what the pouch contained, she was sure he would take it, killing her with no more thought than he had killed her papa.

Alissa took a pained breath and resolutely pushed the memory of her papa to the back of her mind. He had died when she was five to prevent Bailic from discovering she existed. Bailic still didn't know whose daughter she was, and if he ever found out, her life wouldn't be worth the rolls she was making. Turning back to her dough, she spread a thin layer of honey across the even rectangle. Living with the danger for so long seemed to have dulled her fear of it.

A faint scent of char slipped into her musings. But it wasn't until Talon chittered that Alissa looked up from her dismal thoughts to find her breakfast burning. "By the Hounds!" she cried as she swung the toasting fork from the fire and vainly tried to brush the black scorch from the toast with a towel. Talon's chittering sounded like laughter, and Alissa gave up. Plucking the slice from the toasting fork, she tossed it clattering onto the waiting plate. Ruined. She stared at it, wondering if she ought to eat it anyway. The last time she refused to eat burnt toast, she was half a mountain away from her home when the sun had set. Omens were useless if ignored.

"Omens," she said with a soft scorn, glancing up and away from her bird. She didn't believe in such things. Alissa eyed Bailic's half-prepared breakfast tray, briefly entertaining the idea of giving the toast to him. Knowing it would result in a series of degrading, half-breed slurs, she rose to throw it away. She had the plate with its crusted char tipped over the slop bucket when Talon chittered a cheery greeting.

"Don't throw that out!" came Strell's voice from the open archway, and she spun around, embarrassed he had caught her throwing food away. His usual early morning, sleepy countenance was stirred to life with an indignant accusation.

"I burnt it," she said, holding out the plate as proof. "We've plenty of bread."

Strell was plains born and looked it, being almost awkwardly tall and thin despite the volumes of food he ate. His hair was dark and gently curling as was everyone's from the desert, nearly as long as hers, and pulled back with a metal clip. Clean shaven, his skin was as brown in the dead of winter as the sun turned hers at the height of summer. They had met in the mountains: she following the pull from her book, he running from the tragic demise of his family in an unprecedented desert flood. Their different backgrounds dictated they were to hate each other, but somewhere, in their joined efforts to remain alive, she had forgotten how. Occasionally, in the deep stillness of the night, she dared believe he might be flaunting the wrath of both the foothills and plains and have grown to truly like her.

Strell came forward, his brown eyes failing to hide his amusement for having caught her in an embarrassing moment. Saying nothing, he plucked the plate from her grasp. Strell never threw out food, often spending inordinate amounts of time making her toss-outs into something edible. It was probably a remnant from his chosen profession and never knowing where his next meal was coming from. Settling himself at his usual breakfast spot, he pulled the jam pot closer. He ladled a huge helping onto the blackened bread and took a bite. "See? It's fine," he said around an ash-ridden mouthful.

Alissa scrunched her eyes as she imagined the acrid taste. "You know, it would be less wasteful to throw out a single slice of bread than to use half a pot of jam to make it edible."

He gave her a half smile and arched his eyebrows. "Not nearly as tasty, though," he said as he caught a drip of jam with his finger.

Giving him a last, pained look, she cut a second slice of bread and set it close to the fire. Strell methodically devoured his breakfast, silent but for the obvious crunches. With a rush of air and warning chitter, Talon dropped from the rafters to Strell's hastily raised fist.

"Morning, bird," he said gruffly, not seeming to mind the pinch of her talons as he offered her a crumb. Alissa watched, amusement pulling up the corners of her mouth, as the kestrel predictably refused. Seeing no meat forthcoming, the bird worried at his fingers, finally retreating back to the ceiling with a helpful toss from Strell. He rose to his feet as he finished his toast, clearly looking for something more to eat. Giving Alissa a sly look, he dipped a spoon in a pot set to warm at the edge of the fire and pulled out a thick, glistening strand of melted sweet. "M-m-m. What's this?"

"That's my candied-apple syrup," she blurted. It was supposed to have been a surprise for tonight's dinner, and her brow pinched in feminine outrage as he stuck the spoon in his mouth. "Stop that!" she protested, knowing he was teasing her but unable to stop.

Strell grinned as he licked the spoon clean. "You aren't supposed to know how to make candied apples. It's a plains secret. Did your mother teach you her recipe? It's a good one."

"Then keep your fingers out of it," she said tartly but was too pleased he thought it good to be angry. Going back to her dough, she rolled the rectangle into a squat log shape and began to cut slices. Strell hovered over her shoulder, trying to snitch a bit of unattended dough. She skillfully thwarted his attempts, surprised when she was unable to find her usual contentment in their silent, long-running game of thief and guard.

She was tired of being silent. Tired of the pattern her days had fallen into. Bailic knew one of them had come in search of the book of *First Truth*. Thanks to Strell's skillful acting and distractions, the man had been deceived into thinking Strell was the latent Keeper, not her. For the last four weeks, Bailic had been trying to teach Strell enough magic so he could open the book for him. And though she had mended all her stockings and made a new skirt while eavesdropping on Strell's lessons, she had learned little about how to manipulate her hidden source and tracings. The idea had been that Useless, the last Master, would secretly teach her, and she would perform the magic for Strell without Bailic knowing, buying time until the Master found a way to kill Bailic. But Useless hadn't returned to teach her anything, Strell was running out of excuses, and Bailic was growing impatient.

It was all Useless's fault, she thought, her lips pressing together in misplaced frustration as she thunked the knife on the table to warn off Strell's reaching fingers. The Master had introduced himself to her last fall with the pseudonym Useless. She would just as soon keep using it, seeing as it seemed to be more appropriate than his real name, Talo-Toecan. Useless had flitted away on his raku, batlike wings with only his whispered promise to return. He wasn't ever coming back. Counting on him was—useless? She should take things into her own hands. Soon.

"I've been thinking," she said slowly, not sure how Strell would react. His cautious plainsman nature made him more inclined to follow a wait-and-see approach rather than her try-and-see philosophy. "The snow isn't that deep yet. We could make it to the coast. Then we won't have to stay the winter here. It's not too late."

Strell took the toast off the fire and set it on a plate for her. "There's snow on the ground. It's too late," he said shortly, stretching to reach the butter tin.

"Still," she said. "If we get enough blankets from the annexes—"

He looked up from buttering her toast, a wary, knowing look in his eyes. "You're thinking about stealing your book back, aren't you." It wasn't a question, and Alissa flushed for Strell having guessed her plans. He leaned halfway over the table towards her. "Just what are you going to do?" he asked. "Go up to his rooms under some pretense and snatch it?"

"Useless isn't coming back," she protested.

"What about the ward on Bailic's door?" he asked. "You'd be trapped until he gave you permission to leave."

Her breath hissed out in vexation. He wasn't even listening. Grinding her teeth, she continued to cut the rolls. "I can break any ward," she grumbled.

"You cannot," he said, shooting a glance at the open archway and the dining hall. "You have no idea what you're doing with your source and tracings."

"I'm not going to go into Bailic's room." Turning from her almost lie, she settled a roll upon the baking stone. "Today," she finished softly.

"And even if you did manage to get out of his room, what's to stop him from taking it back? It's winter, Alissa. There's nowhere to go! The coast is a three-week trip from here in good weather. The snow is up to my knees."

Alissa wouldn't meet his eyes. "I'm tired of waiting," she said plaintively.

"But to risk your life for it? It's just a book."

"It isn't *just a book!*" Alissa shouted, unable to fathom herself just what kind of a hold it had on her. Ever since pulling it from its hiding spot, it seemed as if it contained something she needed. But she wasn't missing anything. Confused and wanting to end the argument, she dusted her hands free of the flour and picked up Bailic's half-empty tray.

Strell was right behind her. "Where are you going? We aren't done with this yet."

"Upstairs to the practice room," she said with a forced brightness. "You're late, you know. Why don't you take the tray up for me?"

"I will, and stop trying to change the subject." He pulled the tray from her and set it down. Alissa slumped where she stood. "Be reasonable, Alissa," he coaxed, his tone abruptly softening. "There's nowhere to run, even if you could get your book. And if he catches you, he'll kill you for it. He's killed for it before."

Miserable, she caught her breath. Reminding her of her papa's death wasn't fair. "I know, Strell," she said. "Just stop." Her eyes flicked to his as he took her chin and gently turned her to him. The soft concern in his expression surprised her. It almost seemed he understood. Perhaps he did. He knew loss. It was easy to forget, when he never let it show.

"I'm sorry," he said gently. "But you had some plan to take it, didn't you?"

She lowered her eyes. There was nothing she could say. If she ever found her book unattended, she didn't know if she could stop herself.

Strell let go of her and turned, seeming as frustrated as she. "I don't know what to do anymore," he said with a quiet urgency, "except wait. Master Talo-Toecan knows what he's doing. He will come up with an idea."

Talo-Toecan, she thought darkly. He was Useless to her, now and forever.

An aggressive hiss came from the rafters, and she glanced up to see Talon's feathers raised like the hackles of a dog. She was glaring beyond them to the open archway to the dining hall. A faint shout echoed into the kitchen, and Alissa and Strell exchanged a worried look. "That's Bailic," she said, putting her untouched toast on his tray. Her appetite was gone.

"Well, there's no one else it could be, is there." Strell

had said it as if making a jest, but he immediately picked up the tray and turned to go.

"I'll finish my rolls and be up in a moment," Alissa said, her earlier bluff and bluster evaporating in the cold shock of reality. Bailic had broken the conditioning that kept Keepers from using their wards to harm, emptying the Hold of students and Keepers with his self-taught lessons of murder with magic. If she couldn't keep her desire for her book hidden, Bailic would realize he was being deceived. Anonymity was her only defense until Useless tutored her on how to use the maze of tracings that lay in her unconscious.

"Will you be all right until I get there?" she asked as he went into the dining hall.

"Yes. I've got it." Strell turned and gave her a tired smile. "I won't forget my lines."

She returned his smile, but it vanished quickly. She had coached Strell endlessly on what her source and tracings looked like so he could answer Bailic's questions properly, but she worried when she wasn't up there to catch any possible mistakes.

"I'll be fine." Strell gave her a solemn nod, clearly pleased to see her slip into the unaccustomed role of meek and mild. The slight clattering of the dishes seemed loud as he left.

She turned back to her rolls and blinked. One was missing. He had stolen it right out from under her nose. It was the second time this week! "Strell!" she called loudly after him. "Burn you to ash!" But a smile crossed her face as his laugh came echoing back. Next time, she would catch him.

A sharp snap broke the silence, and she pulled her head up, wondering what it was. The kitchen was empty except for her and Talon. But the small bird was staring at the narrow door leading to the expansive kitchen garden. It was really more of a walled-in slice of wood and field, but there were a few herbs that had yet to go wild.

The tap came again. She straightened, not in fear but curiosity. Glancing at Talon, she wiped her hands free of flour. It had sounded almost like the peck of a bird. She tiptoed to the door and held her breath as she leaned closer, listening. A third tap echoed thinly. This time she heard a small rattle as something clattered against the stone sill on the other side of the door.

Someone was throwing stones at the garden door.

Immediately she reached for the handle and pushed. It wasn't Bailic, and it wasn't Strell. That only left one presence: Useless.

A thrill of excitement tinged with relief went through her as she stepped outside into the cold, clasping her arms around herself. He hadn't forgotten her. The postdawn chill seemed to catch in her nose, and puffs of air marked her breathing. The sun was shining on the upper reaches of the Hold, but the ground was still in shadow. She looked across the silent lumps of snow the dormant vegetation made. Where was he?

"Here," a low, deep voice whispered, and her gaze darted to the tall, unclimbable wall surrounding the garden. The wall stood higher than two man lengths, and perched upon it like an errant goat was Useless.

The raku was in his human form, dressed in a yellow shirt with overly expansive sleeves and a matching pair of trousers. He had no coat, but he wore a sleeveless vest so long it went down to cover his unseen boots. It was bound tightly to his waist with a black scarf, the ends of which reached the top of the frozen wall. He let a handful of pebbles drop, and Alissa struggled to pull her eyes from his hands. His fingers were long, looking as if they had four segments rather than three. His eyes, too, couldn't hide his raku nature and were a startling gold. Though not seeming old, he clearly was far from youth, his short cap of white hair and eyebrows making him appear older than his lightly wrinkled face would make him look otherwise. Even standing atop the wall he possessed a quiet strength that Alissa envied. And he had promised to teach her.

"Useless!" she exclaimed, knowing he wouldn't be here if Bailic could see him from the practice window. She gathered her skirts to step into the snow, but a rough sound stopped her.

"No," he said, motioning her to stay. His eyes traveled up the Hold's tower, and his thin lips pressed together as if in worry. "Tonight," he whispered. "Wait up for me."

"Tonight?" she repeated, then caught her breath as the Master dissolved into a gray mist. There was a tug on her awareness, jolting her. "Useless, wait," she cried, stepping out into the snow as the mist grew and solidified into the massive bulk of a raku.

She stopped dead in her tracks with an instinctive fear. He was as large as six horses put together, with teeth as long as her arm and eyes as big as her head. She swallowed hard as the sinuous beast turned his head to her and raised an impossibly long finger to his snout, clearly admonishing her to be quiet. His muscles bunched under his golden hide, and Alissa stepped involuntarily back to the threshold as, with one downward push of his wings, he became airborne. The Master headed east over the trees towards the unseen, abandoned city of Ese' Nawoer, a morning's walk away.

Alissa bit back a cry of surprise as Talon darted out over her head with a screech of outrage, following the huge raku as if driving it away. Tonight? Alissa thought as her toes turned cold and the chill settled into her. He was coming back tonight?

2

An irregular drumming shifted the air as Bailic waited, his pale fingers tapping the arm of the chair. It was the only noise in the narrow practice room. "He will be late again," Bailic said, not caring that he was talking to himself. He rose to stand before the row of tall windows. Meson had once told him the roofs of the long-abandoned city, Ese' Nawoer, were visible from here. For Bailic, though, the spectacular view was a blur of blue, brown, and green in the summer, shifting to blue, brown, and white in the winter. Right now it was gray with the unrisen sun.

His nearly pink eyes were almost useless and abnormally sensitive to light, but it was only in the strong sun he could see much of anything. Even so, he avoided the sun as his transparent skin burned frighteningly fast. His hair, too, was the color of faded straw instead of the dark brown all plainsmen had, and so he kept it cut close to his skull to minimize its tendency to make him look old. As if to make up for his lack of color, he had taken to wearing black. Reluctant to abandon his stolen Master's vest, he wore it open over his traditional Keeper garb of a gray, wide-sleeved tunic and trousers. He had donned the soft-soled shoes the Masters had insisted on behind the Hold's walls, not out of respect but for his occasional need for stealth. A puckered scar ran from behind an ear, across his neck, and under his shirt. It had been a parting gift from Talo-Toecan more than a decade ago, and it still hurt when the air was damp. Raku score was long to heal.

The windows here were large even by the Hold's standards, and if not for the wards on them, it would be frigid.

Until the wards fell with the first spring rain, the only thing
to pass them would be the amber morning light the Masters of the Hold had delighted in. Beneath the openings
was a wooden bench running the entire length of the room.
It lent the chamber the feel of a roofed balcony. This had
once been a pleasant spot in which to study or practice.
Now it was empty and hollow looking, all the amenities
stripped away.

Well, almost all, Bailic thought as his eyes slid to the
soft chair tucked by a distant window. Positioned to catch
the first ray of sun, the chair was a silent reminder of the
girl. It had appeared the second day of the piper's instruction amid much consideration and shifting.

Bailic's eyes narrowed—the only show of disgust he
would allow himself—as he recalled the pathetic display
of the piper and girl discussing at great length the chair's
final placement. It was her cursed bird who finally settled
the matter by swooping in to settle on the back of the chair
and preen in the morning sun. So now it sat just beyond the
limit where his sight began to blur to inconsequentiality.

His chair was tucked into the darkest corner. A third seat
sat alone at the long, black table, scarred from centuries of
students' abuses. It was the piper's. Bailic remembered it
was as uncomfortable as it looked, and still the infuriating
man kept falling asleep in it.

As he waited for the sun to rise, Bailic sat ramrod
straight on the edge of the long bench and fumed. A short,
white thread decorated his sleeve, and he plucked it off,
drawing it through his fingertips to gauge its quality. First
rate, of course. There was nothing else the girl could have
found in the annexes to work with.

His ill temper softened as he let the thread fall. The
leavings from her stitching had been finding their way to
the hem of his sleeve or sash for weeks now. It wasn't right
for a commoner to listen to the instruction of a Keeper, but
the sight of her bowed head and flashing needle was a bittersweet reminder of his sisters, a contented gaggle of con-
summate skill and gossip. He ignored her, as the one time
he commented on her work she hadn't shown up the next

morning. And the sight of her domestic serenity was a pain that served to temper his resolve further.

Her silent presence in the corner had become an unexpected reminder of all he left behind, all he escaped, all he couldn't return to. He was a plainsman, but his pale skin and hair ultimately forced his expulsion before reaching twelve summers; he looked too much like a foothills grubber to be accepted. Reviled and shunned by his own parents, he fled to spare them the exorbitant bribe price necessary to "quietly escort" him from the plains. One of his few regrets was that he had tried to get them to love him, even as he ran away.

Unwilling to live among the barbarous foothills people—as if they would have let him—he had wandered into the mountains. It was to have been a noble trek to his death. Instead, he found the Hold, his maturing abilities drawing him as heavy skies draw rain. Here he met Meson, and after gaining a broken nose and cracked rib, learned a grudging respect for the smaller but tenacious folk the foothills produced. His resentment had lingered, hidden even to him until Meson showed his true, traitorous nature by charming away the only woman Bailic could love: a dark, beautiful woman from the plains who didn't care that his skin was paler than the moon and his hair was the color of straw.

Meson, the coward, had abandoned his responsibilities as a Keeper while Bailic stayed and became more powerful under the tutelage of the Masters. It was then that Bailic's idle thoughts began to spill from his fantasy to his reality. He would take what the Masters taught him, bending it to rule the plains and foothills so as to make a place for himself. But not until he taught them the meaning of pain, giving them tenfold the hurt they caused him. They were deserving of it.

The two factions were well balanced for conflict; they hated each other almost as much as he despised them. But war never materialized. They were just clever enough to know where to draw the line. Bailic needed something to tip the scales. The abandoned city of Ese' Nawoer would

do nicely. He was sure the book of *First Truth* was powerful enough to wake the cursed souls there, and then he
would demand their allegiance as history claimed was
his due.

He would send them into the foothills and plains, plant-
ing the seeds of madness. The souls of Ese' Nawoer would
whisper their fears and guilt into the thoughts of the un-
suspecting, inciting war. The delicate balance between the
plains and hills would crumble, and they would be at each
others' throats by summer's end. When their numbers were
sufficiently reduced, he would save them. They would call
him the great peacemaker, and he would use his strength to
drive the souls of death back into the mountains. But
everything has a cost. He would have their allegiance for
their freedom from death's hounding, or they would return
to their hell.

The book's power, though, was merely a promise when
it was closed. Only someone it claimed could open it, and
then only when enough lore was gained to insure its
knowledge could be utilized. With the exception of Talo-
Toecan, the piper was the sole individual who could access
the book, and the piper was late—again.

Frustrated, Bailic ran his hand over the short bristles
atop his head, ending with his fingers clenched at the base
of his skull. Progress the last four weeks had been thin. It
should go faster now that the basics were out of the way.
Especially if Bailic continued to ignore the painstaking
philosophies the Masters had pounded into their students
along with the more desirable skills.

"Will he never get here?" he said as he willed his anger
away. He wished he could send a sharp thought to hurry
the irritating man along, but he hadn't taught him wordless
speech and wouldn't bother. The Hold's ward of silence
prevented Keepers from communicating this way unless
one or both were beyond the fortress's environs, a good
morning's walk in any direction. The ward had been a
blessing when the Hold was full, helping to keep the sub-
liminal background murmur of everyone's thoughts to a
minimum. Now the ward was a nuisance. It had never

stopped the Masters from talking silently amongst themselves, though.

A Master couldn't speak silently to a Keeper at all, and Bailic thanked the Navigator and all his Wolves for that. Just imagining the voiceless threats and nightmares Talo-Toecan would inflict on him made him uneasy.

The thought of Talo-Toecan pulled Bailic's gaze to the windows, and he wondered if he ought to carry the book with him instead of leaving it hidden in his room. He knew the wily raku wouldn't break his word, but making a tight deal with him was difficult. That Bailic was still alive proved he had been successful. There was no loophole in this bargain. Bailic had made sure of it.

Talo-Toecan wouldn't attack Bailic as long as he remained in the Hold. This was a small concession on Bailic's part, seeing as it was winter and only an insane man would go out for anything other than wood. Bailic had also forced the raku to agree to not steal the book back, as well as contact or otherwise interfere with his tutoring the piper to open the book. The promise had been pulled from the angry Master under the threat that Bailic would burn the book and the girl holding it at the time, to ash. Talo-Toecan had bent to his every demand, not willing to call Bailic's bluff. It had been a satisfying encounter with the usually domineering Master.

In return, all Bailic had to do was keep from wringing the piper's neck while he struggled to stuff enough wisdom through his thick skull so that the man could open the book. It was clear the plainsman knew he was relatively safe, as he had begun to find small ways to irritate Bailic. The piper's companion survived under the same protection. But once the book was open, the agreement would be ended, and he could do what he wanted with them. In turn, Talo-Toecan could do what he might to Bailic. The prospect didn't worry him. He would be privy to the Masters' greatest lore. The student would become the master, as it had been since time immemorial.

And so he spent his mornings with the piper. Eventually the man would open the cursed book, and Bailic's plan could move forward another slow step, but move forward it would. He had first emptied the Hold of its interfering Keepers, as messy and time consuming as that had been. Then he had persuaded almost the entire clan of Masters to their deaths in a search of a lost colony, a feat he once would have claimed was impossible. Most recently he acquired the book, only to find he couldn't open it.

Bailic rose to his feet as the sun's first rays spilled into the room. Frustration washed into him as if driven by the beams of light, and he strode to the door. "Piper-r-r-r!" he bellowed into the hall. "Where, by the Hounds, are you?" He lightly divided his thoughts to send his awareness to search the Hold. Bailic felt his lips curl as he sensed the plainsman's presence on the stairs, slowly making his way to the practice room. Ceasing his motion, Bailic took a pose with his back to the sun and his hands on his hips, knowing he made a formidable shadow.

There was a small scuff, and the fuzzy image of the plainsman hesitated at the doorway. He heard a heavy sigh as the man entered and set the breakfast tray on the table. "You're late, Piper," Bailic said, not bothering to hide his contempt. It disgusted him that such a man as this was both the access and the obstacle to his desires.

"Yes, I know." Strell collapsed in his chair and slumped, clearly not caring.

"It's the third time in as many days," Bailic continued.

"My apologies." It was just shy of belligerent, and Bailic seethed. The piper stretched to reach the tray with the tea, and using a single digit, Bailic slowly pulled it out of his reach. His eyebrows rose mockingly as the piper stiffened.

Bailic poured himself a lukewarm cup of tea, briefly entertaining the idea of warming it back to a drinkable temperature. Reluctantly, he didn't. The piper might be quick enough to see the resonance of the ward's creation on his own tracings, deep within his unconscious. In effect, he would have inadvertently taught the man the easy ward. And Bailic would just as soon keep this ward to himself for a time, if only to deny the piper one of the pleasures of being a Keeper.

"If you're ready?" Bailic asked dryly as he set his cup on the small, round table next to his chair. It would keep until after the lesson.

"Uh-h-h . . ." Strell grunted, pouring out his own drink and swallowing half its contents.

"By now you should be able to find the network of tracings spread in your thoughts—with your eyes open," he added.

"Yes." Yawning, the annoying man stretched his legs under the table.

"Perhaps we may begin to make some progress. I had expected that in four weeks you would be further along." Bailic placed his palms on the table and looked down at Strell, anger trickling through him. "Talo-Toecan is laughing at me. You will do better."

The piper sat up with a dramatic sigh.

From the pocket his deep sleeve made, Bailic took a small, unadorned wooden box and placed it on the table. The piper picked it up and thumbed the latch. "Don't open it!" Bailic shouted. "Or I'll have to air out the room for a week!"

Clearly unnerved, Strell set the box down and hid his hands below the table. "What is it?"

"It's the smallest dusting of source." Squinting, Bailic turned to the windows, forcing his breath to come slow in the effort to keep his want from showing. It was hard to let even this small bit slip through his fingers without claiming it for himself and adding to his strength. "It's not enough to do much with," Bailic continued. "It was all I was able to find. Besides," he said mockingly as he turned back, "I won't give you anything to increase your strength. It's enough to practice with. If a Master were your instructor, you'd have none until your schooling was all but complete, so consider yourself fortunate. It's yours until I take it away." Bailic smiled in anticipation. "And I will take it away."

The man looked at the box with a wary curiosity. "What do I do with it?" he asked.

"Pick it up," Bailic instructed, shaking his head as the piper cradled the box as if it were a grasshopper that might bite him. "Now unfocus your attention—shut your eyes if it helps. You should be able to see the source with your mind's eye beside your tracings. Try looking sideways for it, as if it is around the corner. It will look as if it's—"

"A sphere of nothing, given shape by a glowing lacework?" the man interrupted, his voice that of wonder. "Wolves take me. It's beautiful. . . ."

"You found it already!" Bailic exclaimed, shocked.

The piper jumped as if startled. "It's gone," he said, staring up at Bailic in dismay.

Bailic adjusted his Master's vest to cover his surprise. Perhaps the piper had an ounce of talent after all. It had taken him several hours to find his source the first time. "It's still there," he said. "As long as you're anywhere near that box. Find it again."

Strell sat straighter, the box gripped tightly with an almost white-knuckled force. His eyes went vacant; his face went slack. "Ah . . ." he breathed, his eyes distant and unseeing.

Not entirely trusting this, Bailic eased forward. His sash hissed against the floor as he circled to stand behind him. "What does it look like?" he asked, making his voice pleasant to lull Strell into being cooperative. "What's beyond the mat of threads that encase your source?"

"Nothing," the man said. "I can't see past them. My focus seems to slide away. I don't think there's anything really there." His eyes cleared, and he looked at Bailic. All trace of sullen student was gone, his usual animosity probably lost in the near shock of finding a piece of glory in his thoughts. "But there is. What is it?"

Encouraged that his student finally seemed to be making progress, Bailic's frustration eased. He gathered himself to explain, then seeing his fingers steepled like his old instructor's, put his hands behind his back. "Force," he said. "Energy. That's why you can't see it. No one can be sure where the threads binding your source into that sphere shape come from. Someone once told me they were made of will, your will, in an attempt to separate your mind from the damaging reality of infinity."

A genuine wonder filled the piper's eyes. "Infinity?" he whispered. "I didn't know that."

Bailic's eyes narrowed. "Of course you didn't. Find it again."

The piper went still, his eyes closing and an odd stillness coming over him as he focused entirely on his inner sight. Bailic remembered how easy it was for a new Keeper to get lost in his own strength until he took it for granted. He almost envied the piper for his naïveté. "Tell me," Bailic said from over Strell's shoulder, "what did you have for breakfast?"

"Hm-m-m?" Strell looked up, his concentration clearly broken. "Burnt toast."

"No!" Bailic shouted, punctuating his word with a hard blow to the table. "Don't drop your inner sight while answering! How many times do I have to explain it?" *Wolves,* he thought. Just when it seemed the piper was starting to understand. "Try again," he said.

A silly, distracted grin spread across his student's face.

"Yes, it's very pretty, I'm sure," Bailic said caustically. "Now, without losing it, tell me what the girl is wearing today."

The grin vanished, and the man met his eyes. "Why do you want to know?"

Bailic's breath escaped in a long hiss. "You lost it again, didn't you?"

"Well, stop asking me questions!"

Leaning close, Bailic whispered with an exaggerated slowness, "That's the whole point!"

Strell's eyes narrowed.

"Once more," Bailic said. "Find your source, and if you lose it again, I will make it seem as if you have hot coals at your feet every time you sit down."

The man's glance shifted from Bailic to the snowfield

four stories below them. "And that is something I want to avoid, yes?"

Bailic took a steadying breath, willing his fingers back to stillness, reminding himself he had promised to not kill him, though the idea was becoming more attractive. But kill the piper, and he would kill his chances at opening the book. "Find it," he said tightly, turning to pace along the windows, using the motion to collect the scattered motes of his patience. For an instant, there had been respect.

He listened as the piper took three slow breaths as he had taught him. Judging enough time had passed, Bailic halted beside the piper, squinting to see the idiotic, half-focused look Keepers were afflicted with while learning how to successfully divide their attention between reality and their thoughts. "What is for dinner?" Bailic asked. "That girl must have something special planned if she sends you up with toast." Bailic shifted the stiff bread with a finger, flicking it off the plate and onto the tray in an effort to distract the piper. He was marginally pleased to see the man's attention hold.

"Candied apples," his student said distantly, his words slightly slurred.

"What's that?" Bailic said loudly, putting his mouth uncomfortably near the piper's ear to try to startle him from his concentration. "You sound like a beggar with no teeth."

"Candied apples," the man repeated, his speech clearer this time.

Bailic drew away, confident the piper had gained a measure of control. "Candied apples," he mused aloud. "Her mother must have been full plains for her to know how to make those. The woman ought to be whipped for teaching it to her half-breed daughter. Still, I haven't had a candied apple in years."

"Then perhaps you ought not to have killed everyone in the Hold," the piper said.

Bailic's breath caught in outrage. Anger gripped him, tensing his muscles and setting his thoughts to form a savage ward to silence the piper. But the sight of his student with his jaw clenched and an unrepentant defiance dissolved Bailic's first flash of anger into guile.

A slow, patronizing smile slid over him, becoming deeper and more satisfying at the piper's obvious surprise at his lack of reaction. Bailic hadn't murdered an entire fortress of Keepers by magic alone. There were other ways to bring a wealthy upstart of a plainsman to heel, and he thought he knew how.

The girl's scandalous mix of plains and hills was obvious, but it seemed the piper had forgotten his standing and taken a fancy to her. Bailic could use this unsavory attachment. He wouldn't risk teaching his student a powerful ward over a lack of respect. He didn't want the piper's respect, anyway. He just wanted him to hold his tongue.

Bailic stepped close. "I could burn you to ash where you sit," he said lightly.

"Then why don't you?" the piper said, clearly knowing he wouldn't.

Bailic nodded slowly, as if admitting the piper had a valid point. There was really nothing Bailic had to say. The answer was sitting up in his chambers, hidden among the scores of other books he had gathered over the years. "You're right, I won't," he said. "You're worth something to me. But there are things you might miss."

The plainsman looked at him from under lowered brows. "There's not much left to me, Bailic," he said, a hatred glimmering behind his eyes. "I've nothing left. My name is worthless. Everything that went along with it is gone."

"Oh. I see. Yes." Bailic gathered his robelike vest to half sit on the table. He shifted his gaze, tilting his head slowly in a confident pose, sending his eyes to the girl's chair.

The piper's face went white. "You touch her, and I'll—"

"You'll what?" Bailic taunted, leaning close. "She is a bred-in-shame half-breed. Your father would throw you into the street; your schism would stone you. Tell me you aren't compromising your high, plainsman values but simply using her."

The piper gritted his teeth, his neck turning red. Bailic leaned closer yet, daring him to say anything. He held the man's gaze for six heartbeats, proving his dominance. "Go on," he said, straightening to his full height and gesturing to the door. "I'm through with you today. Go find your slattern. Practice holding a conversation and your inner sight simultaneously. If you show no improvement tomorrow, I'll repeat the exercise with you myself."

Strell's chair grated harshly on the floor as he got to his feet. A look of controlled hatred suffused him, and Bailic smiled in satisfaction. If he couldn't have respect, he would have hate. After hate came fear.

"Take the tray with you," Bailic said, nudging it. "I'm not a chicken. I don't eat bread crumbs. I'll be down momentarily to supervise her until she gets my breakfast right."

The piper said nothing, his stiff expression giving clear indication he knew this unusual attention to the girl was to punish his behavior. Bailic watched the plainsman take the tray and leave. He was pleased to see the box of source gripped tightly in the piper's hand. It, too, could be used to manipulate the man, for a Keeper would rather die than give up a source once seen glittering in his thoughts.

It was going to be a good morning, after all.

3

A slippered foot nudged her ankle, and she jumped awake, struggling not to grunt.

"You're not falling asleep, are you, Alissa?" Strell said.

She shifted in her fireside chair to give him an annoyed look. "Course not. He could be here any moment."

"I'd wager you miss him because you fall asleep."

"Strell, there is no way I'm going to fall asleep." She pointed to the half-emptied pot of tea on the hearth. "If you want to go on to bed, go. I'll be all right." She leaned to swat his foot as he threatened to push her again.

"No. I promised I'd keep you awake, and I will."

Alissa gave him a smile as she tugged her blanket back up to her chin. The fire made an arc of light just large enough to hold their chairs, leaving the rest of her small room in shadow. It was in the Keepers' hall on the eighth floor—her papa's old room, actually. The Keepers' hall was one of the few places Bailic hadn't stripped of belongings in his decade-long search for the *First Truth*. He had been rightfully concerned about running into a lethal ward left by someone he had murdered. The room offered Alissa a measure of protection, as Bailic wouldn't cross the doorframe. Strell had the room next door, but his chair sat before her hearth as it had ever since their first night in the Hold. Apart from this fall when with weighted ropes Bailic covertly moved it back to Strell's room to cause a rift between them, his chair had remained there, instilling Alissa with a heavy feeling of stability.

Talon wheezed in her sleep from her nearby perch. The bird had returned from chasing Useless with half her tail feathers gone. Most of her day had been spent in an exhausted sleep, waking only to hiss thinly at Bailic. He had found fault with Alissa's toast and invaded her kitchen. It wasn't until noon that he finally left with a bowl of porridge in his pale hand: just enough honey, just enough milk, made with tea instead of water the way he insisted plainsmen took it. It sounded awful, but she tucked the knowledge away to surprise Strell with some morning.

Bailic had left her a wreck of shattered nerves and quick temper. It took Strell all afternoon to bring her back to her usual self, a task he took seriously, actually blaming himself for Bailic's unusual attention. He eased her raw emotions away by playing her favorite songs on his pipe. The sun had set with her feeling very content, but she couldn't sleep now. Useless was coming.

Strell leaned to stir the fire. He stood up, considering the flames for a long, silent moment. "Here," he said suddenly, slipping a hand into a pocket to bring out a fold of yellow cloth. "I've been meaning to give this to you. It was supposed to be for the solstice, but I forgot. Then it didn't seem right . . ." His voice trailed to nothing. He had nearly died while freeing Useless from the prison deep under the Hold that day. "You should have it," he added.

"For me?" She beamed, not caring it was a month late. "You made me something?"

"Uh-huh." He sat down on the edge of his chair and leaned close. "Open it."

He extended the fabric, and Alissa took it, her fingers touching his for an instant. She glanced to see if he noticed, flushing at his knowing look. Wondering what he could have made that was so small, she carefully opened the cloth. Nestled among the folds was a thumbnail-sized charm. It looked like it was made from spun thread, the color of gold. "Oh, Strell," she breathed, entranced. "It's beautiful!"

He smiled and looked to the floor, seeming embarrassed. "It's for luck," he said as he glanced away. "It's a luck charm. I wove it from a lock of your hair."

"Mine?" Alissa touched her head, her eyes wide in surprise. "When did you—"

"Ages ago," he said with a rush, his brow creased in worry. "You were asleep. I wanted it to be a surprise, and if a charm isn't made out of hair—"

"It doesn't work," she finished for him, smiling to show she didn't mind. It was done, and she didn't want him to think she didn't like his gift.

Marveling that such an exquisite thing existed, she undid the ribbon that bound her hair and pushed the strands impatiently out of her way. She looped the ribbon through the charm and tied it loosely about her neck. The bit of gold rested well above the pouch of dust she kept hidden. Alissa smiled as she looked at the charm against the dark blue of her dress. "Thank you," she whispered, reaching out to touch his shoulder for an instant. "I like it."

"Good," he said as he knelt to poke needlessly at the fire again.

Satisfied all was right with the world, Alissa leaned back and watched the flames. She felt her breathing slow as she relaxed in the new warmth of the stirred coals. Strell returned to his chair, and they kept a companionable silence until her head snapped back as she nodded off. Struggling to focus, she looked to see if Strell had noticed. His eyes were shut; his breathing was slow. It shifted his loosely curling hair as he exhaled, and she fought the urge to arrange it.

"Asleep," she murmured, not surprised. Rising, she pulled her shawl tightly about her shoulders. It seemed Useless wasn't coming. Disappointed, she went to her shutters and pushed them open. They squeaked loudly, and she turned to see if it had woken Strell, but he seemed all the more settled. Talon, though, fluffed herself in the sudden chill with a grumpy dissatisfaction.

Alissa leaned halfway out her window and took a slow breath, enjoying the chill that burned her lungs only because a fire was near. The full moon on the snow made it bright, and the few stars were tiny. Hers was the only window in the Hold without a ward to keep out the cold. She broke both hers and Strell's while removing the ward Useless had put between her and her source. The ward had been for her protection, but irked he would dare do such a thing, she had tried to remove it. Her attempt not only shattered the window wards but her mind as well. The uncontrolled release of force had torn through her thoughts, burning her tracings to what she had first thought was an unusable ash. They had since healed. She and Strell had put the shutters up shortly thereafter. Deciding to ask Bailic to replace her ward as he had Strell's would be foolish.

A gust of wind blew back her hair, and her head snapped up. Squinting into the brief gale, she saw a raku's fearsome shadow ghost from behind the Hold's tower in a hiss of leathery black angles and sharp teeth. She stared in awe as the house-sized raku turned against the full moon and circled the tower.

Talon darted out over her head. "Talon. No!" she cried. She spun back to her fire. "Strell! Wake up. Talon is going to get herself killed!" But Strell didn't move. Torn between shaking him and watching the demise of her bird, she stood frozen at the window as Talon dove at the raku. A wickedly clawed hind foot slowly reached out, black in the moonlight. Talon gave a startled squawk and dropped. Useless followed with an almost unheard rumble. Alissa's breath caught. Talon. He was going to eat Talon!

Come back! she thought, a frantic shout nearly slipping from her, but she could do nothing. Shifting suddenly, the bird darted for height, leaving the raku grasping air. Useless was too massive to keep up with her lightning-quick maneuvers, but it would only be a matter of time.

Alissa's hand went to her mouth as the raku feinted a swoop to the left, flinging his tail—*Wolves, it was as long as the rest of him*—into Talon's path. The bird slammed into it, falling neatly into a waiting claw. Together they dropped to the forest beyond the garden wall.

Her heart pounding, Alissa flung herself back inside. "Strell!" she cried, shaking him. "Burn you to ash. Wake up!"

The plainsman frowned in his sleep, saying nothing. Giving up, she grabbed her hat and coat and ran downstairs to the Hold's door in a terrified flurry of silence. *The Navigator's Wolves take that raku!* she thought as she shrugged into her coat. Useless couldn't eat Talon. She was her friend.

Pushing open the thick doors of the fortress, she raced into the snow to stop at the edge of the clearing. "Which way?" she agonized, the night's silvery silence hard upon her ears. Over her thudding pulse and rasping breath came a faint chitter. "Talon!" she called in relief, spinning about only to halt in confusion.

Useless, in his human guise, was striding out from under the distant trees. He had hidden his Masters' attire under an ill-fitting wool coat, and his tall height stood out sharply against the snow and moonlight. Grinning wildly, he waved a hand for Alissa to stay where she was. On his other hand sat Talon. The bird's noise increased as she caught sight of Alissa, but the kestrel made no move to leave her new perch.

"Hush, little warrior," Alissa faintly heard Useless admonish as he drew close. "You'll wake the Hold. All are asleep inside. Let's keep it that way." Talon obediently ceased her caterwauling, but in no way could Alissa say the bird grew any calmer.

Useless took Alissa's elbow as he came alongside, and without missing a step, began walking her back to the Hold. Flushing, she dug in her heels and tugged her arm free. "What are you doing? You were chasing Talon. I thought you were going to—"

"Eat her?" Useless finished. He began to laugh, and Alissa stiffened. "We were playing! She wouldn't make a mouthful."

"A mouthful!" Alissa yelled. "Talon is my friend!"

His mirth vanished. "She's a bird. And don't shout at me. Here." Taking Alissa's hat, he placed it lopsidedly upon her head. "Put this on before you get cold." Abnormally long fingers encircled her upper arm, and she found herself moving forward.

Alissa stumbled into motion, halting in confusion before the formidable wall surrounding the Hold's garden. Standing straight and unbowed, Useless ran his eyes over the sterile expanse. "This seems about right," he said, tossing Talon into the air. The bird flew up, then down to land upon Alissa's shoulder. Useless frowned at them for a long moment before turning to run his fingertips across the frosted stone.

Reaching up, Alissa touched Talon's feet to reassure herself her bird was safe. "What are you doing?" she asked, her voice still shaky from her recent fright.

"Looking for the door."

"Oh." Alissa turned to scan the blank stone for anything unusual.

"This may take a moment." His eyes on the wall, Useless shifted three steps to the right. "I usually fly into my garden, not crawl in like an insect."

"Or a Keeper," Alissa said as she set her palms firmly against the uneven surface. There was a familiar pull on her awareness followed by an inaudible click as the lock disengaged and the stone swung out to reveal the tangled remains of the long-fallow garden.

Useless stared at her. "How did you know?"

"Someone wrote 'Here' on the wall." Pleased she had bested him in this small matter, Alissa pointed out the thin scratchings.

"Humph!" He leaned forward, squinting to see it in the moonlight. "Impudent students," he grumbled. "After you." The Master gestured stiffly, and she stepped inside. "We can talk at the firepit. Do you know where that is?"

Alissa nodded, looking up at the Hold's tower to place herself. Useless shut the door to make it all but invisible. The hem of his coat turned dark from the snow as he picked his careful way amongst the dormant vegetation. Alissa followed, trying to memorize where in the rambling garden they were. It might be useful knowing a second way out.

"There," Useless said softly, almost to himself.

Alissa nodded. Hiking up her skirt, she stepped down

into the huge firepit and brushed the snow from a bench. Strell had served her dinner here last fall to try to make up for having twisted his ankle and leaving her with all the work. His attentive behavior had left her flustered, not knowing what to think. All that remained of their evening under the stars was black, snow-dusted charcoal. That, and her memories. Alissa hid a smile, remembering she had fallen asleep on his shoulder, waking to the sound of his heart and the warmth of his arms around her. It had been a most pleasant evening.

She gingerly settled herself on the cold bench. Useless took the seat beside her, and Alissa's eyes widened as she saw his hands. His fingers *did* have an extra joint. Seeming to realize she was staring, the Master hid his hands in his sleeves. As suddenly and unexpectedly as a sneeze, a fire burst into existence in the ashes of the old. Before she could comment, an ugly teapot appeared in the snow. Startled, Alissa divided her attention to take a peek at the web of tracings that lay silent within her unconscious. Useless had made a ward, and the pattern of tracings he used would resonate upon her own, showing her a part of how it was done.

A smiled eased over her as she examined her mindscape. The faint resonance showed a multitude of intertwining lines, joined at several spots and sprawling in just as many directions. *That doesn't look too hard,* she thought as the subtle luminescence faded. *Perhaps, if I—*

"Don't even think to try it," Useless murmured as he filled the pot with snow and set it right in the flames. "You're far from ready. Now," he said firmly. "I will be brief, as it's not prudent for me to be here. Is Bailic trying to teach Strell enough lore to open the book as I hoped?"

Alissa nodded. "He gave him a source today. Not much. A pinch, perhaps."

"Really?" Useless said, his eyebrows raised in surprise. "I wonder where he found even that much?" He held his hands out to the fire, his long fingers almost amongst the flames. "It can't do the piper much good, seeing as he is not Keeper stock, but commoner."

Alissa frowned. Strell's tracings might be a useless, defunct scramble of dead ends and tangled knots, but to call him common was insulting. Talon pinched her shoulder, responding to Alissa's ire, and she moved the bird to a nearby leafless shrub.

"As it stands," he continued, "I'm not actually barred from my Hold, just from killing Bailic while he hides here. I won't be staying, though. It wouldn't be . . . prudent."

Alissa shifted on the cold stone. "Can't you just take the book and we all leave?"

"No. I gave my word. It was either that or he would have burned you to ash."

"But it would be so easy," she cajoled. "It's just up in his room."

Useless raised his eyebrows. "You're asking me to break my word?"

Though shamed, Alissa refused to drop her eyes. "Well, I never said I wouldn't take it."

"Go ahead," he said, his disgust obvious. "Save me the trouble of keeping you alive."

"Bailic doesn't scare me," she said boldly, and Useless shook his head.

"Bailic murdered every last Keeper," he said. "Killed or drove away the students, and destroyed what remained of my kin. I'm sure *you* could manage, though." Useless rubbed his long-fingered hand over his eyes. "I'm going to lose this one to outright stupidity," he murmured.

Anger trickled through Alissa.

"You," he demanded, "will lie low. Use your ears, not your tracings, which you have untimely discovered. If you care to eavesdrop upon Strell's tutelage, Bailic can impart at least the basics of their use to you, if not the reasonings behind them." He turned severe. "But along that same line of sight, I want no more tampering with your neural net. I understand you managed to remove the ward I put about your source. You must have burnt your tracings quite proper."

She dropped her gaze with a flush of guilt. "How did you know?"

"Strell told me, but I had already guessed. The entire Hold shook," he accused. "You could have taken out all of the eighth floor with your unauthorized tinkering. It was luck Bailic thought it was Strell. See that it doesn't happen again.

Alissa looked up, stifling a surge of irritation. It was difficult to listen while he sat dictating orders as if he had the right to. Seeing her scowl, Useless chuckled. "Get used to it," he said shortly. "You're only a student, one of many who have come and gone."

"Like my papa?" she snapped, immediately regretting it.

"Yes, like your father." Useless winced, his eyebrows bunching together. "Meson was an excellent student, almost a friend, but he couldn't get past the wings, so to speak. Always with him, there was an awe, or reverence. It gets tiresome." Rearranging the fire, he watched her over the low flames he had stirred up. "You, I see, didn't inherit that as you did his gray eyes. It's fortunate Bailic is so nearsighted, or he might guess you were Meson's daughter by the sight of them alone." He hesitated, frowning. "Yours are almost blue, though. Not as distinctive as Meson's. Still, I would advise you to keep to the shadows."

She couldn't help but be pleased he had noticed. It was her opinion, too, that her eyes were blue, but her gaze dropped at the reminder of how easily their deception could be broken.

"I wish I could have warned him of Bailic's treachery," Useless continued. "But when he returned my book, I was already trapped under the Hold. And Keepers and Masters can't speak silently between each other as they can between themselves."

"We did," she said bluntly, recalling his disastrous attempts to frighten her home before she reached the Hold. Being able to tell that someone was in her thoughts had shocked both of them, and she had driven him from her mind with a surprisingly potent force.

"Yes," he said. "It shouldn't be possible. Your thought patterns must be laid out . . . differently." Useless drew back, blinking at her like an owl with a sudden thought. "How much did Meson tell you of being a Keeper?"

"Nothing," she said. "But I was only five when—when he left." Feeling alone, Alissa curled her feet under her, cold and damp in their slippers.

"Yes, and Strell told me your father taught you how to read."

Alissa nodded. "Me and my mother both. Well, he started, but she finished it."

"Why did he bother?" Useless said, more to himself than her. "He couldn't have known that early you had inherited his neural pattern and were bound to the Hold. He must have perceived something in you. . . . I don't know. You aren't like any other Keeper I have known."

Embarrassed, Alissa looked down, but he continued, clearly not expecting her to answer.

"You don't let your fear dull your temper, and how, under my Master's Hounds, did you find your source and tracings in your thoughts when no one told you they existed? It's almost as if . . . You remind me of—"

Alissa raised her head. Useless was regarding her with a peculiar mix of dismay and delight. His scrutiny continued as she leaned to fuss with the fire so as to have something to do. "Tell me," he said abruptly. "You like Strell's music?"

"Yes," she blurted, wondering at the sudden shift in topics.

"He says you fall asleep."

She shrugged. "His piping is very restful—usually."

Useless nodded. "Growing up on a farm, you must have had a lot of pets."

Alissa stared at him. *What kind of question is that?* she thought. "No. We couldn't even keep a cat in the barn. Everything that could, ran away."

"And you like the cold, I see?"

"I adore it," she said sarcastically as she hunched into her coat.

"Yes, of course." Useless's thoughts were clearly somewhere else. "That book you found last month, you seemed most reluctant to give it to Bailic when you pulled it from the well, despite knowing if you didn't, you would die right there in the woods."

Alissa fidgeted with the hem of her sleeve, trying to deny her stab of longing at the mere mention of it. Giving the *First Truth* to Bailic had been the hardest thing she had ever done. "I'm going to get it back," she said. "It's mine."

"It's my book, not yours," he said, a marked softness in his gravelly voice.

"That's not what it said!" she shouted, then put a hand to her mouth, shocked at her outburst.

"Just so," Useless said mildly. "Perhaps *my* book did, at that. It would explain many inconsistencies." As if taking on a heavy burden, he shook his head and sighed in resignation. The ugly pot over the flames began to steam, and much to Alissa's astonishment, Useless pushed on the seat of the bench beside him. The seat slid off with a grinding sound to reveal a small stone box within it. She eagerly leaned forward as he took out the box and opened it, slumping back when she found it contained only tea leaves. Unaware or uncaring of her disappointment, Useless set the pot to brew, shut the box, and replaced the seat. There was a tug on her thoughts and a ward so quick she hadn't a chance of memorizing the pattern resonating in her unconscious. Two brown cups equal in ugliness to the pot appeared. "If I may, Alissa," he said slowly, "I would like to look at your tracings. To see . . . ah . . . if the burn across your tracings that you received while removing that ward has healed properly."

She narrowed her eyes, wondering at his shift in tone from dominating to almost respectful. "You'll have to put your thoughts into mine?" she asked warily. She didn't like that. Every time he did, it left her afraid he might see more than what she wanted him to.

He nodded. "The technique becomes easier with practice, a teaching tool, a common event between instructor and student. But if you can't manage it . . ." He let the challenge hang.

She took a deep breath, willing her unreasonable fear away. Useless wasn't going to hurt her. "What do I do?"

Glancing up at the dark sky, Useless drew his legs up under him. He eyed her tightly, grimaced, and finally nodded. Cross-legged upon the bench, he hid his odd hands among the folds of his coat sleeves. "If you would find your tracings?"

"All right." Her pulse quickened in anxiety, and she divided her attention to visualize her tracings with her mind's eye. The thin, spiderweb-like lines seemed to melt into existence in a fantastic tangle, fracturing off in every direction. The pathways were dark and still as they were empty of power, barely visible against the blue black of her consciousness by way of the thin streaks of gold that ran through them, seeming to glint where the tracings joined and crossed one another.

Close beside them, but seeming to be half an angle away, was her source. The sphere of power was enveloped by a tight weave of shimmering threads. She couldn't tell what lay within the gold, almost white, hollow ball. Alissa's breath slipped easily from her as she reveled that she was intact, her tracings no longer burned to an unusable char by her own stupidity.

Useless's eyebrows rose. "You have them?" he accused. "Your eyes are still focused."

"I can close them if you like."

"No, that's fine," he said remotely. "If you're ready, we can try." He looked to the fire, and Alissa's eyes slammed shut of their own accord as his presence materialized within her thoughts. Instantly, a wave of affronted panic washed through her, and she found herself struggling to keep from mentally lashing out at him. For a terrifying moment she kept her lethal response in check, then another. With a gasp, Alissa felt a surge of power around her source, an instinctive reaction to drive him out with a blast of mental fire.

His thoughts vanished from hers, and she sagged in relief. She opened her eyes to find Useless staring back, his amber eyes round and unreadable, seeming to glint in the firelight. "This isn't a good idea," he said slowly. "I've never begun with someone as untutored as you."

"No." She gulped, her pulse beginning to slow. "I—I can do better. I almost had it."

"Better?" he grumbled. "You must be entirely trustworthy, or I can't stay."

Trustworthy! Alissa thought, affronted. "Maybe if you didn't storm in so high and mighty, I might be more accommodating!" she said, not wanting to admit she couldn't control herself.

The Master's face tightened. "Again," he demanded, goaded into trying once more.

Alissa closed her eyes and found her tracings, surprised to realize she was scared. If she couldn't do this, Useless would teach her nothing. She shivered as much from anticipation as the cold. Her breath came fast, and she tensed. Burn her to ash. What if she couldn't do it?

There was a sigh, and a markedly cautious thought slipped between hers, a hint of presence that slowly grew to a whisper. His unusually submissive presence made it easier, and it took only a moment of struggle before she mastered herself. Slowly she exhaled. *"See?"* she thought, shoving her primitive thoughts away. *"I can do this."*

"You're sure?" Useless asked into her mind, giving Alissa the impression of settling himself. *"Well, let's see what you can manage."*

Alissa was silent, trying not to squirm as she felt his light thought among hers. *"I'm going to set up a ward,"* he explained. *"If your tracings are fully . . . er . . . healed, there should be an echo of it reflecting on your neural net. Do you see which circuit is resonating?"*

"Yes," she thought nervously as several loops began to shimmer. They formed a convoluted pattern sprawling in six directions whose end and beginning were the same.

The glow faded and was replaced with a more complex form. *"How about this one?"*

"Uh-huh."

"Really? How about . . . m-m-m . . . this?"

"Yes. What does it do?"

Immediately the glow vanished. *"Never mind that."* There was a slight hesitation. *"I would say you healed properly."*

"But what do the patterns do?" she persisted, then brightened. *"That's how you make a ward, isn't it!"*

Clearly uncomfortable, Useless muttered into her thoughts, *"It's very complex."*

Alissa felt a thrill of excitement. *"Do I have to set up that crossed loop first?"* she thought, then pierced through the weave surrounding her source. A shimmering dart of force shot to her tracings in an elegant S shape. It looped back in a mirror image of itself to her source to make a glowing, twisted loop.

"Stop! Shut it down!" Useless exclaimed, his thoughts slamming into hers.

Frightened, Alissa broke the connection. The crossed loop faded as the force vanished back into her source. He fled from her thoughts, leaving her with a unexpected sensation of loss. Alone again, she looked up to see him with his head in his hands, muttering at the fire. Something had upset Talon, and the small bird was grousing, shifting in agitation from foot to foot.

"Old fool," she heard Useless grumble as if he had forgotten she was there. "I should have known by the way she is yammering on about my book."

"It isn't your book," Alissa said with a sudden rush of dismay.

His head came up. "It most certainly is," he said, sounding affronted.

"It's mine!" she cried in alarm. It was as she had feared. Now that Useless was free, he was going to take it. She hadn't crossed the mountains and trapped herself with a madman for the winter so Useless could claim it for himself!

"That will be enough, student," he said calmly to the fire. "It's my book."

"You gave it to my papa!" she cried, fear pulling her to a stand. "He gave it to me. It's mine! I won't let you take it."

Useless turned to her. "What did you say?"

"I won't let you," she repeated shakily, a tinge of self-preservation lowering her voice.

He rose in a single, fluid motion, drawing himself up to his full height. "Sit down."

"No," she whispered, feeling her face go white. She wouldn't let him tell her what to do.

"You will sit down!" Useless said, taking an unnerving step closer.

"But it's mine!" she exclaimed, past caring what happened next.

In a breath, he went still. His arm dropped, and he slowly exhaled. Terribly afraid, Alissa stared at him. "You will, student," he said softly, dangerously. "If you look to me for instruction, you will do as I say, or as I say not. I will teach you what I want, your instruction proceeding as fast or slow as I deem fit. This isn't from malice or dominance but to save . . . your . . . hide." He stepped back, crossing his arms before him. "There will be no constraints or wards to stop you, only your word. But you will put yourself under my discretion, or I will leave for good."

He would leave me? Alissa thought, panicking. She would learn nothing, have nothing. Bone and Ash, she cursed herself as she felt her throat tighten and her shoulders slump. "I don't know if I can," she whispered, her fear washing from her in misery.

The Master blinked, his anger vanishing in surprise. "Excuse me?" he said, incredulous.

"I *said,*" she shouted, furious at herself, "I don't know if I can!" Alissa slumped on the cold bench. There was a lump in her throat, and she angrily wiped a tear of frustration away with the back of her hand. She had been so close, she thought bitterly. Now she would have nothing.

Useless's brow furrowed, then he chuckled, easing back to his seat. "M-m-m," he said. "I imagine any other answer from you would be false."

"You mean you're not angry?" She wiped her eyes and stared at him incredulously.

"No, just concerned." He paused, considering his next

words. "You see, it's a rather dangerous turn for you. You're standing in a threshold, so to speak. It would be wise to push you through, and I would, except for one thing."

"Bailic?" she guessed, darting a glance at the tower, dark above them.

Useless resettled his robes. "No, he isn't an issue. It's the present state of the Hold."

That made no sense whatsoever, and Alissa patiently waited until he noticed her silence and continued. "I am one and alone. It's too risky. Someone should be here to help in case complications arise, and from what I have read, they always do."

"I thought you taught my papa," she said, becoming more confused.

"Um . . . I did," Useless stammered, "but each student has their own peculiarities."

"I see." Alissa eyed him warily. There was something off about his words.

"And there was always someone to seek counsel from," he continued as if trying to convince himself. He certainly wasn't convincing her. Useless eyed her warily. "I do believe I have had enough of you tonight. Expect my return on the extremes of the moon's drift; otherwise, I'll be searching. Someone besides me may be left."

Alissa pulled her coat tighter, not trusting his rapid shifts of emotion. "There is," she said hesitantly. "I saw a raku just outside the foothills this fall. It was my third day out from home, and it scared me into a puddle of pudding."

"It must have been a feral beast," Useless said, his gaze going distant into the flames.

"A what?" she asked.

His eyes went sad as he leaned to rearrange the fire. "A feral beast. Masters are subject to few ills, but one we share with men is that of madness. Whether by accident or punishment, sentience will occasionally be lost. Unable to remember, they exist as any predator. We watch over them, trying to keep them from the lands of men. It's of these unfortunates your conventional idea of rakus being beasts come from. But they're not truly insane, just unaware."

"They never recall themselves?" Alissa asked in a small voice, trying not to imagine Useless's strength unbridled by wisdom.

"Never," he asserted, sounding angry but not at her. "It's something we don't talk about, as they all have names, though they don't hear them anymore."

"I'm sorry." Useless seemed so sad, Alissa wished she hadn't asked for an explanation.

"Was he a younger beast?" he asked.

"I . . . I think so."

"It was probably Connen-Neute. He was an astonishing student, much potential. Here," he said, sketching a figure in the snow with his finger. "This is his name. It shouldn't be forgotten, now that he doesn't know it." Useless sighed. "I wonder what drew him from the mountains and into the foothills?"

She leaned to study the simple figure, grateful he thought enough of her to teach it to her. Useless's fingers drummed a slow, intricate pattern on the stone. Unsure of what to say, she waited until he looked up with a faint, mirthless smile. "Go," he said. "It's cold."

Alissa dutifully stood and gathered her skirts. With a final nod to Useless, she began to pick her way along the snow-covered path to the kitchen. She looked back before rounding the bend in the path and saw him unawares in the bright moonlight. Chin in his hands, he was contemplating his fire, the two unused cups beside him. He looked worried. Without knowing how, she sent a wisp of an understanding thought to him. He jumped but didn't turn.

"Go, young one. My troubles aren't your concern," she sensed in her thoughts, light and sure as spider silk. It startled her, and she hastened to the kitchen. Hesitating at the door, Alissa unintentionally caught more of his thoughts which confused her even more.

"Old fool," she heard him complain. *"You know better than to jump into a novice's thoughts like that. She had every right to char you proper—but she didn't. Where did*

she learn her control?" Alissa felt him sigh. *"Curse you, Keribdis. Convincing the Hold to chase your rainbows to punish me has brought the Hold's downfall twice over. I wasn't trained for this. It would be done perfectly if you were here. She guesses far too much. Totally out of control. I've never worked with* children *before."* He hesitated. *"Burn me to ash if that wasn't fun, though."*

Then the faint touch was gone, and Alissa was left with her disconcerted thoughts, alone once more in the empty, silent kitchen.

4

"Just look at it, Alissa. It's perfect!"

Smiling thinly, Alissa levered herself up onto the long, black table and wrapped her arms about her knees. It was frigid down in the Hold's second kitchen unless the sun was out. The large room was at the end of one of the short tunnels off the great hall, unused for what looked like decades with its empty hooks and cupboards. "It's cold," she complained, her voice echoing off the flat stone walls. "You won't be able to work the clay. Your fingers will stiffen up."

Plainsmen lived or died by how skilled they were in their profession, and the chance to practice his original family craft of clay work seemed to have become an obsession since Strell found the large barrels of clay three days ago. Upon discovering the small jars of what he claimed were powdered glazes, setting up a potter's stead was a foregone conclusion. He needed good light to work by, a convenient water source, and a kiln, though he claimed he could make do with a smolder pit in the garden, whatever that was.

The light was too dim in the upstairs kitchen. Any of the countless practice rooms had enough sun but no water. The same went for the dining hall. That left only the annex kitchen. Alissa just knew he was going to spend all his time down here. And as it was too cold for her to keep him company, her days would soon stretch long and lonely.

"Too cold? Maybe," was his muffled reply. He had crawled partway into the largest oven to estimate its size, and his long legs stuck out, looking like a spider's. "But I won't be down here unless the sun is bright, and you know how warm it gets then." Slowly he backed out of the oven, humming a child's tune.

Alissa gave him a dour nod he couldn't possibly see as he had turned to the narrow windows high overhead. "It's hard enough finding wood for our rooms, the kitchen, and the dining hall," she grumbled. "If you use that oven as a kiln, you're going to need a lot of wood."

He stood with his hands on his hips looking tall, confident, and happy. "I won't need to have a fire but once every week or so." Singing softly, he peered down the kitchen's well, listening to his voice echo.

"There's probably no water down there," she predicted, hoping he would abandon his latest diversion and come back with her to the warm upper rooms. Strell reached for the cracked bucket tied to an even more ancient-looking coil of rope. Curious despite her glum mood, she hopped off the table, the thin soles of her shoes making a hard landing. Their heads nearly touched as she and Strell peered down into the shadows of the well. "Careful," she advised. "That rope looks thin in spots."

"Nonsense," he cried as the faint sound of the bucket finding water reached them. "It'll hold. Besides, I'm not going to fill it. I just want to see what's down there." Ignoring the dubious arch of her eyebrows, he turned the large crank, drawing the bucket up. The pulley's piercing squeaks seemed to go right through her head, until there was an audible snap and an even louder splash.

"Ah . . . oops." Strell stared mournfully down into the depths as Alissa laughed, then covered her mouth in embarrassment. It really wasn't funny.

"Oh, Strell," she said quickly. "I'm sorry." But he was peering into the well, apparently not having heard even her laugh.

Talon left her perch to land upon Strell's shoulder, crooning softly. "Sand and wind," he sighed, eyeing the frayed end of the rope. "Now I'll have to find a hook."

Alissa slumped as she finally admitted how much this

meant to him. She would be selfish not to help. "I know where there's another bucket," she offered.

"No. I should get that one out, or it's going to molder down there and contaminate the well." He sighed, peering into the black. "Hounds. I really wanted to try to find a wheel today. Now I'll have to play fisherman." A dark hand ran through his mop of brown tangles as he glanced at the ceiling to estimate how much light was left.

"Tell you what," Alissa said cheerfully, "I'll find a wheel for you, and a new rope, too."

"No, that's all right," he said. "I know it's too cold down here for you. I'll find everything all right. Why don't you go have a cup of tea or something?"

Her eyebrows went up, and her mouth went down. She wasn't sure how she should take that. It sounded patronizing. Strell glanced up at her silence, and recognizing the cast on her face he quickly added, "To warm you up! You know the annexes better than I do. I'm sure you could find everything faster, but you, Alissa," he leaned to lightly tap her nose, "look positively chilled."

Alissa blinked in surprise, then smiled at the attention. "Why don't we both go look?" she suggested. "At least until we find a hook and rope."

Pushing himself from the well, Strell headed for the tunnel archway. "Castoffs?"

"Dry goods," she said confidently as they left. Talon stayed behind, peering down into the well. Strell was humming, and she smiled as the last of her ire at his attention being focused from her slipped away. He hadn't been in this good a mood since . . . since . . . She hesitated. She hadn't ever seen him this happy before. And who knew? Her mother had wanted a nested set of Hirdune bowls. Perhaps Alissa could get them for her now.

5

"Wait! Strell?" she called, but he was gone, his rope and hook draped over his shoulder. She had agreed to find a potter's wheel for him while he fished his bucket out from the kitchen well, but there was one problem. "I don't know what it looks like—exactly," she finished softly. Alissa gazed at the empty mouth of the tunnel, debating if she should follow him and ask, but decided she would probably know one when she saw one.

She slid from her perch on a bale of linen and ran her eyes over one of the Hold's glorified closets. There were four levels in the dry goods annex, their open balconies overlooking a central work area on the ground floor. The tall, narrow room was lit by the slits in the distant ceiling, angled to maximize the light reflecting in. It was bright, if not necessarily warm, as there were no wards here on the windows.

Feeling slightly put out, she wandered over to the Hold's stash of leather. She would look for Strell's wheel, but first she wanted to find a swath of leather to make a new hat. She was blissfully knee deep in the supple sheets when there was a small scuff, and she knew Strell had returned. Perhaps he had fished his bucket out already and had come back to help her. "Strell?" she called loudly to the unseen floor. "What exactly does a potter's wheel look like?" But it was Bailic's voice that echoed up, and she stiffened.

"Don't you know?" he said in a smooth, mocking voice. "Your lack of education is appalling. But even you should know it won't be with the fabric."

Alissa's face warmed. She went to the railing and peered down to find Bailic gazing up in her general direction. His pale skin looked all the more obvious against his black Master's vest. "Good afternoon, Bailic," she said warily. She steadied herself, hoping he would go away quickly. She felt almost naked without Strell beside her to serve as a ready distraction.

Using her voice to orient himself, he focused on her and gave her a slow nod. Silently he turned and wove his way past the mesh screens and barrels of waste cloth towards the tall cupboards behind them. "I can't imagine what you want with a potter's wheel," he said. "But if you help me find what I need, I'll tell you where one is."

Her refusal was hot on her tongue, but she hesitated as he turned his painful-looking eyes to her. They were rimmed in red from the sun's glare, and he was squinting. A slight feeling of compassion whispered through her. But it was the idea of not having to admit to Strell she didn't know what a wheel looked like that prompted her to ask, "What are you looking for?"

Bailic rubbed his wet eyes and opened the cupboard to reveal stacks of bound paper. "High-grade paper. The ink dries faster on it." Touching a sheaf of paper in what almost looked like a caress, he took a sheet, creased it sharply, then ripped it down the center. His eyes closed as he breathed deeply of the cut. "Second grade," he mused, hardly audible. "You can tell by the smell." And the scraps fell to the floor in a whisper of sound.

"If I find some for you," she said, "you'll tell me where I can find a potter's wheel?"

"Yes," he drawled as he took a second sheet. It met the same fate as the first, and the twin pieces of white drifted down.

Alissa pulled her shawl closer as she descended to the first floor. "All right," she agreed.

"Done and done," Bailic said, pulling back from his reach for another stack. He stoically waited until she was before him. "This shelf," he tapped a finger on an empty one. "This is where I found it before. There is a symbol etched upon the face. Do you see it?"

Alissa edged closer, reluctant to get too near him. "Yes," she admitted. The faint tracings were too light for Bailic to see and too small for his fingers to discern. It read, "High-grade."

"Do you think it within your capabilities to match that symbol to another just like it?"

"Yes," she said shortly, not liking his tone.

"We will see if you're as clever as you would like to think," he said. "Find it."

Willing to play the game of ignorance, Alissa dutifully reinspected the high-grade stamp and tried to match it to the rest, ignoring that she could read that all the remaining shelves were second and third grade. "Nothing like that mark here," she said and closed the cupboard with a dull thump. The next cupboard was the same, as was the third. Bailic, who had moved himself and his tender skin to a shadow, was beginning to visibly chafe by the time she had been through all the cupboards and hadn't found any. Shrugging, Alissa met Bailic's forbidding frown.

"I was right," he muttered. "Either you are half-witted, or I have used it all. I'll check again by hand tonight." He turned on a heel and headed for the archway.

Alissa stood waiting. "Where are the wheels, Bailic?" she called.

"Hm-m-m?" He didn't even slow, and she felt her face redden.

"The potter's wheel," she prodded. "You were going to tell me where one was."

Bailic hesitated in the mouth of the tunnel. "The agreement was that if you found the paper, I would tell you where it is. You didn't find any, so I don't have to."

Alissa's jaw dropped. "You know but won't tell me? It's not my fault there's none here!"

"Even so." He plucked a thread from his sleeve and dropped it with a look of annoyance.

"But that's not fair!" she cried.

Bailic took three quick steps toward her. His face was

red, and the scar that ran from his ear and across his throat stood out sharp and obvious. "Be still," he snarled, and Alissa backed away, frightened. "An agreement is an agreement. Because you don't like the outcome, it doesn't follow it will shift itself to please you." Turning, he strode away, his long vest furling about his ankles.

"What a pile of sheep dung," Alissa muttered as he disappeared, disgusted for having tried to help him. Snatching up the torn pages, she sniffed at the ragged edges. They smelled like paper. Bailic was right, she thought sourly. A potter's wheel wouldn't be here. She would try the castoffs annex next door. Alissa tucked the sheets in one of the cupboards and followed Bailic's path back to the Hold proper.

As she stepped from the tunnel into the great hall, she heard the faint sound of Bailic's door slamming. "Maybe I should just tell Strell I don't know what one looks like," she said with a sigh, but remembering Bailic's words of scorn, she decided not to. "I can find it," she said boldly, stomping to the head of the last tunnel and feeling her way down its black, gently sloping path. "I know it has a wheel on it." With that, she stepped into the chaos that was the castoffs.

She stood for a moment, her confident smile fading as her eyes went to the distant ceiling. The narrow storeroom was jam-packed with clutter. This was where Bailic piled everything that wasn't fastened down, and the mess was atrocious. Even if she knew what she was looking for and somehow found it, they would never be able to get it out of here.

Pride kept her from admitting defeat. She yanked the tarp off the nearest pile to find footstools, covered to keep their embroidered colors from fading. Struggling slightly, she tucked the cover back. The next revealed a mound of glorious tapestries, and she flipped through them until their weight overwhelmed her curiosity. The third tarp was tied, and she peeked under it to find empty frames. Wondering what Bailic had done with the pictures, she reached for the next.

Alissa continued toward the back of the annex, finding

baskets, jars, chamber pots, curtains, shelves, everything.
It was nearly time to begin supper when she reached the
cooling shade of the far wall. Turning about, she put her
hands on her hips and blew a strand of hair from her eyes.
Ashes, she thought. The clutter was overwhelming. She
was making no headway at all. Tired and disheartened, she
pulled a badly gouged end table from the mess, set it next
to a battered trunk, and sat down. Her head thumped back
against a stack of slatted crates, and she watched the light
sift through the still air.

It was cold in the shadows; no one could have been
back here in ages. Alissa's eyes drifted across the tower of
trunks. It looked as if someone had packed up their entire
life and piled it away to be forgotten. She leaned closer to
the trunks, feeling the beginnings of a frown. Something
was written on each and every one.

"Connen-Neute?" she whispered, recalling the figure
Useless had shown her when he explained the Master had
gone feral. Stiffening, she half turned and inspected the
crates behind her. They were labeled the same. She was sitting among a feral Master's belongings!

Alissa stood up, wiping her hands nervously on her
skirt. The tower rooms where the Masters once lived were
full of possessions, but everything had been protected by
painful wards that cramped her fingers and singed her
thoughts with even an accidental touch. The day she had
investigated the tower had ended with her incapacitated by
an agonizing headache caused by the repeated jolts of
power across her tracings. She hadn't been able to pick up
a thing. But here there were no wards at all. Maybe.

She touched a trunk with a tentative finger and smiled.
No ward—it wasn't even locked—and so she lifted the lid
to find it was full of books. Her smile softened as she
breathed in the scent of paste, sinking to her knees to run her
fingers over the bindings. Books were rare, but her papa had
always brought her one from his frequent trips. At least,
that's where her mother said they had come from. Opening
the cover of the first, Alissa found "Connen-Neute" written

in a childlike scrawl. A feeling of sad remembrance filled her as she read the title.

It was a book of short, humorous stories of a misguided squirrel and his efforts to remain calm in the most trying of circumstances. Whenever the poor thing had lost his temper, he had ended up in a terrible stew. Alissa remembered her papa reading to her from this. It had gone a long way in teaching her four-year-old spirit the difficult art of self-control. Her smile faded, and she closed the book with an uneasy snap. What had her papa been doing with a copy of a raku child's book that taught self-control?

Next was a book that compared the symmetry in nature to that in mathematics. This one, too, she had studied from, and beginning to frown, she dug deeper. There was a slim, unfamiliar volume about music, an entire stack devoted to the movement of the stars, an enormously thick one concerned about the dynamics of closed populations, and another on how to manipulate them to achieve a desired trait. Three loose-leaf volumes were penned by Connen-Neute himself and seemed to consist entirely of notes referring to the craft of paper production. Half the trunk contained book after book of dates, accomplishments, and activities that she idly riffled through until realizing they were Connen-Neute's private journals. Flushing, Alissa put everything away and shut the trunk with a thud.

"All right, then," she whispered as she stood and tucked her hair back behind an ear. Her eyes slid to the crates, and spotting a familiar word peeping from between the slats, she bent closer. "High-grade?" she breathed, her eyebrows rising. Not believing her luck could be that good, she cast about until she found an easel and used one of its legs to pry open the crate.

"Paper." Grinning, Alissa gazed at the stacks bound with a thick gray ribbon. This would explain the carefully written notes she had just found concerning its crafting. Clearly, Connen-Neute had mastered the art of papermaking, and if a Master bothered to learn how to make something, it was going to be the very best.

Alissa teased out a single sheet and tore it in two.

Taking a slow, deep breath, she fancied she could smell almonds. "Odd," she whispered, and tried it again. Once more the rich scent of stored sunshine mixed with the gray, cold smell of forgotten memories.

The torn paper went into her pocket, and she lifted out a bundle. If Bailic wanted more, he would have to ask. Terribly pleased, Alissa clambered across the abandoned furniture and practically danced her way to the great hall and up the stairs to Bailic's room. Standing before his door, she smoothed her hair and knocked politely, if not smugly.

"A bargain is a bargain," came his muffled voice. Smirking, she knocked again.

"Go away!" Bailic shouted.

This time she pounded the door with a fist. "You don't listen very well," she heard. "Perhaps if I box your ears it will help."

The door was yanked open, showing Bailic tight with anger. "Your paper," Alissa said dryly as she dropped the heavy package at his feet. It hit the floor in a loud thump, startling even her. He quickly stooped to pick it up and set it on a nearby table. His ink-stained fingers ran lightly across the gray ribbon to untie it. Still having not said a word, he predictably tore a sheet in half.

"This is Connen-Neute's work," he breathed, his eyes distant. "Where did you find it?"

"Good enough?" she said, refusing to follow him past the one-way ward on his door.

"Yes. Yes, it's fine, but where was it? I thought the last had been used ages ago."

"Where is the potter's wheel?" she demanded.

Bailic chuckled, and Alissa froze. "You learn fast, girl." He met her eyes. They looked almost normal in the half-curtained darkness of his room. "I can see why the piper has allowed himself to tolerate you," he said, arching his eyebrows in a way that made her decidedly uncomfortable. Drawing herself up, she took a casual step back, tugging her shawl closer.

"An agreement is an agreement," he sighed, "and you seem to have gotten the better end of it—this time. He rubbed gently at the scar on his neck, and she felt a stirring of unease. "I enjoy a good bargain. I used to live for them, you might say, being a plainsman. Would you be interested in another?"

"No." Not caring if Bailic could tell she was scared, she backed to the stairs.

"Indulge me," he said with a simper. "At least hear me out."

She nodded. If she didn't humor him, he might not tell her where the wheel was.

"That wasn't so hard now, was it?" Bailic leaned confidently against his doorframe and crossed his arms. "I can do much for you," he said, "almost as much as you can do for me. Your eyes are very keen. The way you found the paper is almost beyond belief. I would never have been able to find it that quickly. When the book is open, stay and be my eyes. I can guarantee your safety for the time you're in my service. Think of it," he said, leaning forward, and Alissa backed up another step. "There *will* be a war. There *will* be a new order. I will instigate it, and I will choose who will prosper and who will fail. Wouldn't it be pleasant," he murmured, "to have the ear of the one making such decisions?"

"I understand," she whispered, feeling ill.

Nodding, he smiled as if she had said yes. "You will consider my offer?"

Thinking only of escape, Alissa fixed her face into a careful neutrality. "Yes."

"Good. I put the wheels in the stables." He hesitated. "Bring me your answer anytime."

Quite sure that was an invitation she would never take up, she left, feeling unclean. She wanted to tell someone what had happened, a confession to purge herself, but she wouldn't tell Strell, afraid he might do something to antagonize the fallen Keeper. Telling Useless would only gain her a lecture. Talon wouldn't care. This, she decided, she would keep to herself. But at least she had found Strell's potter's wheel.

6

"Late again, Piper?" Bailic stood alone in the practice room while the sun rose beyond the surrounding hills. He wasn't surprised. But that didn't mean he was going to accept the piper's excuse.

Bailic forced his tension away as he topped off his cup of tea from the cloth-covered pot. He had found it here waiting for him along with his breakfast: porridge made with tea instead of water. At least the girl was up in a timely fashion. He might keep her when all was said and done. Someone who knew him might be pleasant, when the world shifted to suit him. And the world was going to shift.

The steam from his cup drifted upward to obscure his already fuzzy sight. Bailic held himself still and sent his thoughts out to find the girl and the piper. The kitchen was empty, as were the stairs. His eyes narrowed as he found them in the Keeper's hall. The rising sun warmed his back, and knowing his limit had been reached, he moved to his chair into the shadows. Slumped in its rigid shape, he leaned to run a caressing finger over the book of *First Truth*, resting on a small table beside him.

Wanting to jolt his student out of his complacency, Bailic had brought it down with him this morning. It would serve as a reminder to the piper as to why he was here and not burnt to ash. An extra incentive, Bailic thought, for his pupil to work harder. His student clearly needed some encouragement.

There had been very little progress since giving the piper that dusting of source two weeks ago. Apathetic would be the appropriate word to describe him. The plains-man seemed to understand; he asked all the expected questions, gave all the right answers. But there had been no movement to actually do anything. Bailic's own instruction had relied heavily upon Tolo-Toecan entering his thoughts and showing him exactly what he wanted. As a Keeper, Bailic couldn't do this. It made things all the more difficult.

Frowning, Bailic set his tea beside the book. There would be improvement today, or he would take it out on the girl. It was a cumbersome way to get things done, though. Perhaps he should go back to his old techniques. He had broken stronger men than the piper. He couldn't kill him, but there were lots of permanent things that weren't fatal. The piper was too sure of his immunity. He needed a reminder of how tenuous his situation was to encourage him to apply himself more stringently. It was likely the man was simply prolonging his lessons until the snows melted and he had a chance to escape.

"But there is no escape," Bailic said, running a finger over the ancient tome. "I will open his mind to wisdom as surely as I will eventually open your clasp."

The book had thwarted his every attempt at entry. Upon first gaining possession, he had concentrated his efforts upon the heavy clasp. After bloodying his fingertips, he had tried his knife. Now his blade lay tucked under his pillow, shattered into three pieces by the book's protective wards. He had been lucky. It could have been him.

With that thought tight in his mind, he had cautiously tried to open it with his own ward. His first, tentative attempts had been met with a mild resistance, but each succeeding ward he set provoked a correspondingly more severe reaction until now even the smallest ward would result in a protective field. Attempting to remove the field only caused the book to strengthen its protection. Trying to touch it before the field dropped on its own would result in a sharp, painful dart of energy lancing through his tracings. The mild singe gave him a headache that could last for days.

"No matter," he crooned. "You're mine." Bailic snatched his hand back as a silver-lined containment field blossomed into existence about the book with a finger-cramping hum of warning. He hadn't even set a ward. It had responded to his unconscious desire alone. With a sharp cry of frustration, he rose and strode to the hall. "Piper-r-r-r-r!" he bellowed.

He stormed back to the book, staring down at it in outrage. "Mine," he nearly spat. It might be as long as sunset until the hateful thing let its protection drop and he could touch it again. Bailic began to pace, spinning as he reached the windows to glare at the book glowing under its silvery field. "I say you are *mine*," he vowed.

7

Alissa fidgeted outside Strell's door in worried indecision. The sun was shining on the Hold's tower already. Soon it would fill the practice room. A tray with a small pot of tea and sweet roll for Strell was in her hands. He hadn't been down for breakfast, and it was too late for their usual meal together. Either he had forgotten to get up or decided to skip his first meal. The latter was a physical impossibility.

Strell?" she called through the door. "Are you awake?"

She held her breath and listened, keeping the tray sideways so she could put her ear close to his door. Nothing. She didn't want to be improper, but deciding she had no choice, she set the tray on the floor and cracked the door open.

"Strell?" she said hesitantly, making out the lump under the covers. The fire in the grate was banked, and it was dark. "Strell. Get up. You're late."

"Late?" It was a sleep-slurred word.

Emboldened in that he seemed to be covered by his blanket, Alissa entered. There was a tingle of a ward left in the sill by a long-gone Keeper, recognizing her and dismissing her as no threat. Her eyes were inexorably drawn to the ominous crack in the wall running from the warded window to the ceiling. The explosion caused by improperly removing the ward about her source had torn through their shared chimney flue, cracking Strell's wall and giving him a slight concussion. Flushing, she dropped her gaze back to the lump on the bed. "Wake up," she said.

"Bailic said he would remove all your hair if you were late again."

"He can't do that," Strell said as he propped himself up on an elbow. "Can he?"

Her brow furrowed as she imagined Strell with no hair. "I don't particularly want to find out." His face was slack from slumber, and he blinked as if struggling to focus. "I'll wait for you in the hall," she said and ducked out, embarrassed. He looked charmingly defenseless while soft with sleep.

Knowing he would be a while, she picked up her tray and went to wait at the landing, but a shout from Bailic drew her to a stop before going three steps. Such a blatant show of emotion from him wasn't typical, and worry flickered through her.

There was a sudden commotion behind Strell's door, and he strode into the hall, unshaven and his boots unlaced. He halted in surprise when she extended the tray to him. "I thought you would be hungry," she said.

"Yes. Thanks," he said as he took it. "It's not Bailic's?"

"No. You're late. He already has his tray."

Grimacing, Strell took it, and they continued down the hall. "Wolves," Strell complained. "He has himself in a state this morning. I could hear him through the walls."

Alissa grabbed his elbow to steady him as he stumbled on the stairs. "I think he's getting impatient again," she guessed.

Strell nodded around a yawn. "I'll become an expert today in fields, at least the theory of them. That should satisfy him for a time."

She returned his smile, but it faded quickly. There was only so much Strell could do, or pretend to do. Useless hadn't given her permission to perform any wards or fields in Strell's stead, saying she hadn't enough control yet. She didn't understand why she had to be good. Even Bailic couldn't expect Strell to get it right the first time.

The silence from the practice room was daunting as they reached the door. An amber light from the risen sun was spilling out into the hall, and Alissa's hopes that they

might make it in time were dashed. She held herself back
a step, and Strell went in first. Eyes lowered, she moved to
her accustomed spot in the sun, not wanting to risk Bailic's
attention by getting her usual cup of tea.

Bailic stood with his arms crossed before him, his
shadow running halfway up the opposing wall. "You're
late," the man said. They were his first words, more often
than not.

"Sorry," Strell said. She watched his fingers fumble to
straighten his collar in the probable hope that Bailic would
drop the subject if he at least looked contrite. Reaching for
the pot, Strell poured himself a cup of tea, pointedly ignoring Bailic's silence. Alissa settled herself into the cold
cushions and pulled her stitching out from between them.
The dress she was working on was primarily black linen,
and when done, she was going to make a matching scarf.

A faint pull, a familiar jittery feeling, drew her attention
up, searching. Her eyes widened and her heart seemed to
stop. Her book. Bailic had brought down her book. It was
on the small table beside his chair. A containment field was
wrapped around it, so strong it was actually visible as a
faint shimmer. What had he done to her book to make it do
that?

Her pulse raced with the thought it was so close, and
with a strength she didn't know she had, she tore her eyes
away. Desperate, she looked helplessly to Strell. He gazed
blankly at her until he followed her darting eyes back to
the book. His mouth opened slightly, and he stared at it.
Burn me to ash, she thought. How could she stop herself
now? It was right in front of her.

Strell casually rocked forward to a stand. Taking his cup
of untasted tea, he brought it to her, breaking her line of
sight with the book and kicking the leg of her chair. She
gave him a tense smile as her gaze was jolted from the
book, resolving to not look at it again. Should Bailic realize her desire for it, he would know she was the Keeper,
not Strell.

Falling into his familiar role of distraction, Strell returned to the table, shifting from his usual spot to block her

view of the book. A flash of indignation took her, quickly followed by relief. She could do this. If she didn't look at it, she could do this. But as she picked up her stitching, the same restless feeling took her. *Ashes,* she thought as her foot started to jiggle. If she crossed the room, she could touch it. Bailic's eyebrows rose at her erratic motion, and she dropped her head and focused on her stitching.

"No excuse this morning?" Bailic said as he turned back to Strell. There was no emotion in his voice.

"I said I was sorry."

Bailic eased across the practice room to lean over Strell as he slumped in his chair. "Sorry won't do, my piper," he said, his anger almost hidden under his smooth voice.

"Hair grows back," Strell said as he met Bailic's eyes from under his lowered brow.

A benevolent smile came over Bailic, and Alissa's heart gave a hard thump. There was an eager intensity to him that said he was up to something. "You're right," the Keeper said. "Fetch me my book."

Alissa's gaze darted to Strell. If he touched the field, the ward it held would burn him. Bailic wanted Strell to singe his tracings—as if he had any that mattered. But it would still hurt and probably give him a nasty headache.

Strell glanced from Alissa to the book, and then to Bailic. "Get it yourself," he said.

"No." Bailic sat on the long, black table. "You get it for me."

"It's under a field," he protested.

"It's not my field," Bailic said gently, as if chiding a child for being afraid of the dark. "It's the book's. It's claimed you. You ought to be safe." He hesitated. "I want to find out."

Strell glanced past Bailic to the open door. "I don't know enough yet. It will burn me."

Bailic heaved a dramatic sigh. "Oh, very well. The girl will retrieve it for me. What does it matter if a commoner is burnt?" He smiled at her, and she shrank back. If she touched her book, she wouldn't be able to put it back down. She knew without trying.

Immediately, Strell stood, his chair grating on the smooth floor. His face was pale with the knowledge of what was going to happen. Alissa shifted uneasily in her chair. It was her fault, she thought. She should have gotten Strell up earlier. She shouldn't have waited so long. What did it matter if she saw his bare feet or that her mother would think it improper for her to be in his room while he was still in bed? Strell was going to singe his tracings. And she could do nothing to stop it. Helpless, she clenched her stitching in her lap and watched Strell move down the row of tall, sun-filled windows to where Bailic kept his chair in the shadows. Her pulse pounded as Strell squatted to bring his eyes level with the shimmering field.

Bailic had spent a long, boring week explaining fields and how they could protect and defend either in or out of one's thoughts. Strell couldn't make a field, but Bailic had made sure he understood them. If he violated the bubble of thought, the ward it contained would burn him.

Or would it? she wondered as Strell scrubbed his hand over his stubbled cheeks, delaying the inevitable. Strell didn't care what the book contained, and Bailic had explained over and over again that intent was often more important than action when it came to triggering the ward a field carried. Alissa had found this to be true to a certain extent. The wards on the windows would burn her fingers and thoughts even when touched by accident. But others, like the one on her doorsill left by her papa, didn't.

"Now, Piper!" Bailic exclaimed impatiently.

Strell took a breath. Screwing up his face, he gingerly reached out

"Please, no," Alissa thought, hoping the book could hear her and understand.

Like a snuffed candle flame, the field extinguished itself as he touched it. Strell jerked his hand back and lurched to his feet. Clearly shocked, he darted his gaze to Alissa, then Bailic.

"Good," Bailic said. It was a short sound, but heavy with emotion. He held himself alarmingly still. Alissa waited, knowing it wasn't over. "Open it," he said.

Strell shook his head and took a step back.

Bailic sent a sly look toward Alissa in an unspoken threat. "Open it," he repeated, and Strell grimaced. Resettling himself before the book, he wiped his palms on his pant legs and reached for the clasp.

There was a sharp pop, and Alissa gasped. Strell snatched his hand back, gripping it protectively in the other. The smell of burnt lightning bit at her nose, and she felt ill. What more could Bailic ask for?

"Get away from it," Bailic said, and Strell backed up, putting space between himself and the book. A hard eagerness had come over Bailic's usually closed face. "Ready yourself," the Keeper said as he scooped up the book. "We're going out."

Alissa's worry shifted to surprise. "Outside? In the snow? What for?" she asked.

"My attempts to wedge wisdom into the piper's skull may shortly become redundant. We're going to Ese' Nawoer. Now."

"You can't leave the Hold. Talo-Toecan can kill you," she said, then dropped her eyes as Bailic focused on her.

"Really?" he said, his voice cold. "I'm taking both of you and the book with me. Talo-Toecan wouldn't dare attack me the last time I held it. He won't this time." Bailic stepped to the door, seeming to be talking more to himself than to them. "I imagine we won't even see his shadow. He won't expect me to go out in the snow."

Strell had eased back to his seat. Eyes on his hand, he opened and closed it as if it wasn't his. "That's because it's foolish," he said softly as Bailic left the room.

Bailic jerked to a halt in the threshold, his head pulling up with an angry stiffness. He turned, his jaw clenched. Alissa shot a pained glance at Strell. Why couldn't he hold his tongue?

"I believe the word you want to use is *clever*," Bailic said tightly. "And you'd better pray to the Navigator and all his Hounds I'm not successful. If I can bring the souls of the abandoned city awake, I won't need you." Bailic's eyes went distant as he gazed out the window towards

Ese' Nawoer. His breath shook as he slowly exhaled. "I've waited long enough," he whispered fiercely. "Snow isn't going to stop me if there is a chance I can start now. You removed the ward from it. Perhaps you can open it if you're in the city."

"But—the snow is up to my knees!" Alissa protested.

Bailic's eyes cleared and his brow rose mockingly. "I'm not leaving you here alone. You'll survive, and if you don't, that's one less half-breed to worry about."

She froze in a nauseating mix of shock and betrayal.

"Bailic," Strell said in sharp warning. He was glaring at him, his muscles tensed.

A sedate smile came over the fallen Keeper. "But that's just what she is," he taunted, shifting her book to his other arm, cradling it as if it were a child. "A bred-in-shame half-breed. We've been over this before, plainsman."

Alissa felt her chest tighten in misery. Her mix of plains and hills was obvious, but to have the reminder thrust upon her without warning was painful. It seemed Strell had found it in himself to ignore her background, but the hatred for half-breeds was so ingrained in both plains and foothills, she was sure Strell would never see her as anything but that odd girl he had met on the way to a legendary fortress. It hadn't seemed to matter before. Now it did. Miserable, she stared out the windows at the cloudless sky.

She heard the sound of Bailic's shoes as he left, and Strell called after him, "You might show some tolerance. Looking the way you do."

"Enough!" Bailic nearly spat, storming back into the room.

A gasp slipped from Alissa as she felt a sharp tug on her awareness. Bailic was setting a ward. Strell choked on his next words, making a terrifying gurgle. He stiffened into immobility as his expression froze into a mask of anger and frustration. Bailic had warded him to stillness, rendering him incapable of everything but the basic movements to keep alive.

As she sat in her chair in horrified indecision, Bailic

crouched to look him face-to-face across the narrow table. "I've been very patient with you," he said softly.

Alissa tensed with fear. "You can't kill him," she said, her voice quavering. "You can't. You won't be able to open the book."

Clearly ignoring her, Bailic rose. He set the book down on the table and crossed his arms. Cocking his head, he eyed Strell, seeming to be deciding what he was going to do. Alissa bit her lip as a small groan came from Strell as he tried to move. His face was turning red with the effort, and sweat had started to bead on his forehead.

"You're right," Bailic said, coming around the table to stand beside him. "Hair grows back. But there must be something. . . . Ah." He bent down and whispered in his ear, "Which hand is it now that uses all its fingers to play your pipe? The right one. Yes?"

Alissa went cold in a wash of panic. "Bailic, no!" she cried, standing up. "He's a minstrel. He needs his hands to play. It's his life."

There was a flash across her tracings, showing her the pattern the ward took in her consciousness, then nothing. Her muscles froze and her pulse raced in fear. Bailic had warded her to stillness! He hadn't even looked at her! How could she fight something that fast?

"Your life, piper?" he said as he pulled Strell's right hand out from under the table and set it on top. It was brown from the sun, made strong by his travel. "You don't need all these fingers to open a book. That's why you are alive. To open a book. And do you know what I'm going to do when you open that book?" he whispered. "I'm going to wake the dead. An entire city of death to dabble my fingers in."

Alissa struggled to move as Bailic lifted Strell's pinky. "Ese' Nawoer was sixteen thousand souls when they built their walls to keep out the refugees from the plague of madness," Bailic said lightly. "Women and children from both the plains and hills went there for help. The mountain city turned a blind eye, refusing them even as their pleas for mercy turned to a savage rage under the throes of madness. The guilt from watching them tear themselves apart against their gates has cursed Ese' Nawoer. They will serve the one who wakes them, and with the book, I can do it."

The Keeper came around to the front of the table and crouched to look Strell in the eyes with a mocking smile. "And do you know what I'm going to do with my sixteen thousand souls? My desperate, cursed, pathetic, guilt-ridden souls? I'm going to send them to the foothills and plains, by ones and twos and threes, until the city is empty. They will infuse their feelings of despair and misery into the minds of the living. It will be as if the plague of madness has returned as they each blame the other and go to war. My souls will drive the living insane. Having Death's thoughts in your own will do that."

Seemingly satisfied, Bailic straightened and took a cleansing breath. "Now, Piper," he said shortly. "I'm not good at this yet. Too much and I'll set your hand on fire, too little, and you will have a stump that will take weeks to fall off. I don't like the stink of decay, so hold still so I can get it right."

The Navigator help me, Alissa thought. *Bailic is jesting. He has to be. He won't do this. This is to scare Strell into obedience. That's all. Strell has to have all his fingers to play his pipe. His hands are his life. Bailic knows that.*

There was another desperate, half moan of a sound from Strell, and Alissa tried to move a foot, anything, not knowing how to break the ward. A sheen of sweat glistened on Strell's face, and he had gone white. *This is enough,* she thought. *Bailic should stop. Stop now.*

Bailic knelt before Strell with the narrow table between them, pulling Strell's hand into the air and leaving it to hang. "The plains and hills need to suffer," he said lightly as he arranged Strell's fingers so they were in his unmoving line of sight. "As I suffered. They treated me as if I was nothing. They forced me out. Showed me what I couldn't have, then laughed at me. What's left after Ese' Nawoer has been at them will beg me to save them. I expect there won't be many, but then, I don't need a lot."

Without warning, there was a small pop and a flash against Alissa's thoughts.

A strangled groan slipped from Strell, and Alissa stared, horrified. The first segment of Strell's smallest finger was gone, as if it had never existed. The smell of burnt hair came to her. There was a strong pull upon her awareness, and she was free. Strell shuddered. A cry of pain seemed to tear from him as Bailic broke his ward. Curling in on himself, Strell clutched his hand to himself and took a rasping breath. "Go away!" she cried, rushing to Strell. "Just go away!" Horrified, she wrapped an unsewn collar around his hand, half covering Strell protectively with her body. There was no blood, but she had to cover it, to hide it. To make it go away, as if it never happened.

Bailic blinked, clearly surprised. It was as if he had forgotten she was there, so enraptured he had been in his butchery. "He won't die of infection, my dear. It's cauterized. I think I did quite well—for being out of practice." He rose from his crouch and slid the book from the table and back into his arms. "You have two, almost entirely whole hands," he said to Strell. "You only need one to open a book. Please. Feel free to give me your opinions any time you like."

Alissa alternated her shattered attention between Bailic and Strell. His hand, she thought. Bailic had done worse than kill him. He had taken away Strell's music, his livelihood, now that he wasn't a potter. Her resolve thickened, tempered by a new hate. She rose to stand between Bailic and Strell. "The Navigator's Wolves will hunt you, Bailic," she said softly, her voice shocking her in its intensity.

"I've been cursed by Keepers and Masters, girl. Your words don't mean anything." Satisfaction in his every movement, Bailic headed for the door, clearly thinking his dominance had been reasserted. He was wrong, Alissa thought.

At the threshold, he turned to Strell, huddled about his hand, and shaking in pain and shock. "We're leaving as soon as I find my boots. Be ready, Piper, or you'll both walk it barefoot." He paused. "I'm going to have to start calling you something else, aren't I?"

Alissa caught back a sob of hate and frustration as Bailic vanished into the hall. "Oh, Strell," she said, turning to him. "I'm sorry. I'm so sorry. I should have woken you. It's my fault."

"Not your fault," Strell said raggedly, still not looking up. "I pushed him too far," he almost panted. "My fault." He took a shaky breath, looking up at her. Alissa drew back, frightened at the hatred and pain in his eyes. "We have to get out of here."

8

Her toes were cold, her nose was frozen, and her knees felt like they would never thaw again. The bright sun was deceiving. It was frigid. With each labored breath, the chill burned her nose and made her lungs ache. Bailic was behind her; Strell was breaking a path. His broad back seemed to remain the same distance away, no matter how fast she tried to walk through the knee-deep snow. "Strell?" She puffed in exhaustion. "Can we stop for a moment?"

Strell pulled up sharp and turned, glancing over her shoulder to Bailic. Coming up alongside, she whispered, "We can do this for three weeks. We can make it to the coast."

He gave her a long, searching look and shook his head. "A morning's walk on a road is not a three-week trip into the wilds. And it would take us twice that in the snow," he whispered back. "We would only make it far enough out to the coast to not be able to make it back."

Bailic came to a shaky halt behind them. "Why are you stopping?" he nearly barked.

"We need a rest." Strell looked pointedly at Alissa, and her eyes widened in understanding. Giving in to her fatigue, she slumped heavily on his arm.

The Keeper's gaze jerked to the sky as Talon landed noisily upon a nearby branch. She had been following them in short hops, undoubtedly making Bailic more irritable than he might otherwise be. He was clearly worried about Useless. "A few moments," the fallen Keeper agreed, pushing his way off the path to the nearest tree.

Leaning against the frost-rimmed bark, he squinted up through the branches, his pale eyes watering from the sun. His breath made fast puffs of mist. Clearly he needed a rest, too.

Bailic was dressed for the weather. A slate-gray coat covered him to the tops of his boots, and a wool scarf kept the wind from his neck. He had on a hat, its brim as wide as the one Alissa had given Strell last fall to replace the one Talon had shredded in a misguided attempt to protect her mistress.

The lump of her book showed from under his coat, and Alissa forced her eyes away. It would be so easy to snatch it and run, but Bailic's threat to turn them to ash if they moved toward it or strayed from his sight kept her from temptation. She thought she could feel the ward that would make good his threat already upon them, set into place as they had left the Hold.

"How is your hand?" she quietly asked Strell, and he frowned.

"It hurts like the Navigator's Hounds are gnawing on it," he said, his brow crinkled in pain. The farther they went, the worse he looked. His coat hadn't been made for deep winter, and his hands were wrapped in cloth as he hadn't found a pair of mittens in time. His injured hand was clenched under his arm, making him unsteady on his feet. She, at least, was prepared for snow. Strell wasn't, and the thought that they would spend nearly a full day in it left Alissa heartsick.

"Go," Bailic said as he pushed himself off the tree. "We're almost there." He glanced mistrustfully up, obviously not as bold as his words had been this morning.

Strell and Alissa exchanged worried looks and lurched into motion. If only she could call for Useless and tell him Bailic was clear of the Hold and vulnerable to attack. But only when the Master put his presence alongside hers in her mind could she reliably hear and be heard. It seemed the Master was elsewhere today. The skies were clear of clouds and raku alike.

The snow seemed to push at her, despite staying in the

path Strell was breaking. She stoically followed him, her head lowered and her eyes upon her footing. Bailic kept close on her heels. It made her nervous, but his eagerness to reach the city was catching. And she, too, was anxious to see the abandoned city. Her father had told her of Ese' Nawoer as a frightening bedtime story. Only later, from Bailic, had she found out it was a true history.

"Sweet as potatoes," Strell said, pulling her from her thoughts, and Alissa came to a halt beside him. Talon quietly swooped down to land upon Alissa's shoulder, and together they stared out from under the last of the trees at the glistening roofs of the city.

"How did we miss that on our way to the Hold?" she whispered, knowing it was from Strell's shortcut through the briars and thorns. It hadn't been a shortcut at all, and they had passed the city without ever knowing it existed.

Before them stretched a wide, open plain surrounding the walled city, the sun glinting off the snowfield in a blinding glare. Dark, slate roofs jutted up over the thick walls, and Alissa half expected to see someone waving a greeting from an upper story. Not a breath of smoke, hint of sound, or trace of smell marred the clear skies.

Bailic came up behind them, scanning the faultless blue of the sky for a long moment from under the safety of the empty branches. "I was right," he said smugly as he squinted and rubbed a mittened hand over his eyes. "Talo-Toecan isn't here. Come on." He pulled his scarf up to his eyes and pushed past them, heading for the set of fallen gates.

Strell and Alissa silently followed. Her eagerness to see the city faltered as she eyed the ominous gap the fallen gates created. The wind kept most of the snow from the wide opening, giving the appearance that people had been at work. The closer they came, the thicker and taller the wall looked, and Alissa stifled a shudder. Her papa once told her all great cities had walls, but the danger must have been terrible to hide behind a wall as tall as this.

Her gaze dropped from the sharp line the wall cut against the sky to the stone slab of the gate still upright. It

leaned aslant against the wall, hanging from the lowest of
its three hinges. Red dust sifted down to stain the snow as
Strell stretched to run his cloth-wrapped hand over the top
of the middle hinge. It was as thick as her arm and bent at
almost a right angle, looking as if it had been broken from
the inside. The other half of the gate lay outside the walls.
There was no crossbar to lock them, and from the look of
the smooth stone, there never had been.

Beyond the walls were empty streets and silent houses.
Alissa stopped at the gates, hesitant to pass them. The wind
gusted to shift the snow from her boots, and she shivered.
Talon twittered encouragingly from her shoulder.

"Look! There's writing," Strell said, pointing to the
large paving stone that served as the city's threshold. First
with his foot, then crouching to use a cloth-wrapped hand,
he brushed the snow from it. Alissa's eyebrows rose as she
recognized a word. It was in the script her papa had taught
her, and she bent to help.

"To Serve the Soul of the Mountain?" she read when
they finished, not liking that at all.

"Come on," Bailic shouted, and she jerked her head up,
startled. He had already entered the city, and his black silhouette was sharp against the snow. Hands upon his hips,
he waited for them in the middle of the road. "We're going
to the center."

Talon left her to settle on one of the roofs, her excited
calls echoing harshly. Alissa half jumped over the engraved stone, not wanting to tread on the words for some
odd reason. Strell took her elbow as she slipped, and they
hurried to catch up.

The street was nearly free of snow by some trick of the
wind. Even more amazing was that the street was paved.
She had never seen such extravagance. The stone buildings
rose up on both sides, coming right up to the pavement,
some two stories high. It looked as if the doors and shutters had been purposely removed, leaving black, gaping
holes. The snow eddied about the barren sills, the sporadic
movement looking like the souls that were said to remain.

She watched in alarm as Strell went to peek into a house. "Empty," he said, his disappointment obvious.

"There's nothing left," Bailic called over his shoulder. He stopped and turned, clearly chafing at their slow pace. "When boys, I and Mes—" He cut his thought short. "I explored much of the city on a dare." His jaw clenched, and he resumed his forward motion.

With her papa, Alissa finished silently for him, glancing up at the black roofs. She watched the vacant, empty doorways and windows, shivering as she was struck by the feeling of walking over her own grave. "Strell," she called as he crossed before her to look into the house across the street. "Don't." The city had her on edge, and she couldn't say why.

"Oh, loosen your tent flap, Alissa," he said as he rejoined her. "No one's left to care."

Bailic turned, his posture stiff with impatience. "Yes there is. And keep yourselves up with me." He waited for them by a patch of snow-slumped vegetation. It was the first they had seen since entering the city, and it spread nearly two house widths. Woody vines as thick as her arm waged a slow, vicious war with what looked like fruit or nut trees, smothering them in a mass of twisting vegetation. It seemed the untidy tangle had once been an orchard or public garden.

Bailic squinted at the sky as they came even with him, and with a frown, he started forward again. Alissa found herself lagging. Her enthusiasm was gone, leaving her reluctant to venture farther among the stone buildings. The snow made it eerily silent. Even the expected birds were missing. The blocks of vegetation interspersed between the buildings became more frequent as they continued until the houses gave way to an immense field. Together, all three stood and took in the vista.

The city enclosed a field so vast that the homes on the far side looked gray and small from the distance. Near the center, a grove of frost-blackened trees marred the otherwise unbroken sight of even whiteness. It was utterly still, with only the sound of the wind over the snow murmuring of past seasons of solitude. Looking at the field, Alissa shivered and couldn't say why.

Bailic waded eagerly into the snow to force a path through it. "Quickly," he called over his shoulder. "We're almost there."

"I don't want to go," Alissa said softly, balking at the edge of the field.

Strell took her elbow, and she jumped. "It's all right, Alissa," he said. "Talo-Toecan said Bailic couldn't open the book, and I know I can't."

"That's not what's bothering me," she said in confusion as she reluctantly fell into place behind him. She was getting the oddest feeling, and she couldn't shake it off. A quick glance back at the empty houses, and Alissa hastened to catch up.

It took longer to reach the grove than she expected, the trees being twice as large as she first thought. Bailic doggedly pushed through the snow ahead of them, moving faster when the snow thinned as they neared the trees' uncertain shadow. Alissa gazed up in wonder at the inverted bowl their leaf-emptied branches collectively made. She couldn't decide what kind of trees they were, but they were old, big, and awe inspiring. Three had fallen to mar the perfect symmetry that once was, their trunks wider than she was tall. The surviving trees' naked branches formed a black lacework that stretched nearly to the ground, doing little to block the low, winter sun. Snow and ice outlined the horizontal branches. Alissa could imagine that in summer, their tall shade encompassed the entire grove. Her tension loosened for the first time since passing the city's gates as the memory of cold stone was replaced by the promise of life.

"You stay here," Bailic said sharply to her, and she stiffened at the reminder of him. "Move from the trees, and you'll be ash. Bother me, and you'll be ash. If Talo-Toecan appears, you'll be ash. Understand?" His eyes were wide and fever bright. Slowly she nodded. As tense and excited as he appeared, she wouldn't give him any excuse.

"You," he pointed to Strell with a trembling hand. "You will come with me."

Alissa and Strell gave each other a sick look.

"Go!" he shouted, gesturing. "Over to the center of the grove. It's the heart of the city, according to the stories."

Strell placed one of his cloth-wrapped hands on her shoulder. "I'll be back in a moment. Everything will be all right."

"I wouldn't count on it," Bailic said, gesturing impatiently for Strell to walk ahead of him.

Alissa managed a smile as Strell gave her shoulder a quick squeeze, and she wondered if a disappointed Bailic might be worse than a Bailic flush with success. Either way, it was going to be a miserable walk back home. But what if he did manage to wake the city?

The two men walked from her, one tall and quick with anticipation, the other tall and plodding from exhaustion. Much as she didn't want to see what Bailic was going to do, she didn't want to be left alone among the trees, either. The sense of presence, not of being watched but of an impending something, was settling about her, making her jittery and anxious to be away.

Alissa stomped a patch of snow flat and sat with her back against one of the fallen trees. The grove was quiet and hushed, giving her the impression of a massive, open building: its floor was the even snow, its ceiling was the interlaced branches high overhead, and its walls were the limbs bowing low nearly to the ground. Even as restless as she had become, the grove was less nerve-racking than the city's barren streets. The solitude here was the natural quiet of sleep, not death or abandonment.

The cold bit deep now that she had stopped moving, and Alissa hunched further into her coat to find some warmth. Though the stark branches looked dead, she could sense the life beneath the smooth bark and knew come spring, there would be flowers and tender new leaves. She could almost see how it must have been when the city breathed with the myriad lives it had sheltered.

Bailic shouted at Strell, and she looked to see Bailic

forcing him to stand such that she couldn't watch what
either of them were doing. Resigning herself to wait, she
leaned her head back against the trunk. "I'd wager this was
a nice place in the spring once," she said softly, feeling the
need to break the silence. Brushing the edge of her boots
through the snow, she found moss, black from the cold.
"The moss was soft and deep," she said, "and the flowers
gracing the branch tips were white." Smiling at her diversion, she closed her eyes, trying to make her imaginings of
the city's past as real as the smooth bark behind her head.
It seemed as if her jittery feeling had lessened in response
to her words. *Like whistling in the dark,* she thought.

"Their intoxicating fragrance fills the field, spilling out
into the city to slip among the streets like a cool breeze,"
she said, settling herself further. "People cast open their
shutters, glad to know that winter is finally put to rest.
Children run into the field to play among the trees.
Leaves, delicately translucent with their newness, adorn
every branch, forming a shifting shadow that is neither too
bright nor too deep. A cool breath. A still point of rest. As
the sun crests the clear sky, the young are joined by the
slowly moving old who tell exciting truths of a history so
far removed from time as to appear as only a fable." She
smiled. She almost believed she could hear the murmur of
an old woman's voice and the eager whispers of attentive
youngsters.

"Later . . ." She sighed as a breath of warmth seemed
to infuse her and set her fingertips to tingle. "As the light
wanes, the children are lovingly gentled to sleep, the moss
and their mother's shawl as their beds, the earth's warmth
as their fire. The stories turn to lost loves and tragically
forgotten promises until the moon rises. Shadows shift and
fall, and the flowers slowly rain down to cover the young
sleepers with a blanket of white.

"Exuberant dances celebrate the coming of a new year,"
Alissa said drowsily, completely involved her daydream.
"The music of pipes and drums weaves an ever-changing,
never-ceasing melody. Gifts are made of the falling blos-

soms, exchanged between the as yet unpromised, a gentle query as to the possibility of a future union of matrimony."

In her thoughts Alissa saw an unremembered face with a lighthearted grace and an undeniable expression of longing. He held a single flower in his hands, a look of desire in his green eyes. Alissa jerked her eyes open in surprise. Far above her, a solitary white shadow was drifting down. Frozen where she sat, she watched it float first one way, then another. She held out a trembling hand, and a flower settled softly into it. A hauntingly familiar fragrance blossomed: the sweet, painful scent of hard-won wisdom, and sacrifice, and love.

The unexplained ache of loss crashed over her, and her eyes closed against a tear. She held her breath, trying to remember, left with the feeling the memory hadn't yet been lived. Slumped with an unknown grief, she opened her eyes to try to find a sense of what was real again. The sun hit the icicles rimming the trees, and the glittery shimmer through her tears made it seem as if the branches were alive with flowers.

A tingling began in her palms, seeming to come from the flower. As she sat in shocked indecision, the tingling turned to a warmth that rose through her arms and filled her entire body, making her as warm as if it were summer. She couldn't help but cry out at the sudden relief from the cold.

A child laughed, and frightened, she scrambled to her feet before realizing it was a slump of snow and icicles falling to the ground. Her new warmth was gone. She felt herself go pale as the west wind slipped under the branches, seeming to tug at her. Silent and unnerved, she stood as the wind died and the hush turned profound. What the Wolves was going on?

Magic? whispered a thought through her, and she shoved it away. But how else could she explain the flower and the one who had given it to her. *He* wasn't from her imagination. *Ashes,* Alissa thought. He had felt like a memory. Her memory. Her desire. Her loss. But recalling a memory you hadn't lived was impossible. Alissa's gaze dropped to the white bloom cradled in her palm. Just as impossible as a flower falling from dormant branches.

She tucked her flower behind her coat front, and the sky darkened as the sun went behind a developing cloud bank. Alarmed, she sent her gaze to Strell. He was looking at her across the distance, his eyes wide in dread. Alissa's confusion shattered in a wash of panic as Bailic snatched the book from Strell and cuffed him into motion. Unusually docile, Strell took the abuse, lagging until Bailic pushed ahead of him, frustration in his every motion.

Alissa held her breath as Bailic stalked past her. "Home," he barked, never slowing.

She fell into step beside Strell. "What happened?" she said in a hushed whisper.

"Didn't you see them?" Strell said, his face ashen. It was the first time she had seen him afraid, and Alissa felt the true beginnings of fear.

"See who?"

"He did it. The Navigator save us, Alissa. He woke the city."

Shocked and confused, Alissa stopped. "But he—"

"He doesn't know," Strell whispered, tugging her into motion. "He didn't see them."

Alissa glanced forward to Bailic. "See who?"

Strell shook his head. "The city," he said harshly as he pulled her into him and whispered in her ear. "It was alive. I saw it when I held your book. Somehow he woke them. He's going to do it. He's going to destroy the foothills and plains, whether the book is open or not."

Her heart gave a frightened thump. "What are you talking about? I didn't see anything."

"Ghosts!" Strell hissed. "I know one when I see one, and the grove was full of them. Dancing, playing games, telling stories. Ashes, Alissa. Tell me you could at least hear the drums. I don't want to be the only one to have seen them."

Alissa shook her head, fear making a quick tremor go through her. She glanced at Bailic's stiffly held back ahead of them. "There's no such thing as ghosts," she said, stumbling as her pace broke from Strell's. "And Useless said he couldn't open the book; only I could."

"Burn it to ash, Alissa," Strell said as he let her go. "Talo-Toecan never said Bailic couldn't wake the city. I'm telling you it's awake. And if Bailic finds out, we're both dead."

Alissa said nothing, trying to find a way to understand what Strell was saying and what it meant to her. She felt her cheeks, stiff with cold, grow even colder. Bailic couldn't have woken the city. He would have known. Not saying anything, she numbly moved her feet, wondering how much worse it could get.

9

"**B**ailic did what?" Useless said, clearly shocked.

Alissa rubbed a hand under her nose. It was closer to sunrise than sunset, and the cold bit deep, relieved little from the tiny fire in the center of the firepit. Talon huddled close to her neck. The smooth feathers pressed against her seemed to make her all the more cold. "He took off most of Strell's finger. With a ward. To punish him."

"Did you see it?" Useless asked, his brow pinched. "The ward, I mean?"

"The ward!" she cried, shocked. "Bailic mutilated his hand, and you're worried I might have learned how he did it? No. I didn't!"

Clearly relieved, he resettled his coat about him. "If all the piper lost was a finger because of his impertinence, he was fortunate. I warned you not to underestimate Bailic's abilities or the depth of his depravity." The Master frowned at her scowl. "Unfortunately, the loss of a finger is not enough to call our agreement ended. Is Strell all right?"

"No," she said, almost sullen. "And then he made us go to Ese' Nawoer." She dropped her eyes, feeling like a child complaining about an older sibling. "He wanted to see if he could use the book closed. Strell says he woke up the city—"

Her instructor's eyes went wide. "Wake Ese' Nawoer? Bailic hasn't the finesse to wake the dead." He harrumphed. "Neither do I. And if he had woken them, he wouldn't be sleeping in my room; he would be planning his next move."

"But Strell saw them," she insisted. "He said the grove came alive with people! Bailic doesn't know he woke the city because he didn't see them."

"Did you see them?"

Alissa winced, embarrassed. It wasn't that she didn't believe Strell, but it sounded so unreal. "There are no such thing as ghosts," she said softly, and it was with no little relief that she saw the Master nod. Last fall, she had said there was no such thing as magic.

"I thought not," he said. "Plainsmen see ghosts when the wind blows the sand. It's their nature. I would be more inclined to believe a fish can grow hair than Bailic can wake Ese' Nawoer. Perhaps we will practice reaching my thoughts from a distance before we call it done, in case Bailic is foolish enough to leave the Hold again."

Alissa reached for the warmth of the fire, glad Useless supported her own beliefs that Strell had been imagining things. The small sack of dust her mother gave her slipped from behind her coat, and she tucked it back. "Bailic said leaving the Hold when the snow was so deep was clever," she said, her eyes on the flames.

Useless harrumphed again. "Trying it once and getting away with it is clever. Trying it twice and getting caught is foolish. He won't do it again."

An uneasy silence descended as Useless removed his box of tea from under the bench. He added a handful of leaves to the steaming pot and set it to brew. The pot and the two cups had come into existence somewhere between Useless landing on her roof to wake her and her making her way down to the firepit. "May I see that bag for a moment?" he said casually. Alissa hesitated in confusion, and he added, "The one you just tucked away."

Startled, she took it from around her neck. Useless held out his hand, and she reluctantly let it slip from her grasp, not understanding her unwillingness. "Ah, this isn't good," he murmured, running a finger delicately over her mother's initials. He handed the bag back, frowning. "As soon as we have a large enough space of time, I'll show you how to bind that source you have so untimely acquired. Until then, don't let Bailic see it. If he takes it, I can't replace it. Such a large volume as you have is typically generated from—ah—ashes. It's a careful secret. Even Keepers don't know."

Alissa settled the pouch back over her neck, tucking it in its usual spot behind her shirt. The unsettled feeling that had gripped her when Useless held the bag eased. "But you're telling me?" she said, glad to know she had been right in what it was.

"I like you," he muttered. "Now," he said, clearly changing the subject. "Let me see you set up the first circuit."

A sound of disappointment slipped from her. Useless might call her tracings a neural net and the first loop the primary circuit, but manipulating them was still something she already knew how to do. "But I know how to set up the first circuit," she complained.

"Then show me how fast you can do it," he said with an infuriating patience.

Alissa thumped her heels against the firepit's bench. "Faster," she said, thinking longingly of her abandoned bed. It was hard to justify leaving it for something she already knew. Learning how to reach Useless's thoughts at will would be far more useful than more practice in setting up her primary loop. Eyes half vacant, half intent, she fussed with the fire. Maybe, she thought glumly, she could make a game of it. The next snap of the fire, and she would go.

Alissa settled herself to wait, easing her thoughts with three slow breaths. The small fire collapsed in on itself with the sound of sliding coals and she jumped, slipping her awareness into her source with a quickness she hadn't found before. The first crossed loop flowed into existence before her heart had finished its beat. She smiled. Holding herself calm had helped.

"Playing with fire?" Useless said. His eyebrows were arched, and suddenly the night wasn't so cold as she blushed. Talon responded to her emotions by pinching her shoulder painfully. "Even so," he continued, "that was ex-

cellent." His brow furrowed in thought. "You have permission to practice this alone. See how fast you can
become before we meet again."

A grin edged over her. Seeing her smile, Useless chuckled. "Actually, it would be a good idea to leave you with a
few other exercises to keep you out of trouble."

"That would be—wonderful," she said, trying not to
sound so blessedly eager. If he knew how excited she was,
he might reconsider.

"I've something in mind," he continued. "It would test
your abilities, stretch your endurance. It's not a ward rec-
ommended so early in your career as a—student, but when
done properly, it will offer you a measure of protection
from Bailic."

Alissa's pulse grew fast. Her first ward. "Show me?"

He grimaced, clearly not convinced his idea was a good
one. "Bailic's faulty decision to name Strell the latent
Keeper was undoubtedly due to seeing the destruction of
your neural net caused by improperly removing my ward,"
he said. "The layout of tracings are notably different between Keeper and commoner, but being a Keeper himself,
Bailic can only perceive another's tracings when invited or
the subject is near to death as you were."

Alissa stifled a tremor. The pain in her mind had sent
her so deep into her unconscious, she never would have
found her way out but for Strell.

"I would like . . ." He frowned. ". . . to give you a ward
to overlay an illusion of scar tissue over your tracings.
Once you master it, even if you should be injured to the
point of profound unconsciousness again, Bailic won't realize you've healed." Turning to her, his golden eyes appeared to flicker eerily in the firelight. "Holding it in your
thoughts would strengthen your stamina, give your eventual fields more staying power. It's difficult, but if the ward
is beyond you, there's no harm done." He hesitated.
"Would you like to try?"

"Hounds, yes!" she exclaimed, dropping her eyes as he
laughed.

With a final glance up at the star-filled sky, Useless

drew his legs up under him. Sitting cross-legged on the bench, he hid his odd hands among the folds of his sleeves. "This will be easier to explain if we move our thoughts to your tracings."

Steeling herself, she nodded and closed her eyes. She heard his grunt of approval, and with a flash of outrage that was surprisingly easy to suppress, she allowed him among her uppermost thoughts. Alissa's shoulders eased down. As Useless had promised, sharing her mental space was getting easier.

"*Now,*" Useless thought, "*you have deduced how to form fields in your thoughts?*"

She nodded, forgetting for a moment he couldn't see. "*Yes,*" she affirmed, forming a bubble of thought.

"*So fast,*" he mused, then louder, "*That's it. For this ward, you need a three-dimensional field large enough to encompass your entire neural net.*"

"*The whole thing?*" she asked, not sure what three-dimensional was but very clear upon the length and breadth of her thoughts.

"*It need not be much mass,*" he thought. "*Imagine a hollow sphere of mist encompassing every corner of your pattern.*"

Willing to try, Alissa focused on the bubble, or field as he called it, expanding it.

"*Good,*" he encouraged. "*Next, set up the primary circuit while maintaining the field. It might take several tries to find the balance of keeping both at once, so don't be discouraged.*"

Alissa recalled her mornings when, while traveling to the Hold, she had practiced the art of seeing both her real sight and that of her mind's eye simultaneously. To walk a stony path without tripping, yet retain her vision of her source, had left her with stubbed toes and banged shins. Eventually she gained the skill of it, but not before acquiring a reputation for being clumsy. Now the practice allowed her to easily hold her concentration as she manipulated the field and the pattern all at the same time. She had the first crossed loop up and glowing as quickly as she could imagine it. Alissa knew she must be grinning like an idiot by now, but she didn't care.

"Um, very good," came his thought, and she grinned all the more. *"If you would, show me what your neural net looked like before your burn healed."*

Alissa hesitated. *"How do I do that?"*

"From your memory," he encouraged. *"Recall it. It will show itself."*

Steadying herself, she cast her memory back to when she first gazed in panic at the charred, twisted remains of her tracings.

"Bone and Ash!" Useless exclaimed out loud, nearly jolting her attention from her tracings. His horror-struck reaction slammed into her in a wave of revulsion, shocking in its honesty. She struggled to hold the memory of the burn in place as he yanked his emotions back, smoothly hiding them. But she had seen, and she now knew she hadn't been a sniveling weakling for nearly accepting Mistress Death's invitation. Rather, it was a miracle that she had survived.

"Alissa," he thought shakily. *"I had no idea. You escaped death from—from this?"*

She examined the holocaust spread before them with its ash and char smelling of cold, twisted metal and snow. After his response, it didn't bother her anymore. She had survived. *"Barely,"* she thought tightly. *"Strell convinced me to find a way back."*

"I didn't realize," Useless seemed to whisper, apparently in awe of the destruction. *"The pain alone would have . . . Even I—"* Shuddering, he let his thoughts go unfinished. *"Everyone gets their tracings burned badly at least once; perhaps now you'll be more careful."* Clearly unnerved, Useless seemed to gather himself back together. *"Well then, if you would turn your attention to your—your tracings."* Alissa heard him take a deep breath. *"I have set up the relevant path in my own network to instigate the proper ward. Do you see it resonating against yours?"*

"Yes," she thought. A simple, wide-flung pattern began to glow faintly, the blue black lines weaving behind her

mind's eye, giving off an even luminescence. The thin lines of gold that ran through the tracings seemed to fade under the increased light.

"When properly set, the ward will bind to your neural net, giving it the look of unusable scar tissue. Draw a trickle of energy from your primary loop to fill the paths I've indicated."

"Like this?" Alissa held everything as it was and allowed a ribbon of force from the first loop to enter the resonating paths. Immediately the lines of gold burst into life, making the larger pattern glow from within. She felt a slight tug. It was unfamiliar, and she resisted it.

"No, don't hold it so tightly," Useless advised. *"You've done it correctly. Let more energy flow, and let the two attract each other."*

Alissa had no idea what he meant by the last part, but she did as he suggested. *"Oh!"* she exclaimed as the field collapsed, binding loosely through her tracings, carrying her vision of destruction with it.

"Marvelous," Useless praised.

She wrinkled her nose. Her tracings looked scarred and unusable. *"It's ghastly."*

"Marvelously so. Marvelously so," he thought as he chuckled. *"With practice and concentration, the ward will remain after you disengage the circuit. Let both go right now. I want to watch you set it up without me helping."*

"All right," she said, casually breaking the first loop. Her pathways returned to their original, pristine elegance as the ward fell. Useless promptly disappeared from her thoughts. Startled, she opened her eyes.

"Set it up! Set it back up!" Useless waved his arms, sending his coat sleeves flapping. If she had known him better, she would say he looked concerned, not pleased, as she would expect.

Alissa replaced the ward, surprised at the ease of it. It had taken longer to explain than it did to repeat. Looking at her handiwork, she thought about what she had done. "Useless?"

"Yes?" he said worriedly. His fingers were almost in the flames as he poked at the fire.

"Did I neglect to fix the force into a state that was stable enough to withstand the change to reality?" She was referring to her disaster that blew out the protection wards on her windows, shook the Hold to its foundations, and put her and Mistress Death on a first-name basis.

"Probably." He looked up, seemingly surprised at the direction of her thoughts.

Alissa reached for the teapot and poured out two scalding cups of tea. "Is that how you make your cups and teapot?" she asked as she held out one for him.

"Yes. It's a large part of it." This time he sounded wary. He took his cup and downed half of it, not seeming to be bothered by its temperature.

Alissa nodded, her vision blurring slightly as she checked to see if the ward was still holding. It was. "Bailic threatened to burn my book. Would he have formed a field about it and a bit of energy and not fixed it?"

"It's not your book; it's mine. And though that would probably work, no, he wouldn't."

She held her tea gingerly, trying to warm her fingers without burning them. "How then?" Alissa glanced from the fire to him. For an instant, she thought she saw horror or perhaps fear in his eyes, but it vanished before she could be sure.

"I'll tell you, but I want your word you won't try it."

Silently, she nodded. Just to know would be enough.

"He would have formed a containment field about it and set the molecules within the field vibrating at the proper frequency."

"Why would he need the field?" she asked, wondering where one could find a molecule and what a frequency was.

"So as to maintain a semblance of control," was his uncomfortable answer.

"I see." Alissa took a tentative sip of her tea. "It doesn't sound difficult."

"It isn't."

She took a slow breath. "So why didn't you fry Bailic when you had the chance?"

"My, aren't we blood-driven all of a sudden," Useless scorned.

Shamed, Alissa dropped her eyes. "It would've made things easier," she said defiantly.

Useless harrumphed. "You think so? Your vision is dangerously shortsighted. Bailic had forged a connection between himself, you, and the book. It was so subtle, I didn't see it until our haggling was all but complete. Had I not heeded his warning and *fried* him, as you suggested, my source's energy would have flowed between the three of you. You would have vanished as surely as Strell's finger, turned to ash by my ignorance and lack of restraint."

Alissa bit her lip, recalling having felt such a connection when Bailic forced them to go to Ese' Nawoer. "I'm sorry," she apologized in a small voice.

"No doubt." Useless fixed a vehement stare upon her, and she shrank back. "You cannot go about shattering everything that irks you, Alissa," he lectured. "What would become of us? Strength would dominate over wisdom. Chaos would bloom as Keepers and Masters struggled for control. There would be no time to progress in gaining knowledge, and so we would dip back to our beginnings, becoming as feral beasts, man and raku alike. That is why I practice restraint."

"But there're no Keepers left," she protested.

"That's exactly what I mean," Useless said. "Bailic has emptied my Hold in his search for dominance. What he lacks in strength, he more than makes up for in guile. You continue to underestimate him. Watch him, Alissa. Be careful. He has emptied the skies of rakus. It's something no man has done in two thousand years."

Her brow furrowed, and she looked away, not liking what he was saying, but knowing better than to disagree openly.

Useless cast his eyes to the sharp stars above the wall. "It wasn't intended to happen like this," he said apologetically. "You shouldn't even have a source to draw upon yet. It puts too much temptation before you."

Alissa looked up, startled at the sorrow in his voice.

"There's much you should have gained first," he said gently. "An entire philosophy of restraint and control to help you tame the beast of power you're catalyzing." Useless turned away, his features tight with concern. "You have to understand how dangerous that marvel tucked away in your thoughts really is. It's capable of infinite possibilities and carries a correspondingly high price. The toll it exacts is paid by not giving in to your desires, which may sound easy, but it isn't. Slow down. See the dark purpose your small miracle of existence can be set to. Your abilities can be used against you without you even realizing it." He sighed, watching his breath steam over his cup.

A twig snapped, and Useless jerked. A chill took Alissa as Talon began to hiss, pinching her shoulder.

"Ashes, Talo-Toecan," came a pleasant, masculine voice from the darkness. "Why do you always insist on seeing the gloom in every situation? You're worse than my grandmother!"

Her eyes wide, Alissa set her mug down and looked at Useless. He looked as surprised as she. "Who are you?" Useless said coldly, "and how did you come into my garden at my unawares?"

"I thought I had a standing invitation," came the unfamiliar voice with a familiar accent. It sounded amused, as if privy to a joke they weren't aware of. "But that was some time ago, even as rakus record it." A shadow at the edge of the firepit shifted, and an elegantly cloaked man stepped to the edge of the light.

IO

"Lodesh?" Useless took a hesitant step forward.

He looks like Strell, Alissa thought as Talon's hissing cut off with a sharp peep. But the more Alissa looked, the less resemblance there was. Finally she decided it was more the cut of his coat than anything else. His hat, too, was like Strell's, or the one she had given him, rather, being large and floppy. There was a flower embroidered upon the brim. In his hands was a staff taller than he, planted solidly on the frozen earth. His feet were encased in a pair of worn, snow-rimed leather boots rising to mid-calf into which his trousers were neatly tucked. The flower pattern was stitched with a silver thread upon the collar of his ankle-length coat as well. She would wager it was also on the heavy-looking ring he wore.

Only now did her eyes reach his face, and she stared, startled by the warm look of amusement and what she thought might be hopeful recognition. His eyes were green, and they glinted roguishly under a carefully arranged tangle of soft, blond waves. Clean shaven, his jawline was square and firm. It was a young face, and she dropped her gaze as he winked at her. With his fair hair and skin, Alissa would say he was from the foothills, but he was too tall for a farmer. Perhaps, like her, he had a parent from both hills and plains. It might explain why his accent was identical to hers, something she had never heard outside her home before.

The man stepped close and clasped Useless's proffered arm. There was a pleasant scent of apple and pine about him. "You look old, Talo-Toecan," he said. "Has it been that long?" He grinned, looking her teacher up and down.

Useless frowned. "You look as you did as a boy, Lodesh, but your city is barren." His face went abruptly still and sad. "It's true, then," he said, letting go of Lodesh's arm and stepping back. "The piper—"

"Sees ghosts when he ought not to, yes," the man interrupted. "But your fallen Keeper had nothing to do with it. Rest easy. I'm here on other business." He gave Useless a long, silent look, and her instructor seemed to slump with relief.

"Strange days," the Master said.

"Strange indeed, when a Keeper must try to fill the slippers of a Master," the man replied.

Useless drew back in surprise. "Beg your pardon?"

"Don't get that stubby tail of yours in a twist," Lodesh said, smiling. "I've come to offer my assistance," and he glanced knowingly at her.

Alissa's eyes widened at the insult. She knew she couldn't get away with half the abuse Lodesh was heaping upon her instructor, but Useless appeared almost pleased. "You will help me rid my Hold of Bailic?" he asked eagerly.

Lodesh shifted his eyes from her. "Ah . . . not exactly. I meant the *other* matter that stands before us."

Useless started. "You know?" he blurted. "How?"

Somber and still, Lodesh nodded a single, slow nod. "I'm a gardener, old friend. I recognize a good graft before the twig is budded, even when it's unexpected."

Alissa frowned. She didn't like being ignored, whether it was by accident or not. Delicately, and with much restraint, she cleared her throat. "Excuse me," she said, rising. "I don't believe we've met."

Immediately, Useless turned and extended a long hand to help her. "Oh, Ashes. Forgive me." He grimaced, but it was clear he was peeved with himself, not her. "Alissa," he said formally. "This is Keeper Lodesh Stryska, ancient Warden of Ese' Nawoer—and a dear friend."

She lowered her eyes, wondering at the title of Keeper,

then at the term *ancient*. He seemed young to her. And what did Ese' Nawoer have to do with him? A faint unease drifted through her, compounded by Talon's odd croon from her shoulder, a mix of warning and contentment. Alissa looked up to find Lodesh waiting, his eyes gazing intently into hers. They were eerily familiar. Somewhere she had seen those eyes. . . . But how? There were no Keepers left. Perhaps Bailic missed one?

"Lodesh," Useless turned, "this is student Alissa Meson—my most eager of all pupils." He said the last rather dryly, and Alissa couldn't help her sigh.

A fresh scent of apples and pine came to her as Lodesh found her hand and took it in his own. It was callused, a hand that knew work. "We've met before, Talo-Toecan," he said, his eyes fixed upon hers. "She just doesn't remember," and then to Alissa, "It's good to see you again, milady."

Her heart gave a thump. "You," she whispered. "You gave me the flower." Now she recognized him. He was from her imagined thoughts of Ese' Nawoer. It was him she had seen before she caught the blossom that fell from winter-emptied branches. Her knees went weak and she pulled away. Strell saw the day she had described: the children, the dancers, the music. Bailic hadn't woken the dead, she had! And this wasn't a man. This was a . . . a . . .

"You've met?" was Useless's startled response. Then he stopped short, blinked twice, and turned to Lodesh. "You gave her a *mirth flower!*"

Talon made a surprised squawk at Useless's loud voice. "There's no such thing as ghosts," she stammered, retreating until the back of her legs hit the bench. She looked frantically from one to the other. "There isn't."

Lodesh smiled. "I don't believe in them, either."

"If Bailic didn't wake them, then you must have!" Useless shouted, clearly angry. "Burn it to ash, girl. How did you manage that?"

"I—I don't know, Useless . . ." she stammered, more confused by the moment.

"Useless?" Lodesh murmured, his smile deepening.

"By my Master's Hounds! How did you do it?" Useless said.

Lodesh snickered. "She calls you—Useless?" he repeated.

Useless shot a dark look at the Warden. "Even I couldn't fathom the way to wake them!"

Alissa's chest tightened. The Navigator's Wolves should hunt her. What had she done? It wasn't her fault. "All I did was imagine what the city was like in the spring," she pleaded, "when the trees were in bloom."

"How could you know what the grove would look like?" Useless accused, his voice finally lowering. "It's been barren for ages."

"I guessed?" she said, glancing nervously from Lodesh to Useless and back. He couldn't be a ghost. She had felt the warmth of his hands.

Useless stared at her for a long moment, his golden eyes unreadable. "Was it really that simple?" he finally said, his temper seeming to subside.

"There was nothing simple about it." Lodesh took her hands again, exerting a firm pressure. The tangy bite of tart apples and pine filled her senses. "It was a lovely day you returned to us. Thank you, milady."

Alissa's breath caught, and her eyes grew round. Embarrassed, she pulled her hands from him. Whatever Lodesh was, he wasn't a ghost.

"Ah," he breathed so that only she might hear. "I'm already too late." His words were somber and forlorn, and she was surprised to find what had to be heartache, true and grievous, in his expressive eyes. "I will have to be patient and wait even longer."

Apparently having missed all of this, Useless grumbled, "At least Bailic didn't wake you. And now that you are awake, what will you do?"

Lodesh straightened, seeming to hide his melancholy so deeply that Alissa wondered if she might have imagined it. "Nothing," he said.

"Nothing?" Useless pressed.

"There's not much I can do, so I choose to wait."

Useless's brow furrowed. "I was under the impression that once woken—"

"I can act against Bailic and possibly remove my curse," Lodesh said, cutting him off, "but my people would still be bound. They come before me. You know that."

The Master shifted his shoulders, clearly not liking what he was hearing. "Aye. I remember," he finally said, and the two eyed her as if she were a fish they were considering purchasing.

Not liking their scrutiny, Alissa glanced about the firepit for a distraction. "Would you like some tea?" she asked, trying to find some normalcy in her outside, nocturnal gathering in the snow with a raku who wasn't a beast and a man who wasn't really alive. She gestured to the bench, her forced smile faltering as she recalled they had only two cups.

"Ah!" exclaimed Lodesh, promptly brushing the snow from next to Alissa's vacant seat. "You have hit upon my one weakness."

"Only one, Lodesh?" was her instructor's sly comment, but he was smiling as he said it, and they arranged themselves companionably before the fire.

Alissa bit her lip, wondering if she should go inside for a third cup. She took a breath to rise, letting it out in surprise as, with a tug on her thoughts, a third cup melted into existence. It was bigger than the first two, and her brow wrinkled as she realized Lodesh had created it. The tracings he had used were subtly different, and the variations gave her an idea of how the task of molding force to matter might be accomplished. "I think I begin to see . . ." she mused as she poured the last of the tea into Lodesh's larger cup. His fingers encircled his mug as she extended it, touching hers for an instant, and she nearly spilled his tea as she jerked away.

"Watch yourself, Talo-Toecan," Lodesh mysteriously warned, grinning at her confused blush. "The beast will be very cunning."

Useless sighed. "I fear for it, Lodesh. Even with your help, I fear for it."

Riddles again, Alissa thought in dismay. But they weren't deliberately trying to keep her out of the conversation. Rather, it was like listening to two craftsmen at market discussing the benefits and drawbacks to a tool or technique. If one didn't have the proper background, they might as well be speaking underwater.

Alissa sat and sipped her lukewarm tea in a wide-eyed silence, hoping they would say something she could follow. Obviously, Lodesh was a man of some importance, even if his city was, as Useless had said, barren. Useless treated him as if he were one of his peers. Almost. Feeling lost, Alissa reached up and touched Talon's feet.

"That's a lovely raptor you have, milady." Lodesh leaned close, his elbows on his knees.

She looked up to find his green eyes waiting. "Thank you," she said, cursing herself as she felt a blush. "Her name is Talon."

"Fitting." Lodesh nodded sharply. "Will she hunt for you?"

"She does, Warden."

"Please, call me Lodesh," he exclaimed, absolutely beaming.

On her left, Useless muttered something dark and exasperated under his breath.

"She does, Lodesh," Alissa repeated, faintly returning his warm look. "She won't eat until I refuse her catch," Alissa added, and Talon chittered happily under their combined gaze.

Lodesh drew back in mock surprise. "Such devotion."

"It seems," Useless interrupted, "my student has a knack for acquiring staunch defenders."

"I can see how that could happen." Lodesh took a last pull on his cup, draining it. It hit the bench with a dull clink. "I really ought not be here," he said. "It wouldn't do for Bailic to find me. I came to pay my respects, but before I go, I have something for you." He reached beside him and took his staff. Inclining his head formally, he presented it to her.

Alissa looked to Useless before she accepted it, waiting until he nodded. The subtle action wasn't lost on Lodesh, and he grunted in what sounded eerily like one of Strell's comments. "Thank you," she said as she took the smooth, reddish length of wood in hand. Its color was reminiscent of the pipe Strell broke a few months ago, the one that had belonged to his grandfather. "My staff was broken recently."

"This one is made of stronger stuff," Lodesh promised, releasing it to her care.

It was heavier than she expected, with an almost slippery feel. The same scent of apples and pine clung to it that Alissa was beginning to identify with Lodesh himself. "It's a well-thought gift," she said, marveling at its simple, understated beauty. "But why?"

He shrugged, and for the first time he seemed discomforted. "You learn Keeper ways; you should have a piece of the mirth trees to show your ties to the city—whether it's abandoned or not. I would suggest keeping it from Bailic's sight. It may bring you luck," he said slyly, his eyes lingering upon the charm that Strell had given her about her neck. "One can never have enough of it."

"Mirth trees?" she mused, her attention on the staff.

"They bloomed for you, milady," he said ardently, "in the snow-swept fields of my city."

Alissa looked up, startled. She couldn't tell if he was serious or not.

Useless cleared his throat. "Rein yourself in, Lodesh," he grumbled. "She's not meant for the likes of you."

"Yes, I know." Lodesh leaned back, closed his eyes, and put an overdone dramatic hand to his forehead. "But one can dream, can one not?"

Her eyes widening, Alissa sat, wishing she could disappear into the frozen earth.

"No," Lodesh lamented. "It's far too late for me—*this time*. Even I can tell her heart has already been lost to someone else and won't be turned by, as you say, the likes of me." Pretending to be crushed, he held his head in his hands and sniffed mournfully.

Useless turned to her, his eyebrows raised in question. Alissa would have liked to have died right there in the garden. She had barely begun to admit the possibility of something between her and Strell to herself. She didn't want the world to know.

All of Lodesh's pretense at sorrow vanished in a small chuckle. "You, old beast, have been too long from the minds of mankind," he said conspiratorially. Apparently satisfied the damage had been done, he stood. "Well, I'll be going," he said cheerily. "Be assured I'll be present when needed." He smiled at her. "Perhaps you might grace my city with your presence again this spring? Remember, you have a standing invitation."

"Good-bye, Lodesh," she said from her seat as he crossed her proffered hand with his own. She was blushing again, hating herself for it. Lodesh seemed inexcusably pleased to see it.

He turned to Useless. "And clear skies to you, Talo-Toecan. Or is it Useless now?" he asked, his face deadpan. "I've been gone so long. Have you taken a new name?"

"She has my permission. You do not," Useless said darkly. "Keep this to yourself."

"Who would I tell?" Lodesh said. "Join me for breakfast? There are things we should discuss." Lodesh bowed with an exquisite flourish, and showing a dancer's grace, he stepped out of the firepit and into the darkness. There was the fresh scent of apples and pine, and the sound of snow beneath boots, and he was gone. Slowly the snow that had been threatening all evening began to fall.

Sand and wind! Alissa thought, straining to catch the last of his whistled tune. She turned to Useless for an explanation, but he was deep in thought, shifting the coals. Lodesh had left his cup behind, and she picked it up. It was so large she needed two hands. Etched upon it was the same pattern that was on his coat, hat, and ring. Now she recognized it as a dim representation of the flower he had given her. The fire settled, and Useless added a good-sized stick to it. It appeared they would be awhile longer. "Strange days, indeed," the Master said to the flames.

"Useless?" Alissa set the formidable cup down. "Who was that?"

His eyebrows rose in surprise. "That was Lodesh."

"Yes, but who is he?"

"Ah, I forgot," he exclaimed softly. "You lack much of the history surrounding your heritage." Resettling his coat, his eyes went distant into the past, staring at the fire. "Lodesh is the last Warden of Ese' Nawoer, or rather, he was—a long time ago. He ranked among the inhabitants of the Hold as second only to the Masters, privy to all our secrets, yet bound only by the laws of man."

She sipped her tea, watching the new snow melt as it hit the surface. The cup had gone cold, and she set it aside, hiding her hands in her coat sleeves as the snow continued to sift down. "But who is he?" she persisted.

Taking a tentative look at the snow-filled heavens, Useless settled back. He added two more sticks to the fire, shaking his head at some private thought. "Did your father ever tell you the tale of the great madness that took the world and of Ese' Nawoer's walls?" Seeing her nod, he took a slow breath. "Well, Lodesh, the unlucky scoundrel, gave the order to build them."

"No," she protested. "That was—"

"Three hundred, and, oh, eighty-four seasons past, yes," Useless finished.

"Then he is a . . ." she began, then stopped. She couldn't bring herself to say he was a ghost. She had seen Lodesh, touched him. Hounds, the warmth in his eyes had made her blush!

"A ghost?" Useless shrugged. "I don't rightly know what he is. The last time I saw him, he was at the end of a long, productive life. I didn't expect to see him again, much less as a young man, at least not until I breathed no more. A ghost, while assuredly not correct, may be the easiest concept to accept until we know more."

"But he's so alive!" Alissa exclaimed.

"Yes," he accused. "Your visioning must have been vivid to give him so much substance."

"But I didn't *do anything!*" she protested.

Useless silently waited until Alissa looked up. "You most assuredly did something," he said. "What its eventual outcome will be, I can't guess. If Bailic realizes the city is awake, he will force you to do his will, and the result will be the same as if he woke them himself. The souls of Ese' Nawoer would do much damage," he whispered, staring into the fire, clearly worried. "This is not good. Lodesh has suffered enough, as have his people."

"I didn't mean to wake them," Alissa began plaintively.

Useless raised a comforting hand. "Hush. I don't know how you managed it, but it can't be changed. Perhaps some good may come of it someday. They're bound to you until you find a way to set them free from their guilt."

"They serve me?" she stammered.

Useless gave a dry cough. "Not really. It's the other way around. There are sixteen thousand souls now depending upon you to find a way to set them free." He looked at her with what she thought might be pity. "It's a fearsome task you have undertaken."

"I didn't know, Useless. I don't want them!"

"It's too late. Be still," he admonished. "They have slept for centuries. They will easily wait a lifetime more until a way can be found to free them." He turned to the fire, and another stick followed its brothers already burning.

Alissa sat and worried. Useless was silent, watching the snowflakes meet their end in the flames, seeming to know she would have more questions. "Useless?" she said softly.

"Yes?"

"You asked Lodesh if he would do anything, and he said no. If I asked him, would he—could he best Bailic?"

Useless shifted and frowned. "If you asked him, he would try. I don't rightly know if he could. All things being equal, I think so, but things aren't equal. Harming, much less killing with one's thoughts, is something Keepers were conditioned to avoid. An entire generation of Keepers have been lost as Bailic honed his skills. Though Lodesh has more wards at his disposal, he would be at a great disadvantage, unaware of what kills outright, what simply maims, what—"

"I understand," she interrupted, shuddering as she remembered Bailic's easy voice as he casually snipped off Strell's finger.

Useless nodded. "Lodesh wouldn't be fast enough to best Bailic's instinctive reactions. I wouldn't ask him to do anything." He hesitated. "The Warden seems to be working under his own agenda. As usual," he added, sounding worried.

Alissa thought this over, her hopes of ending her difficulties so easily, dashed. "Useless?"

"Yes, young one?" This time he sounded tired.

"Lodesh knows you, yet you said you never expected to see him again."

"Yes," he offered cautiously, seeming unsure where this was headed.

"How," she said, then hesitated. It was rather personal. "How old are you?" she blurted.

"I've lost count."

"Please . . ."

He sighed. "Let me see. I was young when I built the Hold, and old when I met you."

"When was that?" Alissa asked quietly.

"Officially? Your second summer. Don't you remember? You turned red and cried until I tickled your nose with a tuft of grass."

"Useless," Alissa cajoled, but she was relieved to see his good humor returning. He had grown so distant when talking of Ese' Nawoer.

"Very well, a short history lesson."

"Your history," she demanded.

"My history," he affirmed, taking a sip of tea. "I completed the Hold long ago."

Silently, Alissa waited.

"Five hundred forty-nine seasons past, minus a few days."

Stunned, Alissa felt her mouth drop open.

"Long, long, ago," he said, an amused glint in his eye.

Her jaw snapped shut. "Do you live forever?" she asked, half expecting he did.

"No, of course not." He smiled. "But change is slow. I have at least a century left."

"A century?" she whispered.

"Maybe more," he admitted, sounding almost guilty.

"Maybe more . . ." Alissa shook her head as she tried to wrap her thoughts around the concept of so long a span. She couldn't do it. The snow filtered softly down in a quiet stillness, alarming in its opposition to her reeling thoughts. It was too fantastic to accept. She had a raku for a teacher who was, at the very least, six centuries old. He was acquainted with a ghost who lived roughly 400 years ago. That ghost, along with 16,000 of his people, expected her to free their souls from a 384-year-old tragedy.

"I can't do it, Useless," she whispered, feeling her breath quicken. "I can't."

"No one is expecting you to do anything, child," Useless said as if knowing where her thoughts lay.

She looked up with a wide-eyed panic. "But I can't. I can hardly keep myself intact. I can't save the world."

Useless smiled softly. "You only need to save yourself. Ignore the rest until you can do something about it."

"Ignore them!" she cried out in disbelief. "All those people? How?"

"May I see your staff?" he asked mildly.

Astounded at his callousness, Alissa snatched it up and held it stiffly out. He took it, examined it for a moment, then cracked it across her shins.

"Ow!" she shouted as pain raced through her. "What did you do that for!"

"Distraction," he said, a smile quirking the corners of his mouth. "You aren't worrying about things you can't control anymore, are you?" Slumping, he turned to the fire. "It's surprising how quickly one forgets when distracted," he said. "At least while the sun is up." He handed her staff back. "Feel better?"

"No!"

"You will," he said. "Lodesh is correct," he said louder. "Your new stick won't break easily. Mirth wood is extremely dense."

Alissa pulled up her skirt to find her shins swelling already. "I can tell," she snapped.

Useless looked away. "One thing I am certain of is that Lodesh never gave away so large a piece of his precious trees before, at least not to my knowledge. It was a thoughtful gift. It's served you well already," he said dryly.

"It's too long," she said, tugging her skirt back down.

"Is it?" He shifted uncomfortably and glanced up into the falling snow.

Useless didn't say a word, but Alissa knew when he started looking at the sky, their meeting was over. She sent her heels to thump against the hard stone bench. "So, you'll tell me how to call you with my thoughts, now?" she said, knowing he wasn't going to.

He shifted uneasily. "It's cold. Why don't we call it done?"

"I'm fine," Alissa said, forcing her arms to unclench about her. He was trying to get out of it, and she wouldn't let it go without a fight.

Useless stood and adjusted his coat. "I'm not. Get yourself back inside before you freeze to the stone. Replace that ward of disguise every time you notice it's fallen. When you can hold it in your sleep, you will have mastered the technique. I'll be back on the full moon." He stepped from the firepit and dissolved in a swirl of gray fog and a tug on her thoughts.

Alissa's eyes widened. He had never shifted form that close to her before. Within a heartbeat, the fog grew to the size of a small barn, solidifying into the massive shape of a raku. Useless swiveled his arrow-shaped head to her with a startling quickness. She gasped, nearly scrambling back in sudden fear, stopping only as she met his eyes. They were seemingly ten times larger, but the soul behind them was unchanged. Her pulse slowed as he waited, undoubtedly seeing how she would react to this sudden, very real reminder of who and what he was. Letting out her breath, she unclenched her fists.

Just so, his amused look seemed to say. He leapt into the air, and with a rush of wind he was gone and among the stars, leaving her to put the fire out and find her unsettled way back to her bed.

II

Lodesh squinted up into the low sun as the frightening silhouette of a raku ran silently across the snow. It was startling, even when expected, pulling forth primitive fears and reactions that had to be carefully soothed. Letting his armful of wood clatter to the ground, he brushed his arms clean of the bark and moss, waiting for his friend to land and shift to his more familiar form.

The reality of sharp eyes for detecting prey and claws meant for tearing flesh melted into a gray mist, swirling down to coalesce into a tired man dressed in a gold-colored, floor-length vest tied tight about his waist with a black sash. From behind the sleeveless vest showed yellow trousers and a matching shirt, the sleeves of which were wide and expansive. "Lodesh!" came Talo-Toecan's call. "I'm surprised. I expected you would have situated yourself in your family's holdings in the citadel, not out here on the field."

Smiling faintly, Lodesh waited for Talo-Toecan to come even with him. "These *are* my family's holdings," he said softly.

Talo-Toecan paused, his golden eyes drifting over Lodesh's shoulder to the ring of impressive mirth trees, well within hailing distance of the sod-covered house. "Yes, of course," he admitted, clearly uncomfortable. "Forgive me. But still, with an entire city to choose from, why Reeve's cottage? Bone and ash. It's almost a hovel."

With a subtle gesture, Lodesh moved them inside before Talo-Toecan's slippers could become any more damp. Shortly after his mother died, Lodesh had been apprenticed to the grove's caretaker. It was a modest occupation for one of the younger nephews of the current Warden. The small house was the only dwelling besides the Hold that Lodesh thought of as home. They entered in a stomping of boots and soft scraping of slippers.

"It's easier to heat," Lodesh said as he went to build up the fire. "Besides, there're more pleasant memories here than at my first and final house, regardless of how tall the ceilings are or how smooth the floor was worked."

From the corner of his sight, Lodesh watched Talo-Toecan's gaze run over the comfortably but sparsely furnished room. The warmth and scent of cooking sausages visibly relaxed the Master even as he stood there, his head nearly brushing the low ceiling. Small, numerous windows had their shutters open to let in the light; the cold was kept at bay with wards now instead of wood and cloth. Propped in a corner was a pair of carefully preserved pruning shears, shining faintly under a new coat of oil. Talo-Toecan stiffened and turned away upon seeing them, undoubtedly uncomfortable with the thought of the man who once worked them.

Lodesh hid his smile as he shook out his coat and carefully hung it by the fire. "I don't think you were ever invited into Reeve's stronghold," he said, draping a rag over his arm to keep it free of splatters as he shifted the sausages.

"No," was Talo-Toecan's stilted reply. "He never forgave me for stealing you away from him, as it were. Once your potential as a Keeper began to show, he knew it was a foregone conclusion. But I think Reeve clung to the hope you would return regardless, even after you left."

Lodesh took a slow breath, keeping his back safely turned. "I would have come back," he said faintly. "I was ready to, but my city needed me more than the trees he taught me to care for." Depressed at the reminder of opportunities that never really existed, he turned to see Talo-Toecan's eyebrows raised in question.

"I'm not complaining," Lodesh said with a thin smile. "The path I chose had its own joys."

The Master gave a soft harrumph and sat at the small table under the window. His elbows nearly slipped off its narrow width. It was as large as the room would allow, and that wasn't much.

There was a tug upon Lodesh's thoughts, and he wasn't surprised to see the plain teapot appear on the hearth. He accepted its arrival without comment, knowing it would be asking too much of the raku's dignity to use the pink, rose-covered pot that had belonged to his adoptive mother. "I can't believe you never took the time to learn to craft anything better than this horrible pot," Lodesh said, filling Talo-Toecan's teapot and setting it to boil.

"It's sufficient," was his short, dry answer. Talo-Toecan held his sleeve tightly to his arm to keep it from dragging as he reached to ladle a portion of the strawberry preserves onto his plate. Lodesh pulled the sausages from the fire, watching Talo-Toecan's gaze stray to the full pantry shelves, then out the window to the tall woodpile just outside the door. "You seem well stocked for only having been among the living since yesterday," the Master said. "One might think you knew you would return."

Lodesh bit back a muffled curse, sticking his knuckle in his mouth to feign having burned it. This wasn't where he wanted the conversation to go. Silently he slid two plates upon the table, his eyes lowered. They were glazed a pale pink to match his mother's teapot and looked extremely out of place. "I'm not a shaduf to know the future," he said guardedly.

"But still . . ." the Master persisted. "When the city was abandoned, they took everything down to the last spoon. Here you have an entire winter's supply of food and fuel safe under protection wards for how long? Nearly four hundred years?"

Lodesh set two dainty but badly tarnished spoons beside the plates. "Reeve made me promise to keep Mother's home as she left it," he said reluctantly. He retrieved the brown sausages, and with his back to Talo-Toecan, he muttered, "I'd rather not talk about it. Reeve and I didn't part on the best of terms."

"Of course." Talo-Toecan leaned back as the cooked links hit his plate in a series of rolling plops. The squat, almost-burnt bread soon followed. The raku's silence told Lodesh more clearly than words that he was unconvinced; Talo-Toecan was just too polite to say anything.

They ate with only the sound of forks and knives to break the guilty silence until Lodesh set his knife down and sighed heavily. "Are you going to tell her?" he asked.

"What, that she is more than she thinks?" Talo-Toecan frowned. "No. Absolutely not. She might believe she was capable of more than she is and bring about her downfall that much faster." He rose, grimacing as he nearly knocked his head on the low support beams. Retrieving the steaming teapot from the hearth, he set it upon the cloth embroidered with hummingbirds and bees. Lodesh's gaze traveled up from Talo-Toecan's hands, conspicuously clenched at his side.

"This is all wrong!" the Master exploded suddenly. "I'll admit I don't know much about how she is to be handled, but I do know this wasn't how it was done in the past. I'm one and alone, Lodesh. I don't know what I'm doing."

Lodesh slipped the tea leaves in to steep, tactfully allowing Talo-Toecan to shout and fuss. Arguing with a raku was never wise. "Things have a way of working out," he offered slowly.

"Perhaps." Talo-Toecan collapsed into his chair, his eyes distant. "But I think I will have to rid my Hold of Bailic soon. If this morning's instruction is any indication, her abilities will proceed quickly to the point where the book's lessons must be absorbed, long before Bailic's miserable life proceeds naturally to its foregone conclusion. Burn me to ash, Lodesh. I don't even know what she did to bring you back. I can't keep treating her as if she were a simple student!"

"M-m-m." Lodesh's eyebrows rose as he watched Talo-Toecan's long fingers stiffly tap the table. It was unusual his friend would show this much of his worry. The silence stretched, and he let it grow, knowing there would be more.

"Do you know what I did her first lesson?" Talo-Toecan finally said. "I nearly got my tracings singed. I was a fool." He laughed bitterly. "No, I was lucky. She is so blessedly quick, holding an innate understanding of the most complex tasks, but with the defenses of a nursling. I would expect her to be . . . Ashes, Lodesh, she carries the cunning and quickness of a wolf, hidden by the daft helplessness of a sheep."

"A wolf raised by sheep," Lodesh breathed, thoughts of the young woman swirling through his mind. She hadn't really recognized him. He hadn't thought she would. To expect her to remember something only one of them had lived as of yet was untenable. But it had cut him to the quick, her wide, alarmed stare at his hopeful look of recognition. He was already too late. Reeve had been right. He was a green-eyed fool. The piper had gained her heart before knowing it was in contention. But that didn't mean the plainsman would be permitted to keep it.

Lodesh jerked from his thoughts as he felt Talo-Toecan's eyes fall suspiciously upon him. The Master had crossed his arms before him, and a scowl creased his brow. "You still maintain your position of wait and see?" he almost accused. "Wolves, it wouldn't take much. Why can't you just shove him out a window for me?"

"Bailic is your problem, old friend," Lodesh said with a chuckle. "I have my city to administer to. It has its own price, coming long before my allegiance to the Hold. If I abandon my people by attempting to end Bailic's life, who will guide them to their own rest? Besides, I don't know if I can best Bailic, and I'm not going to risk dying again. Not so soon."

Without getting up, Lodesh moved the empty plates to the windowsill. "A spirit can do very little—the odd bad dream, perhaps a book falling off a shelf, souring milk, small things—but one with flesh on it?" He flushed. "Can do so much more." He looked out the window. "I will wait." Talo-Toecan's chair creaked as he leaned back. The sound drew Lodesh's attention. "Fear not, my long-lived friend." He smiled thinly. "You will find a way around your promises. You always do."

"If you refuse to help me, that's your choice."

It was clearly an accusation, and Lodesh's eyes grew hard. "I said Bailic wasn't my responsibility. I never said I wouldn't help," he said sharply.

The Master's breath hissed out and he stiffened. Lodesh met his glare with a mocking, questioning look until Talo-Toecan relaxed, recalling his unusual circumstance of having his hat in his hand. "Anything you would see fit to do would be appreciated," he said. "I would spend my time seeking help. I have searched from my prison hoping to find another Master to free me. Now that I'm loose, my range has expanded to include the plains and much of the western sea."

Lodesh grew still, refusing to return Talo-Toecan's hopeful look. "Wouldn't someone have returned by now had they been alive?" he asked, swirling the pot to brew it faster.

"A Master?" Talo-Toecan frowned. "No, an absence from the Hold for twenty years isn't uncommon. But I fear Bailic's plan to kill them by enticing them to search for a mythical island succeeded admirably. If any were alive, I should have reached at least their thoughts by now. But I'm still going to search."

Silence wedged stealthily between them, relieved by the hissing fire and the call of a jay sounding faint and unreal through the warded window. Lodesh stirred uncomfortably. "They're gone. Let them go," he said into the dismal hush.

"I can't," came Talo-Toecan's distant voice, his eyes on the Hold's tower. "I'm a foolish old raku, Lodesh, clinging to maybes and somedays as tightly as a small child does." Avoiding Lodesh's eyes, he reached for the tea and filled both their cups. "Sometimes, in the still point of the night, I can almost hear her."

"Keribdis?"

His eyes on his long fingers encircling his cup, Talo-Toecan nodded slowly.

Lodesh cleared his throat. "Ah, well," he said overly loud. "You must continue to listen."

The Master glanced up sharply, seeming embarrassed by his admission. "Did Redal-Stan ever tell you of his one and only prophecy?" he said, pointedly changing the subject.

Lodesh's eyebrows rose. Redal-Stan had been both their teacher, although admittedly not in the same century, and the cranky Master had never mentioned such a thing to him.

Talo-Toecan smiled with a dry humor. "He once spoke to me of a great friendship that would arise behind the walls of the Hold, destined to end at the hands of a woman. It would be a lover's triangle, the fallout of which would change the very course the Hold would follow." He paused and sipped at his tea. "The two men fall into contention over her favors. One ultimately betrays his friend, giving him a burden he cannot surmount."

The Master took a slow breath. "Redal-Stan told me to watch for this triangle, claiming it would be the turning point of the Hold. He said the Hold would prosper as the triangle does, or die as the triangle does. I fear, old friend, I have failed in heeding his warning."

"How so?"

Reaching to clean the lip of the jar of preserves with a cloth, Talo-Toecan frowned. "Bailic and Alissa's parents were such a triangle. I was there when it both began and ended, and though I strove to avoid their inevitable conflict, my efforts only worked to worsen it." Having only tasted his tea, Talo-Toecan pushed the cup away. "I imagine the worst has fallen, that the Hold has dipped to the point where it can no longer stand. I'm the only one left," he agonized, his sharp features suddenly creased with emotion. "Alissa's potential will be lost."

"She won't be lost," Lodesh said with an undying certainty. "You already have my help."

Talo-Toecan met his eyes briefly. "What can you do, Warden? You have no wings."

"No wings," Lodesh agreed, "but I can bring something no other could."

The Master shifted with an obvious embarrassment. "It won't be easy. I broke the holden after I escaped. It wasn't built to imprison a sane Master, and I couldn't allow it to remain intact if I was the only one left."

Lodesh shrugged. He hadn't planned on using the Hold's cellar anyway. "Will you accept my help or not?" he asked.

"Of course. I have no choice."

"There is always a choice," Lodesh said, tensing at the wash of pain that came and went, no less intense for its short duration. Again Talo-Toecan fixed him with a sharp look, and Lodesh managed a small chuckle. "Redal-Stan was many things," he softly quipped, "but a shaduf wasn't among them. Alissa isn't lost yet. And besides," he cajoled, "shadufs can't see into the future your long-lived existences cast. Redal-Stan has no way of knowing what may or may not happen. He was just giving you something to worry over after he was gone from this earth."

Talo-Toecan settled back with a grimace, his knees hitting the underside of the table to rattle the cups. "Maybe," he grumbled, blotting at the tea that slopped over. "But he seemed most adamant about it."

Giving him a sharp nod, Lodesh drained his cup. "How often will you be checking up on them?"

Talo-Toecan settled himself. "I have promised Alissa to return upon the full and new moon to repair any damaging ideas Bailic imparts to her through his instruction of Strell. I dare not come any more frequently than that. Not until I devise a way to get rid of Bailic."

Trying to appear disinterested, Lodesh took up the teapot and refilled his cup. "Would you like me to check up on her on a more regular basis? To allow you the opportunity to range farther afield in your searching—of course."

As if recognizing that more was being said than what actually was, Talo-Toecan leaned back with a wary look. "Just how substantial are you, Lodesh?"

Lodesh immediately rose to tend the fire. This wasn't a topic he cared to explore just yet, and most assuredly not with Talo-Toecan. Alissa, perhaps, when she finally remembered him. If she remembered him.

Behind him, he heard Talo-Toecan's fingers tapping on the table. Then they stopped. "Yes," the Master said guardedly. "Check on them both, if you would. Every third day or so. I'll sleep better, if nothing else. Just don't get caught. Bailic might—misunderstand."

Relieved, Lodesh turned. He would have checked upon Alissa regardless, but now he had an excuse, should Bailic spy him. "I will run up a flag if your presence would be an asset."

"I know you, Lodesh," Talo-Toecan said with a watchful tone. "I would think twice about letting Alissa know of your visits."

"Not tell Alissa when I'm there?" Lodesh froze indignantly. "You want me to skulk about like a thief?"

Talo-Toecan made a scoffing sound of amusement. "She would want you to stay, and Bailic would ferret you out, even within the span of an afternoon. The less she knows about you right now, the better. Strell, too. If Bailic guesses you're awake, he will undoubtedly find a way to use that information against Alissa." He grimaced. "You and your city."

Lodesh's brow furrowed, and he exhaled slowly. His citizens. They were as vulnerable as Alissa and held just as much potential. "Yes. Yes you're right," he said softly, not liking it. "I'll be as subtle as a mouse upon my visits."

"Good." Talo-Toecan stood with a smile. "Thank you for breakfast, Lodesh. Next time, I'll bring the sausages."

Lodesh allowed himself a small laugh as he escorted Talo-Toecan to the door. "That would be fine," he said. "But make sure the pig is truly dead and not just stunned. It took me three days to get the mess cleared up last time, and I don't think Nisi ever truly forgave me."

12

"Come on, Alissa," Strell pleaded. "You've been at it all afternoon. It's time to quit."

Alissa blew the mud-clotted strand of hair from her eyes in frustration and glanced up from the misshapen lump of clay that was spinning before her. "Almost done," she grumbled.

"That's what you said before," he said gently, and her jaw clenched. She was determined she should have at least one something worth going into the kiln by sunset.

Strell shifted awkwardly from foot to foot. "I'm going up to get the water. It should be warm by now. Remember, you promised you would stop when the sun was off the wall."

Seeing her tight nod, he left. She listened to the scuff of his steps fade, then raised her eyes to the band of sun. It was creeping far too fast. She bent back over her work and lost herself in the clay. It could be considered a bowl in the loosest of terms. It was round, in a warped sort of way. It could hold water, in theory. She supposed it might be suitable for, say, a slop dish? But it looked nothing like the simple, elegant forms that Strell had produced earlier today, one right after the other, all disgustingly perfect, all disgustingly alike. Lacking a full pinky hadn't diminished his talents as a potter at all.

There was a small scuff in the tunnel, and she acknowledged his appearance with a heavy sigh. He had a teapot in each hand. Giving her a smile, he poured the steaming water into a bucket, warming the frigid water from the annex kitchen's well to a bearable temperature. Strell had

cleaned up ages ago using the cold water. It was his unspoken hope the promise of a warm wash would entice her
away from his wheel.

She certainly needed a wash; she was a mess. There
were splatters of dried clay in her hair. Her skirt, once a
vibrant blue, so fine as to be worn only on market day, was
now a dingy gray in most places. It had grown distressingly damp. The hem was dragging against the spinning
flywheel, long since ragged from its continual contact with
the rough stone. Her knee was sore from constantly kicking the wheel up to speed, and her hands were cramped
and stiff as was her neck. And, yes, she was cold, too.

"There you go!" he called cheerily as the last of the
water went into the bucket. Alissa hunched into herself and
gave the flywheel a stiff kick, ignoring him. The distinctive *churrch* of an apple pulled her head up, and she stared
at Strell; he was deliberately ignoring her. She hadn't eaten
since breakfast, skipping her noon meal because cleaning
up was so much a bother. Only now did she realize how
hungry she was, and her stomach rumbled.

"Got one for you, too." Strell held it up. She smiled her
thanks and extended a mud-slicked hand, but he grinned,
placing it out of her reach. "I want you away from that
wheel first. You've hardly left it alone the last three days."

Alissa's smile vanished as she weighed her options.
Warm water and food, or more cramped fingers and cold,
gritty clay. Shaking her head, she shifted on the hard stool
and leaned back over her bowl. "You're going to have to
do better than that," she said.

He sighed. "How about you choose the first three tunes
I play tonight?"

Shocked at his offer, Alissa glanced up. His face was
twisted with a sudden pain, and she looked away before he
realized she had seen it. Strell couldn't play anymore. The
stub Bailic had left of his finger was too short to reach
the pipe without contorting his entire hand. It misaligned
everything, preventing the easy flow of music Strell had
worked so hard to achieve. She had heard him trying late
one night. His abrupt wrong notes and awkward hesita-

tions had filtered through their shared chimney flue. She had listened, helplessly clenching a pillow to herself in misery. He hadn't played a note since.

"No," she said casually, not wanting him to know she knew he couldn't play. Clearly his hurt was too raw for his pride to accept her concern. He would probably call it pity.

His breath came in a quick heave, and he busied himself with his back to her. "How about I make you dinner in the garden again?" he offered.

"Tempting, but it's too cold," she said, not looking up. One side of the bowl was definitely higher than the other, and she took a wooden knife to trim it away. "Why do yours always turn out so nice?" she grumbled, eyeing the apple core he had left behind on the table. *Burn him to ash.* She could smell its sweetness from here.

He squatted to wipe a piece of imaginary dust from one of his bowls. "I started learning to throw a pot when I was two."

Alissa nodded her acceptance of that and turned back to her disaster. One side of the bowl's wall was thicker than the other. Her lower lip between her teeth, she tried to even it out. That only made the bottom lopsided. "But still," she accused, hoping there was a simple secret she only needed to worm out of him, "it's been years since you left home. When you sat down the other day, it looked as if you had been practicing all week! The clay took shape as if it wanted to please you."

Strell came back and reclaimed his apple core. "Working clay isn't anything you can forget how to do. That is, once you know how, and besides," he paused, nibbling the apple down to nothing, "I was the best of my siblings."

She gave him a dubious look. "The best?"

He bobbed his head, smiling with an obvious pride.

"Why did you bother?" she asked. "You knew you couldn't stay."

Frowning, Strell tossed his core into an empty bucket. The soft thump as it hit seemed unnaturally loud for the tiny bit he hadn't eaten. "Yes," he said hesitantly. "I had known I was going to leave ever since my eighth year, although I didn't know why." His eyes went distant in thought. "I can't blame my parents for not telling me. Being expelled from the family craft to fulfill a pact made decades ago is shameful, even if the agreement was made with a shaduf. I think the only reason my parents respected my grandfather's promise was to ensure the shaduf's forecasting wouldn't change and cause my family name to become forgotten again." His distant look cleared. "But," he continued lightly, "my brothers and sisters didn't know I was leaving until the summer I left."

He sat on the table to watch her. She was silent, knowing he wasn't done yet. The creak of the spinning potter's wheel was the only sound, that, and the occasional muttered curse. She could tell he was having a difficult time watching her. His hands twitched, and his thumbs locked together as they had been when he worked the clay earlier. Wondering if it might work better that way, Alissa linked her thumbs and he visibly relaxed, not aware he had given her the subtle pointer.

"The reason I wanted to be the best," he continued, "was so I could take my grandfather's pipe when I left."

"That was the one you broke, right?" she said, and Strell winced as he nodded. Alissa pulled her jar of water closer. It had been a marvelous pipe, possessing a tone she had never heard before. Strell had broken it in a fit of temper and left it for scrap. She hadn't been able to burn it, and now it lay on her mantel next to her flower from Ese' Nawoer. "Your parents wouldn't just give it to you?" she asked, recalling him once saying he was the only one who ever played it.

"Oh, no!" He reached to halt her hand's motion as she dipped her leather rag into the jar of water to dampen her clay. "I had to earn it, just as my father and his before that—and if you add any more water, your bowl will fall completely apart."

"Thanks," she said, squeezing the water back into the jar.

"Sarmont wanted it as well." Strell sighed and rubbed his nose. "He thought he would get it, too, seeing as he was the eldest. But he didn't know I had been practicing in secret."

"Secret?" she mumbled, trying to even out the top again.

"Yes. That way Shay wouldn't break my fingers as she did Sarmont's."

Alissa looked up, shocked. "Your sister broke your brother's fingers over a silly pipe!"

Strell chuckled and leaned back. "Yes, indeed. But we could never prove it was anything more than an accident. Backed a wagon right into his hand as he was shutting a gate."

Alissa arched her shoulders painfully. "Why? You said no one but you could play."

"It's not just a pipe, Alissa," he said softly, his eyes intent upon hers. "It's the right to claim the profits of my entire family's efforts, so don't lose it, all right?"

Her mouth opened, but nothing came out. "You want it back?" she finally managed.

"Keep it." Strell dropped his gaze. "It doesn't mean anything now that they're—gone." His eyes flicked to hers and away. "It may sound an odd way to choose who will run the clan's affairs for the next generation, but it does ensure the quality of work continues. And it's safer than the way a lot of houses decide who assumes the leadership."

"It's a problem?" she asked. Most hills children set up a farm next to their parents in the rare instance it was necessary.

"It can be a very large problem." Strell sighed. "There are many family names that have disappeared from treacherous schemes and betrayals."

"You're jesting," she said, and he shook his head. "Why?"

Unable to meet her eyes, Strell turned away. "I have noticed," he said slowly, "that you prefer your apples skinned when you have a choice."

Startled at the shift of topics, she nodded.

Strell rubbed the back of his neck. "Even the wealthiest plainsman leaves the skin on."

"Meaning . . ." she prompted.

He took a careful breath. "We would starve if we made a habit of throwing a perfectly edible rind away."

Alissa went cold. The wheel spun, all but forgotten. Food was plentiful in the foothills. Scraps, or even the slightly imperfect parts, went to the sheep. She had never imagined it was that much different anywhere else.

"Carrying a chartered name, I never went hungry," he said, "even in early spring. Being able to trace one's lineage back to one of the original families to settle the plains does have advantages. But many aren't so skilled as to meet the cost of grain at market."

"I'm sorry," she apologized in a small voice. Hounds, she must have looked so arrogant.

"Oh, Alissa," Strell said as he leaned to tuck a wisp of hair behind her ear. "I didn't tell you to make you feel guilty but so you would understand why Shay would find cause to break our brother's fingers. Sarmont was a better potter than her, but he was loose with his money. He would've gambled the family's assets away. I think Father asked him to throw the contest, and when Sarmont refused, Shay 'explained' it to him."

"So what happened when you won?" Alissa asked meekly.

Strell rubbed his nose. "Shay had Sarmont beat me to a paste until I granted her the power to act in my stead while I was gone—had a paper drawn up and everything—but if I was staying, I think she would have accepted it."

"Oh." Alissa felt ill. She would have never guessed the plains were that bad. "All the plainsmen I have seen were thin," she said hesitantly. "None looked starving."

He nodded sharply. "Only the wealthier families are allowed to trade directly with the foothills. A starving man has a very short temper, especially when surrounded by food." His eyes dropped. "It would create too many problems. If you get thin, your name loses its chartered status. It's very rare you get it back."

Alissa was silent, only now understanding why Strell put so much pride in his name.

"Don't think too badly of Shay or my family," he said

in a rush. "She was only doing what she thought best. There were the rest of my sisters, and aunts, and all the children to think about. It's difficult," he said, his eyes downcast, "living on the edge of abundance, never being allowed in. A bad decision can often mean the loss of an entire season's work."

"I'm sorry, Strell," she apologized again. "I had no idea."

"Don't be. Not many from the foothills know." He smiled faintly. "Your innocence of the true state of affairs was intentional, and now that you know, you will keep it to yourself."

Astonished, she blinked. "Beg your pardon?"

Strell hesitated, then slowly exhaled. "What do you think would happen if it was widely known the plains are, at times, full of famine and want?"

"There would be an outpouring of goods!" Alissa asserted.

He shook his head. "The price of grain would go up."

"No," she demanded.

"Yes," he whispered, his gaze distant. "The hills would band together and boycott our goods, trying to starve us out. Not willing to allow our children to go hungry, we would undoubtedly steal what we needed, laying waste to what we couldn't carry away."

"Hounds," she said, knowing he was right. It was all she could manage.

"Hush." Strell stood up, clearly wanting to end the discussion. "The plains and foothills have been bartering for years. They won't stop now."

He went back to his bowls, and knowing how hard it was for him to talk about his family, Alissa bent back over her work to give him some privacy. The wheel had almost stopped, and she kicked it back up to speed. Her bowl was the furthest thing from her mind, and so she promptly bumped it, gasping as it collapsed in the quick sound of slapping clay. "Oh, no," she moaned. "Now I have to start all over." Alissa's eyes went miserably to the wall. The sun was gone.

Strell silently cocked his head at the ceiling and the disappearing light. He smiled and turned away, pretending he didn't see.

"Thanks," she said shyly. Still not meeting her eyes, he made a small noise. Alissa thought he was pleased she was showing so much interest in his first craft, despite his efforts to get her away from his wheel. He did have a point though. It had been three days, but she was as bad now as when she started. She was cold and hungry, and the daft thing was never going to look the way she wanted it. "Strell?" Her whisper broke the quiet, and he turned. "Will you show me how?"

He broke into a soft grin and nodded. Alissa began to rise so he could take her place, but he motioned her to stay. Much to her surprise, he pulled a stool up across from her and sat down. His long leg went out, and with a few practiced kicks, the wheel was spinning. "Here," he said as he reached out and took her hands into his own. Her eyes widened at his touch, and together, with her fingers between the clay and his, they gathered the mangled bits of clay into a small hill.

"Do you feel it humming?" he asked. She nodded, not sure what to make of his casual contact. But it did seem as if the clay under her palms was humming. "That means it's centered," he said. "Now, notice the continuous pressure needed to change its shape." Their hands shifted, and she started as the edge of her palm found the gritty, spinning wheel. "As with any endeavor, it's always best to lure changes from the bottom," he said softly, his eyes fixed upon the clay. "Starting in the middle only ruins the beginning and the end, much as it does a good story."

He leaned closer, his head almost touching hers, and she stiffened. Strell nodded. "Yes. That's better. If you're hesitant, it will rebel and run away from you. But if you're too bold, it will do the same. Clay requires more of—an enticement?"

Under their combined pressure, the hill turned into a perfectly circular, squat column. Her eyes were drawn to his mutilated hand. Their fingers were intertwined, making his pinky difficult to find. Up to now he had tried to hide it, refusing even to let her see it closely and make sure it was healing properly, but here, trying to teach her his first craft, he had allowed himself to forget. A small knot of worry in her began to ease.

"But if you have a gentle firmness," he continued, "and know exactly the limits of your mastery, it will respond willingly to anything you ask." Their joined thumbs sank into the clay to make a well. Beneath his fingers gray with mud, the hollow cylinder thinned and rose to become a delicate vase. She watched, enthralled with how easy he made it seem. It was more like magic than a skill. "And perhaps," he said, preoccupied with his task, "create something you might never expect."

His other foot went out, and using his heel, he slowed the flywheel until it was barely moving. Taking her finger, he traced a close spiral from the bottom up. She allowed him to shift her hand, letting him do as he wished, wanting him to know she didn't mind.

"My father," he said softly, "maintained much as a fiery-tempered woman, clay had to be forced into obedience." He paused, eyeing the gently moving spiral. "I disagree. I believe clay must be charmed, thereby not forfeiting any of its own temperamental spirit, but rather lending it to the potter's skills, supplementing it, allowing him to craft far more that he could make alone."

The wheel stopped. In the new hush, Alissa look questioningly at Strell. He was contemplating their work, more content than she had ever seen him. Her heart went out to him, knowing his music had been a large part of him and now it was gone. Perhaps he could find solace in being a potter again. A sigh slipped from him. His lips parted and he blinked, clearly only now realizing their hands were yet intertwined. Still, she smiled, and seeing it, he relaxed.

"You see?" he said, his voice pitched lower. "It's a matter of gentle firmness joined with a willingness to let the clay show you its own desires, and the ability to meld those desires with your own."

She nodded, her pulse quickening with the question of what would happen next.

"I think we should keep this one," Strell asserted softly, and she nodded again, waiting. His head tilted, and he leaned closer to her over the clay. Her breath caught.

But then Talon winged in, landing on the table before them in a backwash of unmitigated hostility. Feathers raised like the hackles of an angry dog, she stalked stiffly forward, growing more and more agitated. Small sounds resembling cracking ice came from her, and Alissa's eyes widened. It was her bird's tiny nails, snapping on the table.

A flash of ire flickered behind Strell's eyes, and he sighed in resignation. "All right, old bird," he grumbled as he disentangled their fingers and reluctantly stood. "I was just showing your mistress the finer points of throwing a pot." Still hissing, Talon fluttered up to the rafters. Her shadow lay upon the table like a cold warning, watching.

Strell ran a length of twine under their vase to loosen it from the wheel. Fingers carefully spaced, he gently shifted it free and moved it to the drying table, covering it with a light piece of damp cloth so it wouldn't dry too quickly and perhaps crack.

Alissa remained where she was, disgusted with her bird's bad timing. It wasn't until Strell began to wash the clay from his fingers that she rose, stiff, sore, and muddy. Ignoring Talon's muttered comments, Alissa cleaned what she could of herself, resolving to do a better job later. She was lost in a mix of embarrassment and frustration when she turned to see Strell crouched by the vase, knife in hand. "There," he said, and extended the knife to her. "Your turn."

"My turn?" she said, coughing to clear her throat as her voice cracked.

"Your name," he prompted. "I can tell already this piece is worth keeping. It will withstand the heat of the fire. You have to put your name upon it before it dries."

"Doesn't that go on the underside?" she asked, sure that was were she had seen such marks in the past.

"Yes. But as we're not going to sell it, it can go anywhere we want. And I do want both our names upon this," he said, glancing nervously to the rafters.

"Oh." Alissa took the knife, glancing at him as their fingers seemed to touch intentionally. Down at the narrow footing were a series of subtle scratches that she recognized as Strell's name. Crouching, she carefully traced hers next to his. "Done," she said firmly, straightening her back with a wince.

Strell bent low, examining her handiwork. He looked at her, then back down.

"Is there something wrong with the way I write my name?" Alissa asked. He had shown her how to write her name in his script on their way to the Hold. She had returned the favor, giving his name the symbol for stone, as in dense, after spending three extra days slogging through briars because of his "short cut." But his script looked so stiff and boring. She had signed the vase as her papa taught her, in a graceful character consisting of a continuous swoop and swirl. It was small, but clearly enough written using the symbol for luck.

"No," he said softly. "It's just that—" He stopped, shaking his head.

"Just what?"

"Your name has the same pattern as your luck charm," he finished apologetically.

Alissa's eyebrows went up, and her gaze went down. Crouching again, she pulled her charm out from a pocket, unwrapped it, and compared the two. "You're right!" she exclaimed quietly, and a chill ran through her. How had the Masters' jealousy guarded script made it into the plains in such a blatant display as a luck charm?

Talon, up in the rafters, finally went still.

13

"Sleep well, Alissa," Strell whispered. Shutting her door behind him, he slumped back against the wall with a contented sigh, smiling in the darkness that engulfed the hall. It was the middle of the night, but he was wide awake. Alissa's restless sleep had woken him not long ago, and he had gone to quiet her as usual. It was the third time in the last four days. He didn't mind, though it made his early mornings all the more difficult. She never woke fully, and so he was free to treat her as he would like. All it had taken was a softly sung lullaby and a gentle kiss on her fingertips, still rough and gritty from her valiant efforts this afternoon.

He grinned as he levered himself into motion, recalling her pathetic attempts at throwing a pot. They had been astonishingly terrible. Her persistence, though, was marvelous. Imagine, he chuckled, suffering three entire days before asking for help! It had been a real test of his willpower, watching her missteps and not offering to show her what to do, but she needed to ask, or his advice would have been disregarded.

Bypassing his door, Strell continued to the stairs, running a hand along the wall to find his way. Something needed his immediate attention, something that required the night's clandestine shadow, an unfulfilled desire.

Desire. Strell's smile deepened as the image of Alissa at his wheel flashed through his mind. Hounds, he had almost managed to steal a kiss. She had looked grand, mudsplattered and cranky, her eyes bright in frustration. And she had asked for help. And he had obliged. And then there had been that warm, inviting look in her eyes, both shocking and delighting him. *Burn that bird of hers to ash for interrupting.*

He didn't care that her background was mixed. His years of travel had expunged his ingrained prejudice of anyone not from the plains. But the harsh reality was, a plainsman joining with a "foothills whore" might result in the loss of their lives; the hate between their two cultures ran that deep. His family, though, was dead, and Alissa's parents had survived being a mixed union. He was sure her father wouldn't have disapproved solely because he was plains, and Alissa's mother would probably be pleased, knowing he came from a chartered name. They could live without recrimination on the coast. Everyone looked different there.

Alissa balanced against him better than any other he had cared to spend time with, and there had, he admitted, been a few. At least one every winter since leaving home. But he liked Alissa. He didn't care what the rest of the world thought.

Hesitating in the lighter darkness at the landing, Strell gingerly felt for the first step. He eased himself down, finding the stair's pattern. Upon reaching the ground floor, he slipped into the dining hall. Something was calling him, drawing him from his warm bed, and he could do nothing but submit.

The light was almost nonexistent as the moon was a thin arc that wouldn't show until nearly dawn. Shadows were thick where none should exist. It was absolutely silent. Even the mice were asleep. Strell skulked through the cold dining hall, his pace quickening in time with his pulse as he went into the kitchen. Ghosting past the banked hearth, he slunk to a cloth-covered plate. There was a single, furtive look behind him, and then, sighing in anticipation, he gently lifted the cloth to reveal two candied apples. "Ah," he whispered lovingly. "There you are." With a quick snatch, he had the plate and was halfway across the room, fleeing his misdeed. Alissa would assume Bailic had eaten them. He would do nothing to change her belief.

Inexcusably pleased, he sniffed deeply, feeling his mouth begin to water as he passed through the dining room to sit upon the lowest stair in the great hall. The first, deep bite of the sugared delicacy filled his mouth, and a slight moan escaped him. His eyes closed in bliss as the juice dripped sticky from him. Ashes. They were perfect.

Apart from Alissa's cooking, he hadn't seen a candied apple since leaving his homeland. They were a plains delicacy. Alissa's mother would've taught her the vigilantly guarded secret. Wolves, but Alissa's recipe was a good one. Worth every stitch of her bride price.

Slowly, the faint aroma of pine came to him, mixing with the apple spice in an unsettlingly familiar scent. Strell's head came up, and he set the plate with the remaining apple on the step and licked his fingers as he tried to shake the sensation of being watched. It was ludicrous, but he was beginning to think the distinctive aroma was the telltale sign of Lodesh.

Strell's mood shifted to a wary watchfulness. He wasn't quite sure what to think of Lodesh, the supposed Warden of the abandoned city. Alissa had shown him the handsome staff he had given her—she had since hidden it in the kitchen behind the apples—and told him about her midnight tea party with Talo-Toecan and the Warden. Part of him was relieved he hadn't been seeing things in the grove of ancient trees and that Alissa, not Bailic, had woken the city, but he didn't like ghosts. The plains were full of them, making his skin crawl and his head hurt.

Even worse, every time he asked Alissa about Lodesh, she blushed and changed the subject. He couldn't help the sharp, surprising flash of jealousy at the thought of someone other than himself charming Alissa, and Lodesh sounded too substantial to be a true ghost.

From the dark came a faint sound, pulling his gaze up and around behind him. He listened, frowning with the effort. It was the whisper of fabric against stone. Thinking Alissa was up and about, he frantically looked for a place to stash the plate. But his guilt turned to astonishment as Bailic's outline hesitated at the top of the stair. "Bailic,"

Strell muttered, brushing his shirt free of the brown of wayward spice. "I should have known."

"Piper?" Bailic seemed uncharacteristically surprised as well. "I wasn't seeking you."

Unwilling to let Bailic loom over him, Strell gripped the banister and pulled himself to a stand. Bailic made his slow way down to halt on the last step. Strell eyed the fallen Keeper suspiciously, clenching his hand to hide his weakness.

"Your night is restless?" Bailic said, no hint to his emotion in his tone.

"Yes." With a false impassivity, Strell stood before Bailic. None of his growing hatred showed, hidden behind years of dealing with contrary landowners and balky innkeepers. Bailic had taken his finger, his music, his chosen way of life, but he would not take his pride.

"My night is restless, too." Bailic's gaze slid to the plate on the stair, and a whisper of a smile drifted over him. "She makes a wicked sugared apple, doesn't she?"

"She does."

Bailic adjusted the long vest he wore open over his shirt and trousers. "She might make them for me, someday," he said slyly, "if she agrees to act as my eyes."

"She hates you, Bailic," Strell said, his voice flat. "She won't."

Bailic's eyes rolled to the far ceiling, an insulting sigh escaping him. "She didn't tell you of our conversation in the hall?" Bailic stepped closer, a taunt eagerness in him that Strell didn't trust. "I asked her to stay and be my eyes when the book is open. She agreed to consider it."

Strell drew back, and Bailic laughed, a soft murmur of sound. "Don't hold it against her," he said. "She's only looking out for her well-being. She knows I'm going to bring the foothills and plains to war. I can protect her." His lips curved into a smile. "You can't."

His jaw clenched, and Strell's grip on the banister grew to a white-knuckled strength. He wondered if the conversation had really taken place or if Bailic was goading him, trying to make him react so he could justify taking off another finger. It wouldn't work. He wasn't a child to be manipulated that easily. "She won't agree to it," he said. "She hates you more than I do."

The fallen Keeper's shoulders shifted, and he leaned confidently against the banister. His smiled deepened. "Really?" Stooping low, he retrieved the plate with the remaining apple. "I'm glad to have found you tonight. There is the small matter of your studies we need to talk about."

Strell tried to make his step backward look casual. His missing digit throbbed in remembered hurt, and he pulled his hand close. Frustration burned as Bailic noticed and raised his eyebrows. Strell would nearly give his soul for five minutes with Bailic as his equal.

"Your skills seem to have reached another unfortunate plateau," the Keeper said, his voice light as he took a bite of the apple. "You haven't shown any progress this last week. What are you going to do about it?"

"I'm trying very hard," Strell said softly, his breathing shallow. "You said yourself I was doing third-year tasks. I can't learn everything overnight."

"Mind your tone," Bailic warned as he brushed his vest free of the fallen sugar crystals with a free hand. "It's up to you how fast you learn. The tasks are third-year only because the Masters were jealous with their secrets. I'm not." He smiled benevolently. "I'm very generous. And I won't wait twenty years for you. You will have that book open by summer."

"Summer!" Strell said, aghast. "That's impossible."

"I hope not, my piper, for your sake." Bailic took another bite with a mocking slowness.

A thick feeling of helplessness, of being trapped, welled up in him. It was a feeling Strell wasn't used to, and he nearly panicked at the unfamiliar tightness about his thoughts. He backed away, remembering the humiliation of being under Bailic's ward, unable to do anything but watch as the Keeper removed the first joint of his finger as easily as Strell might a dandelion head.

But pain came to pass, and his music was already dead, killed in his effort to keep Alissa safe. It was a sacrifice he didn't regret. What did it matter now if he had nine usable fingers or eight? Bailic's threats of more mutilations were empty. Strell drew himself up with a new courage. "You've taken away everything I cared about already," he said, his voice harsh.

Seeming unruffled, Bailic took another bite of the apple, his attention focused entirely on the sweet. "Not quite everything," he said. "It's foolish to become attached to anything, especially that girl you brought with you." He placed the last bite of apple in his mouth and chewed reflectively. "I do believe I'm going to keep her."

Strell's eyes widened. "She won't stay once the book is open," he said, as much to assure himself as deny Bailic's claim.

Bailic pushed the plate at Strell until he took it. "I never said she was going to like the situation. I only said I'm going to keep her." He turned as if the conversation were over and took a step upward.

"You agreed to leave her alone," Strell said as he followed him. "You got the cursed book. Leave her alone!" he shouted, not caring if he tempted Bailic's anger or not. The Keeper paused, and Strell came to an abrupt halt below him.

"The agreement with Talo-Toecan ends when the book is opened," Bailic said. "I'm not going to break my word." Leaning over him, Bailic whispered, "I don't need to. But what if she should knock on my door—again? Who am I to coldly turn such an innocent from my chambers—a second time?" A white eyebrow rose. "I'll not be accused of being rude."

Strell's throat tightened. He couldn't attack Bailic. The man would take his entire hand off. But his guile and distractions weren't working anymore. He couldn't protect Alissa from this! Strell's blood pounded in his temple, and he took a ragged breath. He couldn't do anything! "I won't let you keep her," he gasped out, and Bailic shook his head.

"Silly man," Bailic taunted. "You'll probably be dead. It depends entirely on how fast you open the book."

"Threatening her won't encourage me to open it," he said, the hurt from his nails digging into his palm breaking into his awareness.

"I think it will. Open it fast enough, and I may reconsider. The longer it takes, the more—fond—I'll become of her." Bailic smiled. "Study hard, Piper."

The taste of failure was as dry and bitter as ash. Bailic's eyes were upon him as he trembled from frustration and helpless anger. His body demanded he rise up and fight, but the memory of pain and the promise of Bailic doing worse to Alissa kept him unmoving.

Appearing smug and content, Bailic watched him struggle with his emotions, clearly aware that Strell was just strong enough of will to keep from attacking him. The mad Keeper stepped close, and Strell's heart pounded as he kept himself from moving. "One last thing," Bailic whispered. "It's true I never break my word, but somehow I always get what I want." He leaned forward until he was a finger's width from Strell's ear. "Somehow . . ." he breathed, and the rich scent of spice washed over Strell. Snickering, Bailic spun about and continued up the stairs, leaving only his last, condescending look to linger in Strell's memory, taunting and ridiculing him.

Standing alone in the moonlight, Strell took a quick, ragged breath and tried to gather his scattered soul. He could do nothing. Bailic would take everything from him, and he could do nothing to stop it. He knew he could make it to the coast, but Alissa wouldn't. He could leave to save his life, but he wouldn't abandon Alissa. Only now did he understand. He wouldn't risk his life for Alissa if his emotions stopped at simple affection. With an emotion that struck him deep, Strell admitted it was for love.

14

"Ouch," Alissa whispered as her needle slipped. She glanced at Strell kneeling beside the fire and stuck the side of her finger in her mouth. Trying to disguise that she had pricked her finger again, she reached for the teapot on the hearth.

"You all right?" he asked, not looking up from the pot of glaze he was stirring.

"Um-hum," she murmured. Topping off her cup, she hid her embarrassment by taking a quick sip. They were spending their evening in the dining hall, and the small arc of firelight did little to illuminate the empty walls. Bailic's tray had been delivered, and as long as they were quiet, they would have the Hold to themselves for the rest of the night. A pile of green fabric lay on her lap. She was making Strell another shirt, as she had nearly two new outfits for herself in her room. Talon was in the kitchen watching for mice. Kestrels generally didn't hunt after dark, but no one had told Talon that.

Alissa leaned to set her cup down on the floor, wondering if her finger was going to stop bleeding anytime soon. Her gaze drifted past the darkness to the stark walls. The long tables made the room seem all the more barren. There were no rugs, no wall hangings, nothing. She hated the emptiness. Bailic had stripped this room along with most of the Hold. She thought he had left the curtains covering the expansive windows to block the morning sun rather than any desire to soften the walls. Wards kept out the wind and cold. When not covered, the windows showed a wonderful corner of the snowy garden.

"You know," she said, breaking their companionable silence. "This would be a nice room if we brought up a rug or two from the annexes. We could even bring up a couple of more comfortable chairs."

Frowning, Strell met her eyes. "Bailic wants the Hold empty. He likes it that way."

A smile crept over her as she imagined the dining hall as it could be. "A little table would be nice for setting the tea on," she said. "And a footrest."

"Not a good idea," he warned, continuing to stir the glaze.

Alissa examined her finger and resumed her stitching. "Bailic doesn't come in here anymore. He only took everything out to try to find my book. He won't care."

Strell said nothing, but he shook his head and settled further on the backs of his heels.

Mildly peeved, Alissa decided she would bring up at least a chair from the annexes, even if she had to do it herself. Sitting on these monstrosities of hard wood was becoming painful. They were all straight-backed, with no cushion at all.

Strell exchanged his pot of glaze for another, mixing it gently to gauge the consistency as it thickened. Alissa watched him with a faint sense of sorrow. Their nights had become decidedly quiet since Bailic removed half of Strell's finger. Strell had replaced his practice of music with the occasional retelling of a story or working on his paints and brushes. Once constant and exasperating, his jests were now few and far between. She would give anything to hear a bawdy tavern tune, sung with the sole purpose to embarrass her.

Strell was being foolish, she thought. There was no real reason he couldn't play something. He could shift the music up the scale and work around that note completely. It had been almost two weeks. He was being a stubborn plainsman, thinking the lack of a segment of finger made him less. He hadn't even let her see his finger, except the one time with the clay. She lowered her head and smiled privately. While teaching her, he had set his pride aside.

She laced another stitch and paused. Perhaps all he needed was a push? Setting her stitching down, she rose and started for the kitchen. Her pipe was in the pantry where she had left it after her and Strell's dinner out in the firepit last fall. She never played it anymore. Next to Strell, she sounded pathetic.

Strell looked up as she reached the black archway. "Where are you going?"

"I'll be right back," she said mysteriously.

Talon blinked at her in what looked like annoyance as she entered the dark kitchen in a scuff of shoes. There was a skitter of noise as the mouse Talon had been watching for scurried into hiding. "The mice will be back soon," she promised, finding her pipe right where she had left it, tucked behind the apples with her staff. Not sure what his reaction would be, she half hid the pipe with her body as she returned to the fire.

Strell glanced up as she settled herself back in her chair. She knew he had seen it as his jaw clenched and his brow furrowed. A splash of glaze slopped over the edge of the small pot as he stirred it too hard. "I'll get that," Alissa offered, snatching up the rag she used to protect her hands from the hot teapot and kneeling beside him. "Hold this for me," she said, extending her pipe to Strell.

He froze, and she looked up from the flagstones. "Take it," she insisted, and he lurched to a stand, the pot of glaze clutched in his hand like an excuse.

"No."

The harsh denial surprised her, and she felt a touch of anger. "You're being silly," she said. "Not every song uses that note."

Strell's face went hard. "You have no call to say anything about this," he said, his voice so cold, she was afraid she had gone too far.

"But your finger almost reaches," she pleaded from the flagstones.

"Almost isn't close enough."

"Look." Alissa wiped up the glaze before it could stain

and got to her feet. "Just hold it for a moment. Show me how close it comes."

His jaw gritted as she stood before him, but he didn't back away.

"Burn you to ash, Strell," she cried, frustrated. "Your finger is half gone. Hiding it or ignoring it isn't going to make it come back! I just want to help. It's my fault Bailic did that to you."

She caught her breath and turned away. "It's my fault, and you won't even let me look at it. You won't let me try to help," she whispered, realizing why she was so adamant he play again. It was because of her that he lost his music. She would get it back for him.

Strell shifted his balance. "It's not your fault I can't play," he said stiffly. "I'm not a piper anymore. There's no reason for you to look at it. It healed fine."

A flash of misplaced anger went through her. She spun back and grabbed his hand. "You're acting like a child," she accused. "Let me look at it." Strell pulled his hand away, making her more upset. "Let me see!" she shouted, taking his arm and pinning it between her arm and her body.

Strell started to pull away, and she gripped his arm all the tighter. She gave him a severe look over her shoulder before turning her attention to his hand. It was as strong as she remembered, brown from the sun with knuckles thicker than hers. His fingernails were cut close and had a rim of clay under them. His skin was warm, rough with calluses. It reminded her of her papa's hand.

Her anger slowed as she leaned to inspect his smallest finger. Only the first joint had been removed. It wasn't much, but it was enough. It had healed well and clean. Strell could have done worse, she thought, loosening her grip as he pulled gently away.

She put the pipe in his hand with a firm determination. "Show me where your finger hits the pipe," she demanded.

Strell dropped his head, the pipe in his left hand. "Alissa," he said softly. "Let the wind take it and go. I've tried to play. I can't."

"I know. I heard. It wasn't that bad."

The look he gave her was almost frightened. "You heard?"

She nodded. "Show me."

His head shook and he backed up a step. "I'm not going to play."

"I'm not asking you to," she said, feeling her pulse race. She would hear him play, even if it took until sunup.

Strell glanced down at the pipe and licked his lips.

"Show me how short that finger is," she said.

He frowned, his brow creasing in a defiant pull. Immediately she softened. "Do this once for me," she said, "and I'll say nothing more about it, even if the Navigator brings his Hounds to earth."

Strell rubbed a hand across his head. He glanced at her suspiciously, moving to sit upon the flagstones. Swallowing hard, he grasped the pipe properly, holding it so it was clear he wouldn't play it.

Alissa sank down beside him. He started to pull the pipe away, and she grasped his arm, shifting until she was so close her leg touched his. "Hold still," she said, leaning over his hands. Her gaze intent, she examined his comfortable grip on the pipe. His fingers curved naturally, leaving a definite gap between his smallest finger and the last hole. The smell of desert was on him even though it was midwinter. Her shoulders eased in the reminder of the summer's warmth. "It's not that much too short," she said softly.

Immediately Strell pulled from her loose grip. "It's enough." He extended the pipe, and when she ignored it, he set it between them.

"Your finger would reach if the hole was on the side instead of the top," she insisted.

"But it isn't, is it," he said bitterly, taking up the fire irons and jabbing at the fire.

A wave of heat billowed out. "So make a new pipe," Alissa said, tired of his sulky mood.

Strell put the irons back with more force than necessary. "Do you know how long that would take?"

"Do you have anything better to do?" she shot back.

Strell frowned, clearly taken aback. "I don't have the proper tools."

"They're in the annexes. I saw them."

"I don't have the right wood."

"Annexes," she said again.

Strell shook his head, a wisp of a smile pulling the farthest corners of his mouth. "You have this all figured out, don't you."

She grinned, but it faded quickly. "I can't let Bailic do this to you," she said. "I can't let him take away your music, your livelihood. Please," she said, taking the pipe and pressing it into his hands. "I want to hear you play. I know you will be good again. It will only take time to figure out the new fingering or make a new pipe so you don't have to."

A wash of relief went through her as she saw his grip tighten on the pipe. "What if it doesn't work?" he asked, sounding afraid.

"Then you haven't lost anything but the time spent."

"But what if it does work?" he said, almost whispering. "What if I can play? I will have given Bailic a way to control me again. I can't let him do that. He might do worse."

Alissa dropped her eyes. "Don't let Bailic take away what you love because of fear. Your finger means nothing. Its loss is a false weakness that only you can make true."

He was silent, his eyes on the instrument. His eyes closed in a long blink, and his fingers, where they rested upon the wood, trembled. "All right," he said, his eyes opening. "I'll try."

Relief so strong it made tears threaten her vision swept her. She smiled up at him. "Play me something?" she said, and he nodded, not meeting her eyes.

He settled himself cross-legged before the hearth as she had seen him hundreds of times before. Not wanting to leave the warm circle of light for the hard chair, Alissa remained where she was, sitting quietly beside him with her hands in her lap. Strell flicked a sideways glance at her and focused upon the pipe in his hands. There was a moment of thought, then he played three notes. Hesitating, he started over, playing them higher. Alissa smiled as she recognized the tune. It was the lullaby they had shared on their way to the Hold, the one she taught him even before they met, camped on opposite sides of a small valley. She had played it to ease her pain of leaving home, and Strell had heard, scaring her when he mimicked it back.

The last of her worry loosened as his first hesitant, unsure notes eased into a smoother pace. Her shoulders slumped, and she closed her eyes before they could fill. He was going to be all right. Strell was going to be all right. Bailic hadn't broken his will.

Slowly the tune became stronger with emotion, the way he used to play for her. His awkward indecisions eased, and the flow became certain. Alissa smiled, curling her legs up under her to be more comfortable. She leaned forward to rearrange the fire, and when she leaned back, she found Strell had shifted to offer her the front of his shoulder to lean up against.

Shyly, hesitantly, she accepted his support, leaning into him as he played, not knowing how much weight he could hold without becoming unbalanced. She dropped her head to rest against him, smiling as he bobbled the melody from surprise. The scent of desert filled her senses again, and she breathed deeply, her eyes closing as she imagined that the warmth of the fire was that of the sun, and she was far from the Hold and the snow and the cold, back in the fields where she had played as a child. Safe.

His music lured her into a deep state of ease as it often did. Slumped against him, she drowsed to the sound of Strell's heartbeat and his music, gentle and slow, never realizing when the music stopped, not caring that it had, and that Strell's arms were now around her. "Alissa," he said, and she felt his breath shift the top of her hair.

"Hum . . ." she said sleepily, not knowing if she said it aloud.

"Are you awake?"

"No," she murmured, uncaring if she was. There was the sound of dry coals sliding and a brief flush of heat.

"Thank you," he whispered, his words accompanied by the lightest touch and breath on her forehead.

15

Alissa searched the rafters as she put the tea leaves in the teapot. She hadn't seen Talon since Strell delivered Bailic's noon tray. It was unlike the small bird to accompany Strell when he took Bailic his meals, and even more unusual for Talon to stay with him afterward. But Strell was ready to fire his pottery and had probably gone directly to his potter's stead from the tower. If he had the fire going, her bird would undoubtedly be with him, basking in the warmth.

Which was exactly where she wanted to be, she thought as she took the copper teapot in one hand and two cups in the other. She could do with a good soak in some warm air. The window wards were wonderful at keeping the Hold from getting cold, but she hadn't been warm, truly warm, in ages.

Her smile deepened as she passed through the dining hall. It was barren no longer. Though Strell had dragged his feet and given her warning glances from under lowered brows, he had helped bring up two lovely chairs from storage. There was a small table between them, and a rug to keep her feet from the cold floor. She was longing to do more but prudently paced herself. Should she push Strell too fast he might not help her, or even worse, Bailic might notice.

The scuff of her shoes seemed loud as she entered the great hall and hesitated, frowning at a small object on the otherwise pristine floor. Curious, she went to investigate. "A nut?" she whispered. She shifted the two cups to her hand with the teapot and bent to pick it up. Seeing another a few steps away, she slipped the first into her pocket and picked that one up, too. A third rested against the tunnel leading to the abandoned stables. There was a fourth lying just beyond where the shadow of the tunnel took over the light. Her eyebrows rose as she spotted yet another farther down the tunnel.

A wisp of a smile quirked the corners of her mouth. What was Strell up to? She let the rest of the nuts lay and followed the trail. It became darker as the tunnel opened up into the long-abandoned stables. Wood replaced the stone underfoot, and the smell of straw long gone bad mixed with the scent of leather soaked in horse sweat. She didn't like horses. And though there hadn't been a horse down here in what looked like decades, she could almost hear the frightened blowing and angry stomping of hooves in her imagination.

Just as she had decided to go back for a candle, her dark-adjusted eyes made out a faint light. She went ahead on tiptoe, curious to see what Strell had lured her down here for. Her slight tension eased as she heard the chitter of her bird and the sharp crack of a nut being broken. The glow of light became obvious as she turned a corner and entered a row of box stalls. From within one came a steady, white light, reflecting off the dark wood of the ceiling and surrounding walls. A faint resonance had set her tracings to shimmer faintly, telling her it was a ward of some kind. It looked horribly complicated. *Useless?* she wondered. The scent of apples and pine eased into her awareness. She reached the stall and halted in surprise as she looked inside. "Lodesh?"

The Warden glanced up so quickly, he nearly fell off the bale of straw he was reclining on. "Alissa!" He jumped to his feet and brushed the shells from him. His green eyes were wide, and he looked charmingly surprised. The brilliant light came from a fist-sized globe hanging in midair. Useless had never told her that was possible!

Before she could comment, the light vanished. She gasped and froze, but then with a familiar tweak on her tracings, a small flame flickered. Lodesh's face was

abruptly illuminated by candlelight. Silently he lit several
more until the large box stall was warm with a yellow
glow. "I, uh, wasn't expecting to see you," he said. "Here.
Let me take that."

He reached for the heavy teapot and cups, setting them
on a slatted box covered by a fine cloth. Eyebrows raised,
she dropped the nuts she had collected into the half-empty
bowl beside the plate of candles.

"I wasn't expecting you so soon," he amended, not a
trace of guilt showing. "It's good to see you again," he said
as he took her hand and drew her forward into the light.
Immediately her bravado vanished in a flush of self-
consciousness and she put a hand to her neckline. She
wasn't used to being treated with this much grace.

Talon chittered merrily from the short wall, and Alissa
ran her fingers over the small bird's feathers in greeting,
surprised to find her with Lodesh. "What are you doing
down here?" she asked Lodesh as she set her cups beside
the teapot and ran her eyes over the small hidey-hole. He
had strewn fabric over everything to disguise the rough
timbers and old dust, enough good material to make an entire dress and underskirt. He must have gotten it from the
annexes. It reminded her of a child's playhouse, only made
from silk and linen instead of rough woolen sheets. "Is
Talo-Toecan here, too?"

Lodesh shook his head, pulling her farther in. "No. Just
me, milady."

Feeling a faint wash of caution, Alissa took her hands
from him. He hadn't answered her question. "I was taking
Strell some tea," she said. "He's next door in the kitchen
annex. Come with me and meet him? We could have tea
together."

"No." His eyes met hers, his look sending a pang of
emotion through her. Her pulse quickened, and she looked
toward the unseen tunnel. That feeling of forgotten memory coursed through her, the same she felt at the grove, and
her heart seemed to clench in an unnamed grief. Her face
went cold. Frightened by feelings that couldn't be hers, she
stepped back.

"Alissa," Lodesh said, his eyes crinkling from worry. "Don't go. Not just yet. I'm sorry. I didn't mean to make you uncomfortable. It's just—"

"It's not you. It's the stables." Alissa looked away from the half lie, glancing at the forgotten brushes and shovels. Horses made her uneasy, but the paradoxical emotions Lodesh stirred in her were far more troubling. But to be frightened by a feeling was childish. And the emotions were gone now.

His worried look shifted to dismay. "I forgot. You don't like horses, do you."

Talon chattered a warning and hopped to her shoulder. Wincing from the claws, Alissa wrapped her hand in the tea towel and moved the kestrel back to the short, rug-draped wall. "No, I don't," she said. Her brow furrowed. "How did you know—"

"Oh. Well." Lodesh turned to relight one of the candles that had gone out. "You were raised foothills, yes? All foothills folk dislike horses, don't they?"

"No," she said. "My mother used to have one, but she told me it broke the fence and ran away shortly after I was born. We never had the need to get another." She scuffed her slipper over a rug. "Horses don't like me," she finished, feeling a sliver of childhood fear.

"My mistake," he said. "Sit with me?" He slipped an arm about her waist and eased her forward to sit on a bale of straw covered in a warm red linen. "Just for a moment? I promise, I won't . . . embarrass you again."

Her brows rose as she settled herself. It sounded like a challenge. "You haven't," she said with a confidence she didn't feel. "But why don't you come up with me? Strell has a fire going. I don't think he believes me that you exist."

Lodesh shook his head as he sat down across from her. His high mannerisms had fallen from him, leaving him, Alissa thought, all the more charming. "I ought not to be here at all," he said. "I'm pushing my luck as it is. If Bailic should run a general search of the Hold rather than a specific one for you or Strell, he'll find me. My presence might be difficult to explain."

"I didn't know he could do that," she said softly, now realizing how Bailic found them so quickly whenever they were noisy.

"The stables offer a modicum of protection," Lodesh continued. "Horses are sensitive beasts. Can't even run a ward to keep out the dust. The walls are partially shielded here, but a concentrated effort, or if Bailic knows who he's looking for, would reveal me. I'll stay here until the afternoon snow is heavy enough to cover my tracks on my way back home."

She smiled. Home must be Ese' Nawoer. It was quite a trek. But then a frown pinched her brow. What was he doing here, sitting in the dark, eating nuts? "You've been here before," she said, feeling a stir of ire. "You've been checking up on me between my lessons, haven't you."

Lodesh seemed to wince. "Please, Alissa. Don't tell Talo-Toecan I let you find me."

He had *been here before?* she thought angrily. "Let me find you?" she said, her voice rising. "Did Useless send you to spy on me between his visits?"

Lodesh straightened. "Um, no, not really, well. Mayhap." His eyes pleaded with her. "Don't tell him you caught me. He would outright tell me to stay away, and I would be bound to listen to him if he makes his request flat out." Lodesh reached across the small space to take her hands, and she pulled away, angry he would try to soothe her like that.

"You have been spying on me!" she shouted.

Talon chittered again from her perch, responding to Alissa's voice. Chagrined, Lodesh sat upon his cloth-covered straw and dropped his head. When he looked up, there was true regret in his eyes. "Yes. I have. It was wrong of me. I promise I'll let you know every time I'm here from now on." He reached out, drawing back as she raised her chin. "Please, Alissa. I only wanted to see you. And I did tell you this time."

Her lips pursed, but he wasn't arguing back, and it

wasn't much fun. She brushed needlessly at her skirt, try-ing to soothe her anger. Useless was only looking out for her, but it still rankled her.

Lodesh shifted uncomfortably. "Here. Let me pour you some tea." She silently waited as he took the pot she had meant for Strell and poured out two cups. He handed her the first, and she met his eyes as his fingers touched hers. She didn't jerk away, her usual embarrassment over-whelmed by the traces of her disappearing anger.

"So-o-o," Lodesh drawled as he eased back to his seat. "How are your lessons going?"

The last of her anger vanished as she saw the comical arch to his eyebrows. Forgiving him, she took a sip of her drink. "Slow."

Lodesh laughed, the sound seeming to fill the small space. "Isn't that the way of it? My instructor, Redal-Stan, once accused me of listening at doors to catch resonances."

"That's awful," she said, smiling at the mental picture of Lodesh crouched at a door.

Lodesh shrugged and took a swallow of tea. "I was."

"Useless gave me a ward of disguise," she said, proud of her first, real accomplishment.

"Can you hold it yet when you sleep?"

She nodded, feeling warm as Lodesh bobbed his head in approval. It was nice to have someone tell her she had done well. "Tell me of Ese' Nawoer?" she asked. "It must have been a grand city, with its orchards and paved streets. Did you ever have festivals out in the grove?"

Lodesh went still. "Festivals?" he said softly. "Such as with music and drums?"

Alissa smiled. "And dancing, with the moon high."

"And the mirth trees blooming?" he said wistfully.

"And the wind, tugging at you to join with it?" Alissa's eyes closed as she imagined it.

"Yes," Lodesh said, and her eyes flashed open at the flat sound of his voice. "Exactly like that." His eyes seemed to grow dusky in the candlelight.

She shifted her shoulders, uneasy at the depth in his

voice. "Tell me of one?" she said as she took another swallow of tea.

"No." Lodesh looked away, refusing to meet her eyes. "Not now. Maybe later."

He looked genuinely distressed, and Alissa reached across the space between them to touch his shoulder. "I'm sorry. I didn't mean to upset you."

His eyes were clear as he looked up at her light pressure. "You didn't," he said as he ran a finger across her cheek. "Even painful memories can bring a moment of contentment."

Her pulse quickened, and not knowing what to say, Alissa leaned back and hid behind her tea. "I should go," she said, setting her nearly full cup down beside the plate of candles.

"I know."

His voice was tired, and she felt bad for leaving him. "It's been nice," she said as she stood up. "Talking with you, I mean. Strell doesn't understand—about Keeper things."

Lodesh smiled at her, but it looked forced, as if he was hiding something. "To share, and know another understands completely, is worth more than gold."

Alissa nodded, feeling as if something more was being said than she understood. Taking the teapot, Lodesh refilled it from a jug he had tucked under a fabric-draped box. "You had better go," he said. "If you promise not to look at your tracings, I'll heat your water back to boiling for you."

She nodded again, not knowing that was possible. Useless always let the fire warm their tea water. There was a brief tug upon her awareness, and he handed her the pot, heavy and warm. "Thank you, Lodesh," she said, pausing in the aisle. "You'll make it back all right? It's getting cold."

His smile grew true. "The longest night couldn't take the warmth from me right now, Alissa. I'll be fine."

Again she hesitated. "Promise you'll tell me every time you come back?"

Beaming, he took her hand and brought it close to his lips. "Every time," he breathed upon her skin. He held her eyes for a moment, and she struggled not to shiver at the dark, serious tone in his voice. He leaned close. The scent of mirth wood filled her. Before she realized his intent, he had touched his lips to hers. Shock shifted to curiosity as a warm feeling rose within her. Denying her first reaction to pull away, she leaned into the kiss, prolonging it. An image of her and Lodesh fell through the layers of her thoughts: a vision of them under the mirth trees, the sound of drums and pipes, her pulse pounding from more than the dance, and an urgency that she had to leave but that she didn't want to.

Her fingers slipped from the handle of the teapot, and it crashed to the floor.

Startled, Alissa jerked away. Her face burned as she dropped her eyes to the rocking teapot. There was a warm coolness to her lips.

"Let me get that for you," Lodesh said, retrieving the copper pot as if nothing had happened.

"Yes. Thank you," she stammered. She took it without looking at him as he proffered it. "I—I have to take this to Strell." She took a step back. "Um, he wants to meet you. It won't take a moment for me to get him. I'll be right back." Fleeing, she nearly ran back to the great hall before he could respond.

Her pulse thudded in her chest as she made her flustered way to Strell's potter's stead, her feet following the familiar path by rote. She held her cooling pot of tea in one hand, gripping it as if it was the only thing that made any sense, only now realizing she had left the cups in the stables. The heavy confusion from Lodesh's kiss still swirled high in her as she reached the annex kitchen and stood blinking in the threshold, watching Strell working the clay at his wheel.

The kiln fire was hot, and he had taken off his shirt. The muscles between his shoulders bunched and shifted as he manipulated the clay with a deft gentleness. He didn't know she was there, and she watched transfixed. The sun glinted on his skin, almost making it seem to glow. Her foot shifted, and he looked up at the small noise.

"Alissa," he said, smiling. Then his brow bunched and

he pulled back from his clay. "What's the matter? You look like you've seen a ghost."

She took a quick breath, struggling to remember why she was down here. "Lodesh," she said, giving herself a little shake. "He's in the stables. You should come meet him."

"He's here?" Strell jumped to his feet, snatching a towel and cleaning his hands. "Show me." Grabbing his shirt draped on an unused table, he stuffed his arms in the sleeves. He took the teapot from her senseless fingers and set it down. Grasping her hand, he pulled her back up the annex tunnel. She stumbled along behind him, wondering why he had never kissed her like that.

It wasn't until they were in the stables that she shook off her befuddled shock and eased her hand from Strell's. "Lodesh?" she called hesitantly as they felt their way in the dark, following the faint glow of candlelight.

There was no answer, and her embarrassment was tinged with relief as they came upon the lavish box stall and found it empty but for a single, lit candle, two cups, and Talon. Strell stiffened as he took in the cloth-draped straw and the plate of candles, all extinguished but for one. He went to investigate, fingering the nut lying on the plate before he set it back down with a harsh clatter. "He hasn't been gone long," Strell said. "The wax hasn't set on the candles that have gone out."

She said nothing. He must have left as soon as she had. She wasn't sure what that meant. "He was here," she finally said. "He was right here. We had tea and we talked."

"Tea?" Strell said, and she looked up at the dead sound in his voice. His jaw was clenched, and he had a look about him that she had never seen before.

Chittering, Talon hopped to Alissa's shoulder, and she suffered the small bite of her claws. "Come on," Strell said, taking her elbow and pulling her back up the aisle and to the great hall. "He's not here now. Let's go back where it's warm."

16

"*Not alone. Not the last. Keribdis. Anyone. Hear me!*"
Alissa woke with a gasp, the last words from her dream resounding in her thoughts. It was dark, and for an instant she couldn't place herself. The dream had been almost more genuine than reality. There had been an icy, dark shore, silver under the setting full moon, the rattle of pebbles washing in the water, and the smell of salt, heavy in the air. It had been so vivid, she felt she would recognize the exact spot in the unlikely event she ever made the journey to the ocean. A feeling of aching loneliness, of a promise ignored, roared within her. It wasn't her emotion, and Alissa studied it carefully before it slipped away. The odd sensation of feelings that clearly weren't her own was confusing, and she sat up.

She was in her room in her chair before her banked fire. The thin light through the cracks in her shutters said dawn was still some time away, but sleep would be impossible now. Besides, Useless was coming tonight, and she was anxious to speak to him. She had a favor to ask.

With an excitement tempered by dread, Alissa rose and put on layer upon layer of clothing, her fingers slow and fumbling from the cold. Irate thoughts of scissors and Strell ran through her mind as she tied her hair back with a length of green ribbon. He still wouldn't cut it for her. Shivering, she folded her luck charm into a length of cloth and tucked it into a pocket.

She went to peek out her shutters, and they groaned in complaint as she leaned out. Dim and faint, the light from the moon setting behind the Hold did little to light the early morning. The frost slipped in to pool about her ankles like water in a snow-melt stream. Talon fluffed herself in the sudden draft, fixing a sharp eye upon Alissa. "Your playmate is coming," Alissa whispered, smiling as the bird began to preen in anticipation of a terrifying game of tag.

As much as it unnerved Alissa, Useless and Talon's predawn diversion had become something of a ritual. Useless was generally it, and their murderously silent, aerial acrobatics left Alissa breathless. Talon had become increasingly inventive in trying to remain out of the raku's grip. It was obvious they spent more time at their play than she witnessed.

Alissa took Talon in hand and crept down to the kitchen without bothering with a candle. The way was as familiar as the old trails about her mother's farm by now. The bird fussed as they entered the kitchen, and Alissa let her out through the garden door before going to raise the fire and start the tea. Her dream had woken her unusually early, and she found herself waiting alone at the firepit with a cooling pot before Useless arrived.

Huddled before the snow-covered ashes, Alissa managed to start the fire with her candle, despite the dampness of the wood. *Useless usually did this with a lot less effort,* she thought sourly as she slipped her mittens back on. Despite her pleading, he stubbornly refused to grant her permission to try it with a ward. Lodesh knew how to start a fire with his thoughts, but using that information to convince Useless would only get the Warden in trouble.

"Where are you, Useless?" Alissa whispered, scanning the purple sky. It was breathlessly still, the icy sharpness seeming cold enough to crack the last of the stars. A few scattered clouds showed gray above the neglected garden's wall, but no Useless. She ran a nervous hand under her nose. Perhaps she had the wrong morning. It was difficult to tell a perfect moon from one just shy of full, and she hadn't seen it at all last night due to snow. But then his silhouette ghosted over the Hold, cutting a familiar swath through the brightening sky.

Ignoring Talon's valiant efforts to distract him, Useless

refused their usual game, landing nearby to shift to his human form in a swirl of gray and a tug on Alissa's thoughts. He held up an impossibly long hand for Talon, and together they made their way to the fire. Alissa rose to her feet and waited. Something was bothering Useless; it showed in his step and his slumped shoulders. She watched the play of emotions over his face as he whispered something to Talon and launched her into the predawn sky. Talon disappeared soundlessly over the garden wall.

"Good morning, Alissa." He smiled in greeting.

"Morning," she returned guardedly.

Useless arranged himself in his usual fashion before the fire, pouring out a share of the dark brew. He sighed contentedly as he breathed deeply of its steam. "You make splendid tea, young one. For this, I'd gladly travel half a continent." Turning to his cup, he lost himself in the steam and took a sedate draught of the scalding liquid.

Alissa shifted uneasily. This wasn't the Useless she had come to know. He said all the right words but seemed preoccupied, as if he were repeating a lesson, not listening to what he said. Seeming to realize she was still standing, he smiled faintly. "Don't worry about me, Alissa. I've had a trying night is all. How goes Strell's tutelage?"

She abruptly sat down, ready to forget his mood. "It's been fields again all week. Internal, exterior . . . He's been over the same things before."

"He goes too fast."

"I'm keeping up," she said and poured herself a cup of tea.

"Yes . . ." Useless drawled. "But you have a real teacher."

Shrugging, she took a sip, wincing as she burnt her tongue. The silence grew awkward as she pondered how to bring up her request. It seemed Useless was content to simply savor her tea, reluctant to mar the serenity with his teachings quite yet. "I have a question," she finally said.

His cup met the stone bench with a small clink. Eyebrows raised, he gave Alissa his full attention. She looked down, embarrassed. Determined to be out with it, she took a resolute breath. "I'm concerned for Strell," she said boldly, her eyes flicking to his. "Ever since Bailic gave him that dusting of source, he has been pushing him. Soon Strell will have to show some tangible results. His acting is wonderful," Alissa pleaded, "but he can't make a field. He can't even see the source Bailic gave him."

"Can you?"

"I—I don't know. I never tried."

Useless reached across her for the teapot, topping off his cup. "You might be able to see it in your thoughts until it's bound into someone's being. It's good to know you're not greedy. Many Keepers would have jumped at the chance to snatch even a dusting of unbound source. In the past, a few unfortunates were killed for it, their murderers not realizing its power was tied to them and them alone—once bound. It's one of the reasons the origin of source is so well guarded. Actually, I'm surprised Bailic managed to give some away."

Alissa's stomach gave a flip-flop. Her own source still lay hidden around her neck, unbound and apparently vulnerable. Content to let things sit as they were, Useless hadn't seen fit to show her how yet. She hadn't known it was so desirable. Against her will, Alissa's hand found the small bag and clutched it possessively. *Bailic couldn't take this,* she thought.

Suddenly she realized she had a nasty choice to make. Asking two favors of Useless in one night wasn't an option. She had worked extensively with external fields during his last visit but had been expressly forbidden to practice on her own, especially in front of Bailic. She could ask to be allowed to manipulate fields alone to cover for Strell, or she could ask how to bind her source to ally her newest, desperate fear. Her decision was absurdly simple.

"Please," she whispered, her eyes nailed to the cup in her hands, "I would ask to be allowed to manipulate internal and external containment fields unchaperoned." She looked up into his unreadable eyes. "For Strell," she quavered. "If he doesn't produce a field soon, Bailic will do something terrible to him."

"Well done, Alissa. Very well done!" Useless shouted, clapping her across the shoulders.

Her tea went flying, and she blankly watched her cup sail into the dark to find the frozen ground with a dull crack. Confounded, she stared at him.

"Here, let me," and he made a new cup from seemingly nothing. It was identical in its brown ugliness to her original, and she held it loosely, not sure what to do. Looking annoyingly pleased with himself, Useless filled it, adjusted his coat, and turned to her, his eyes dancing.

"What?" she finally got out.

"You asked, young one. You asked."

"But I thought . . . All I needed to do was ask?" she sputtered.

"No." He grinned. "Asking wasn't enough. You were willing to forgo the safety of your own source for that of someone else. You're starting to think. That," he said firmly, "is why I will allow you to do as you want."

Feeling like she had been tricked, Alissa sullenly held her cup to try to warm her hands through her mittens. "Strell means more than a stinky bag of dust."

"Really?" Somehow he managed to sound worried and incredulous at the same time.

"Well, anyone would," she added, so it wouldn't seem like she cared.

"M-m-m-m." Useless became very still. His eyes went to the ground, and he slumped his shoulders passively. "So . . ." he said softly. "You wouldn't mind if I took your source back?"

Alissa's cup of untasted tea spilled across the packed snow as she stood. "Don't you dare," she spat, shocked at the vehemence in her voice. She scowled down at him, clutching her small bag of source. It was hers. He wouldn't dare. Instructor or not, it was hers!

He chuckled, his docile posture vanishing. "Alissa, sit down. I was jesting."

"It wasn't funny," she said tightly.

"No, it wasn't. I'm sorry. Sit down." He seemed pleased by her temper, making Alissa angrier still. But she sat, and with sharp, abrupt motions, refilled her cup. "I apologized, Alissa," he said. "I simply wanted to see if you understood the value of your source."

"Do I?" she asked bitterly.

"Offhand, I would say . . . m-m-m . . . yes."

Alissa glared into the dark, ignoring him.

"We should get started if you're going to accomplish anything tonight," he said brightly.

Knowing her temper would do her no good, Alissa set her cup aside and settled herself.

"Watch," he rumbled, making a dramatic and absolutely needless gesture toward the fire. The flames flickered and died. There was no pull on her awareness or resonance upon her tracings. It had been done entirely with a field, without the aid of his source and tracings. She might not have noticed his field at all but for his warning he was going to do something.

"You used no ward for that," she said into the sudden dark.

"Correct. It was an impervious field. A permeable field has no effect on fire."

Alissa pulled her coat tighter, chilled. "Bailic never mentioned impervious fields."

"He wouldn't. Keepers are generally taught only permeable ones."

"But you're telling me."

He grinned, his teeth startling white in the darkness. "I like you." His smile quickly turned into a laugh, and the sound of it rolled out into the garden to fill the broken space with the warmth of his good humor. From somewhere, Talon answered him.

"That's nice." She smiled thinly. "But what's the point?"

"The point is, I snuffed the life from the fire, and because I didn't use my source and neural net, there was no resonance upon yours to give me away. My actions were harder to sense. It gave me a measure of stealth. Use an impervious field carefully, if you use it at all," he warned, his features grim with shadow. "It will take the life from anything without the skill to break it."

"Oh . . ." Alissa's eyes widened as she realized what a powerful weapon Useless had given her. It had felt like every other field she had made, only tighter in concentration, thicker. No wonder Bailic had never been told. They were potentially deadly.

"Good," Useless said, seeing her understanding. "Now, Bailic knows, as all Keepers do, or—ah—did, of permeable fields. It's all they're taught. An impervious field takes more concentration, but it's by no means beyond their capabilities. Don't make one when he is close enough to sense it. If Bailic sees one, he will realize they're possible. That knowledge is something I wouldn't wish him to have. Permeable fields are adequate for anyone."

"What if a Keeper figured impervious fields out for herself?" she interrupted.

"She was asked to forget." Useless frowned until she looked away. "Permeable fields are sufficient to contain even the more wild reactions such as this." With a tweak upon her tracings, the fire blossomed into existence. She shifted closer to the flames in gratitude.

"And, as you have also guessed," he continued dryly, "a permeable containment field is used to carry matter or energy from your thoughts to reality."

"Like the cups you make?"

"M-m-m, or that wonderful explosion of yours last fall," he finished slyly.

Chagrined, Alissa shut her mouth and found great interest in the fire, but not for long. "The energy used to create something—once it's fixed into an object, can it ever be returned to your source?" she asked.

Useless bobbed his head, swallowing a gulp of tea. "Yes. The task uses an impervious field so Keepers generally don't know it. But by far," he said, pointedly changing the subject, "a field's most popular use is serving as a stepping-stone from one's thoughts to one's reality."

"To create a ward," Alissa asserted.

"Yes." Useless rubbed his smooth chin in thought. "A field gives a ward a place in which to act." Seeing her dubious look, he added, "It's much easier than it sounds."

She caught her breath. "Show me?" she asked eagerly.

His eyes narrowed, considering it. "You've seen the pattern of tracings in your thoughts required for a ward of stillness from Bailic, no doubt?"

Alissa felt her pulse quicken as she nodded, remembering the horrible morning Bailic had removed Strell's finger. It was a pattern she would never forget.

Useless grimaced. "Set up the ward by allowing a thin trace of your source to enter the proper paths. If you have it correctly, the pattern will resonate upon my own tracings."

Immediately Alissa sent a small thought to pierce her source to set up the first loop, or circuit as Useless called it. From there, she directed the flow to the proper tracings. Her network glowed with a scintillating pattern, and she held it as her instructor's eyes went distant and unseeing as he looked for any mistakes. His eyes cleared and he grimaced, slumping as if in defeat. "All right," he agreed. "You have it properly."

Alissa grinned. She knew she had.

"Let me see." Useless gazed about the garden. With a pleased sound, he rose and went to a stand of milkweed plants gone to seed. Breaking off one of the half-open pods, he returned and sat down. "Your father and Bailic loved to play this," he murmured, opening the brittle case farther. A few tufted seeds were still within its embrace, and Useless teased them forth. With a breath of air, he sent them aloft. They slowly began to fall, drifting on the draft from the fire.

"Catch them," he whispered intently.

Grinning, Alissa stood and plucked them from the air with her fingers.

"Very amusing, Alissa," he said sourly. "Next time, use the ward."

"I don't need a ward to catch them. A field alone would do it."

Useless inclined his head in agreement. "True. A ward

of stillness is only effective upon creatures who can move, but as there isn't even an insect to practice upon, you will pretend and use the ward as well as the field."

"How will I know if I get it right?" she pressed.

"I will tell you," he all but growled.

A sigh slipped from her as she released the two bits of down, watching them drift closer to the flames. Still standing, she focused her awareness around first one, and then the other, encasing them each in a tidy field. Holding them thus, she set her tracings glowing and directed the flow of energy into the proper channels to set up the ward. As soon as the pattern was full, there was a pulling sensation. Yielding to it, Alissa felt an eerie disorientation as the pattern she set seemed to exist in three places: her thoughts and the two fields. With a snap that thrummed through her existence, her pathways went dark, leaving only the first loop glowing brightly.

"I did it!" Alissa cried in delight. It had been almost absurdly simple. The tufts of fluff hung motionless, an arm's length from the fire.

"If this wasn't practice," came Useless's voice, "you could loose the field, and the ward will remain upon the person, or in this case, the seeds."

Eager to try, she eased her concentration until the field vanished. The fluff fell with her ward. After all, it was only the field that had stopped them. The wards were just for exercise.

"I said 'if,' student," and the seeds froze, stopped by his field. "Catch them again before they get too close to the flames.

"Fields are temporary," he continued as she did just that. "They fade as does your attention. Implemented properly, the wards are permanent until removed by someone skilled in such things. Now again, please." His eyes closed, but Alissa knew from painful experience he was aware of everything around him.

She set the seeds drifting with a puff of breath. Before they had moved a hand's width, they were frozen, caught by field and ward.

"Excellent," was his response. "Try going for the one nearest you first, then the other in separate attempts."

This was harder as she had to set the pattern up anew after the first was away, but soon she had it. It was fun, and she continued practicing, enjoying the novelty. Alissa felt his eyes upon her for a long, quiet moment; then he reached out a thought and snatched the tuffs with his own field and ward. "Hey!" she shouted, more than a little miffed.

"It's a contest," he said smugly. "He who catches both, wins."

"Oh." Alissa smiled. *A game,* she thought. Two breaths later, and five losses down, she changed her mind. Useless was fast. Wickedly so.

Almost as if he were reading her mind, he arched his eyebrows. "Yes, it's easy, but it takes practice to become proficient. Don't make the mistake of imagining you're anywhere near Bailic's skills. He would retaliate before your ward was even finished. You can be sure," he warned, "the result would be unpleasant. Move against him, and all previous agreements would be dissolved. He would be free to act in self-defense." Useless scowled. "Such as it is. You would not be granted a second opportunity."

Gulping, Alissa looked at her shoes. The fluffs reached the flames, and in a flash of brilliance they were gone.

Useless nodded. "Just so," he said quietly. "Shall we move on to your source?"

"My source?" Alissa's head came up. She had thought she would have to wait for another two weeks.

"Course," he said gruffly. "I'm not going to let you run about my Hold any longer with a city's ransom around your neck. You seem to have the barest whisper of control. We will bend the rules a bit." His hand went out expectantly, and Alissa's elated look froze. She stared at him, afraid of what he wanted. "Please," he demanded gently, "I would see it for a moment?"

She reluctantly lifted the small bag over her head, snagging her wretchedly long hair in passing. The cord had become gray and thin from use. The sack itself wasn't much better. His earlier jest hadn't been appreciated, but the worst part was she didn't understand why she was so adamant about it remaining in her possession. The bag clenched in a tight fist, she stiffened, her eyes narrowing suspiciously, distressed and confused at her unusual mistrust.

"Please, Alissa," he said reassuringly. "I only wish to ascertain if there's enough to warrant your potential. Upon his leaving the Hold, I gave your father additional source to protect my book if necessary. I assumed he would bind it, but apparently he didn't, as it's in your possession. But if you would rather not allow me . . ." Useless let his words trail off into nothing. His hand closed upon air and dropped. It was a well-taken, unspoken, threat.

Alissa had to trust him implicitly; she felt her life might depend upon it. Just the hint of suspicion could poison her thoughts against him, beginning the long spiral down to the mistrust and paranoia that Bailic wallowed in. Her pulse pounding, Alissa forced open her mittened fingers, and the small bag fell into his waiting grasp. As his hand closed about it, a feeling of loss rose black and thick, shocking her with its crushing potency. She clenched her eyes shut against a wave of vertigo. Stifling an urge to strike him, she forced her eyes open, struggling to suppress any and all emotion. She would get it back.

"Thank you," he said softly, his eyes locked upon her wide eyes. He shifted his gaze and focused entirely upon her source.

Aching for it to be over, Alissa clasped her arms about her knees and tried to keep her breath even as his brows furrowed and he sent the smallest tendril of thought around the bag. His golden brown eyes widened, and Alissa reached out to grip his arm tightly.

"What is it?" she demanded, dizzy with the sudden motion. She couldn't seem to take a deep enough breath, and she trembled with the effort to do nothing. The want to rise and tear her source from his grasp was so strong she could almost taste it, bitter on her tongue. Her trust in Useless was the only thing that stopped her.

"Nothing. It's fine. You're fine. It's just that . . ." Useless broke his concentration and turned to her. "It's all there," he whispered, "and nearly bound. You've taken the first steps unknowingly." His amber eyes opened wide in what looked like absolute horror. "Here! Take it. Take it back!" he shouted, shoving the pouch into her hands.

Alissa clutched for it, nearly dropping it in her frenzied haste. The teeth of mistrust that had been steadily worrying her, urging her to lash out, finally loosened. She sat curled up about her source, trembling, not daring to look at Useless, waiting for the pounding in her skull to slow. When she finally looked up, he had his head in his hands and was muttering to himself. Alissa caught the name "Keribdis," and what she thought was "recklessly trusting," and what might have been "ancient cretin."

"Excuse me?" she rasped, thrusting a hand out to catch herself against the bench as she nearly tipped over.

Useless shook his head. His eyes were weary, and he looked old sitting on the stone bench in the fire's light. "I beg your pardon, Alissa," he whispered. "I wouldn't have asked had I known. Your restraint is . . . quite considerable, considering your few years, and very appreciated."

She managed a deep breath, her vertigo easing into memory. "I don't understand."

His brow pinched in embarrassment, Useless cast about as if for something to do. With a small sound of relief, he grabbed the teapot, draining it into his cup. "Your source is nearly bound," he mumbled around his mug as if that would explain it all.

"You already said that." She sighed, wondering if a straight answer was impossible.

"I shouldn't have asked to see it, much less gauge its value," he said. "I'm truly sorry."

"Why?"

"Because," he said patiently, "your soul is intertwined about it. To lose it would be to become half, less even." Useless turned away. More to himself then to her, he added, "How you could stand its loss for even that moment, I don't understand. I couldn't. I'm sorry."

"I've been lost before," Alissa said in a distant voice, and he turned to stare at her. "Mistress Death has put her mark on me. I've seen her, recognized her. You, Useless," she smiled thinly, "look nothing like her. Forget it."

His head drooped. "Lost before," he breathed into his cup. "That might explain it.

Alissa looked to the sky. Dawn was only moments away. Breakfast would be late to the practice room. She didn't care. "Do you suppose you might tell me how to finish the task?" she asked, sure now the answer would be yes.

Useless blinked. "Er—make a field around it. That's all that's needful at this point. The rest is instinctive—I think. But, Alissa? Use an impervious field. You will want all of your source, not just what a permeable field will retain."

"But Keepers don't know them," Alissa said, beginning to form the complex containment field. "How would they properly bind their source if they . . . they . . ." Her thought melted to nothing as her field became complete. The exterior world grayed to an absolute as she plunged deep into her thoughts, feeling out of control, but knowing she was more aware than she had ever been before. All that remained was her glittering source. As irreversible as two drops of water coming together, it merged with her unconscious self, humming into every corner, backwashing at every turn, defining the edges of her existence with the tang of glittering tingles. She had thought it hers before. It hadn't been, but it was now.

With a frightening wrench, her source collapsed back into its more familiar vision of a shimmering sphere set somewhere between her thoughts and reality. It was positively the most glorious sight, and it could never be taken away. Ever.

Alissa opened her eyes, struggling to focus. Useless was sitting before the fire, his long fingers laced about his cup, hiding it. As she straightened from her slump, he turned to her. "How—how long was I out?" she mumbled, seeing the day was noticeably closer.

"Not long," he reassured her. "Feel better?" His gaze

went distant to the horizon, tactfully giving her time to find her bearings with a modicum of privacy.

"Rather," she answered wisely, shaking off her daze. Slowly, she loosened her cramped and stiff fingers from around the empty bag, looping it over her head from long habit.

"Alissa?" There was deep concern in his voice. "Be careful. What you have accomplished this morning was needful, but it also put you into greater peril. You have my permission to explore permeable fields freely on your own. Bailic moves too quickly, but you may try what he requests of Strell concerning fields and wards." His eyebrows rose. "I expect you will be most careful. I'm sure the wards won't be anything to give Strell much strength and so will be innocuous enough."

Alissa's eyes widened, and the last of her contented daze vanished in surprise. This was the most leeway he had ever given her. And she hadn't even had to ask!

"Be sure to keep at least a raku's length between you and Bailic when practicing alone," he continued. "He will feel you create a ward if he is closer than that, and unless Strell is nearby to take the blame, Bailic will realize it's you. Think up and down as well as horizontal," he admonished. "You can set a field and ward in place anywhere within a raku length of your person. When performing in the piper's stead, be sure you remain at least that close to them both. That way Bailic will sense the creation of your wards and assume it's Strell."

She nodded, hearing in his words his desire to be gone.

"Very well," he said firmly, "where is that bird? I want to play." Useless scanned the skies. He gave a little jump and turned to the thick shrubbery and the unseen door of the kitchen beyond. His eyebrows rose, and he took a breath to say something but then shook his head and smiled. "Behave yourself," he said as he stepped out of the firepit. In a swirl of gray, he shifted to the form he had been sired as.

"Wait!" Alissa cried, and ran up to him, stopping short at his feet, shocked again at how big he was as a winged monstrosity. She couldn't help her gasp as he dropped his head to see her better. His fathomless, golden eyes were as large as her head, stunning in their depth. Alissa could almost forget his sharp teeth and creased hide. "Thanks," she mumbled, feeling her face redden as she gave his neck a quick, embarrassed hug.

He arched his neck back, blinking in an obvious surprise, and she added, "For—for coming back that first night. For teaching me," she fumbled. "For not . . ." Alissa paused, thoroughly miserable in her lack of finesse. How do you thank someone who not only opens the door to your potential but then rips it from its hinges so it can never be shut again?

Useless dropped his head, filling her senses with the warm scent of wood smoke. He couldn't speak aloud in his present form, which was probably just as well. His teeth showing in what was undoubtably a smile, he pointed a wicked-looking talon to the firepit, and she obediently backed up. There was a last, long, unfathomable look, then Useless departed, raising twin maelstroms of snow and ice and last year's leaves.

She was left behind, nailed to the earth among the weeds, watching as Talon screeched defiantly and dove at him. Beating his wings furiously, Useless struggled for height, lashing his hind foot out when Alissa's tiny defender got near. He rose above the Hold, turning a luminescent gold from the sun that had yet to reach the tower.

Alissa dismally turned away and slowly knocked the fire apart using the stick she kept for the purpose. True, an impervious field would have put it out faster, but, as Useless would have said, not needful. Grabbing the empty pot, three cups, and her extinguished candle, she made her somber way to the kitchen. Behind her was the whoosh of Useless's passage and the screams of her bird. They were being noisy today, almost as if they didn't care if they were noticed. Alissa just hoped Bailic didn't see Useless. The fallen Keeper wasn't blind after all, just ill of sight.

Rounding a turn in the path, Alissa almost ran into the suspicious man himself. "What?" she stammered, gazing in shock at his tall figure, thin and black against the snow. "What are you doing out here?"

17

"That was what I was going to ask you, my dear." Bailic squinted into the sky, bright with the newly risen sun, tracking Useless and Talon's motion through the air behind her.

Chilled, Alissa clasped her coat closer, desperately glad she had heeded Useless's warning to behave and extinguished her fire mundanely. It would have been over right then had she gone back on her promise and Bailic noticed. *Restraint and self-control,* she thought fervently. *Such a small thing between success and failure, life and death.*

She winced at Talon's screams and wondered if Bailic had seen anything. Then her resolve firmed. *She* had done nothing wrong. *She* could be in the garden if she wanted. It might look questionable, but he couldn't prove a thing—could he?

"We were worried," Bailic said tightly. "Let me help you into the kitchen with your—tea."

She extended the empty pot, and his watering eyes flicked to the three cups in her hand, one cracked from its impromptu flight. "Those are Talo-Toecan's cups," he said, drawing back in a mix of anger and alarm. "He was with you?"

Tossing her head, she brushed past him, her eyes on the kitchen door. "He likes my tea," she said over her shoulder. "He sports with Talon. We talk."

Bailic hastened after her. "You give him messages?"

Alissa nervously kicked open the door. "Talo-Toecan wouldn't break his word." The proper name for her in-

structor felt odd upon her lips, but she couldn't call him
Useless before Bailic. It was *so* undignified.

Seeming to regain his confidence, Bailic followed her
in. "He generally finds a way to circumvent it, regardless."
With a final glance outside, he pulled the door shut, sealing out the morning light and setting them in the twilight
of the cooking fire. Alissa's last sight was of Useless, spinning madly in an attempt to outmaneuver Talon. Her bird
was getting quite good, she mused, until a harsh sound
from Bailic brought her back to earth. She, too, would
have to do some quick maneuvering to get out of her latest
spot.

She knew she should be worried but couldn't find it in
herself to be. Useless had known Bailic was there on the
path. That's what his surprised look toward the kitchen had
been, and why he told her to behave, and why he was so
obvious in his cavortings this morning. Still, caution was
warranted, and Alissa frowned as she hung her coat and hat
by the hearth.

Deciding to volunteer nothing, she swiftly prepared a
tray for three. Bailic leaned upon the mantel and watched
her, making her fingers slip and drop things. "Here, allow
me," he said, intercepting her reach for a fresh pot of tea.
"You have had a busy morning already, my dear."

Unease settled over her as Bailic carried the tray up to
the narrow practice room. She walked beside him, empty-
handed, beginning to worry that Useless's confidence had
been misplaced. Bailic had all but ignored her for the better part of three months. Ever since gaining possession
of her book, it was as if she didn't exist. Whenever they
did exchange words, it was, "You there," or, "Girl." Now
she was back to, "My dear," and she could almost smell
the 'ware fires burning.

Her fears were confirmed when, upon reaching the
fourth-floor landing, he needlessly stopped to rest at the
window there. She couldn't very well leave him, and so
she was forced to wait. "What an interesting pouch," he
said. "Odd. I never noticed it before."

Before she could stop herself, Alissa's hand rose to

clutch it possessively. She had forgotten to tuck it out of sight. Mentally kicking herself, she tried to make her actions more natural and changed the motion to that of removing the sack from around her neck. It was empty. What harm could it do to let him see it now? "It was a gift," she said. "Want to see it?"

"Yes." He set the tray on the sill with a clattering of dishes and held out his white hand. It was hard to let the ratty cord slip from her fingers and drop the bag into Bailic's grasp. It had held her source, her will almost, for so long it was hard to accept that it was really empty. "A gift, you say?" Bailic murmured, his smile going wise. "But it's empty." He traced her mother's initials with a thin finger, his manner distant and knowing.

An uneasy feeling slid through Alissa as he handed the bag back. She could hear Talon screeching, sounding loud even through the ward on the window. Bailic turned and picked up the tray. Feeling as if she had let something slip, Alissa followed, holding herself a step behind him.

"Here she is, Piper," Bailic called, blinking at the glare of the sun-filled chamber. "Safe and sound, just as I predicted."

"Safe and sound?" Strell jumped up from a far window, relief flashing across him. "You said she had probably tripped over her feet and fallen halfway to the kitchen!"

"A jest, my dear." Bailic simpered as he placed the tray on the empty table.

Strell choked back his next outburst, probably recognizing how Bailic had addressed her. She shrugged helplessly as Strell met her worried eyes. Bailic was too confident. He was up to something.

"She was downstairs dallying the morning away," Bailic continued. "But here she is. And with tea!" Showing a meticulous care, Bailic poured the strong brew into all three cups. Feeling ill, Alissa sat stiffly in her chair. Strell, grim and wary, sat in his. Bailic sat on the window bench with his back to the sun and watched them both with an expectant arch to his eyebrows.

"You forgot your cup!" Bailic exclaimed, and he leapt

up to play the congenial host. Alissa's eyes lowered as he drew close, and the small click of the cup touching the bench beside her made her tense. "Or have you had enough tea already?" he finished dryly.

With a roar that shivered the tea in the cups, Useless skimmed past the windows. Bailic dropped to the floor with a half-recognized curse. Strell's cup slipped from him, tea spilling in a fantastic pattern. He lunged after it, missing. The cup fell off the table. There was no crash of pottery.

For a moment, no one moved. Slowly, Alissa leaned to look under the table. Strell did the same. Bailic was already on the floor. All three of them gazed in wonder at the cup, hanging in midair as if, well, by magic, or in this case, a containment field. It wasn't her, it couldn't be Strell, and obviously it wasn't Bailic. That left only one presence.

"Talo-Toecan!" Bailic got to his feet and stared at the ceiling. "Leave. Or our agreement is ended!" There was a snort of amusement from the roof, and the cup hit the floor to crack in two. "What has gotten into him, buzzing the tower like a demented bat," Bailic snarled, tugging his gray shirt straight.

"It wasn't agreed he had to shun the Hold, only Strell," Alissa said sharply. Bailic whipped about, his eyes glinting dangerously. Wolves, she thought, a breath too late. When would she learn to keep her mouth shut?

Bailic pointed a shaky finger at her. "You're right."

Strell, who had been kneeling on the floor, silently sopping up the tea, cleared his throat in warning. At that instant, there was a tug on Alissa's thoughts as someone nearby used their tracings. A fourth cup materialized silently next to the pot. Almost, Alissa could hear Useless laughing in her thoughts. Then his shadow raced across the snow, and he was gone.

Bailic must have felt the pull on his tracings as well, for his lips curled in disgust as he noticed the new addition, but with a shuddering breath, he caught his temper, hiding it.

Not sure what to think, Alissa took up her mending left

yesterday between the cushions. There was a clatter of broken pottery on the tray followed by the creak of a chair, and Strell, too, was in his place. Bailic began to pace before the windows, speaking in his best lecturing voice as if nothing had happened. "As you have been told uncountable times, Piper, fields can serve three purposes."

Alissa tried to ignore him. Bailic was as interesting as an argument on the proper weather in which to plant beets. As her fingers shifted her needle in the rhythmic, soothing dance of repair, her thoughts drifted, predictably settling on her lesson this morning and her success in gaining permission to manipulate fields unchaperoned. It was an odd feeling, asking leave to do something that was so much a part of her, but over the past weeks, Useless had impressed her quite thoroughly about the dangers of experimenting on her own. Her disastrous attempt to remove Useless's ward last fall had clarified his arguments, and she was quite prepared to listen. She trusted him implicitly, almost more than she trusted herself.

The only thing they continually disagreed upon was the speed of her progress, or in her eyes, the lack thereof. Useless countered each of her arguments with skill and finesse, leaving her wondering why she hadn't seen it his way in the first place. For Useless, she would be patient, polite, and well mannered. But her newfound reasonableness, as Strell called it, seldom extended any farther than the shallow pit in the garden. Try as she might, her temper still got the better of her. Strell, though, took it in stride. In fact, she swore he sometimes riled her on purpose.

Lost as she was in her sewing and thoughts, she was ill prepared when Bailic's hand slammed the table. Alissa jumped, painfully stabbing her finger.

"Come now, Piper," Bailic nearly snarled in frustration. "It's not that difficult!"

Finger in her mouth, she looked at Strell. He had hidden his clenched fists under the table, trying to hide his repressed anger. Alissa glanced at his mutilated right hand, thinking there might be some fright mixed in as well. "I'm trying," Strell grated. "Perhaps if you showed me what you want I would understand."

Bailic rubbed a hand through his rigidly short hair. Abruptly he spun and strode to the table where he kept her book, maddeningly near. Ignoring it, he opened a drawer and took out a small box. Three sharp steps later he had it on the window seat and was lifting the lid.

Alissa put her needle down and leaned forward to see. Dust? she thought in astonishment. It was dust, the same stuff domestics fight all their lives to eradicate. Apart from the stables, it was the first she had seen since she left home. The common areas of the Hold were kept blessedly dust free under a nightly sweep of a still-functioning ward. Yet, here was a box of it.

Bailic took a healthy pinch, shut the lid, and much to her amazement, blew the dust into the air. The sun streaming in through the tall windows was suddenly full of breathtaking sparkles. "Pay attention," Bailic snapped, a harsh counterpoint to the visual delight he had created. With no warning, a section of sunbeam coalesced into a small sphere as the dust inside was packed closer under the obvious influence of a field. Abruptly it was released; the motes were again free. "Now you," he commanded as he sat stiffly on the bench, pointedly watching them both.

Strell sighed and stared at the shimmering blocks of sun.

A flash of excitement went through Alissa. She had permission; she could help Strell. For a moment she considered the hows and whys. It was only a field. It was different from catching a milkweed puff, but not that different. Trying to look interested but not intense, she focused her awareness around a small section of sunbeam. Her field shrank and gained definition. A globe of shimmering dust hung in the air, looking like a spot of sun. "Strell!" she shouted, simultaneously dropping the field. "You did it!"

"I did!" he said, his eyes wide. "I really did!" He smiled, and Alissa beamed proudly.

Bailic shifted on the hard bench. "So it would appear."

He opened the box again, and taking a handful of dust, he flung it into the air. The sunlight glinted, thick with the fine powder. Too light to settle directly, it eddied and swirled, making the room seem to glow. A field went up, larger than any Alissa had held before, almost encompassing the room. It quickly shrank, and Alissa shivered as she imagined she felt an eerie sensation as it passed through her. Soon it was the size of a pumpkin. She thought Bailic was done, but the field began to shift and change.

Strell's mouth dropped open, and Alissa blinked in surprise. A face was taking shape in the dust. Alissa looked at Bailic, not believing he was the cause of it, only to be stunned by his expression of entrancement. The lines of anger were gone. A wistful look was in his pale eyes. Grace and refinement, dignity and ease; this was the man he could have been had his revenge not led him to empty the Hold.

Reluctantly, Alissa returned her attention to his sculpture. It was a woman, she decided as it gained definition. Young, almost a girl, with a single long braid. She had a narrow chin and a laughing mouth. She looked familiar, and Alissa leaned forward. It was her—her mother!

"Who is she?" Strell asked, jerking Alissa back to herself. Her face went cold, and she shrank into the cushions. She had been a heartbeat away from telling Bailic exactly whose child she was. Strell had saved her again, but how did Bailic know what her mother looked like? Alissa's thoughts returned to Bailic's sly manner in the hall and his finger tracing the initials on her bag. Bailic knew her mother? Shocked, Alissa put her hand to her middle.

"She's no one," Bailic said through a slow exhalation. His smile was gentle as he raised his hand to touch his vision. Just before contact, his eyes went hard, and his arm dropped. The containment field collapsed, and the dust diffused into a shimmering pool of shattered desire.

"Now," Bailic said bitterly, "I will eat, and you," he pointed at Strell, "will practice." Snatching a roll of bread, he settled into his chair and watched Strell with intent eyes.

Feeling shaken and ill, Alissa tentatively began making fields, letting each one dissolve before beginning the next. Strell had his eyes fixed to the sunbeam, playing his part well. Whether his fascinated look was contrived or not, she couldn't tell; it was a curious sight. Alissa was watching, too, as any interested observer might. It was monotonous though, and after a time she picked up her stockings and began to stitch, one eye on her fingers, one eye on Strell. Her fields needed no chaperoning; she knew what they were doing.

As she worked, a whisper of presence slipped stealthily into her uppermost thoughts, almost unrecognizable. The slight pressure was easy to ignore, but it increased to a niggling tickle. Perhaps Useless had returned and was calling her. Frowning, she set her stitching aside to look out the window. The eerie feeling vanished, leaving her uneasy.

Too much going on this morning, she thought, rubbing her hand over her eyes and gazing out over the wooded valley below. Ese' Nawoer's rooftops glinted in the sun, barely visible behind the trees at this low height. A cloud bank was building, and she wondered if it was going to snow again. It never seemed to stop. The sun, though, was warm and comforting, so she resettled herself and resumed her work.

But the feeling slowly crept back. With a sudden revulsion, Alissa recognized the dusky sliver of thought as Bailic's. She froze for a horrified instant, then forced her fingers to resume their work. It was a struggle not to react, to drive him from her with a blistering thought. If Bailic realized she could sense him, he would know she was the Keeper. Apparently he wasn't satisfied with Strell's latest performance and was trying to reach her thoughts.

What the Wolves is Bailic doing? she thought. Useless assured her Bailic couldn't see her tracings or hear her thoughts. With a slow, even breath, she recalled her mother's teachings and relaxed, but he was as hard to ignore as a spider on her arm. Her eyes fixed upon on her sewing, she continued making and collapsing the fields.

Easy, she thought. *Find that calm, still point.* If Bailic saw her insulted anger, it would be over.

Finally, he withdrew. None to soon, either, for the longer he stayed, the harder it was not to drive him out. She disguised her shudder by stretching. But then she got to thinking. Perhaps she could send a questing thought out, too? If Bailic noticed, he would assume it was Strell. Useless hadn't said she couldn't. What harm could it do?

Alissa gave a warning cough to Strell to let him know she was going to try something. His foot tapped out the beat to a song she recognized, and she bit her lip in an effort not to smile. It was from a child's jumping rhyme called, "I'm Ready If You Are." Mindful of her dual role, Alissa continued her mending as her thoughts went out, a whisper of awareness barely recognizable even to her. Curious as to her limits, she first went to Strell.

That's interesting, she mused, for she couldn't make any sense of the emotion she found. She lingered, trying to sort through the confusion of conflicting sensations, puzzling until her perceptions seemed to shift ninety degrees and fall into place. With a jolt, Alissa realized Strell was worried to the point of distraction.

She glanced at him, startled by his casual slouch. It was as if his only care was the small spheres of dust, shimmering in the sun. His toe, however, was moving ever so slowly, tracing a small arc on the floor. It was the only show of his worry. Frowning, she looked deeper. Beneath that was a darker emotion. This one she recognized easily. It was fear, but not for him, no. It was for her and what she might be planning!

Face scarlet, she withdrew, bending her attention back to her stockings. She had no business poking about Strell's emotions as if they were wares on display. His turmoil was anything but obvious, but Alissa could see it now that she knew it was there.

She couldn't do this! she thought taking a chill. Strell didn't even know what she planned, yet had agreed to suffer the consequences if anything went wrong. She had never realized what failure might mean until she saw his near panic. And it wasn't even for him. He was more concerned about her after Bailic killed him, than about himself being killed. Ashes! What the Wolves had she been thinking!

Alissa forced herself to take a deep breath, trying to keep her fingers steady as she laced another shaky stitch into her stockings. Her curiosity was going to be the death of them both. Immediately, she yawned to tell Strell she had changed her mind. His foot became still. Slowly his posture changed until he was truly relaxed. He actually sighed, seeming to droop. Alissa glanced at her work, wincing as she realized she would have to take it all out and start over.

"Piper," Bailic shouted, causing them both to jump. Alissa allowed the field she was holding to collapse as if in surprise. "You aren't thinking of falling asleep again, are you?" he drawled in his most insulting voice.

"No," Strell said darkly, hiding his right hand under his left.

Bailic sauntered closer, his gold sash furling about his ankles. "Once more," he demanded, hands aggressively on the table.

Alissa couldn't help but form a tiny field, just before his nose.

"Enough!" he snapped, squashing her field with his own. It disappeared with a sharp pop. The sudden emptiness hurt. She gasped, quickly turning it into a sneeze. It was, after all, rather dusty. Hiding her face, she fumbled for a cloth.

"That wasn't necessary, Bailic," Strell croaked hoarsely, recognizing her sneeze for what it was and feigning to be hurt.

Bailic's attention went back to Strell, and the fallen Keeper leaned across the table until he was a hand's breath from Strell. The dust glowed and danced about them, adding an unreal feel to the frozen tableau. Alissa sneezed again, a real one this time, and the dust vanished. All three froze in the sudden change. Thinking she had unintentionally done something, she panicked.

"The sun is gone," Bailic said irately as he straightened. "Your lesson is almost done."

She sagged in relief as she realized what happened. The massing snow clouds had finally caught the sun. As its light was lost, so was the dust.

Bailic sneered at Strell. "The lesson is ended when you get the dust back in its box." He shook his head in disgust and left.

"The lesson is ended," Strell mimicked softly, "when you get the dust back in its box."

"Quiet," Alissa admonished. "He'll hear you."

Leaning the chair back on two legs, Strell looked out the open door. "I don't care."

"Please, Strell," she pleaded. "My morning has been hard enough already."

"Oh, right." Strell's chair thunked back to a normal position. He looked at his hands and took a deep breath as if settling himself. "What kept you this morning?" he asked as he reached for the breakfast tray and took a hunk of cheese.

Her worry vanished, and she grinned. "I have permission to manipulate fields on my own," she said. With a casualness she didn't feel, Alissa went to the table to retrieve a helping for her own breakfast. If she didn't, Strell might forget and eat it all. He had before.

"I gathered that. High time," he grumbled.

"And," she continued, terribly pleased, "I have bound my source!"

"That's nice." He pulled the tray closer. It appeared he was far more interested in his breakfast than her news. "Do we have any of those sweet rolls left downstairs?"

"Strell!" she cried. "Don't you care?"

Turning a brown eye to hers, he raised his eyebrows. "Course," he mumbled, making a decorative pattern on his bread with the jelly. "Good for you."

Alissa pouted. Strell didn't seem to care at all. "Good? It was glorious."

"If you say so." He took a large bite. "M-m-m-m. Would you pass me the tea, please."

"Urrg . . ." Alissa stormed to the window and watched the first snowflakes, gritting her teeth at his casual disregard. Lodesh would've understood. Lodesh would've been happy for her.

There was the sound of liquid filling a cup followed by a noisy slurp. "Cold," he muttered.

"Well, don't expect me to warm it for you," she said. "I don't know how yet." She spun about, catching his startled look. Anything was better than his indifference, and she frowned.

"You could do that?"

"Probably, but you'll never know." Deciding to ignore him, Alissa sat at the long window bench and watched the snow put a fresh layer of white on the black branches. Down below was the well where she had found her papa's book, its mouth dark and perfect amid the clearing Useless had torn in order to land. The raw gashes of earth were softened by weeks of snow, but she could tell by the depressions where trees had once stood. It was her opinion she had made very little progress since they had been uprooted. Useless seemed pleased at her snail's pace, but she wasn't. Insisting theory was harder than practice, he had severely curtailed all her attempts at wheedling any practical information from him.

She would take Useless at his word, she vowed silently, and figure out all there was to know about fields. That trick Bailic did, sculpting the dust, had been incredible. It must have taken years to master. Clearly, fields were a lot more versatile than Useless had led her to believe.

And how, she wondered, did Bailic know her mother? It seemed the world knew her.

"I'm sorry," Strell whispered in her ear, and she jumped, not having heard him come up behind her. Turning round, she could tell he was, and her anger started to subside. It wasn't his fault he didn't understand. He handed her a cup and sat down before her. "I'm really glad you got permission to do fields alone." He sipped his drink and grimaced. "You've no idea."

Relenting, Alissa smiled. "I don't think Bailic would have waited another two weeks for you to produce a field."

"No." Strell looked at the view, lost in thought. "He wouldn't have."

They sat and watched the day grow darker as the snow swirled down thicker and more violently. It was an odd sensation, watching the cold and not feeling it, one she had grown to appreciate in the short time she had been behind the Hold's walls.

"You were going to try something," Strell asked. "What was it?"

"Nothing." Alissa felt her face warm. She could have gotten them both killed. The only good to come from it was knowing Strell cared about her. That pleased her to no end, and she couldn't help her faint smile.

"Come on," Strell cajoled, clearly misunderstanding her look. "What were you going to do? You know I'll get it out of you eventually. You may as well tell me now."

"Well," she hedged, "Bailic was trying to reach my thoughts."

Strell's lip curled in distaste. "Past the Hold's ward of silence? He can't do that."

"Yes, I know." She flushed again. "I thought he might be catching on to our ruse, so, um." She hesitated, not sure how he would react. "So I thought I might try to see—"

"What?" Strell shouted. His cup hit the bench. "Are you moonstruck?"

Alissa looked up. He had stood and was staring down at her, his face aghast. "Well," she said in her own defense, "if Bailic thought he could see my tracings, I was going to try to see his."

Strell's eyes widened. "You *are* moonstruck!"

Her shoulders slumped. There was no graceful way out of this. Her idea had about as much merit as a dip in an iced pond. And if yelling at her made him feel better, she probably deserved it. Besides, the stronger his reaction, the more he probably liked her, and she wondered how upset he would get. "Well, I didn't try it," she said, sneezing.

"I can't believe Talo-Toecan gave you the go-ahead for

that. Maybe I should have a chat with him!" Strell paced to the far end of the room in long, agitated steps.

Alissa smiled as she pictured Strell confronting Useless over her tutelage. "He didn't give me permission," she said softly.

"He didn't?" Strell said, aghast. "What under the Eight Wolves were you thinking?"

"I wasn't," and she sneezed again. This was getting ridiculous, and she formed a field encompassing most of the room. She was going to finish the lesson right now.

"She wasn't!" Strell cried to the ceiling, arms upraised. "She admits it! What the Wolves brought you to your senses?"

Strell had worked himself up to an almost comical state. He must really like her, she thought, delighting in the knowledge. Wanting to avoid the higher concentration of dust she was about to create, she stepped to the end of the room, planning on letting the field slip over her as soon as possible. Slowly, she began to contract it. Oddly enough, she felt no sensation as it passed through her. She had expected something and was disappointed. Still, her air was now dust free, and she took a deep, cleansing breath.

"Well?" Strell shouted from the far end of the room.

She beamed hugely at him. His hair was wild, and his eyes were dark with emotion. Tall and lanky, he looked absolutely splendid in the dark green, almost black, clothes she had stitched for him. "Well what?" she asked pleasantly. She honestly couldn't remember what his question had been. Somehow it had slipped her mind when she met his fervent stare.

"What brought you to your senses?" he asked again.

"It was you, Strell," she said, remembering the storm of emotion she had witnessed. *He cares,* she thought, and her entire being seemed to resonate with the knowledge. *He cares, perhaps as much as I do for him.*

"Me!" he exclaimed, and then Alissa's field passed through him.

Strell shivered, blinked, and reached out to steady himself against the wall. His eyes went blank, and he struggled to focus. Concerned, Alissa quickly shrank the containment field to the size of her hand. Leaving it to float in midair, she went to Strell as he leaned heavily against the wall. "What," he whispered, his eyes soft and distant, "was that?"

"My field," she said, hesitating in her reach for him. She had felt nothing when her field passed over her, but obviously this wasn't the case with Strell. He was positively shaken.

"For a moment I thought . . ." He swallowed. "Never mind," he mumbled, turning away. "I have to go. I—I'll see you later—to help with the noon meal." Still not meeting her eyes, he left.

Alissa remained alone in the once-bright room. Her eyes went to the gray globe of dust hanging forgotten in the air. Tentatively cupping her hands around the faintly swirling sphere, she moved it to the box. She looked inside, not really seeing what it contained, and shut the lid with a loud snap. Only now did she collapse her field.

The snow swirled and eddied, falling so thick as to hide the nearby woods from view. Its insulating layer only added to her feeling of uncertainty, and she began to gather the cups on the tray to return them to the kitchen.

The lesson, apparently, was over.

18

Strell lay in his bed, staring at his ceiling. He had been in peaceful slumber for hours, but now he was wide awake. Always, at about this time, Alissa would stir, and he would go to quiet her. His body had come to expect the nightly interruption and had woken him in anticipation.

He contorted in a quick spasm as he tried to stifle a cough. Ever since this morning in the practice room with the dust, he had been fighting a cold. Alissa had plied him with concoction after concoction—some tasty, some not—in her effort to make him feel better. He had stoically accepted her fussing, growing more and more despondent. Finally realizing she was making things worse, though she didn't understand why, she quit. They spent the rest of their evening before the dining hall fire, talking of nothing, until Alissa's eyes drooped.

Having since admitted to himself that he saw Alissa as far more than a friend, he had, over the last month, subtly shifted their evenings together out of her room as was proper. Most of their free time was spent in the dining hall. It was more of a pleasant workroom now, with her needles and thread and his wood shavings.

A faint smile eased over him as he recalled having found the long, black tables shoved up against the far wall. Alissa had shifted them from their accustomed position while he had been busy in his potter's stead, covering them with her scraps of leather and cloth. He had quickly moved his own slice of chaos out of the kitchen to join hers.

He was crafting a new instrument. The debt he owed Alissa for returning his music to him could never be repaid, but making himself a new pipe with which to play for her was a start. One corner of the room was littered with his chips of wood and discarded tries. There were the beginnings of several fine instruments tucked away in a basket under the table, but he hadn't quite got the positioning of the last hole correct. He didn't mind. Half the pleasure of his work was knowing Alissa was busy beside him.

With her sewing to keep her occupied, the kitchen nearby, and her overindulgent chair before the fire, it was a wonder Alissa ever went to her room. Everything she could ever want was right there. Strell felt himself droop as his depression returned. Right here at the Hold.

Strell dismally tugged his blanket free of his bed and wrapped it about himself. He went to awaken his fire, settling wearily upon the warm flagstones. All day and evening his thoughts had revolved around one thing. Could he, or rather, should he, tell Alissa how much he cared for her?

Wiping his nose and snuffing, Strell slumped as he recalled the heavy wave of emotion that had crashed through him in the practice room as her field went over him. It had been as if her entire being slipped into him, warm and comforting as his beloved desert. He knew without question Alissa would reciprocate his love, she only needed to recognize her feelings for what they were. It was only the shock that had kept him from proclaiming his love for her right then and there, and he had fled, trying to sort out his confusion.

He had spent the rest of his morning sweeping his courage into one moment of truth. Full of hope and promise, he sought her out, determined to tell her. But then he found her sitting cross-legged upon her worktable in the dining hall practicing her new game of fields, and his resolve scattered with a feeling of hopelessness. She looked so right there, so happy and content, enjoying the skills that he couldn't ever hope to match. It was then he knew he had no right to tell her of his love. And the realization tore at him.

She belonged here. Here at the Hold she would be a

Keeper. Born to it, she now could live it, reaching her full potential under Talo-Toecan's tutelage. Someone, probably the old Master himself, would make an end of Bailic. The Hold would return to life, and she would remain, while Strell would leave. He knew he wasn't a Keeper. Either of his crafts needed people, and he wouldn't ask her to abandon her place here for the uncertain life behind a wandering minstrel. He couldn't do it, not after what he had seen and experienced this morning. Her gift was too strong to allow her to shackle herself to him.

Twisting awkwardly, Strell withdrew from a pocket a fold of cloth. His fingers stiff with the cold, he opened it to reveal the fragile charm he had crafted from the leftover spun gold of Alissa's hair. It matched the charm he made for her in every way but one. His wasn't of luck but of something vastly more precious: love. He smiled faintly. Alissa's eyes had glowed in pleasure when he had given her the luck charm. Eyeing his own version, he wondered if he had been wise to have made such a thing, old woman's fantasy or not. Carefully, he folded it back in its cream-colored cloth and shoved it back into a pocket.

Ashes, he thought miserably. What was he going to do? He had overcome the prejudice of two worlds for nothing. He was born to a chartered name, able to trace his lineage back to the first families to settle the plains, and still he wasn't good enough for her. Not if she was a Keeper.

If it wasn't for Bailic, he would leave with the spring thaw, before things became more complicated. But he had to wait until Bailic was dead. He would see his Alissa safe from the insane man or die in the attempt. And death was beginning to look like a distinct probability. It was ludicrous to expect their farce to continue much longer. It was luck that had gotten them this far, and when that ran out, it would be over.

Strell closed his eyes. He would lose either way. If Bailic prevailed, his crazed, mixed-up life would be over. If Alissa succeeded, his reason for living would be forever out of reach. It was a difficult position to be in but one he was willing to endure. After having seen her delight yesterday as she practiced her fields, catching one of Talon's feathers as it drifted, he couldn't bring himself to ever tell her of his feelings. It would only make things worse, however things turned out.

His room darkened as the moon was eclipsed by a cloud, and in the sudden blackness, Strell sat on his hearth and brooded. He was accustomed to marriages of convenience. In the plains, a girl married the best she could to help insure she and her children wouldn't go hungry during the long, cold winter. Starvation was too common to exchange safety for desire. It was what he was raised upon, and he accepted it, but that didn't mean he liked it. Lodesh would probably step in when he stepped out.

Strell frowned, unable to stop a tight feeling of rivalry. He had been keeping a close eye upon the stables lately, having sprinkled sand on the floor to know if the Warden ever returned. But there had been no sign of the man, and for that, Strell was glad. He hadn't liked it as Alissa stared into the dark box stall covered in rugs and fabric to make a cozy nest, looking as if she had been deserted.

It was obvious that Lodesh was protecting Alissa in a way that Strell couldn't. The thought made him envious and angry all at the same time. Strell ought to be able to protect her. Otherwise, he didn't deserve her.

He slumped, pulling his blanket tighter. There was the wind behind the storm, he thought dismally. He didn't deserve her. And what could he offer Alissa? Nothing. Even his name had lost its worth.

Faint through their shared chimney flue, he heard Alissa's muffled noise, right on time.

"There you are," Strell said through a sigh, rising from his huddled position. Not bothering with his boots, he crept through the darkness to her room. Lulling Alissa back to sleep was a pleasure. She never woke up, and so he was free to treat her as he wished he could openly. It was a dangerous game he played, but this he wouldn't change.

Strell cautiously opened her door, catching the faint scent of pine and apples. Poking his head past the frame, he darted his gaze to the corners of the room for a glimpse of Lodesh. There was no one, and he finally decided the smell was from the flower Alissa had found at the walled city of Ese' Nawoer. The frail-seeming thing was in remarkably fine condition. Alissa had flatly refused to throw it away, and so it sat next to his grandfather's broken pipe on the mantel. Flushing at the memory of the night he broke it, he tiptoed over the threshold to meet Talon's icy stare. "Be still, old bird," Strell admonished. "I'm here."

Talon settled her ruffled feathers, satisfied now that Strell was present. Still, she never took her eyes from him as he gently placed a forgotten blanket over Alissa's rumpled form.

"Alone," she mumbled, thrashing her arm to undo Strell's work.

"Hush, you aren't alone," he said, tucking the blanket back. He cringed, hoping she wasn't going to wake up. He didn't have on any stockings. It might be hard to explain.

"No. . . . He's alone, all alone." Alissa frowned, deeply asleep.

He? Strell thought. "Who?" he asked, bending low to catch her words. She was tossing forlornly, her hair covering her face, and he knelt next to the chair she always slept in. He gently put his arms around her, as he had vowed he wouldn't any longer while she was awake. Breathing deeply, he closed his eyes at the smell of sun and meadow, wishing he didn't have to go back to his cold room.

"Alone," she whispered, her voice taking on Talo-Toecan's odd accent. "I cannot do it alone."

An icy dread slipped through him, and he drew away. In all the nights he had gentled Alissa back to sleep, this had never happened. Her hands shifted restlessly, and he took them into his own. They were cold. She grew still, but her brow was furrowed, and he daren't leave yet.

"I will lose her. It's beyond me," Alissa sighed. "The Hold is empty; the holden is broken. I can't hope to catch the beast alone, much less break it. There must be someone!"

Her eyes flew open at her shout. Unseeing, they stared, almost black in the dim light. Slowly they closed. "Hush, you're not alone," Strell repeated nervously. He knew now it was Talo-Toecan calling his lost companions, but the Master probably didn't realize Alissa was responding. It would explain her restless sleep the past months. Talo-Toecan must be very close tonight for her to be reacting so strongly.

Strell's brow furrowed as he stood and gazed down at the peacefully sleeping young woman. He was fairly certain that Alissa was the "her" in, "I will lose her," and that left him afraid in a way Bailic's threats never could.

The beast Talo-Toecan spoke of might be Bailic, but it lacked the usual accompaniment of death threats, and Strell was uncertain. Perhaps he should seek Talo-Toecan out and ask, the bargain with Bailic be cursed. Strell dropped his eyes in frustration. He knew it would only make matters worse, and a knot of worry settled about him. There was little he could do to help Alissa. He knew all too well that the purpose he served was solely one of distraction, and even that was becoming ineffective.

Reluctant to leave her, he peeked out at the night through her shutters. The moon shadow cast by the mountain behind him stretched long over the woods as if protecting the land between it and the unseen city. In a startling smack of feathers, Talon streaked over his head into the bitter night. Strell stumbled in, biting back a curse. He couldn't believe the bird would be able to navigate in the dark, much less be in such a hurry to do so.

Squinting after her, Strell felt his chest tighten as suddenly a much larger patch of stars was eclipsed by a dark shadow. It was Talo-Toecan, swooping silently over the Hold to land at the edge of the woods. Talon hovered, looking like a gnat next to his monstrous form, finally landing out of sight among the trees. The raku's silhouette showed well against the snow despite the distance. His great eyes seemed to glow, reflecting the unseen moon, and Strell shivered as the Master turned his gaze upon the Hold. Bird and raku kept a silent watch.

Strell flushed. His presence in Alissa's room was terribly improper, made more so by the late hour. Assuring himself his intentions had been honorable, Strell shut and latched the shutters. He returned to her, sleeping soundly in her chair before her fire. "Sleep well, my love," he whispered, but he dared not touch her, not with Talo-Toecan standing so near. "You have stronger guardians than I." For a long moment he gazed at her as if he were never to see her again. Finally he turned and left, clutching his blanket about him, slumped with loss.

When he was no longer necessary, he would go.

19

"**B**ye, Papa," Alissa whispered. She turned away, the tears brimming, but too much a part of her to fall. With feet slow and heavy, she made her way from the ice- and thorn-covered pile of rock at the base of the Hold's tower that marked his grave. Bailic had never cleared the rubble of his fallen balcony. Her papa was under it. The snow was thick and would soon obscure that she had been here. Bailic would never know; she would just as soon keep it that way.

She tugged her coat tight about her neck and peered up at the tower, gray in the diffuse light. Icy pinpricks melted into cold drops as the snow fell upon her upturned face. It was hard to tell in late winter, but she thought the tangle of canes was a wild rose. *Papa would have liked that,* she thought as she turned to find her way back inside.

It was seldom she could slip completely away from Strell, but he had stormed down to his potter's stead shortly after his morning lesson. Bailic had been especially brutal in his sarcasms, and Strell was undoubtedly working his frustrations out on the clay. He had become markedly more careful with Bailic, and holding his tongue clearly grated on Strell's independent plainsman upbringing.

Slumped with more than her feeling of sad remembrance, she halfheartedly tugged the Hold's black, inner set of doors open and slipped inside. Talon landed upon Alissa's shoulder in a flurry of wings and noise, scolding her. Although it had been more difficult, Alissa managed to avoid her bird as well. "Hush," she murmured, ignoring the nonstop harangue. Talon gave a final chitter and flew to the rafters as

Alissa entered the kitchen, apparently convinced her scolding had done some good. Alissa stomped the snow from her boots and filled her copper teapot. She put it over the fire, too dejected to bother taking off her coat. Slouching on a stool, she traced a slow arc on the floor with her foot, waiting for the water to heat.

It seemed something more than Bailic had been bothering Strell lately. She thought the beginnings of his mood could be traced to the afternoon she had found Lodesh in the stables. Though she had immediately taken Strell to meet him, they found the stables empty. Strell hadn't been the same since.

And Lodesh was avoiding her. True to his promise, he let her know when he came by leaving an acorn for her to find. She uncovered a new one every third day or so in the oddest of places: tucked in her shoe, behind the rolling pin, jammed in her thimble. The stables were empty whenever she looked, and she hoped she hadn't said anything to offend the Warden. She loved secrets, and at first, finding a nut was like sharing in a mystery. Now she was tired of the game and wanted to talk to someone.

As she sat in the warm, comforting quiet of the kitchen, Alissa wished she didn't have to sneak out beyond the garden's walls to her papa's grave. Having only a pile of rubble to remember him by was depressing. There was his pack, but that was in the closet under the steps in the great hall. The door was warded shut, and had been since they arrived.

Alissa's foot went still. Slowly, she straightened. Strell had gotten past the ward by jamming the door behind Bailic, preventing it from locking. Perhaps the door was still open?

A sly, casual glance to the ceiling told her Talon was preening, apparently satisfied Alissa would be doing nothing of interest as there was a pot of water over the fire. Very quietly, Alissa stood and left. Talon, she was sure, wouldn't approve.

Her pulse quickened as she made her stealthy way to the great hall to stand before the door to the closet under the stairs. She eyed the thin cracks in the wall, a small grin easing over her as she spied a bit of green fabric peeping from between the stones. Apparently Bailic hadn't bothered to investigate the door after Useless had escaped, either. With a last, furtive glance toward the kitchen, Alissa pried the door open and cautiously peered inside. There, lying in the dust by a stack of torches, was her papa's pack.

Pleased but rather depressed, Alissa slipped into the half-light under the stairs and knelt before it. She tugged at the knots holding the pack shut, finally running to the dining room for a knife. There was a slight cramping of her fingers as she cut the knots free, and she jerked her hands away. Her papa had warded it. That was why Bailic hadn't touched it. Then she shrugged—her papa would never make anything that could hurt her—and she confidently opened the pack to pull out a familiar pair of cream-colored boots. Smiling faintly, she set them aside. It was no wonder she had prized hers so greatly. She hadn't consciously known it, but before Strell turned her boots that horrid brown with his water-proofing grease on their way to the Hold, they had been identical in color to her papa's. Next came a thick blanket. She brought it to her nose and breathed deeply. The tears pricked as it smelled of home even now. Taking a slow breath to keep from crying, she set it down and continued.

All told there were a spare set of clothes—eerily identical to the first outfit she had stitched for Strell—a cup and bowl crafted out of stone as was her mortar, a length of rope with several immovable knots, and myriad minor objects. It was all fairly typical, mirroring her own abandoned pack. Near the bottom she found a fold of paper, and after reading the salutation, she tucked it in her pocket with a rush of grief. It was for her mother. As she sat in the dust becoming depressed, Talon found her.

Hissing and flapping like a fear-maddened beast, Talon dove at her from the great hall. Alissa's eyes widened in shock. "Talon! No!" she shouted, hunching into herself. The bird's claws reached skin when Alissa snapped out of her astonishment and shoved her out of the closet. Talon sprawled awkwardly on the smooth, polished floor, squawking indignantly as she struggled to regain her wings. Alissa lunged to the door and pulled upon the handle. The sounds of her kestrel's fury cut off abruptly as the door grated shut.

"Hounds!" Alissa whispered, staring through the new darkness at the unseen door. Her heart was pounding, and she felt queasy. Talon had never done that before! What demon had whispered into her ear?

Fumbling in the black for her papa's fire kit, she lit one of the torches. The light jumped, responding to a draft she hadn't noticed before. With a faint stirring of excitement, she peered down a square hole in the floor. This had to be the passage Strell told her about that led to Useless's cell. Useless had been his typical, closed-mouthed self when she asked him how Strell had freed him. Strell, though, had been free in his account, so much so she sometimes questioned the truth of it. One thing he had mentioned was this stairway. "And pillars engraved with the script I can read," she whispered, curiosity pulling at her.

The breeze shifting her hair smelled of snow, and she wondered how long it would take to find the stair's end. It might be useful knowing a third way out of the fortress. The cramped stairway seemed awfully dark and wet, but the thought of something to read was irresistible. Taking a resolute breath, Alissa prudently tucked the knife in her pocket and started down.

The air in the stairwell was cold and damp above her boots, and she shivered, glad she still had on her coat. She began to shiver, and just as she decided to forget the entire thing and return to the upper rooms, the steps ended and a narrow, cramped tunnel began. Holding her torch before her, she followed it until it opened up into a small room, one end blocked by an enormous gate. The bars were set so far apart, it would be easy to slip between them. There was the sound of dripping water, and the smell of outside was thick in the chill air. Alissa went to put her torch into the wall holder, but the last one had been jammed and she couldn't free it. Resigning herself to holding it, she stepped closer to the gate.

Beyond was an echoing blackness relieved by the hint of huge pillars. Her light stretching over the smooth stone floor didn't reach far, smothered by the dark. She hesitated, biting her lip as she looked at the metal rods. Slowly she reached out to touch one. There was a flash of unseen power, and she nearly jumped out of her skin. They were warded, she thought dryly, her finger in her mouth.

Grimacing, Alissa eyed the distant glow of sunlight behind the pillars. She could tell they were engraved, but she was too far away to see what even the closest said. It irritated her, the not knowing, and she eyed the rods with a wary distrust. Strell said he had passed between them, not just in, but out as well on the western gate. He said they were warded for Useless only.

"Maybe if I don't actually touch them," she whispered, and she carefully sent a finger dead center between two. There was a tingle of warning but no pain, and so she stuck more of her arm behind the gate. Wiggling her fingers, she withdrew her hand and sent her foot to try the same. Still only the warning. Her breath hissed out in exasperation as she looked at her torch. It was burning well. There should be plenty of time to see what some of the pillars said and make it back upstairs before it went out—if she could get past the bars.

Lips pursed, she took a wary step back. Her finger was singed, but not badly. It didn't even hurt anymore. She flexed it, eyeing it in the dim light. Strell had passed through the gate, so she should be able to as well. Nodding sharply, Alissa boldly stepped between the bars. A strong wash of caution coursed through her, shocking in its intensity. She shivered, but once through, she looked about the gigantic cavern with a growing feeling of awe.

Her eyes rose to the distant ceiling, decorated with myriad muted colors and soft shapes. The pillars, though, were far more interesting. Holding her torch high, she squinted to read the first. A smile lifted the corners of her mouth as she realized they were books, stretching to the heavens. Before her satisfied eyes were the comforting whispers of stories and adventures she had heard all her life. She almost turned around to get Strell. But the light beckoned, and Alissa headed for it, reading snippets of well-known and new stories as she went. The pillars, rising like some strangely symmetrical forest, were both eerie and comfortable. She halted in wonder as the last slipped behind her. It was as if she could see the entire world.

It wasn't snowing on this side of the mountain, and the clear skies revealed the distant horizon. It was nearly flat. She had never seen such a thing before, and it looked wrong. In great undulating waves, the land flowed away, the hills between her and the unseen sea dwarfed by the one she now stared in wonder from. The ocean was lost in the gray, but she could sense it was there, just out of sight. Then Alissa looked down, and gulping, took three steps back. It took all her courage to cautiously peek over the edge again. There were clouds between her and the ground. Her knees went weak, and her hand went to her stomach. The floor at the opening was ragged, showing where the hinges holding the gate against the mountain had once been. The thought that Strell had actually climbed out onto the surrounding rock made her ill. Unnerved, she turned to the sound of moving water, her eyes slowly adjusting back to the torch-lit darkness.

The icy plinking led her to a tremendous cistern behind a retaining wall thicker than she was wide. Steady drops plunked into it, shifting the surface to look like rhythmic echoes of sound. Her gaze rose to the source of the water, and her mouth opened in astonishment. Hanging high above the pool was a fantastic array of worked stone in the shape of a cone. There was the faint whistle of wind through its honeycombed channels, and with a feeling of wonder, she realized the structure had been designed to capture water from the very air itself!

Amazed at the skill necessary to craft such a thing, she dipped her hand and took a taste of its result. The water was warm, and she shivered. The surface disturbed by her fingers rippled gently against the circular walls, looking more like mist than liquid in the soft dusk. Drying her hand nervously upon her coat, she gazed at the ceiling, squinting to make out the swirls of color.

She set her torch down to lever herself up onto the retaining wall to get a closer look at the ceiling, but hesitated as her torchlight fell upon the cistern's wall and the thin tracings of words chiseled there. Immediately she crouched to read them, having to pull her torch so close, the smoke stung her eyes. Her brow rose as she realized it wasn't a story or tale, but names! Her unease forgotten, Alissa circled the pool, holding her torch before her.

"Dom-Crawen," she whispered. "Redal-Stan." She continued with a growing excitement, recognizing the names Useless had scratched in the snow and made her memorize her last lesson. "Sloegar," she mused, wondering why they were abruptly singular, not hyphenated. The names spiraled around the cistern in overlapping rows. Alissa followed, her finger tracing lightly down through the ages. Almost to the end, she paused. "Keribdis," she breathed, taking a chill as she recognized another. The male names were hyphenated, the female names were not.

Immediately she went to the masculine rows to find Useless's name. "Talo-Toecan," she said, smiling. There was a good handful after his, but it was the last that caught her attention. "Connen-Neute," she said, frowning. Useless had told her he had gone feral, and there was a shallow circle etched around his name that most lacked. Alissa frowned, thinking it must be a designation of some sort.

His was the last on the masculine list, and she pondered it for a time before sitting down to put it at eye level. It didn't seem right that the last Master named upon the wall would be recorded as feral. Being contrary, she used the knife to scratch the name, "Useless," after it.

Pleased at the result, she awkwardly went to stand upon the wall. Holding her torch high, she craned her neck to stare at the ceiling. The additional height seemed to make the difference, and she could see now that it was decorated with pictures of rakus. One had brown eyes instead of the usual gold, and she pondered the incongruity as she circled the pool from atop the thick wall. Her feet made a small scuffing hiss against the pillars and floor. On impulse, she looked up, breathing a soft, "Hello-o-o-o." She smiled as her echo whispered back. Taking a deeper breath, she called again, louder. She set the torch down and clapped once to try and gauge the echo's interval. Her papa had once taken her to a cliff, showing her how, if she paced it right, it would sound as if the mountains were singing with her. Smiling at the memory, she started to sing, her voice bouncing wildly among the pillars and ceiling. She chose a tavern song, easy to sing and not required to adhere to any particular tone to sound good. It was known by farmers and plainsmen alike, thought they each had their own versions. Regardless if it was sung in the plains or foothills, it always revolved around an addle-brained man out to make his fortune and his continuous predicaments.

> "Taykell was a good lad,
> He had a hat and horse.
> He also had six brothers,
> The youngest one of course.
> His father said, 'Alas, my boy.
> I've nothing more to give ye.'
> His name forsook, the path he took,
> To go to find the blue sea."

Alissa's eyebrows rose and she turned to the darkness, hearing in the echo of her voice, the deep tone of another singer.

> "Taykell sought a treasure,
> To give his name some worth.
> The one that he'd been born with,
> Now stood with a huge dearth.
> Told of one that he might find,
> He searched the total land.
> Was found, but lost, to pay the cost,
> To forge a copper band."

Someone else is down here? she thought. And it sounded like Strell!

20

L odesh pushed aside the thin, lacy curtain on the window with a single finger. "Good," he breathed upon seeing the morning snow swirling down in a muffling, gray stillness. He had been hoping to get to the Hold today, and the snow would help cover his tracks. Deciding to eat later, he quickly packed a small sack of whatever was handy. He dropped an acorn to leave for Alissa into his pocket, and after a hurried check on the fire to assure himself his guardian's dwelling wouldn't go up in smoke in his absence, he left, warding the door from long habit.

Looking to the center of the field, he whistled. The sharp sound died quickly in the sifting snow. Lodesh grimaced, turned, and stomped towards the western edge of the city. He didn't like it when he forgot he was alone. He'd have to make the journey on foot. His horse was long gone, and the wild herd had abandoned the field when the first stone for his cursed wall was laid. They hadn't been seen since.

He walked west through his empty city, stoically ignoring the black windows and barren shop fronts, unable to prevent the names and faces that once went with them from swimming up from his thoughts. He should have stopped the wall's construction right then, he thought dismally. But he had been young and inexperienced, relying heavily upon the whispered counsel of frightened men and women. Wishing that his foresight could have been as clear then as it was now, Lodesh passed through the broken west gate and continued through the hushed woods until the tower materialized, appearing as if by magic from the swirling snow.

The small prints of Alissa's boots decorated the steps, and he smiled, feeling the stiffness of his half-frozen cheeks. Apparently he wasn't the only one using the snow to their advantage today. A quick mental sweep of the great hall, kitchen, and the Keepers' dining room told him the first floor was empty. Satisfied, he knocked the snow from his boots and slipped inside.

The stillness that gripped the Hold was absolute. A hot, metallic scent hung like a pall in the air, and he wondered what Bailic was up to. There was a sudden rush of wings. Alissa's bird landed on his wrist, having dropped from one of the balconies overlooking the great hall. "Hush," he soothed the agitated bird, hoping she wouldn't pierce his coat with her talons. He wasn't surprised to see her. The bird had an uncanny knack for finding him, serving as a silent witness as he made his hurried checks upon Alissa.

With the small bird perched on his arm, Lodesh followed the stench of burning metal into the kitchen. His eyebrows rose as he saw the copper teapot, black and tarnished from going dry over the flames. Flinging Talon to the rafters, he pulled the pot from the fire. Alissa would be furious. It was made from enough copper to forge a score of wedding bands, and she was meticulous in its care. Smiling for having caught her in a forgetful moment, Lodesh dropped the acorn into the pot. She would be embarrassed for him knowing she had scorched it, and he loved to make her blush, even if he wouldn't be there to see it.

His promise fulfilled, he sent his thoughts through the Hold to find her. Her room was empty, and so he moved his thoughts to the dry goods. Alissa liked the smell of leather and was forever poking about for the odd bit of adornment for her new clothes or her room. She wasn't there, either. Feeling cold, Lodesh sent his thoughts to Talo-Toecan's old rooms. With a sigh of relief, he found only Bailic.

Concerned, Lodesh returned to the great hall and did an entire sweep of the fortress. Starting in the uppermost chambers in the tower, he worked his thoughts down through the rooms and halls to finish in the annexes. He found the piper in the students' kitchen at his potter's wheel, but no Alissa. She wasn't in the Hold.

Talon had followed him out, and frowning, he soothed the bird on his arm as he recalled Alissa's footprints had been leading into the great hall, not out. Nevertheless, he sent his thoughts to the garden and the surrounding environs. Perhaps she had decided to take a walk in the snow, unlikely as the prospect was—Alissa's aversion to the cold was like none he had ever seen—but the garden and overgrown fields and pastures were empty. She was nowhere. Nowhere at all.

Lodesh's unease grew as he recalled the forgotten teapot. "Where is she?" he whispered, and Talon took flight to land on the floor at the foot of the stairs. She hopped around behind it, chittering as if urging him to accompany her. Not sure he quite believed what the bird must be doing, Lodesh followed. With an increasingly tight feeling, he watched the bird flutter reluctantly to the closet under the stairs and peck at the nearly invisible seam.

"No," he whispered, feeling his face pale. Immediately he unlocked the door and swung it open to find an empty pack, its contents set aside in several piles. Lodesh sent his thoughts to the holden and found, to his dismay, that she was already behind its imprisoning bars. "Oh, Alissa," he breathed, his eyes flicking to the hole in the floor. "Your curiosity will be the end of us all."

"Alissa?" came Strell's faint call from the students' kitchen.

Lodesh took a quick breath. Stepping into the closet, he shut the door behind him, sealing himself in the darkness. There was no need to involve the piper just yet. Slowing his thoughts back to calm, he set them to form a soft glow of light, cupping a hand about the luminescence so as to keep it with him. The stairs were slick, and as he peered uneasily down into the damp, he wondered what he would find at the bottom. He had been told of this passage as part of his Wardenship but had never been invited into the holden, thick with tradition and stately ceremony.

He began his descent with a resolute grimace. The way

was tight, damp, and very uncomfortable. His imagination put the walls closer and the ceiling lower with every step, but he continued, keeping his thoughts on Alissa instead of his mild claustrophobia. Soon the sound of water came to him, and still unsure as to how he would handle the situation, he slipped around the last turn and peeked into the small anteroom he had been told was there.

Blackness upon blackness soaked up the thin glow from his light. He listened, a smile coming over him as he heard Alissa's faint singing. Being careful not to touch the bars, he slipped between them. As a Keeper, the bars couldn't prevent him from passing back through, but they would stop Alissa. No need for her to know that, though.

He didn't agree with Talo-Toecan's wishes for him to stay away from Alissa—Lodesh would do what he wanted when it concerned her—but lately he had been avoiding her for his own peace of mind. There, in the stables, it had almost seemed as if she remembered, speaking of his mirth trees and moonlight. Her words had torn at him worse than the winter's cold. He hadn't expected that when he had lured her down to the stables. Like a fool, he had hoped her casual acceptance would shift to true recognition if she only talked with him. But her gentle speech and innocent touch only left him despondent. She was her, but not.

Lodesh shifted his pack higher as he strode to the square of light that was the western gate. Leaving acorns for her to find was his cowardly way to keep his sanity. Now, though, she had gone and gotten herself stuck behind a warded gate. He had to make sure she was all right, and if he kept their conversations to mundane topics, he could pretend she knew him.

Anticipation quickened his steps as he followed the sound of her voice to the far end of the spacious cell. A smile crossed him as he recognized her song. Thinking to surprise her, he joined his voice to hers, sending it to echo among the thick pillars like a forgotten memory.

21

"Strell?" Alissa said in astonishment. She spun towards the eastern gate. Her foot rolled on the discarded torch. She slipped, and with a small shriek, she toppled into the water. Just before she hit, she heard, "Alissa!" Then there was only the rush of bubbles as she sank. Her skirt and coat weighed her down. After a brief struggle, she realized her only chance was to either get out of them or push off from the bottom. *"Useless!"* she shrieked with her thoughts, praying her teacher might hear her, not knowing if he had or not. Reaching him from a distance was not a certainty, despite their practice, but possible. Lungs aching, she struggled with her coat tie. Her feet hit bottom. Relief flooded her—she half expected the pool to be bottomless—and she kicked off, angling to the edge.

She reached the surface and gasped in a lungful of air and water. Choking, she felt the water threaten to slip over her head. She grasped for the edge. A strong hand fumbled into hers. Another tight grip fastened on her arm, and she was pulled to the side. Hacking and coughing, she was dragged to hang over the cistern's wall. Alissa struggled to breathe, trying to clear her eyes. The hand upon her shoulder had all its fingers. It wasn't Strell.

Still choking, she pulled away.

"It's me, Alissa," a resonant, clear voice said, and she slumped in relief.

"Lodesh?" she wheezed. "What are you doing down here?"

"Watching out for you," he said, a curious softness to his voice.

Water dripped from her to puddle as she righted herself and slid her feet to the floor. Her relief turned to embarrassment. "I don't need anyone to watch over me," she said, even as she tried to take her first, good breath.

Lodesh took a step back. He ran his gaze over her as she slumped against the cistern wall. A hint of a smile drifted over him. "Yes, milady. You do, or you wouldn't be soaking wet."

For a moment, she could say nothing. Frowning, she pulled her hand from his. She hadn't even known he had taken it. Her pulse was racing, but if it was from Lodesh or her efforts to keep from drowning, she didn't know. Tugging her coat and skirt free of the wall, she lurched to a stand, unbalanced from the weight of her soaking clothes.

Lodesh picked her torch from the floor. She had dripped over it, and it was out. "I don't think I can make this burn," he said. "Why don't we go to the western gate and consider your options. It will be warmer in the sun."

Alissa ran her eyes over herself disparagingly. "Yes. I'm rather wet, aren't I. But I think I should go upstairs and hope Bailic and Strell don't catch me on the way."

"You can't, Alissa. The gate won't let you back through."

Surprise shocked through her. "Strell made it past the bars on the western gate," she said. "Before Talo-Toecan ripped it from its hinges, Strell climbed out and opened the latch. He told me."

"Yes, well, he's a commoner."

Her eyes narrowed. Warden or not, he need not be insulting. "Strell is the last of a great house of artisans. He comes from a chartered name," she said. "He's not a—a—commoner!"

"He is, milady," Lodesh said as if it gave him pleasure. "I meant it as no disrespect, simply a classification. The wards on the gate respond to the complexity of one's tracings."

His calmly spoken words stood in sharp contrast to hers, and she dropped her eyes, flustered. She had no right to yell at Lodesh. "I'm sorry," she said. "I really ought to learn not to shout at my rescuers."

Smiling, Lodesh took a small step closer. "Let's go to the sun. You'll dry faster."

Alissa didn't move, a drift of worry building within her. "Can't you unward them?"

He shook his head, regret in his eyes. "Only Talo-Toecan can do that. I'm sure he is close about and will get you where you belong. If not, perhaps we can climb out of here."

Alissa felt herself go white. "He's going to be so angry with me."

"Probably. But we have to get you dry before we do anything."

He took her dripping arm and gingerly set it across his own, leading her to the drop-off as if she were a grand lady, not half drowned. "Yes, thank you," she mumbled. She numbly followed his lead, her thoughts on what Useless was going to say. Her coat was a soggy, slimy mass of wool and leather, weighing heavily on her, and as they found the patch of sun, she took it off. It was going to dry to an unusable stiffness. She just knew it.

The opening that faced the sky was warmer than it looked as the wind was directed past the cavern rather than through it. Settling herself on the sun-warmed stone, she was struck by a sudden thought. "Lodesh? You followed me down here, knowing you would be stuck behind the gates, too?"

He took a breath as if to speak. Slowly he let it out. "Yes. I guess I did."

"Thanks," she said shyly as she untied her hair ribbon and tried to shake her hair out.

He sank down beside her, sitting in the sun. "I'm sorry for making you fall in."

"It wasn't your fault," she said, grimacing as she squeezed the water from her sleeve.

Giving her a quick smile, he took the pack off his back and removed his coat. He leaned close and gallantly draped it over her shoulders. It smelled like mirth wood, and she breathed deeply. "Would you be interested in joining me for my noon meal?" he asked lightly.

It was obviously a ploy to distract her, but Alissa's looked up, intrigued. "You have something to eat?"

Clearly pleased, Lodesh opened his pack and spread a small kerchief between them. From his pack he produced a large wedge of cheese, a greasy-looking sausage, and a battered biscuit beginning to crumble. He handed Alissa the cheese and half the biscuit.

Alissa went for the cheese first, wrinkling her nose at the faint smell of sausage on it. She was raised foothills and had never eaten meat. Foothills farmers kept sheep, pigs, and goats, but they sold them to the plains. That the plains ate them only proved they were hard up for food. She had never eaten anything with feet, and she wasn't going to start now. Slightly queasy at the lingering smell, she set the cheese aside to concentrate on the biscuit. Lodesh saw her distaste and chuckled. "I make no apologies for my diet," he said, his pleasure in consuming the nasty little morsel obvious.

Trying to ignore him, Alissa sent her eyes to the view. She could almost imagine she could see the sparkle of water on the horizon. "Have you ever been there?" she asked wistfully as she blotted a crumb off her soggy knee.

"Sorry?" came Lodesh's confused voice.

Alissa blinked and turned to him. Strell would have known what she meant by the tone in her voice and the direction of her eyes. "The sea," she repeated. "Have you ever been there?"

"Ah, yes. Once or twice."

"What's it like?" She sent her eyes to the distant horizon, waiting.

He shrugged. "People are born there, they live, they work, they laugh and cry. And when they die, those they leave behind mourn their passing. It's much the same as anyplace."

"Oh." It wasn't quite what she was looking for, and unsure what to think, Alissa picked up the cheese and took a bite. "It's a shame you can't make tea appear with those cups of yours," she said, half jesting.

Lodesh surreptitiously cleaned his fingers of grease on the kerchief between them. "Well, even the most skilled Master can't make food or drink."

Creating things from one's thoughts was a topic Talo-Toecan avoided like the plague. Alissa felt a smile come over her as she realized Lodesh might be a font of information if handled correctly. "Why not?" she asked, forcing her voice to be casual.

Lodesh hesitated. "You won't try it?"

"No," she agreed lightly, a thrill of anticipation going through her.

"To craft an object with your tracings," he said, "you must first master its creation with your hands. And since only a tree can make an apple, you can't craft one with your thoughts."

Alissa frowned. "I make bread. Why couldn't I make a loaf of it with my tracings?"

"No, you misunderstand." He met her gaze, and she flushed. The devious light in his eyes made it clear that, not only did he know she was charming information from him, but that he didn't mind. "When I was learning to craft a cup using my tracings, I first made innumerable cups on a potter's wheel. Then, when I was satisfied I could make them in my sleep, so to speak, I secluded myself from all possible distractions and crafted a final one. I was focused solely upon its creation to such a degree that it became my entire world for the space of time it took."

"But it takes weeks to make a cup," Alissa protested, nibbling the cheese to nothing.

"True," he admitted. "But since time is what you make of it, you can string the pertinent memories together, skipping the space where you're simply waiting. Now, when I go to create a cup, I simply relive those memories. The ward harnesses my thoughts and gives them substance. The result is what you see before you." With a tweak on her awareness so quick she hadn't a hope of seeing a pattern mirrored in her tracings, a cup materialized on the smooth floor.

"So in theory I could make a loaf of bread," she asserted doubtfully as she picked it up.

"Probably not. The more components an object has, the less likely you will be successful. A cup is made of clay, glaze, heat, and lots of effort. True, the glaze is often formed of many things, as is the clay, but in your thoughts, they're one thing. Bread is flour, lard, yeast, milk, and any number of things. They exist in your mind as separate identities, no matter how much you would like to believe it otherwise. It would be too difficult. Most Keepers only manage one or two objects," he said. "Masters have more time and so generally have a lots of things they can make. But if you observe closely, you will note they specialize in only one medium. One may craft things of wood, another of clay, a third of fabric. It's easier."

"Talo-Toecan seems to excel in everything," Alissa said, sure he had an answer for that.

"Yes, well, he doesn't care what anything looks like and skimps on the time spent perfecting each object. His bench has splinters, the stitching on his cushion is loose. He glazed his cups that ugly brown because he was too impatient to find anything better."

"M-m-m-m." Alissa thoughtfully turned Lodesh's cup over in her grip. "So every cup you make is identical to the last one you crafted by hand?"

"Exactly right," he agreed. "That's why you don't imprint a form upon your consciousness until you're sure you can make it the way you want. Once you have a form, you can't replace it with anything similar, or it falls apart because your thoughts weren't decisive enough."

"Oh!" she teased. "So every cup you make will have that spot of glaze missing from the underside of the handle?"

"Missing!" Lodesh shouted. "Where?" He took the cup from her, and his shoulders slumped. "Oh no," he moaned, and Alissa's eyes widened as he threw the cup out the window. "I never noticed it before. Now I'll see it every single time."

"The ward," she said, ignoring his distress, "draws from your source, uses your memory to fix the energy into your idea of a cup, then turns your thoughts to reality."

"Ah—yes," he stammered. "But please, Alissa, don't try it. It's very complex and draws upon many diverse areas of practice you have yet to be introduced to."

"Doesn't it use up a lot of source?" she asked.

His head bobbed. "Yes, as a matter of fact, it does. But as Warden, I've been instructed how to circumvent that problem."

"How?"

Talon streaked into the cavern, chattering wildly. They turned to see a dark shadow cover the opening. "Look out!" Lodesh shouted. He lunged, grasping her around the waist and pulling her into the shadow at the edge of the opening.

A huge gust of wind buffeted them. Alissa impatiently brushed the hair out of her eyes, gasping as a raku was suddenly standing where she had been only a moment ago. "Useless," she cried as she disentangled herself from Lodesh and struggled to her feet. "You heard me!"

He shifted to his human shape in a tight swirl of gray mist, solidifying with his arms crossed disapprovingly. "Why are you wet?" he snapped, glowering down at her.

"I fell into the water," was her soft response, and Lodesh snickered.

"Into the cistern!" he cried, looking aghast, and Alissa winced, resigning herself to a lecture. Talon took refuge upon her shoulder but silently winged out as Useless gave the bird a black look. "What are you doing down here in the first place?"

She shrugged. "I saw a hole in the floor; I went down it." His eyes grew dark, and his lips pressed together. "You never said I couldn't!" she said defiantly.

"Didn't you feel the warning on the bars?" he demanded.

"Yes," Alissa protested, "but they didn't hurt me."

Lodesh came even with her, brushing his clothes free of imaginary dirt. "She was unaware the warnings were for her," he said mildly.

"Stay out of this, Warden," Useless said coldly, and Lodesh raised a placating hand and took a symbolic step backwards. Alissa blinked in surprise but became all the more determined the day wouldn't end with them looking like errant children.

"Your curiosity," Useless said, "hasn't only endangered you, but Strell and the Warden."

Lodesh cleared his throat. "I was never in danger. And you did ask me to keep an eye on her," he said, then stiffened at Talo-Toecan's warning finger.

"Lodesh pulled me out," Alissa said, beginning to become angry. "I would have drowned if not for him."

Useless turned to her, his eyes carrying an anger she had never seen before. "I heard you taking instruction from him," he accused, and Alissa felt herself go pale, suddenly afraid.

"He, um . . . I—" she stammered, realizing her mistake. "I'm sorry," she said, honestly contrite. "I wasn't thinking."

Lodesh drew himself up. Placing one arm before him, one behind, he executed a formal bow. His eyes never left her teacher's. "My apologies, Master Talo-Toecan. It was harmless information, weighted to pass the time. I accept the penalty you see fit for my—choice."

"There is no such thing as harmless information, Warden," Useless said, and Alissa held her breath. "She is *my* student." Leaning close to Lodesh, he barely breathed his next words. "Respect my authority in this matter."

Lodesh's green eyes went still. "Of course, Master Talo-Toecan."

Useless made a sound of dissatisfaction. He turned away, took a breath, and straightened, seeming to have put the matter behind him. "I'll take you both out by air," he said softly. "I'm not going to remove the ward on the eastern gate. You will not come down here again. And if you do, you won't be able to get out without my help. Understand?"

"Air?" came Lodesh's faint whisper. "Er, Talo-Toecan? I would be the first to admit you are a strong flyer, and the largest beast the skies have seen, but either one of us will be too much for you to carry."

Useless raised his eyebrows and eyed Lodesh. "I managed the piper," he finally said. "And I will have built up a great deal of momentum by the time I catch you."

"C-catch?" Lodesh stammered.

Alissa pulled her contrite eyes from the floor and was shocked at Lodesh's paleness. As she watched, the self-assured man went whiter still, taking a step back. "Er—thanks, Talo-Toecan, but I'll go back the way I came."

Useless turned to him, a savage humor in his eyes. "How?" he questioned harshly. "You can't pass the gate. Correct?" The Master leaned close and looked at Lodesh as if he were going to strike him if he disagreed.

Lodesh glanced at the drop-off frantically. "Ah, yes. Right."

Useless eased back and adjusted his sash. "Just so. You will both go by air."

Lodesh shot a furtive look behind him. "If you must punish someone, punish me. But don't do this to Alissa. She's only a child."

"I am not!" she said loudly.

"There's no other way," was Useless's firm decision, and Lodesh cringed. "I will take Alissa first, as is proper for the lady she deems herself."

"Alissa," Lodesh apologized. His hands taking hers tightened spasmodically. "I'm sorry. I didn't think he would get this angry."

Alissa stared at him in confusion. "What?"

"He's going to take you by air. . . ."

"So what?"

"Jump," said Useless.

Slowly, Alissa blinked. "I beg your pardon?"

"Jump," he repeated.

Her eyes went to the drop-off. White in the bright light of

the afternoon, she could see clouds, big puffy ones, looking small as sheep between her and the unseen ground. Only now understanding, she took a step backwards and shook her head. "No."

"I don't have time for this," Useless growled, and saying no more, he picked her up and threw her out in a flurry of skirts and kicking ankles.

Her stomach dropped. Alissa tried to scream, but the force of the damp wind in her face forbade it. Her ears hurt, and for the first time she was thankful for her wretchedly long hair as it covered her eyes. She could see nothing. *Useless,* she thought frantically, *he will catch me.* On that thin cord, her sanity hung, but he didn't, and just as she was beginning to believe he had, in his anger, decided to let her perish, there was a terrible snap. Now she screamed, her surprise, prohibiting any other response. The wind blew back her hair. Realizing how close he had let her come to the ground, she shrieked again.

The trees were a bare wing's length below her.

Useless climbed furiously, and her ears popped. He began to dip and swoop in a horrendous example of the worst drunk at the best of markets. Alissa's belly rolled. As the Hold came underneath them, he dropped like a stone, pulling up at the last moment to lurch to a landing at the uppermost balcony in the tower. There was a tug on her thoughts as the ward was disengaged from the window, and then they were through.

Breathless, Alissa nearly collapsed as his grip about her middle loosened. She staggered to a stand on the wide balcony. Useless dropped her wet coat from between two talons before shifting to his man guise. His expression was decidedly smug. "Oh, Useless!" Alissa cried. "Can we do it again?"

He stiffened, his satisfied air evaporating, scowling in disgust.

She leaned over the railing to estimate the drop. "If I jump from here, can you catch me?" Turning, her elated smile vanished at the anger in his face.

"Get yourself out of this tower," he said darkly as he

proffered her coat. "Don't ever go back down there again. Do I make myself clear?"

"Why?" she asked, her curiosity stronger than her alarm at his obvious anger. "What's down there I shouldn't see?"

Useless took a wrathful breath, then seemed to slowly collapse. "Nothing," he said softly. "There's nothing down there you shouldn't see." Shaking his head, he slumped further into himself. "You frightened me out of a hundred years with your call. Why didn't you answer me?"

Her eyes widened. His anger was from his fright. She had worried him. "I couldn't hear you," she said. "I wasn't sure you even heard me."

"Hm-m-m. We will take care of that directly. Meet me at the firepit tonight. You will practice until we get it right every time."

Alissa started to smile but then squashed it. She was in disgrace. Her extra lesson wasn't a reward. "Yes, Useless," she said meekly. She wiggled out of Lodesh's coat and handed it to Useless, shivering in the sudden chill.

Apparently satisfied, he turned to leave but hesitated, looking at her with pleading eyes. "Did you really fall into the cistern?"

She nodded, and he passed a worried hand over his eyes.

"Don't tell anyone, all right?"

Mystified, she nodded again, guessing she had violated some raku taboo. Lodesh, though, hadn't seemed to think it was a problem. Besides, who would she tell?

"I'm going to get that Warden out," he grumbled. "You would do well to leave him alone. You showed a horrible lack of discretion in allowing him to instruct you on the theory of wards of creation." He smiled faintly, as if in a memory. "Not that I can truly blame you." He stepped lightly to the top of the thick railing of the balcony, and Alissa gasped, reaching out for him before he turned and smiled reassuringly. There was a strong tug on her tracings as he shifted. As a raku, he dropped into space. Feeling left behind, she stood and watched as he circled the tower, thoughtfully replacing the ward on the window before he left.

22

"Wake, child."

It was a soft whisper in her thoughts, but Alissa was warm, so she ignored it.

"Wake. I'm here," it came again.

"No," she mumbled, burrowing down among her blankets, determined to remain asleep. She was having such a nice dream, about a warm sea. It was the third such dream this week.

"Alissa." It was loud and impatient. *"Wake up."*

"Go away, Strell. I'm fine," she said around a sigh.

"Strell?" the voice thought incredulously. *"I'm not Strell. Wake up!"*

The last word was a veritable shout in her mind, and Alissa jumped. Her room was empty except for Talon, blinking at her from her perch. From habit, Alissa looked to see if her ward of disguise was still in place. It was. It had been weeks since waking to find it gone. Pleased, Alissa tugged her blanket over her shoulders and rose. "Looks like I have another lesson," she whispered to Talon as she minced barefoot to her shutters.

The cold pricked at her nose and slipped under her blanket as she leaned out into the night, or perhaps it was early morning. It was hard to tell. By the waxing, crescent moon rising, she thought morning. The stars that did show were few and becoming fewer as the snow clouds that threatened all of yesterday finally reached the Hold.

She took a deep breath and exhaled, watching her breath steam as it met the cold air. Though spring was officially two weeks away, the dampness held a hint of it, filling her with a thrill of expectation. Spring had always been her favorite time of the year.

"When you're through tasting the night, come to the garden," arose Useless's dry thought.

"A moment," she thought back. Once intermittent and not under conscious control, her skills at voiceless speech at a distance were improving. She could now hear Useless and be heard as she wished despite the Hold's ward of silence. When she had asked Useless about this incongruity during her intense lesson on nonverbal speech, he had abruptly changed the subject, saying only that Bailic ought not to be able to hear her, even if she should go past the ward's boundaries, and not to worry about it. His put-offs were happening a lot lately, and she was tiring of them.

Lately, their meetings were sporadic and unpredictable, as Useless had begun holding class whenever the mood struck him. Her lessons were delightfully more frequent, but they invariably occurred in the dead of night. Alissa didn't care when they met as long as they did. Judging by the lack of acorns, Lodesh's visits had stopped completely, and she hoped she hadn't gotten the Warden in trouble.

She dressed for the cold with as much haste as she could. Useless would let her light the fire if she hurried. "Coming?" she asked Talon. The bird fluffed her feathers and sank down, her bright eyes closing. "Last chance," Alissa warned as she slipped her luck charm into her pocket and her feet into her boots. Apparently it was too early for a game of chase, and so Alissa left. If Talon wanted, she could still leave by the hole Alissa had notched out in her shutters.

Ghosting down the hall, Alissa ran a finger over Strell's door in passing, wishing him peaceful dreams. He looked so tired lately, blaming it upon restless sleep. The Hold was silent; only the small sounds of her boots disturbed the darkness as she made her confident way. She caught sight of herself in the mirror at the landing and paused, having to lean close to see in the dark.

"Mother would never recognize me," Alissa said, feeling a stab of homesickness. Dressed as she was in such fine clothes, she looked far from the foothills-raised girl she was. Practically everything she had on was new, crafted from materials of an almost unreal quality. There was no second-rate fabric to be found in the annexes. As a result, her clothes had none of the usual telltale signs of foothill frugality. They were extravagant, making her at least look like a well-mannered lady. Only her ugly boots, her coat, and Strell's dilapidated hat remained of her old clothes, and eyeing the hat sourly, she resolved to do something about it—someday.

"Student . . ." Useless called wearily.

"I'm coming!" Alissa ran down the remaining stairs. Slipping into the dark kitchen, she filled a teapot with water. Two cups were next, and she skidded out into the darkness, her coat flapping loose about her ankles. Useless could supply either piece of crockery, but the kitchen was full of them, all distressingly alike. They didn't need any more.

The night was marginally lighter than the halls, and it was bitterly cold. Alissa hurried down the path's frozen turns until she was before Useless. The fire was yet unlit. She had made it in time.

"Good morning, student," Useless intoned seriously, his voice rumbling through the dark. "Would you care to light the fire?"

"Good morning, Useless. Yes, I would, thank you." Grinning like an idiot, Alissa formed a containment field about the wood. An immeasurable moment later, energy slipped coolly through her thoughts, creating a ward that set the very molecules of the wood vibrating so rapidly they ignited. Well, that's what Useless said; she only knew it worked. The first time she had tried it, the wood was consumed in a startling instant. Useless had harrumphed, thrown more wood on the ash, and told her to try again. Her control was improving, though, and tonight her fire began with a satisfying whoosh. Pleased, Alissa waited until the blue-hot flame shifted to its more normal orange before she set the pot to boil.

"Quite nice." Useless edged closer to the flames. "Very

efficient use of your resources. Just enough and no more. Have you been practicing?"

She nodded.

Useless sat and closed his eyes. "It shows."

Glowing from the praise, Alissa sat as well. She kept her eyes open, however, eager for whatever tonight's lesson might entail. Each midnight session brought her closer to what she imagined a Keeper was capable of. It seemed the more she knew, the easier everything became. But it was never enough. She always left hungry for more of Useless's teachings.

The water slowly warmed, and Alissa waited, knowing there would be no instruction until Useless had a cup of tea in his long fingers. She could have made the water boil now as quickly as Lodesh, but she didn't. *Patience,* Useless would say. *Use the time given you. Instant gratification teaches nothing and cheats yourself.* So she sat, trying not to watch the pot. Instead, Alissa gazed up at the star aptly named after the Navigator, the hub of the night sky. It was disappearing behind the thickening clouds, and she held her breath to see if it would show itself before she needed to breathe again.

Much to her relief, Useless hadn't ever brought up her "error in judgment" in allowing Lodesh to impart the theory behind wards of creation. Her teacher's attempt at punishment had failed miserably, and Alissa thought he was reluctant to discuss the incident at all, preferring to let sleeping rakus lie. If the truth be told, he hadn't answered any of her questions concerning what she had seen down in the Hold's cellar, spouting a dazzling plenitude of doubletalk and jargon that left her blinking in shock. Alissa had been hesitant to ask again, not wanting to subject herself to such a disgraceful display of twaddle a second time, but she had one burning question she hoped he'd explain.

"Useless?" Alissa's breath slipped out to obscure the now-visible star.

"Yes, Alissa?"

"Down in the cavern," she lowered her gaze, "that pool of water . . ."

"The cistern, yes," he prompted warily, opening his eyes.

Alissa straightened, encouraged. "There were names engraved upon it?"

"Yes. The names of Masters." Useless's golden brown eyes went softly into the past.

"There weren't very many," she said. "Rakus have been around since mankind can remember. I would have thought there would be uncountable more."

Useless smiled faintly. "They are names of Masters, not rakus."

"They aren't the same?"

"They are, and they aren't."

Patiently she waited.

"The names inscribed on the cistern are only the last seven generations of rakus," he said. "Before that, we couldn't read or write."

"You were all feral?" she said with a gasp.

Useless chuckled. "By my Master's Wolves, no! We have been sentient for as long as mankind, perhaps more. But it has only been the last few generations we acquired the wisdom to shift to a form that can hold a pen and focus upon paper. Our weaker kin has given us a great gift, and we have striven to repay it by instructing those who possess a partially functional neural net on the use of it. The names you saw are Masters, not rakus. They're inscribed only after the first shift to a human form has been accomplished. Until then, their names are only a promise."

"Still, there were so few. . . ." she pressed.

"Sentient or not, we're still carnivores, and large ones at that. The surrounding land can only support so many of us."

She thought about that, recalling her mother's small flock of sheep and the constant threat of inbreeding it posed. "Doesn't that," she stammered, feeling constrained, but needing to know. "Doesn't that pose a problem, with—with who you may join with?"

Useless politely ignored her blush. "Yes," he said with a sigh. "It does. We keep a close record of ancestral ties,

and there is the occasional new bloodline that usually results in a slight population explosion."

"New bloodline?"

"Yes." Only now did he seem uncomfortable.

"The feral beasts?" she asked, remembering Connen-
Neute.

"Ah—no," he muttered. "Unions between Masters are
often prearranged far before maturity is reached," he said,
clearly changing the subject.

"Marriages of convenience are barbaric," Alissa interrupted. Strell held a similar belief, and she wondered if the
plains tradition stemmed from here.

Useless eyed her warily. "Be that as it may, it's a neces-
sity. No one has complained yet. The two intended are
schooled together. They're usually pleased with the situation.
If not, changes are made. Our population is . . . ah . . . wasn't
so small that mobility was nonexistent."

Alissa nodded, surprised he had explained it so fully. It
wasn't often he imparted anything concerning his background. She had one last question though, and she stirred
uncomfortably.

Useless sighed. "Yes, Alissa?"

"The circled names?" she asked, her eyes on the
ground.

"They went feral. Yes."

"I'm sorry," she whispered, wishing she hadn't asked.

Again silence fell. The water began to steam, and seeming ready to forget the matter, Useless reached for the pot
and asked pleasantly, "How goes Strell's tutelage?"

"Very well, as you probably guessed." Relieved he
hadn't turned despondent as he usually did upon recalling
his feral kin, Alissa drew her legs up under her and arranged
her coat so more of her was under its concealing warmth.
"Bailic has covered myriad minor wards in quick succession as you predicted."

Useless gave her a curious, sidelong glance. "His instruction follows his own training, but he goes dangerously
fast, seeking to find what triggers my book. He incorrectly

imagines if Strell knows enough, the book will open to him, allowing access to its lessons."

The mention of her book sent a thrill through her. It was rare she could pry any information from Useless about it. She forced her features to be casual, fearing he would say no more if he knew how interested she was. "So, what does open it?" she asked, poking at the fire in a vain attempt to appear nonchalant.

"Right now, it's you," he said softly. "You could have opened it the day you found it." Reaching for the stone box of tea he kept secreted in the bench, he added a generous handful to the steaming water. "Knowledge," he said regretfully, "means nothing to it, only potential." He sat back and closed his eyes, unaware of or more likely disregarding the effect his words had.

Confused and hurt, she frowned. She had thought it closed to her. She could have snitched uncountable times. Bailic had it out almost every morning, tantalizingly near on that small table by his stiff-looking chair. "Why didn't you tell me before?" she asked in a small voice.

"You hadn't the willpower to resist, had you known." Useless smiled. "You do now."

Alissa went to protest, then closed her mouth. He was right. She would have snatched it. Bailic would have realized she was the latent Keeper. They would have ended up dead. Still, being second-guessed was infuriating.

Ignoring her sour expression, Useless poured out the tea. His eyes meeting hers over his cup were glinting in amusement. He settled back, his long fingers laced about the cup. A few flakes of snow began to sift down. "I'll teach you a small oddity tonight," he said suddenly. "You may find it of interest as you creep along at Bailic's pace. Mayhap it will come in handy." His eyebrows furrowed in warning. "Just don't rely on it."

"I thought you said Bailic goes too fast," Alissa said as an obscure portion of her tracings began to resonate in response to his ward. Quickly, she memorized the pattern.

"He does," was his short answer. "Now this," he continued, "is a ward of obscurity, and it helps to keep you from notice. It isn't a certainty. A keen eye will spot you every time."

Alissa's eyebrows rose, and she stared at him. He looked the same except for the few flakes of snow now resting upon his shoulders and knees. "I can still see you," she finally said.

"I said it was of obscurity, not invisibility, child."

Flushing, Alissa set her first loop glowing and filled the proper channels. "Like this?"

There was a faint touch on her thoughts as Useless dropped his ward. Now that his tracings were empty, they would resonate to show what lines she was using. His eyes grew distant as he examined the pattern for any mistakes. "Exactly," he said, his gaze again sharp and clear. "You have it correct, as usual."

Unreasonably pleased, she reached for her abandoned tea. *Cold,* she thought and warmed it with a second ward. The two patterns used some of the same lines, and so it was possible to set up the second without disengaging the first.

Useless raised an eyebrow at her steaming cup and hid a smile. "Has Bailic mentioned the ward of illumination I showed you?" She shook her head, and he frowned. "I'm surprised." Running a free hand over his short-cropped hair, he glanced into the snow beginning to fall in earnest. "It's just within his grasp. I'm certain he will soon. Feel free to perform as he asks. The wards he gives Strell are simple enough."

"He ignores most of the wards you have taught me," Alissa said. "I think he's afraid to give Strell more than he himself can easily overcome."

"Yes, well. A lot of them Bailic doesn't know."

She blinked in disbelief. "They aren't that hard."

Useless gave her a long, unnerving look until she dropped her gaze. "Not everyone has a complete pattern, Alissa," he admonished gently. "There's much diversity among Keepers, many gaps and severed connections. A pattern won't resonate in one's thoughts if it's not complete, so it remains unseen and unknown. The one I just gave you is like that, so you may use it freely, even when Bailic is within a raku length. A single misconnection keeps that pattern from completion in him." Useless shook his head. "So close."

"But I can do it," Alissa pressed.

"Obviously. That's why I like you." Grinning, he topped off her cup. "Patterns that aren't beyond Keepers that we wish to keep to ourselves must be implemented with care, lest a Keeper pick them up by accident," Useless said. "It's a necessary bit of deception for everyone's safety, but most of all, their own. You can't learn what you don't know is possible."

She did, Alissa thought as she took a warming gulp of tea. "It must be frustrating," she said aloud, thinking of her own stymied desires for knowledge.

"They never know they lack," Useless said. "But their children stand a fair chance to be as they, or much more rarely, a touch more complete in their tracings."

"Really?" That was interesting. Each generation was better than its precursor.

"Yes, but just a touch," Useless explained. "It's a process that spans hundreds of years before even a minor change is apparent."

Alissa mulled that over. It explained a great deal as to why she was here. Her papa had been a Keeper. She had stood a good chance of being the same. "Useless?"

"Yes-s-s," he drawled, examining a snowflake that had landed upon his fingertip.

She paused, not sure how to phrase her question, wondering if she would like his answer or if he would give one. It had been bothering her for a long while, and she felt that now was as good a time as any to broach the potentially touchy subject. He was unusually free with his information tonight. Worried, Alissa drew her knees up to her chin, hiding under her coat. "Useless? Where exactly do I fit in?"

Still lost in the crystalline perfection on his finger, he replied, "Why do you ask?"

"You say Bailic goes too fast, but I'm creeping at the same pace. You teach me things you say no Keeper should learn, and . . ." She gestured helplessly, not sure how to continue.

"And you want to know why." His snowflake vanished with a puff of breath. Sighing, he turned to face her. "My book has called you to the Hold. It's that simple. I wish to leave it at that." His attention returned to the fire, effectively ending the discussion.

Ignoring his improper reference to *her* book, Alissa sat and stared at him. She would stare all night if need be. He would tell her more.

Useless drained his cup. With nary a glance in her direction, he filled it. This, too, he finished silently, but his feet were beginning to tap an irregular beat, and his brow held the shadow of a frown. It wouldn't be long before he broke. Alissa had used this technique upon her papa and remembered the signs.

"Oh, very well," he finally relented, seeming irritated at himself. "Latent Keepers are naturally drawn to any conglomeration of Masters upon maturity. In the past, a lucky set or two were born at Ese' Nawoer and learned their craft as children. You," he pointed a long finger accusingly at her, "were not called by the Hold. You were called solely by my book."

"My book," she muttered.

He glowered, saying nothing until she dropped her gaze. "As I said," he continued, "you were called by *my* book. Uncountable Keepers have read it, any number have held it when I was busy elsewhere, and a precious few understood a fraction of its contents, your father among them." Useless paused. "Perhaps he understood more than I realized."

Then he shook his head and fixed her with a severe look. "I'll admit only that you have the potential to use the wisdom it contains. That," he said, shutting his eyes, "is all I will say—so don't ask anymore." But he wasn't done quite yet, and as he leaned back, he added, "It's this potential that prompts me to divulge more of my secrets than normal. That, and I like you. You make me laugh." The last was almost inaudible, and Alissa wasn't sure how to take it.

Clearing his throat, Useless shook the dusting of snow from his overcoat. "Now, I understand Bailic has shown Strell how to start a fire?"

Alissa nodded absently, deep in thought.

"Good. You may, with caution, extinguish them with an impervious containment field."

"Really?" she blurted, all thoughts of her unique situation vanishing.

"Yes, really." He smiled. "Just don't show Bailic such a field by error; he would have no compulsion against using it improperly."

Recalling Bailic's rapture when he removed Strell's finger, she vowed to be very careful.

"We will call it done for a time," Useless said, scanning the snow-filled skies. "You will be pleased to know there will be no more instruction until the snow is gone."

"What!" Her head came up and she stared at him aghast. "No more lessons? You can't!"

"I can. I will. I just did. It's cold out here. It has gotten ridiculous."

"I don't care!" Alissa wailed. "Come inside. Bailic will never know." It was an old argument. One she had yet to win.

"He would know," Useless all but growled, but he was irritated at Bailic, not her.

Her lips pursed. "How?"

"He would smell me." He touched his nose, and Alissa slumped. "So," he smiled, "you have a brief reprieve from new lessons. Be content practicing what you know. Just keep a trace of thought upon Bailic when you do."

Alissa hadn't much to show for her interrupted sleep, and she couldn't stop her heavy sigh. Halfway to a stand, Useless changed his mind and sat down again. "Before I go," he asked slowly, "was Lodesh exaggerating about the direction your desires have taken?"

Silently, her face turned red. She had been hoping he might have forgotten the night Lodesh first met her in the firepit, teasing her with bemoaning his fate in that he was not meant for her, and that her heart had already been lost to another.

"Ah. I can see he wasn't." Useless shifted the coals about, leaving his stick to burn. "Go gently, Alissa," he warned. "Make no ties with Strell that can't be sundered easily."

"Useless!" It was all she could manage. It was so embarrassing!

"It's for the good of both of you. You're irrevocably tied to the Hold in ways you can't imagine yet. I can't change this. You wouldn't have me change this, even if I could." Seeing her defiant look, he shook his head sadly. "Once Bailic is gone, Strell can't stay. It isn't safe."

"I'll go with him then," she said, her chin upraised.

Useless shook his head, looking grim and determined. "If you leave before I decide you have control over yourself and your mouth, I will be forced to hunt you down." He paused. "I am obligated to burn your tracings to permanent ash rather than let a rogue Keeper access to the hills and plains again." His eyes closed, and he shuddered. "Not again."

Alissa stiffened, knowing enough of his cursed sense of honor to realize he would, apologizing all the while. Only now did she see the trap she had built and fallen into, and her jaw clenched. Frustrated and betrayed, she could say nothing.

"I won't apologize," he said softly. "It's hard to be forced to stay until someone else decides, freeing you to follow your heart. That's how Ese' Nawoer came to be."

There was true regret in his voice, and her anger slowed at the empathy in his eyes.

"Only Keepers may safely choose to reside behind the Hold's walls," he said, "Masters as tradition dictates, and students, always, until they attain what status they can. It's a lengthy process, spanning decades. Ese' Nawoer began as a small group of wives and husbands caught as you now seem to be. Slowly it grew into the stature you see today, imposing even as a ruin. It was lovingly ruled over by a hereditary line who, not surprisingly, were strongly influenced by their Keeper standing. Lodesh was the last of them. He was the best—is the best."

Useless's eyes began to glow with a distant passion, and she listened, eager to learn more of the past he usually hid from her. "Once the Hold was full and alive, with many comings and goings," he said. "Ese' Nawoer served as a willing support staff, providing all we could wish in goods and services. We couldn't stop them. It was the reason for their existence in their eyes, and when Ese' Nawoer fell, the Hold began to follow."

Staring into the past, Useless slumped. He looked tired and worn out. His dream, having seen its zenith, appeared to be over. "Perhaps my idea of such a stronghold wasn't really a good one," he whispered.

"Perhaps you only need to modify it," Alissa suggested gently. It made her uneasy, seeing him this despondent.

His eyes grew large in astonishment at her softly spoken words, and his somber mood fell from him like water. "Harrumph," he snorted. "I'm going. Mind what I have said," he warned sternly, but she could tell his thoughts were elsewhere. "If not for yourself, then for Strell. You don't know everything yet." He stood and moved out of the pit, his head tilted in worry.

"Useless?" Alissa rose, reaching out after him, and he paused. His dark silhouette stood quietly as the snow drifted and fell, swirling about him as if he were already gone.

"It—it will be all right," she fumbled, searching for words, finding all inadequate.

"Mayhap," he replied, and he was gone in a flurry of snow, wind, and loosed power.

23

The faint, pleasant smell of apples and pines met Alissa as she slipped through the darkness heavy on the stairs. She would have thought it was Lodesh, had she found even one acorn since Useless had discovered her and the Warden together under the Hold. The scent was probably from the staff Lodesh had given her. She had gone to fetch it from under her bed where she had taken to keeping it lately, and she was on her way back to the dining hall. The walking stick was too long, standing well over her head. And as all of Strell's woodworking tools were out, she was going to shorten it to a usable length.

She ghosted down the last of the stairs, spurred on by the welcoming glow of firelight spilling into the great hall. Pausing at the archway, she smiled at the domestic sight. A pot of tea sat brewing on the hearth. Two empty cups waited on the footstool before the fire. Talon was dozing on the back of her chair, her favorite perch since Alissa and Strell had brought it up from storage. Strell was slumped in his chair, staring at the fire. Alissa's smile slowly faded. He looked unhappy, and she frowned as he sighed and ran a hand through his mop of dark hair. *Strell is unhappy?* she thought in confusion. *Strell is never unhappy, even when he should be.*

Twisting awkwardly, he reached deep into a pocket to withdraw a wad of cloth. He carefully unfolded it to reveal a small bit of gold lace about the size of a coin. She could see little else, but she could tell it was fragile from the tender way he held it. "What do you think, Talon?" he said. "Is there any way under the desert sun, or should I just burn it along with the rest of my hopes?" Rising to his feet, he crouched before the fire, considering the drop of gold in his palm. Talon chittered as if uneasy. "Oh, Alissa," she heard him whisper. "What will I do without you?"

Alissa froze. Eyes widening, she stepped back into the shadow and fought with her twin emotions of delight and misery. She had known Strell liked her, but to admit his emotions might go as deep as hers had seemed so senseless, she had denied the possibility. Alissa took a breath to go to him, to tell him it was going to be all right, that she would go with him to the coast, or he would stay here with her. But Useless's warning shocked her feet to stillness. She couldn't abandon the Hold; it held half of what made her alive. And Strell couldn't stay. Either of his two crafts needed people, and the nearest was a month's journey away.

Still, she couldn't stand in the great hall all night, so she straightened her shoulders and scuffed her feet loudly as she entered the dining hall. Strell jumped to his feet, one hand deep in his pocket, the other waving weakly at her. "Hey there," he called.

"Tea ready?" she asked, unable to look at him.

"I would think it probably is."

Alissa watched from the corner of her eye as he took the pot off the fire, but it was as if his distress had never existed. *He isn't that good of an actor, is he?* she wondered. But upon recalling their success in duping Bailic, she realized he probably was.

"Look what I found in the pantry!" Strell said. His voice carried a hint of forced cheerfulness as he held up a familiar cup.

"It's Lodesh's," she said dismally. She had hidden Lodesh's cup ages ago, not wanting to risk Bailic seeing it.

Strell's smile seemed to freeze. "Oh. I probably shouldn't use it then."

"No," she said. "I don't think he'd mind."

His eyes flicked from her to the cup as he poured out first her cup, then his. Still not saying anything, he took a quick sip from the larger cup. "I wish I could have met him," he said, his tone giving no indication of his mood.

Alissa knelt to tend the fire, immensely relieved that "Lodesh the Bold" was staying away from "Strell the Impressionable." All she needed was for Strell to pick up Lodesh's disarming ways. Strell was charming enough. He didn't need any help. Settling back on her heels, Alissa replaced the fire irons and gazed glumly into the bright flames. A sigh slipped from her as she settled back into her chair.

"What is it?" Strell asked gently.

"Nothing," she mumbled, hiding behind her cup. She couldn't tell him. She couldn't bear it if he should love her, and he still had to leave.

"Come on," he cajoled. "You know you'll tell me sooner or later."

"It—it's my staff," she blurted. "It's far too long." Alissa snatched the offending piece of wood from the floor as if that would make her story less of a lie than it was. With a saucy flip of her tail, Talon abandoned Alissa for the rafters.

Strell leaned forward, sending the scent of the desert to fill her senses. "So cut it."

"You're right." She jumped up, trying to distance herself from him.

"What! You're going to do it now?" came Strell's cry.

Avoiding his eyes, she nodded. "If I wait, I might lose my nerve. Mind if I use one of your saws?"

"Go ahead," he said with a puff.

Alissa slowly moved to the end of the long worktable loosely designated as Strell's. Wrapping her staff in a fold of cloth, she placed it in a vise and spun it tight. Secured as it was, she half expected Lodesh to appear and demand to know what she was doing. Talon forgave her for her falsehood and fluttered down. Hopping to the clamp, the small bird tugged on the fabric.

"It is mine," Alissa said, feeling as if it wasn't right to cut the valuable wood.

His back to her, Strell snorted and slurped from his cup.

"Which one?" she mused, looking over the myriad tools neatly laid out. There were quite a few to choose from. Strell liked tools, and he used them all, even if another would do. He kept his treasures well oiled and sharp, looking better now than when he had found them. Alissa's hand went to a fine-toothed saw with a bright red handle.

"Try the red one," advised Strell, not bothering to get up.

Shooting him a look he couldn't possibly see, Alissa grasped it and positioned herself. She gently pulled back to start the cut, wincing as she did. It didn't seem proper to mar the smooth finish. The saw slipped smoothly over the wood to leave barely a mark. Dense wood, indeed. Frowning, she tried again using more force but getting the same result. She stared at the wood, then the saw. Maybe she should use a different one.

"Are you sure you have it right side up?" Strell called from his chair.

"I know how to use a saw, Strell." With a faint feeling of exasperation, she looked to see if he was watching, then checked to see if it was tooth-side down. Once more she drew a line across the staff. Absolutely nothing. *Burn him to ash*, she thought, *Lodesh must have warded it.*

Strell chuckled, and Alissa's eyes narrowed. She looked up at Talon, who promptly closed her eyes and pretended to sleep. "Would you like to try?" Alissa asked him sweetly.

"No. It's your stick." But he got up and sauntered over to watch. Apparently he found something amusing in her struggles, and he peered over her shoulder at her lack of progress. Her lips pursed, she tried again. Still nothing, and she blew her hair out of her eyes, jumping when Strell tucked it behind her ear. "Here, let me," he said, unable to resist anymore.

"No," she said, her pulse quickening from his touch. "Like you said, it's my *stick*," and she set the blade to try again. Strell was reaching out as she spoke, and so they pulled back on the saw together, his hand atop hers.

With a loud *chirrch*, the saw bit deep. Startled, she

dropped her hands and stepped back into Strell. He gripped her shoulders tightly in order to keep them both from falling.

The scent of open skies and hot sands enveloped her, and her breath caught. Wide-eyed, she stared up at him, fighting her emotions of desperation and desire. He couldn't stay. She couldn't go. There was nothing she could say, frozen by her indecision.

"Are you all right?" Strell said, his brown eyes seeming to hold a twin emotion.

"Yes." She hesitated, not moving from his impromptu embrace. "Yes. I am."

Strell took a breath as if to say something, then slowly let it out, his gaze falling from hers. Saying nothing, he stood her upright, not releasing his strong grip on her shoulders until he was sure she had her footing.

The unmistakable scent of pine and apples had grown strong, and Alissa glanced at the black archway for Lodesh. But the aroma was solely from the wood itself. Strell shifted awkwardly from her, bending to examine the new cut. Talon hopped close, and they eyed the scoring together. "See," he said, sounding unsure. "All it took was a little muscle."

"Please," she gestured, "you do it." Miserable, Alissa stepped aside, so torn she didn't care if he could cut it or not.

Repositioning himself, Strell took the saw and drew on it. *Chirrch,* and he was halfway through with no effort at all. *Chirrch,* nearly there, and *chirrch,* he was done. The waste piece fell partway to the floor and stopped, caught by Alissa's field.

Strell eyed the length of wood hanging in midair. "Sweet as potatoes," he said warily. "That was easy."

No it wasn't, Alissa thought in dismay. *It was exceedingly unfair and probably Lodesh's idea of a jest.* Giving her a staff that was too long that only Strell could cut wasn't very nice. Thinking of a few choice words she would put in the Warden's ear the next time he dared show his face, Alissa loosened the clamp and removed her staff.

She stood it upright, deciding it came to a reasonable height. Not that she was going anywhere anytime soon to use it.

"Uh . . . Alissa?" Strell broke into her thoughts, and she turned. "Do you want the leftover?" Pointing to the length of wood still hanging above the floor, he shrugged.

"No, you can have it."

"Thanks." He reached out, and as his fingers encircled it, she dropped her field. "I'll try one more time," he said, sighting down the length of wood. "Such a pipe this will make," he breathed, striding over to his tools.

"Right now?" Alissa complained. How much worse could the evening get?

"Why not?" he said over his shoulder.

Depressed, Alissa returned to sit in her chair before the fire. She had stockings to mend and a hem that needed putting in on her latest skirt, but nothing seemed worth doing. Eyes closed, she concentrated on the flickering warmth of the flames, trying to imagine spending her evenings without Strell. She didn't know what she would do.

Strell worked for a time in silence. It was dark in the far corner, and Alissa set up a soft sphere of light over him. It was risky, as Bailic hadn't yet shown Strell this ward. But Talon warned them whenever Bailic came down. With a twinge of guilt, Alissa belatedly ran a mental search for Bailic as she had promised Useless she would, finding him safe in his room.

This ward was tricky, for light was only a breath away from her source's energy in the raw, so to speak. It was nearly the same thing she had done when she burned her tracings last fall, but now the reaction was firmly encased in a strong field and controlled by a ward. When done, or in the unlikely event her field broke, the energy would flow harmlessly back to her source through the proper channels, hardly a drop of it depleted. Never again would she make the mistake of harnessing such a huge amount of energy without a place to put it when done. Oblivious to her contribution, Strell puttered contentedly.

"Strell?" she said into the companionable silence.

"Hm-m-m?"

Alissa glanced out at the garden through a gap in the curtains. The snow had a thick, treacherous crust from the repeated thawing and freezing of the last few days. Though the accumulation had been steadily decreasing, it was apparently still too deep for Useless. "Tell me about the sea?" she mused aloud.

"The sea?" Strell stuck a stylus behind an ear.

She stretched for her cup and took a sip. "Yes. I've been dreaming about it."

Strell stopped working, set down his tools, and turned. Just noticing her light, he blinked in surprise. "Are your dreams frightening?" he asked, his expression blank. "Do they wake you?"

"Hounds, no!" she exclaimed, laughing.

"Oh." With a grunt, Strell returned to his work. "The sea is flat at times, and at others it's full of motion. It can be blue, or green, or even a dirty white, depending on the sky."

"Is it warm?" Alissa asked, her eyes shutting in her effort to picture it.

"No." Strell pulled his stylus from behind his ear and scratched a mark. "I've heard if you go far enough south, the sea warms, but the coastal people seldom go there."

Alissa shivered for some reason. "The sand is warm then."

"Sand?" he exclaimed softly. "No, it's rocky beach."

"All of it?"

He squinted, holding his progress up to her light. "Most."

"Well, the gulls fly above it, don't they?" she said dryly, determined at least part of her dreamscape was correct.

"Course," he mumbled absently.

"And the breeze is fresh and tangy, smelling of salt and purple sea plants."

"Uh-huh."

Her eyes had shut in her effort to visualize it, and she smiled faintly. There was a small scrape of noise as he abandoned the table and brought his work to the fire.

"And," she continued more confidently, "when the sun rises, it flashes green through the water."

"Uh . . . no." Strell sat down, his chair creaking softly. "But it's said if you go out far enough, weeks and weeks, occasionally you will see such a flash when it sets."

"Never when it rises?"

"No."

"Why would anyone go out that far?" she asked.

"Very big fish full of oil and fat."

"M-m-m." Alissa thought that over as Strell worked quietly in his chair. Curious as to what he was doing, she opened her eyes. "Oh!" she blurted upon seeing he was polishing his old pipe. She thought he had been fiddling with his new piece of mirth wood. Evidently, he was done for the night, and Alissa dropped the ward glowing over the worktable.

His fingers slow and methodical, Strell ran through his warm-up piece, "Taykell's Adventure." She couldn't help but smile as she recalled the first time she had heard him play it when she had been stuck at the bottom of a ravine, and she sang the words of one of her favorite verses:

> "The blushingly fair maiden,
> She had some brothers four.
> And scowling quite nastily,
> They met him at the door.
> For though her mother liked him,
> He found he couldn't stay.
> He had to charm, so to disarm,
> Or soon be on his way."

Strell gave her a quick grin and switched to a quick, sharp-noted dance tune. The fingering was too complicated, and she winced as he ceased playing it at his first mistake. Slightly red-faced, he took up a sad lament, gently filling the room with its ethereal beauty. The tune never came close to using the last note. It was mournful, speaking of loss and regret. Alissa had never heard it before, and it washed over her in a sudden tide of emotion.

"That sounds like my sea," she said with a sigh when he finished.

Strell blinked in astonishment. "It's a coastal tune telling of a young woman's regrets at having fallen in love with a seafarer."

"What's so bad about that?"

"The sea," he explained, his eyes wide and serious, "is a jealous and spiteful mistress. Those souls who hear her seductive whisper the clearest and respond to her call are often consumed by her passion, never to return to their true loves who wait for them on the shore."

Thinking she might understand, Alissa dropped her eyes from Strell's intent gaze. "Oh."

"Here, let me play another song of the open waves," Strell suggested. "I should practice them more, and you might get a better idea of the perilous beauty that makes up such a wild and tempestuous mistress. She can be so many things, one would think she would have uncountable names, not just the simple one men call her by." He lost his gaze in the fire and began to play.

Alissa sat up straighter, determined to catch every nuance of it. He had been to the coast; she hadn't. His songs were the closest she would probably ever get to it, and she was intensely curious about it these days. But Strell's playing had its usual relaxing effect, and after three or four songs, she found herself slouching. "Are there no happy songs of the sea?" she complained as he stopped to wet his throat.

"Many," he admitted, and he launched into another melancholy tune. It was simply the most sorrowful rendition of emotion she had ever heard from him, bringing tears to her eyes and stirring her with a rush of unfulfillment. She felt an aching need to go and see for herself the rolling mass of wind and waves, to taste the salt in the air, and to know that tomorrow would be nothing like today, the horizon never changing, but never really the same. She couldn't let Strell leave her! she thought suddenly. She had to go with him.

With a sharp intake of breath, Alissa realized Strell had

done this on purpose. He had chosen each song, each melody, to provoke the restlessness she was now feeling. She should be angry, but she wasn't. She would have done the same had she possessed the skill. "Strell," she said softly, her vision swimming and a catch in her throat. "I can't go."

His music abruptly ceased, his deception having been realized. "I know," he said, his voice level and centered, his eyes riveted upon the fire. "I can't stay. As soon as this game between Talo-Toecan and Bailic is over, I'll be gone."

Although his words were spoken gently, they hit Alissa hard, and she struggled to keep her breathing even. To hear it, admit it openly, made it terribly real. It was no longer possible to pretend their friendship hadn't grown into something stronger. And they would soon part ways.

Numb and empty, Alissa listened to Strell's music rise into the silence. But then his melody broke harshly, and he played nor spoke no more the rest of the night.

24

There was a gentle pull on Bailic's thoughts as the window wards went down. He was expecting it, but still it caught him unawares, and he started. No longer would the Hold see that all remained warm inside, at least not until next season's first hard freeze. The piper, he thought snidely, would have a cold night, seeing as he hadn't taught the man how to ward windows.

Setting his quill down by the remains of his supper, Bailic looked out into the dark. The soft hiss of the rain came slowly to fill his room, bringing with it the biting smell of wet stone and yellowing vegetation too long without the sun. He closed the book he was studying from, rising to stand at what was left of his balcony. Mist, damp and cold, drifted in to caress the tight scar across his neck in a soothing balm. Later he would put up a ward to keep the rain out, but now he stood with his eyes closed, enjoying the sensation on his sensitive skin. The moon would be full tomorrow. Tonight its near perfection was hidden behind the rain. He could see little of the night. He wished he could. It smelled glorious. Come morning, even the last drifts of snow taking refuge in the shadowed places would be gone, and his prison would become less secure.

Bailic brushed the beads of condensation from his long Master's vest to leave a dark stain. He wasn't worried about the piper leaving. The man's tie to the book wouldn't allow it. Bailic had watched him still its aggressive protection ward with a simple touch. It was obvious the *First Truth* had a claim upon him. Still, with the lower passes open, the temptation to take the book and run would be

strong. It was definitely time to remind the piper of his tenuous position.

Bailic had finished most of the basic wards, and still the
book remained closed. The piper's skills had grown surprisingly fast, leaping ahead to eight- and ten-year tasks
just this week. It only proved Bailic's belief that the Masters dragged their students' lessons out to prolong their
slavery. He would begin some of the more complex wards
tomorrow. It wouldn't be long before the book was open,
but encouraging his student to work all the harder would
be both productive and a pleasure. Harassing the girl
would do nicely.

Pleased with the idea of inflicting some harmless torment, Bailic sent out a thought to find them. "The scul-
lery," he muttered. "Precisely where they belong." He spun
about and reached for his tray. Taking it down would be a
convenient excuse to visit the kitchen. He had never returned his trays before, but he felt the need for a reason to
enter their domain.

Bailic froze, his hand outstretched. Burn him to ash!
What, by the Wolves, did he need an excuse for? The Hold
wasn't theirs. Fighting to keep his anger in check, Bailic
stormed out and down the stairs. A frown twisted his lips
as he reached the open walkway above the great hall. It
was cold without the window wards, but that wasn't what
bothered him. It was the thin, white ribbon stretching in
graceful curves from one end of the great hall to the other
along the outside of the railing on the fourth-floor walkway.

"I should have taken out the rings," Bailic said, fingering the loops of metal hammered into the stone that the
ribbon was draped through. Divesting the fortress of its belongings had given him a sense of control over the ancient
stones. The Hold's seasonal banners had gone into storage
the morning after he imprisoned Talo-Toecan. Seeing them
up again made him feel as if something had shifted without his knowing. Even the color was right, white for the
melting snow.

Brown for furrows churned, Bailic thought, slipping

into the simple rhyme he had learned as a student. Green for solstice turned. Red for the first frost / White for winter's loss. Gold for dreams realized / Blue for my true love's eyes. Bailic frowned. Or green, or brown. Occasionally gold if a Master sang it. It was never pink.

"Talo-Toecan must still be having tea with the little wench," he growled. How else would they know white was the proper color—and had been for the better part of four hundred years? Even the timing of its appearance was right. Only a Master could have guessed the window wards would fall tonight. The ribbon hadn't been there yesterday. To have hung it earlier would have been bad luck.

Bad luck. Bad luck. The words hammered at Bailic as he stomped down the remaining stairs. Apparently he had allowed his guests too much freedom. They were starting to undo his careful assault of the Hold. Their domain, indeed! Thoroughly disgusted, he stepped to the floor of the great hall, stopping stock-still as his shoes tread not upon stone, but fabric. He looked down in disbelief. It was too dark to see properly, but he knew by the familiar give beneath his feet that the large rug depicting the ever-changing path of the sun had been replaced. His pulse pounded, and he took a calming breath before he strode into the dining hall.

"Great stars above us!" he gasped. He hadn't been here in weeks. The room was nearly back to its original state. The tables were out of place, but everything else was nearly perfect. Everything was as it had been almost twenty years ago: the floor coverings, the drapes, the small table before the hearth, even the picture hanging above the fireplace, the one done all in blue that gave him the shivers. How had they known? It was perfect.

Almost, he seethed. There were two chairs before the fire instead of the traditional one. "And the smell—of mirth wood," he whispered, forcing himself to relax as he breathed deeply of the pleasant aroma. It was everywhere, mixing with the musty, earthy smell of the garden that ghosted in with each billow of curtain.

He knew the scent well as his Keeper status had allowed him to possess a rather large piece of it, nearly as long as his finger. It had been on a chain around his neck until a Keeper he briefly "entertained" one afternoon ripped it from him, claiming he had no right to it anymore. In his rage, Bailic forgot to take it back before literally burning the Keeper to dust.

The fire was only a tongue of orange, and he slipped through the gloom to the table to investigate. It seemed the piper was making something, as Bailic could discern the shapes of saws and drills. Wood chips littered the floor, and he scooped up a handful to bring to his nose. "Yes," he whispered. "It's mirth wood." Shavings of it were lying about as if it were a common wood to be shaped and worked. With a shock, Bailic realized the plainsman was using mirth wood to make a pipe. Where did he get enough for that?

The answer was obviously Talo-Toecan. It wasn't a breach in their contract, but it was close. Bailic's eyes rose to the archway leading to the kitchen, the flame shadows cast by the cooking fire flickering upon it. The chips fell slowly through his fingers, clattering down in a cascade of rustling fragrance.

"Listen to that rain, Strell," he heard. "The window wards have fallen." There was a masculine comment and the noise of water splashing followed by a feminine shout of dismay.

"Piper!" Bailic barked in frustration.

The laughter and splashing ceased. "In the workroom?" Bailic heard, then, "I'll see."

The lanky silhouette of the piper appeared in the shadowed archway, followed shortly by the smaller form of the kestrel. The agitated bird hovered until Strell raised a hand to provide her with a perch. Together they stood, blocking the way. "Yes, Bailic?" the man said, keeping his mutilated hand behind his back.

Bailic sneered, glad to see that lesson had been learned. "You will meet me in the garden tomorrow," he said on the spur of the moment.

"In the rain?"

"It won't be raining tomorrow, Piper."

Strell nodded suspiciously. "Why outside?"

Bailic looked Strell up and down disparagingly. "I'm going to attempt teaching you the difficult task of shifting the source's energy to that of light," he said. "I simply don't want to have to scrape you from the walls if you get it wrong."

"It's that dangerous?" Strell's eyes grew round.

"You will arrive well before sunup," Bailic continued, stepping to stand toe-to-toe with the surprised man. He wanted to torment the girl. It was the reason he had come down here. "I want to see how bright a light you can manage."

A worried frown crossed Strell, and his eyes grew vacant.

"Early, Piper," Bailic growled, "or I will roust you out from beneath your warm covers myself. Now, *get out of my way!*"

There was no ward behind the command, but Strell stepped aside, seemingly dazed by Bailic's demand of an early meeting. "Wait!" Strell cried as Bailic whisked past.

But it was too late, and Bailic strode into the brightly lit kitchen with a satisfied air. He stopped short, giving Strell a black look as the annoying man almost crashed into him. "Where is she?" Bailic muttered.

Water was standing upon the floor by the abandoned sink, half full of dishes. In the center hearth, a cooking fire burned low and even. A teapot hissed over it. The room was suspiciously lacking the girl.

Bailic's fingers drummed against his crossed arms. He sent a thought to find her, but her hiding spot was so close, it seemed as if she were still in the room. Perhaps in the garden . . . Well, he wasn't going to chase after her in the rain. His hand slapped on the table in disgust, jolting the bird into motion. The wicked thing flew to one of the unused hearths and fluttered over nothing until she finally settled upon the mantel. A chill took Bailic as she glared into space. Then she turned her anger to him and hissed, all her feathers raised.

"Tell the girl we will be meeting at the firepit," Bailic said, his eyes riveted to the bird. "She already knows where I expect her to put the breakfast tray." With a last suspicious look, he spun on his heel and left.

"Something isn't right," he muttered as he crossed the dark hall. "I don't like this, not at all."

25

"Strell," she whispered, then rolled her eyes. Why was she whispering? The whole idea was to wake him. Alissa moved to his hearth to see if any of his coals lived through the night. She shivered as she cupped her hands close over the small spot of orange she unearthed. It was cold without the wards—they had fallen last night—and in the dim glow of the predawn, she looked about Strell's sparse room.

He had never done anything to change his quarters as she had, and there was little to mar the stark, stone walls. With the exception of the crack in the wall, his room looked nearly the same as when they found it. Alissa felt slightly ill as she realized he could leave at a moment's notice and there would be nothing to show he had ever been here. Grimacing, she turned back to Strell. He had buried his head in his blankets, and he looked nearly immovable. "Strell." She stood up and dusted her hands. "Your lesson."

"Uh?" came his muffled groan.

She gently shook his shoulder. "Come on," she demanded. "I told you that second pot of tea last night was a bad idea."

"Uh." He rolled over, her proddings beginning to have an effect.

"I'm getting my hat," she threatened. "If you aren't up when I get back, I'll—I'll . . ."

"You'll what?" Strell mumbled, his eyes open but by no accounts focused.

"I don't know," she huffed, "but you won't like it."

"Uh-h-h-h."

With a final harrumph, Alissa left to open her shutters. The thought of her room remaining stuffy as the rest of the Hold was being swept clean of winter's staleness was intolerable. The shutters creaked open, and Alissa leaned out into the icy stillness that spilled in to pool about her feet. There was a bright twinkle of a fire burning in the pit in the garden. Alissa pulled herself back in, not liking Bailic in her classroom.

She snatched her hat from the bed—she had finished it yesterday; it matched the one she had given Strell perfectly—and returned to Strell's room. Peeking hesitantly around the open door, she wasn't surprised to see he hadn't moved. "Hey!" she shouted, her hands on her hips.

"I'm up!" He jumped, his eyes flashing wide and unseeing. "I'm awake." Rubbing his stubbled cheeks, he sat up and swiveled until his feet touched the cold floor. His bare toes poked out from under his trousers, and Alissa hastily spun around, flushing.

"I'll wait in my room," she said, watching him from the corner of her sight.

"Whatever suits you." He held up two mismatched stockings in the semidarkness. Then realizing they weren't on him yet, he tucked his feet back under his covers.

Alissa couldn't help her grin as she returned to her room, pleased to find at least one moral conviction ran the same from plains to foothills. Knowing he would be some time, she settled herself cross-legged before her fire to practice her latest diversion.

Her breath eased from her in a slow sigh of concentration as she formed a field just above the low flames. Bailic's ability to use fields to sculpt dust was incredible, and Alissa had spent the better part of last month trying to figure out how he managed it. All her fields came out as spheres. She had some success by overlaying one field upon another, thereby giving it the illusion of a different form, but the more fields she had up, the harder it became. It would be years before she could maintain more than a handful at any given time.

But she kept at it. Not with dust, though. That had given

Strell a bad case of farmer's fever. So instead, Alissa used the flames of a fire. She hadn't told anyone, especially Useless. It wasn't breaking her word as he had given her permission to explore fields freely, but somehow she didn't think he'd approve of her playing with fire.

Alissa made her field as permeable as possible without it falling completely apart. It was difficult, much more so than making an impervious field, and it was only her incessant practice that made it look easy. The shape of her thoughts became apparent as a tongue of flame curled up the top of the field. Feeding upon itself, the fire's heat filled the entire sphere to make a fist-sized swirling globe of red and orange. It was a useless trick, she thought, but pretty. Alissa overlaid a second sphere partway through the first, and the flame reached higher than normal, channeled by her field. On a good day, she could hold four fields at once.

There was the small scuff of booted feet, and Alissa looked up as she let the fields collapse in a wash of guilt. Strell couldn't be ready so soon! But he smirked good-naturedly from the door. "Hounds," he said around a yawn. "What time is it? The middle of the night?"

Alissa's eyebrows rose as she took him in. "You haven't shaved."

"Later, later," he said, rubbing the prickly looking stuff. "Can't keep Bailic waiting. He's already in the garden. You can see the fire from my window, and nearly hear him grumping, too."

Alissa rose, relieved he hadn't noticed the odd shape of her fire. "Let's go then."

The predawn sky showed only a lighter blackness through the occasional window, doing little to light their path down the dark stairwell. It didn't matter. The way was as familiar to her as the trails about her parents' farm.

"Where's Talon?" Strell asked as they reached the walkway overlooking the great hall.

"Kitchen. We ladies have been up long enough to make rolls."

Strell grunted, giving her a nod. "Mind if I make dinner

tonight? I've got a meal I want your opinion on. It's kind of a tradition in my family. Made entirely with carrots to honor the new season."

"Hounds, yes. I'd love it," she gushed, then paused. Everything made from carrots? What kind of tradition was that?

"Talon," Strell called as they entered the kitchen. He looked up at the rafters, and the bird dropped to land upon his wrist. "What did you catch this morning?" he murmured, sending a thin finger across her age-faded markings. Talon hopped to Strell's shoulder, settling herself by his ear where they compared whispered notes. Alissa shook her head in amusement as she checked the breakfast tray.

Strell yawned as he shrugged into his coat and reached for the tray. "I'll take it."

Smiling her thanks, Alissa grabbed three cups. Much to Strell's disappointment, she prudently left Lodesh's cup behind. Strell would have to make do with, as he called them, Talo-Toecan's thimbles. "What a beautiful day it is," she exclaimed quietly as she opened the garden door and Talon launched herself into the freshly washed heavens.

"Is it?" grumbled Strell. "It still looks like night to me."

"Don't be such a goat," she said cheerily, her gaze going deep into the clear, transparent-seeming skies. "Spring is here. Can't you see it?"

"It's too dark," he groused. Stifling another yawn, he hunched deeper into his coat.

Alissa gave him a friendly shove and moved eagerly ahead, the toes of her shoes quickly going damp. She should have put on her boots, but she hadn't been able to find them, and she really didn't care; the morning was so grand.

Now that the snow was gone, she would begin to see what surprises Useless's garden would provide. As overgrown and neglected as it was, there were bound to be a few delights among the weeds, and she itched to get her hands dirty in the finding of them. The warm, coastal rain had finally made it over the first of the mountains last night, leaving behind only soft, black earth. Even the ground was thawed where the sun had been upon it yesterday.

"Good morning, Bailic!" Alissa called happily as they rounded the bend.

His head jerked up—he was clearly startled at her pleasant voice. Strell seemed surprised as well, and he gave her a long, questioning look before he set the tray down. The clinking of the dishes sounded comfortable and right among the dripping branches and long, wet grass.

"Morning," Bailic returned cautiously, apparently not knowing what to make of her cheerful disposition. He turned to Strell, who, Alissa would admit, looked half dead, as he was unshaved and still in the rumpled clothes he had on last night. "I'm glad to see," Bailic continued, "at least one of you is prepared for the day's lesson. Unfortunately, it's the wrong one."

"I'm here." Strell slumped heavily onto the bench. Balancing her roll on the rim of her cup, Alissa retreated to the farthest corner of the pit. The sun was on the peak rising high above the Hold, turning the gray stone a marvelous gold. She could almost see the light creeping down the mountain, growing ever closer to the fortress. Soon it would reach her room to fill it with the strong spring sun, warming the old stones to life.

"Set up your primary loop, Piper," Bailic said, jolting her from her reverie. "You'll eat later."

Alissa reluctantly brought her attention back from the faultless skies. It only took a moment to do as Bailic demanded, but he continued to drone on and on about field strengths, and proper channels, and the perils of setting them up incorrectly. She ignored him, as did Strell.

Just as well Strell wasn't listening, she thought. Bailic wasn't explaining it very clearly. It was obvious he wasn't confident in the process. She just wished he would get on with it. As if responding to her desires, Bailic's globe of light blossomed into existence to throw the shadows from the firepit. "Oh!" she exclaimed, remembering to be impressed.

Strell looked up, half a heartbeat behind. He, too, looked convincingly awed by the light.

"You see," Bailic said, a patronizing lilt to his voice. "It's difficult, and it uses a lot of source, but it does impress the commoners."

Alissa frowned at his last words and looked to see what tracings Bailic was using. Her source was barely touched when she created a ward of illumination, and she couldn't imagine even Bailic would be so miserly over such a minuscule loss of strength. Well, no doubt, she mused, finding a long stick and poking it into the soft earth. He wasn't using the most efficient paths. All that waste. No wonder he used candles instead of his skills. His source would be depleted within a matter of years.

Then she recalled what Useless had said about broken paths and fragmented neural nets. This was obviously the case here. It was a wonder he could create the tricky ward at all. Rather ingenious actually, and her estimation of the pale man begrudgingly went up. The ward was hard enough without the handicaps he had to circumvent. Something near to pity went through her, and she shifted, not comfortable with applying the emotion to Bailic.

"You see the resonance?" Bailic said, and Strell nodded. "Then try it," the pale man demanded as his light vanished.

"I'm—uh—not sure I have it," Strell said uneasily.

Alissa's eyes rose to Strell. Perhaps he thought she hadn't been paying attention, and so she cleared her throat to let him know she had been listening.

"Sand and wind," Bailic griped. "You're slower than a beggar with a full belly."

"I don't want to make any mistakes." Strell's jaw clenched. "You said it was dangerous."

Alissa thumped her heels against the side of the bench. A ward of light dangerous? Maybe, but not if you knew what you were doing.

"If it makes you feel better, close your eyes." Bailic arched his eyebrows. "Well?" he mocked, almost looking eager for Strell to make a mistake and turn them all to ash.

"Give me a moment." Strell frowned and closed his eyes. His elbows were propped up on his knees, and his head dropped into his hands.

Alissa quickly set up the proper paths, and her containment field snapped into existence as the cold pathways filled. Immediately there was the eerie sensation of being in two places at once as the intricate pattern existed simultaneously in her thoughts and in the field. Unlike most wards, this one required constant maintenance; it remained securely connected to her conscious until disengaged. The sensation of vertigo faded not because the ward left her thoughts to make the leap to her field, but rather because it became overshadowed by the impressions from her other, more frequently used senses. A soft glow enveloped them just as the sun reached the Hold's roof.

"Good," Bailic grudgingly admitted, his confidence in Strell's nonexistent abilities restored. The man frowned up at the Hold. Alissa could imagine his thoughts were in the same vein as hers. It wouldn't be long until the sun reached the garden, and the lesson would be over.

"Drop your ward and begin again," said Bailic, his eyes fixed to creeping beam of light. "Implementation and dissolution are more important. Maintaining is easy."

Alissa licked her fingers clean of the last of the sticky rolls and did as he asked. The glow of her light mixed with that of the rising sun, illuminating the outskirts of the firepit. *Crocus!* she silently exclaimed as she spied a small bit of yellow peeping from beneath a barren shrub. Glancing at Bailic—who was watching the encroaching light—she decided she could investigate. It was well within a raku length. The last thing she wanted to do was to step out of range and have that resonance fade.

A delighted smile stole over Alissa as she touched the small flowers in a welcoming caress. They were cold and silky. Bending low, she noticed the stiff leaf of an iris poking up bravely from crowded roots half exposed.

"Make it brighter," Bailic said ingratiatingly, and Alissa did, not bothering to turn around. Moving to a nearby tangle that was once a flower bed, she knelt, feeling her knees grow damp and cold. She didn't care. The earth was coming alive again, filling her with a deep sense of purpose and peace. Her hands went willingly to dig the choking weeds from the soft, new growth hidden amongst last year's dead-looking clumps of vegetation.

"Brighter," she heard distantly, and she made it so.

Alissa knew from sad experience her fine new clothes would be ruined with the dark stains of soil. She couldn't help it. When she saw disorder, she lost all sense of responsibility. Her clothes were her best no longer, and she didn't care.

"Phlox?" Alissa whispered, puzzling over a familiar-looking leaf before clearing a large swath of weeds from around it. It was sensitive at times of pushy neighbors.

"Thyme." She nodded confidently at the tiny leaves already emerging from the tougher, main branches. She ran a gentle finger over the tenacious herb. This one would need no help from her, and she smiled at it, wishing it well.

"Brighter, please," Bailic said, all but forgotten, and so it was.

"Mint!" She beamed, and knelt down where it was, overwhelming a nearby patch of something she couldn't identify yet. Brimming with a vengeful enthusiasm, Alissa bent low and ripped out great handfuls of the aggressive plant from around its gentler companions. The smell of fresh spice rose up, and she nearly burst with her happiness. It was spring at last, and she willingly surrendered herself to the dirt and soil, content to set the small space by the firepit to rights as Bailic silently watched.

26

"Good," Bailic grudgingly admitted as the piper's sphere of light winked into existence. "Drop your ward and begin again. Implementation and dissolution are more important. Maintaining is easy."

Bailic glanced at the light creeping down the face of the Hold. He didn't want to be in the garden when the sun found the small patch of earth he was standing on. "Make it brighter," he commanded of the piper, who was slumped with his head cradled in his hands in concentration. Bailic shrugged his coat closer. It was cold, and the acidic smell of ice rot caught in his throat. Once he found the man's limits, he would call it done, retreating back to his fire and books.

He was almost done with deciphering that second volume he had found explaining the effective use of fear and superstition as a tool. He was eager to reread it. It was obviously the Masters' benign strategy for keeping the masses out of the mountains, but he imagined it could be used to drive them from their homes as well—if used properly.

He sank down on the bench, stiffening at the expected cold of the stone. As he watched, the girl abandoned them to muck about in the dirt. She was getting her clothes dirty, Bailic thought with a smirk. *You can take the girl off the farm . . .*

A slight noise drew his attention to the long row of silent windows where the Keepers once had their quarters, and he gazed at them, frowning. Something was different. The sun shone strong, illuminating the shutters on Meson's window so well it seemed as if Bailic's fuzzy sight had cleared. One of them hadn't been fastened properly, and it tapped an irritating, broken rhythm against the wall in the freshening breeze.

Bailic stared at it, his brow furrowing. Meson never had shutters on his windows. No one did. They weren't needed. Once the Hold dropped the window wards for the coming summer, everyone made their own as needed or got someone else to do it if they weren't skilled enough. That was why Bailic replaced the ward in the piper's room that he had blown out four months past. The wards had fallen just last night. There hadn't been time to make shutters. Why, Bailic wondered, did the girl have shutters on her windows?

Shifting slightly, he looked at Strell, silent and unmoving in his deep concentration. "Brighter," he said quietly, and the small, but well-constructed sphere doubled in its intensity.

A cold sensation slipped through Bailic as he realized he had never checked Meson's old room for damage the night the Hold shivered to its foundations. But how many times had he listened to Meson moan and gripe about the injustice of having to share a chimney with the room next door? The force could have easily blown out both their windows by going through it. That would mean the force the piper had manipulated was tenfold stronger than what Bailic estimated.

His breath quickening, Bailic went to stand beside Strell. Could the man be sandbagging, Bailic wondered, capable of far more than he witnessed? Bailic watched him take another slow breath. So relaxed! he thought in alarm. How could he be so relaxed when he was channeling enough source to burn out his entire network? Then Bailic heard a slight sigh, and he bent closer.

"He's not relaxed! He's asleep!" Bailic whispered wildly. He straightened, a stab of fear slicing through him, leaving him open to the icy breath of doubt. *Who?* he thought. *Who is making the ward?* For it couldn't be the piper, not asleep as he was.

Bailic sent a frantic thought out, searching for any presence besides himself, the piper, and the girl. His mental search was more accurate than his vision, but he also scanned the skies for the golden menace he feared was behind the ball of light. But the heavens were clear of beast and cloud, and he sagged in relief. *It isn't Talo-Toecan*, he thought. *That only left . . .*

"The girl?" He winced, turning to her small figure bent low over the slushy muck. It couldn't be her! She wasn't even listening.

"Brighter, please," he whispered, and the sphere glowed brilliantly, almost rivaling the sun. The form kneeling in the mud held no sign of the concentration needed to perform such a task, but someone was working the ward. He watched as, with a happy sound, she shifted her attention to a patch of mint. She began tearing out great masses of it as if ridding the world of a great injustice.

Not caring if the sun burnt him, Bailic edged closer. Running his hands nervously down his Master's vest, he methodically calmed himself, making his mind blank to examine his tracings for the telltale signs of resonance. With the true beginnings of fear, he found no answering glimmer in his thoughts. None at all.

Bailic froze. Whoever was making the ward was using a pattern he didn't have. He had discovered in his earliest, and ironically, bloodiest interviews with peers unwilling to share their secrets, that every Keeper varied in the way their tracings were connected. These differences were apparent in only the most complex and therefore seldom-used tasks. That was why no one had realized it, and their Masters never felt the need to tell them. Resonance only occurred when a perfect match for the ward in question was found. Whoever was working the ward had a more precise network. They were potentially stronger but not necessarily more cunning.

"But the girl?" he whispered. It was unthinkable he could have misjudged so badly. Deathly still, Bailic watched her continue her weeding, oblivious to the dangerous thoughts that raced through his mind.

"The piper wears Keeper garb," he asserted, still wanting to deny the truth. Bailic stared at the girl. "But she made his clothes, right in front of me, and I never noticed." She, he realized, was the one who blew out the windows and cracked the Hold's wall, burning herself into the death state that he brought her back from. She recovered the book from the well where Bailic assumed her companion told her it lay concealed. She had shared tea with Talo-Toecan, leaving him thinking it was nothing more than a report of the piper's progress. *She,* Bailic snarled silently, *is creating a ward that is so bright, it casts shadows stronger than the sun!*

It is her, he realized, the depth of his folly crashing down upon him. Then, the blissfully content figure of a slight girl raised her face to the sky, adjusted her new Keeper's hat, and smiled at the sun. For the first time, Bailic saw his young guest in the full morning light, and he saw, with no uncertainty, the color of her eyes.

"They—are—not—blue," he seethed. "They are gray, as were her father's!"

Thick fury roared through him, shocking him with the violent, smothering wash of black rage. His face twisted as he stiffly moved to stand before the oblivious girl. With a violent shudder, he shackled his deadly emotions, a part of him amazed at the strength needed to turn them aside, wondering where he had found it. He consoled himself with the thought he would be able to give them free rein soon enough. He had been manipulated badly, but he realized his mistake in time. The piper would pay for his interference, just as Talo-Toecan's student would suffer for her audacity, but not yet. There was a book to open, and he had just found the key.

Clenched to an unbearable tightness, he leaned close. "Well, my dear," he rasped, and the girl spun as if having forgotten he was there. Her eyes grew round as she took in his anger.

"W-what?" she stammered, and she shifted to rise.

Bailic lunged, twisting her arm behind her back, forcing her to remain where she was. "No you don't," he whispered harshly into her ear. "We have an appointment to keep, you, me, and a good book. You know the one, don't you, Alissa Meson?"

27

"Strell?" Alissa squeaked; her throat had gone too dry for more. Bailic pulled up sharply on her elbow, and pain shocked through her. Gasping, she bent low to the ground to escape it. The fresh smell of mint rose to fill her senses. Her light winked out of existence.

"Ah, ah, ah," Bailic admonished. "Let's not wake our dear minstrel. He looks so-o-o-o tired." There was a twinge upon her awareness as a ward of what she prayed was only sleep settled over Strell. From habit, she looked to see what tracings were used. Bailic frowned at her intent expression. "You are the clever one," he said bitterly, seeming to know what she was doing. "But apparently not clever enough." He roughly pulled her up and spun her about to look her in the face. "You see he is under my field?" he spat.

Alissa's heart pounded as her eyes flicked to Strell and back, unwilling to look from Bailic for more than an instant. He knew. Bailic knew. Nothing could save them now.

"He's mine," Bailic threatened. "Don't try anything, my dear, or he will suffer for it. Everyone who underestimates me is dead. No need for you to join them yet."

She thought back to Bailic's rapt expression when he had incinerated Strell's finger, and her knees nearly buckled. Bailic was insane. He would kill Strell with no compunction.

"Yes." Bailic pulled her closer, his pale eyes narrow and tight. "You finally understand. And look closer. See that connection between your piper and me, formed by my field and ward?"

Silently she nodded.

What do you suppose that is?" he asked lightly, his face twisting.

She licked her lips. "I—I don't know."

"You don't know." He smiled indulgently. "Let's just say, if I die, he dies, too. So don't try any tricks Talo-Toecan may have taught you."

"Useless!" she called silently in her thoughts, only now recalling him.

"Come on," Bailic said, and she gasped as he yanked her arm so hard her hat fell off. "There's something you need to do."

"Useless!" she thought again as she stumbled into motion. If he was too far away, he might not hear. Bailic didn't seem to notice, for which she was thankful, but neither did Useless.

From the tangled brush came the soft call of a songbird. It was answered by its mate, and for a moment the two carried on a gentle duet, standing in dark contrast to her own desperate situation. Alissa's pulse grew fast. She had to get away. He was going to force her to open the book. It was hers! Bailic couldn't have it! Twisting suddenly, she struggled to break free.

"Stop it!" Bailic hissed, pulling her tightly into him.

Terrified, she gave a violent lunge, stomping on his foot. He let go in surprise. Alissa scrabbled across the sodden earth on all fours, only to find her feet pulled out from under her as she tried to rise. Her face went into the mud, and she bit back a muffled cry as her chin cracked into the ground. Tears welled up from the pain.

"I said, stop," Bailic whispered coldly, his knee on the small of her back. "I'm not going to warn you again. The next time, the piper suffers."

"You wouldn't dare," she countered boldly into the ground. "You have an agreement!"

"My agreement?" He snorted. "That old raku finally made a mistake." Bailic bent so close his breath shifted her hair, and she stiffened. "The arrangement ends the moment the book is opened. I'll be free to do whatever I want with you. Talo-Toecan has no way of knowing when the book is opened. You," he smiled as he pulled her back to her feet, "were never as secure as you thought, and now your piper is dreaming his last dreams."

She stared at him, fear knotting her stomach.

"His life hangs upon your cooperation. If you fail me," he said, beginning to drag her to the kitchen door, "I'll kill your piper as you watch. I assure you, it will take some time and be very degrading. It's been a while since I've tortured anyone, but it's not the sort of thing one forgets how to do."

With a savage kick, Bailic pushed the door to the kitchen into the wall with a resounding crash. They entered the silent, empty room in a clatter of muddy shoes and stumbling feet.

"I'd wager you all had a good laugh over it, didn't you? Poor old Bailic," he raved as they crossed the dining hall. "Can't see the first thing before him, all this time blinded by the distractions of a commoner!"

She was helpless to do more than stumble behind Bailic as he hauled her up the stairs. Her thoughts wove frantically between her need to escape and her need to protect Strell. Bailic held her more tightly in his poisonous grip than he might realize—or maybe he did.

"Talo-Toecan thinks I'm a fool," Bailic spat, his face twisting as they reached the fourth-floor landing. "He has been tutoring you all winter! Right under my nose!" Jaw clenched, he reached out a pale hand and tore her white banner from its moorings. She watched it writhe down to make a gentle contrast on the enormous rug she and Strell had wrestled into place yesterday. Her and Bailic's muddy tracks showed strongly upon its soft, muted colors. "I haven't taught that man a thing," Bailic raged. *"You've* been doing everything! *Everything!"* he shouted, applying a savage pressure to her arm and twisting it far beyond its usual span of movement.

"Ow, ow! Stop it. Bailic!" she cried as she half knelt under the pain.

"Useless!" she screamed into her thoughts. *"He's taking me to the book!"*

Enraged, Bailic spun her onto the floor. As she sat there, clutching her bruised arm, she silently heard Useless's frantic answer, and she nearly cried out in relief.

"I'm coming," she heard. *"Don't open it, Alissa, whatever it costs. We aren't prepared."*

"You're a lying, half-breed, slattern," Bailic growled, and he lunged. Panicked, she skittered backwards, managing to avoid him for all of two heartbeats. But for all his frail looks, he was stronger, and he caught her as easily as Talon catches a grasshopper.

"Filth from filth. No better than your mother," he muttered as his fingers dug into her shoulder and he dragged her to her feet. "All this time it was you. Your piper was very clever. He had convinced me, but—he—fell—asleep!" Beginning to laugh hysterically, he halted, trembling. "You were betrayed by the one who tried to protect you!"

No, she thought as Bailic pulled her up the stairs. It was her fault, losing herself in spring as if she were safe at home. And with that, her situation became irrefutable.

She was at home.

Her parents' small farm in the foothills was her birthplace, and for her first years, it had been her home and school. Now the Hold was her home, and she would die here, very shortly.

"Useless. Please!" she cried silently in despair. *"Bailic linked himself to Strell. I can't use an impervious field, or Strell dies, too. Please! We're almost there."*

"I'm coming," came Useless's firm thought. *"Don't open that book. You won't be able to contain it. I'll lose you to the beast."*

Stumbling, her shin hit the stair, the pain going all but unnoticed in her fright. She reached out a hand to stop her fall, and Bailic yanked her up, impatient at their faltering progress. *"I don't understand,"* she sent wordlessly.

"I'm sorry," Useless whispered into her mind. *"I thought we would have more time. I was going to explain. . . . I tried to begin."*

Bailic halted suddenly, a mere flight from his room. Gazing at Alissa with a mix of hate and avarice, he grew frighteningly still. Alissa's breath caught, and she stiffened in terror. "I would wager," he speculated mildly, "that you have a source. You must have one." He leaned close, and she tried to back up, hitting the stairway's wall. "That explosion last winter had to have been supplemented. "Tell me," he crooned, "did Talo-Toecan let you bind it, my dear, or is it still—vulnerable?"

"It's beyond your reach, Bailic," she whispered, half crazed with the fear he might know a way to tear it from her.

Snarling, he jerked her up the last few steps.

"Useless!" she shrieked in her thoughts as she saw his open door.

"Just use the accursed field, Alissa!"

"I can't," she sobbed, and Bailic shoved her across the threshold. The tingle of Useless's own ward, perverted to Bailic's use, heralded her arrival. She was trapped. Catching herself against a table, she took a shaky breath, leaning heavily on it. He took a step towards her, and she shifted to put the table between them. Her wide eyes never left his as she felt her way around it. Behind her, a chair hit the back of her legs.

"I actually asked you to help me," he said and shoved the table into her. Knocked off balance, she sat down in the chair as he had planned. Her heart pounded as she looked frantically for a way to escape.

Now in his room, Bailic seemed to slow, taking the time to rub the dirt from his knuckles with a cloth. Alissa's eyes dropped to her hands. They were clenched in a white-knuckled fervor, and she forced them apart. *"Useless, please hurry,"* she begged. *"He will kill Strell."*

There was no response, and Alissa began to think she was alone. Then, almost she could believe closer, was his thought, *"Soon."*

"Don't feel too bad, my dear," Bailic said as he dropped his rag. "Your father couldn't outfox me, either." He leaned closer, his elegant features softening in a mock sadness. "He was a two-faced, back-stabbing, foothills devil, and I killed him, too."

She swallowed hard. "I know," she said with a quavering voice, stalling for time. "Talo-Toecan made me relive it, to try to scare me away."

"What!" The word was sharp, and she jumped, hating herself for the small gasp that slipped from her. "Talo-Toecan allowed you to relive a memory? Of your father's? I waited for years to be shown that skill. He never—"

Horrified, Alissa watched his eyes go black as his pupils grew large, and his hands, stiff at his sides, clutched spasmodically. He looked to the ceiling and tensed. She shrank back, trying to put more distance between them, even if it was only a finger's width.

"No," he groaned, closing his eyes. "It will wait," and with a wracking shudder, he turned away. Now his manner shifted to the other extreme, and his shoulders drooped. Slowly he spun on a heel. A small sound slipped from Alissa at the smile he had taken. "Relax, my dear," he all but sighed, moving to a shelf. "Let me find a little light reading for you. You do read, don't you?" He chuckled. "If not, well, the piper has lived an exciting life, if not a long one."

"*Useless,*" she whispered, feeling the beginning of the inevitable end grip her.

"Perhaps this will help you decide?" Bailic said as he brought forth her book and placed it softly before her. Alissa's heart seemed to stop. Reeling from the shock of having it so close, she nearly passed out. A feeling of separation overtook her, and she stared hungrily at it, her breath coming fast and shallow.

"*I have claimed you,*" the book whispered in her thoughts alone. "*You have claimed me.*"

"Useless," she moaned. Her fingers twitched and reached, and she felt her will to resist begin to slip gradually away.

Bailic grinned, sure of his victory. "Yes, it's useless to resist, so why try? Open it."

"Alissa, no!" Useless pleaded in her thoughts, almost unheard.

"We have waited long enough," the book crooned into her thoughts alone.

"You're mine," she breathed, and she ran a finger over the latch. With a small sound, the metal clasp parted. A warm tingling began at her fingers. Her vision blurred. Her breathing became shallow.

"I am what will make you unbroken," the book nearly sang through her mind.

Bailic bent low. "Open it," he whispered urgently, his breath a warm touch on her cheek.

"Alissa!" Useless called frantically. *"I won't be able to bring you back!"*

"Now," the book commanded.

"Now," Bailic breathed as her fingers ran below the heavy leather binding.

"Now," she agreed, and uncaring of the consequences, she opened the *First Truth*.

28

B ailic reached for her book with a triumphant cry.

"Don't," she said sharply, and he stopped, frozen where he stood over her. She had used no ward; his surprise halted him. A silver glow had flickered into existence about the book, and as Alissa sent her fingers to brush over the fine tracings of print, the light played about her fingertips like ripples in a still pool. Dabbling them in the silky sensation, she identified the glow as a thought or memory given substance. The words on the page only served to contain the memory, much as a field gave a ward a place in which to act. She smiled with a quiet satisfaction as she realized she didn't need to read the book. She could live it.

Bailic's frustrated presence hovered over her shoulder, rightly afraid to touch what she had claimed. Her book wouldn't stoop to speak to him. He had to be content with the printed word. Besides, she thought smugly, he couldn't begin to understand.

And with that sentiment, Alissa abandoned herself to the book's memories, allowing them to freely enter her own. A wave of warmth rose to become her world, bringing a gentle lassitude. It was the first lesson, and she absorbed it as a dark rock absorbs the summer sun.

"It's nonsense," she heard Bailic's distant whisper.

"No," she sighed, unable to stop herself. "It's heat." And she sank deeper into the drowsy, alert state, the scent of broken rock thick in her senses. "It's hot sand, butterfly wings over dry, summer grasses, sunbaked cliffs, clouds of moisture, and the rain that falls from them."

"Alissa," came Useless's unwelcome voice echoing in her mind. *"Stop. Be content with the first lesson."*

"A candle flame on a moonlit night," she continued, ignoring him, "the wind over the water, and the spinning of the earth and stars."

"It's energy," the book explained needlessly, *"in its most humble of forms. No matter what state it takes, it's the same. At rest. In motion. It's always the same."*

"Yes," she whispered, familiar with the concept. It had been a common thread binding her lessons at home. "I see what it is."

"I don't understand," Bailic muttered, and at the sound of his voice, her heightened awareness dimmed until she remembered where she was. Opening her eyes, she ran her finger past the unseen but not unrealized pages, skipping to the next lesson. Alissa felt the memories her fingers touched turn gray, and the shimmering glow surrounding the book shifted to a pearly translucence. It did nothing to obscure the single word upon the page before her.

"Substance?" Bailic said. "What kind of wisdom is that?"

The last remembrance of heat slipped away, and Alissa shivered. It was replaced by a sensation of presence, not a person or even a thing, just a lack of nothing. "Substance," she repeated as it enfolded her in its vast strength and her eyelids drooped of their own accord. "What a small word for so large a concept."

"Explain it," he demanded, his voice thick with irritation.

"I'm almost there, Alissa," came Useless's thought, grating upon her.

Uncaring of her imminent rescue, Alissa let the pearly gray thoughts slip freely through hers. "It's the air," she explained to Bailic, safe in the knowledge he would never grasp the significance. "It's the earth. It's you and me. It's what makes up the trees that flower and bear fruit, but not the light that gives them life. We're all made up of the same material, just put together differently, and it can be changed." This, too, was an idea that had run through her earliest schooling, so fundamental and basic, it hardly seemed worth repeating, but the book made it so clear, she knew it would forever change the way she perceived even the simplest thing.

"*Yes,*" the book agreed. "*Go. You're almost there.*"

Dazed, Alissa turned to the last page. It was blank. The book's thoughts turned from gray to black. Her fingers resting on the page appeared to be lost in a night so dark as to be impossible.

"What does it mean?" Bailic demanded.

Bewildered, she stared at the obsidian page, smelling the cold of old snow. "I—I don't know."

"*Thank the Master of us all,*" came Useless's intruding sigh.

"*Come,*" the book whispered seductively. "*You know enough. I will show you the rest.*"

Useless's cry of anguish was almost unnoticed as Alissa met her book's invitation with a resounding, "*Yes!*" As soon as her answer was uttered, she was overtaken by a feeling of perfect disconnection. There was nothing to see, or feel, or even comprehend. As if blowing out a candle, her world vanished. It was almost Death, but having seen the dark maiden once, Alissa knew it wasn't. Even so, it was only Alissa's will that kept her from crossing to join her. "*What is it?*" she asked her guide, unable to even speculate.

"*This? This is time,*" came its unshakable answer. "*All that has been, all that might be, can be seen from the now. You simply have to know—how far back to look.*

"*All three are related,*" the book asserted. "*Can you see this, energy, mass, and time?*"

"*Yes,*" she answered, knowing exactly how they were related. It was so simple once shown.

"*And one is in essence the same as the other?*" it continued.

"*Yes.*"

"*Then I give you the first truth. You decide what it means. Energy,*" it lectured, "*can be transformed from state to state, but in the doing, nothing can be allowed to*

*be lost or added. Mass is much the same in its own fash-
ion, changing function, but not its most basic form. And
time? Well, time is relative. It's what you make of it. Control that, and you can shift between the two brothers of energy and mass."*

"You mean by using my tracings?" Alissa thought in
disbelief.

"Yes," the book responded, somehow sounding devious. *"Use your tracings to manipulate the constraints of
time, and you can turn your mass to energy and back
again."*

"But what good is it?" she asked, seeing clearly the
how, just not the why.

"Try it." The book seemed to chuckle in her thoughts.

"Try it?" Alissa repeated, becoming even more confused.

"Try it . . ." came its taunting whisper.

"Try it," she said aloud as her world slipped into existence in a rush of color and sound. She felt out of breath,
and taking a gasp of air, Alissa snapped completely out of
her dreamlike state. The book's thoughts were lost, returned to the pages of her now quiescent book. Its work
was done and it called no more, but she remembered.

The ebony glow surrounding her book faded to gray,
then silver, then flickered out of existence. Staring at the
book, she wondered why Useless was so concerned. This
knowledge wasn't enough to harm anyone. Most of it she
had known already.

Bailic lunged across the table, pulling her book from
her slack fingers. Clutching it to himself, he backed to his
desk, his eyes wild. "What does it mean?" he shouted, all
but incoherent.

Oddly unconcerned, Alissa gazed up at him, calm and
centered for what she thought was the first time in her life.
She didn't need the book anymore. Its lessons had been engraved into her very essence. The heavy sense of peace it
had instilled in her was difficult to shake off.

In the expectant hush, there was a small *ping* of something hitting the floor. What looked like a small, gray coin

had fallen from the binding of her book. It bounced twice and rolled to her feet, circling in noisy, ever-narrowing rings until it fell onto its side with a clatter.

Alissa's hand automatically went out to pick it up. Barely bigger than her thumbnail, it sat lightly in her palm. It glistened a soft gray that, even as she watched, turned a luminescent gold from her warmth. Examining it in the profound stillness, Alissa frowned. It looked familiar, teasing from her the memory of the scent of birch seeds and mud—and her papa.

"What is it?" Bailic said, huddled in the corner with her open book pressed against him.

Squinting, Alissa held it up between her finger and thumb. The sun glowed brilliantly through it, and she smiled at the pretty little thing. Then she remembered. Her papa had tucked it there, just before he left to return the book to the Hold. He hadn't known what it was, either.

"Take it," her book taunted, *"in an impervious field as you did your source. Bind it to your being. Quickly! Before you lose your chance!"*

"Alissa. No!" Useless shouted in her thoughts, and from outside she heard the passage of his wings.

Like a child caught with her hand in the cookie tin, Alissa grabbed her treasure and made it hers, loath to, as her book had said, lose her chance. Her impervious field cracked into existence around it, and she stiffened and gasped. "No!" she shrieked as her entire network awoke. Every channel hummed with the energy explosively released from her source. She hadn't done it. It was out of her control, and it burned like ice but didn't destroy. Destruction would have been a blessing compared to this.

"It hurts! Please, make it stop!" she silently screamed, and then collapsed. Her last sight was of Bailic, clutching her open book to himself, his face a mask of utter astonishment.

29

Bailic froze as the slight frame of Alissa stiffened. Her eyes grew wide as if in shock, and her mouth opened in a silent scream. Then, with a soft sigh, she collapsed onto the table. He hesitated, not trusting this at all. Drumming his fingers upon the back of the book, he moved a cautious step closer, wondering what, by the Wolves at the Navigator's heel, had just happened.

Her explanation of the book's contents had confounded him. Though the pages were full of the raku's script, she had lingered on only the first ornately written word of each section, skipping the pages between. He hadn't even seen the final page, obscured as it was in the eerie blackness that enveloped both the book and her fingers resting upon it. It was as if his eyes refused to acknowledge anything was there, sliding away with a greasy feel. And then she turned to him with that contented, self-assured look he recognized from his younger days as a student. Her attitude was reminiscent of a Master of the Hold, and it had shaken him.

"What a Keeper you would have made," he said, edging to where she sat crumpled as if she had fallen asleep at her studies. Placing the open book on the table, he leaned over it. "It's a shame you didn't take me up on my offer." He tilted her head, looking for any likeness to her mother, finding it in the shape of her cheekbone and the length of her lashes. "But I can't suffer you to live now. Someday your experience will give you the upper hand." Gently, regretfully even, he turned her face to the table again.

So intent was he on his thoughts, he almost missed the

sudden absence of sunlight spilling over the floor. The shadow was accompanied by the smallest sound of scraping stone from the broken balcony. But it was only when Talo-Toecan shifted that Bailic fully realized he wasn't alone. He snatched the open book to him and scrambled back until he slammed into the wall. "It's mine!" he shouted, unable to keep his voice from cracking in fear.

"Drop it, and you're ash," Talo-Toecan said tersely. All but ignoring him, The Master strode to the girl. A fleeting look of distress passed over him, appearing out of place on the stoic, sedate bearing Bailic's old instructor always showed the world.

Bailic hesitated. This wasn't what he had expected. To be dismissed as if he was no threat was infuriating but also disconcerting. His confusion was multiplied threefold as a smartly attired man in Keeper garb appeared in the doorway to his room. There was the scent of mirth wood, and Bailic ground his teeth. He was rapidly losing control of the situation.

"It's time then?" the stranger said, giving Bailic a secret, sideways grin.

The Master looked up. "She was completely unprepared. I've served her badly."

"Ah," the man replied cheerfully. "It may yet work out."

"Who," Bailic snapped, "are you?"

Talo-Toecan stooped and picked up the girl, cradling her easily with her head slumped upon his chest. "We must get her from behind these walls," he said, ignoring Bailic.

"Stop!" Bailic shouted. "You broke your word, Talo-Toecan. No one," he threatened, "is going anywhere."

The man whistled in surprise and spun round on his heel. There was something akin to astonishment in his eyes. Talo-Toecan looked up as if aware of Bailic for the first time. "The book is open," he intoned. "The agreement is ended."

Ended! Bailic thought wildly, struggling to push his fear aside. He had forgotten, but he still had the book. Talo-Toecan would have killed him already if he felt confident there was nothing to lose by doing so. The game wasn't over yet, and Bailic tightened his grip on the ancient tome, knowing it was the only thing that kept him breathing. "If you kill me, I take your precious book and the piper with me."

"Don't count yourself safe, Bailic," Talo-Toecan said coldly. "I simply don't have the time to rip your throat out at present. I'm here for the child. You have *never* been of any consequence." Talo-Toecan dismissed him with a contemptuous look and stepped to the door.

It had to be a ruse! Bailic thought frantically. He was alive and untouched. The beast had to be bluffing. "Stop!" he demanded. "She's mine."

Talo-Toecan whipped about. Hatred glinted behind his eyes, and recognizing it, Bailic blanched, feeling a sweat come over him. "Lodesh," the Master said, his eyes never shifting from Bailic's. "Take Alissa out."

The elegant figure received Alissa's limp form with an almost imperceptible bow. There was a last grin at Bailic, and the man stepped over the doorframe. The whispered sound of his feet faded. Outside, the courting birds broke into glorious song. It went all but unnoticed as Talo-Toecan, now empty-handed, focused his entire being on Bailic.

"The ward on my sill," Bailic stammered, "it's broken?"

"Aye, not merely dismantled as when you found it." The Master's eyes flicked to the book in Bailic's grip. "I'll deal with you later. I'm busy now, but know Alissa is not yours."

"She is!"

The Master's eyes narrowed. "You misunderstand. I'm not bargaining with you. I'm telling you. She—isn't—yours. Nor the piper," he continued, "nor even her bird, whom I have secured lest she sully her nails trying to tear your eyes out. I'm through with you—student. Go scrape the front steps free of moss as penance for your transgressions." Talo-Toecan turned his back upon him, gazing past the shattered balcony into the spring morning.

Dismissed like an errant schoolboy, Bailic stood, trembling with rage. *Student, indeed,* he seethed. *Scrape the front steps.* Talo-Toecan ranked his ambitions as a student's prank. "You may be through with me, winged demon," he said with a snarl, gripping his book with a white-knuckled strength, "but I'm not done. Hear me, beast? I'm not done!"

"Get out," Talo-Toecan growled, not turning around.

Bailic left. Stumbling through the muck of spring, he went east to Ese Nawoer, cursing the mud that weighted his feet, cursing the sun that burnt his skin, cursing the fact he had no horse, but most of all, cursing that whore child of a foothills girl. The book was an awkward load, heavy to begin with, but matters were made worse because he carried it open. He knew that to shut it meant his death; its protective influence would end. But his anger gave him strength, and it wasn't until he was amongst the chill, shadowed streets of Ese' Nawoer that he slowed, his footsteps hissing to shocked stillness with what he found skirting the edge of his awareness.

They were here, he thought with a thrill striking deep within him. The souls of Ese' Nawoer. And they waited for direction; he could feel it. Like the scent of sand-scoured lightning after a desert storm, he could feel them, and their guilt and despair filled the chinks in his hate until it was strong again.

Bailic's laugh echoed from the buildings until it sounded as if the city laughed with him, mocking and triumphant, full of ironic failure and last-moment treachery. Let Talo-Toecan mourn over his last Keeper like a woman over spoilt soup. He had a city of dead to raise.

"Come, then!" he cried into the faultless sky. "I'll be ready for you, Talo-Toecan!"

30

"Talo-Toecan?" Lodesh called. "I've found the piper!" Jiggling impatiently, he waited as his longtime friend descended on wing from his rooms to the garden below. Lodesh glanced worriedly at Strell. The gangly man was under a ward of sleep, sitting with his head cradled in his hands. If the afternoon went as Lodesh thought, the piper would be sorely tested today—as would they all.

In a swirl of gray, Talo-Toecan shifted to his human shape and stepped to the firepit where Lodesh had arranged Alissa on the bench in the sparse shade of an overgrown, leafless shrub. "I will have to fumigate," Talo-Toecan said around a sigh.

Lodesh straightened in astonishment. "Beg your pardon?"

"My room." The Master slumped onto the bench, showing all his 855 years. "You saw it. Ink stains on my desk. The furniture has been replaced with that horrid, stiff wood. All my unwarded papers and books have been rifled through." Disgust twisted his face. "He stacked wood in my bedchamber to the ceiling. I'll never get the slivers out." Talo-Toecan gestured weakly. "His writings, though . . . It's a shame. Astounding ideas. But he wanted to implement them dangerously fast—and for all the wrong reasons."

Quite sure he wasn't comfortable with the direction the conversation had taken, Lodesh cleared his throat, and when Talo-Toecan looked up, he nodded questioningly at the piper.

"Let him sleep," Talo-Toecan said. "He will gain nothing by watching Alissa go insane."

Lodesh smiled faintly. "She may yet best the beast. Don't lose her until she's truly lost." Snatching her hat from the weeds, he tucked it under Alissa's head as protection from the damp. It looked new, cut to the traditional Keeper style, and his eyebrows rose. If it was Alissa's—as it must be with that sprig of mint tucked in the band—this might have been what gave them away.

Shrugging, he seated himself at the fire, stretched in the sun's warmth, and closed his eyes. A shutter banged in the wind to shatter the peaceful quiet, and he cracked an eyelid at it. "We still need a third," he reminded the despondent Master. "As you say, two have no chance, but with three, we might hold her until a way can be found to return her awareness."

"It's a very thin maybe," Talo-Toecan grumbled.

Lodesh sat up, interested again. "Can you remove Bailic's ward?"

"I taught it to him," the Master said. There was a small resonance across Lodesh's tracings as the raku broke Bailic's hold on the piper. Strell stirred, rubbed his chin, and looked up, blinking profusely.

"My," Lodesh quipped, running his eyes over Strell's rumpled clothes and stubbled cheeks. "Rather a scruffy looking fellow, isn't he?"

"Talo-Toecan?" Strell said, his voice cracking. "By the Wolves. What are you doing here? Where's Alissa?"

With tired-looking eyes, Talo-Toecan pointed out her small figure on the cold bench. Strell rushed to her side, skidding to a halt, his hands outstretched, seeming not to dare touch her. "Is she all right?" he asked frantically.

Talo-Toecan sighed. "No."

"Bailic! Where's Bailic?"

"On the road to my city," Lodesh said, not pleased at how much the piper cared for her. Strell wasn't the only one who liked the young woman, but Lodesh wouldn't push his own claim until she remembered him.

Strell ran his gaze over Lodesh, clearly confused. "Who are you?"

Lodesh concealed his feelings with a hard-won expertise. "Talo-Toecan, how much time do we have?"

The Master glanced at Alissa and frowned. "A bit. Knowing her, it won't be long."

Smiling, Lodesh approached Strell. "Then allow me to introduce myself. I am Lodesh Stryska," he gave Strell one of his extravagant, citadel bows, "Keeper of the Hold and Warden of Ese' Nawoer." Taking a half step back, he regarded the dazed piper with an amused expression.

"You're Alissa's Lodesh," Strell breathed, his eyes darting from Lodesh's ring to the city's seal around his neck, and finally to the silver flower embroidered on his shirt.

"Aye, most assuredly Alissa's."

Strell flushed as if having forgotten his manners. Clearing his throat, he inclined his head slightly. "I'm Strell Hirdune, the last of the family once carrying that name, Keeper of nothing, Warden of even less." Grimacing, he met Lodesh's proffered palm with his.

"Hirdune!" Talo-Toecan rose from his seat. "That's the erratic line Keribdis has been trying to erad—"

"Hirdune, Hirdune," Lodesh interrupted, looking at the sky. "I've heard that name before. Ah, yes," he exclaimed, brightening. "My youngest sister, the headstrong snippet, ran off with a man from the coast by that name. A craftsman of some sort, away to make his fortune."

Talo-Toecan stopped short, clearly unaware that Lodesh was trying to distract the piper. "Lodesh," the Master said. "You're jesting. There's no Hirdune in your ancestry."

"I'm sorry," Strell apologized. "It must be someone else. I'm from the plains, and my family has been gone these seven years."

"No." Lodesh rubbed his temple, lost in thought. "It was, oh, three hundred eighty-eight years past—I believe."

Strell blinked.

"Warden," Talo-Toecan warned. "Has he not suffered enough?"

Grinning, Lodesh clapped Strell on the back. "Sit down. I'll explain." He took Strell by an elbow and led him to the bench. The piper dragged his feet, seemingly loath to leave

Alissa. "We have time," Lodesh assured him. "And we can sit so as you can see her."

Though obviously unconvinced, Strell sat, perched on the edge of the bench. Talo-Toecan resettled himself as well, poking at the fire with a short stick, his fingers almost amongst the coals. Lodesh eyed the two cups with their cold tea, and mumbling of thimbles, made a cup of his own. "Would you like some tea?" he inquired lightly.

Talo-Toecan sighed in exasperation, and Strell jumped to his feet. "Tea?" the plainsman shouted in frustration. "Do I want some *tea*? I want to know what's going on!"

"Piper," Talo-Toecan grumbled, "sit down."

"No! I have *sat*. I have *listened*. I have watched as things progressed until—" With a tormented cry, Strell sank down. "It's all my fault," he whispered. "I fell asleep."

"You fell asleep!" Talo-Toecan pulled away from the bright embers, his eyes glinting dangerously.

"Right in the middle of Bailic's lesson, and now she's dying," finished Strell, his expression haunted and empty.

Lodesh's gaze shifted from the incensed Talo-Toecan to the piper. "No one said she was dying," he interjected.

"She's not?"

"Here." Lodesh shot a warning glance at the raku, who was muttering voiceless threats under his breath. "Let me explain. Talo-Toecan uses such big words, it makes my ears hurt. There's nothing you can do right now," Lodesh asserted gently as Strell gazed at Alissa. The emotion-filled look of the piper wasn't wasted upon him as it was on Talo-Toecan, and Lodesh felt a stab of shared sorrow. "As you guessed," he said as Strell met his eyes, "Bailic finally made the correct assumption."

"I fell asleep," Strell said with a moan.

"Yes, you fell asleep," Lodesh said sharply. "It's done. Let it go. It was a miracle the deception lasted this long." Faintly, he added, "Be glad it wasn't fear or cowardice that betrayed you." For a moment there was silence, broken by the trill of a bird convincing his ladylove of his charms. "Anyway," Lodesh continued as the serenade ceased,

"Bailic gave her the *First Truth*, and push gave way to pull."

"I still don't understand," Strell whispered.

The plainsman looked so confused that Lodesh couldn't help but smile. Turning to Talo-Toecan, Lodesh set his cup down, placed his hands quietly in his lap, and formally asked, "May I give him the knowledge of what has passed?"

The Master grimaced. "Might as well. I don't expect we'll survive to speak of it again."

Strell paled. "I didn't know the book was that dangerous."

"It isn't," Lodesh said dryly. "He's being histrionic." Talo-Toecan's eyes narrowed, and Lodesh leaned toward Strell. "Can you keep a secret?" he whispered, and Strell stiffened in surprise.

"Lodesh . . ." Talo-Toecan said in annoyance.

"Well," he exclaimed, his eyes wide and wondering in mock concern. "I had to take a blood oath. Shouldn't he be under *some* kind of obligation?"

Talo-Toecan regarded Strell tiredly. "We don't have trappings for a blood oath. And I think our good piper will know to keep his mouth shut."

"Really?" Lodesh said with a false innocence.

"I will hunt him down if he breathes a word to anyone not already wise to it—providing we survive, of course."

Strell gulped. "I promise. Just tell me."

Giving Strell a sidelong glance, Talo-Toecan threw his twig into the flames. He looked at Alissa, then back to Strell, clearly waiting until he was sure the man was listening. "Not all rakus are sired as such," he said, his golden eyes locked upon the piper's. "A rare few, usually the most inventive, the most headstrong, are born to man; only later do they find their wings."

Strell's face went slack, and he began to blink slowly.

"There you go again," Lodesh complained, slapping his knee in disgust. "Always starting at the end, never the beginning."

"Alissa isn't a Keeper of the Hold?" Strell whispered.

"No, not anymore," Talo-Toecan admitted. "She never really was, actually."

Strell gulped, seeming unable to say the words. "She's a . . . a—"

Lodesh jumped to his feet, unable to contain himself. "Yes, my good man!" he shouted. "She's a Master of the Hold. A dreamer of the skies!" Taking a grand pose, he made an elegant flourish towards Alissa's small, mud-smeared shape. "A golden menace," he continued, "that sends terror through the hearts of the bravest men." He paused. "She will be—a raku."

"She always has been," Talo-Toecan interrupted, shaking his head at Lodesh. "Being a Master isn't a state of being but a state of mind, quite literally. Alissa was born human with a neural pattern commensurate with that of a raku's. She just needs a push to become one fully."

"Uh . . . How?"

Lodesh grinned at the disconcerted piper. "It was Talo-Toecan's book." Then he turned solemn. "Are you sure, Talo-Toecan? You really want him to know the entirety, not that drivel you usually feed your students?"

Talo-Toecan gestured absently, his gaze lost in the fire.

"Very well." Lodesh refilled his cup. Glancing at Alissa, he decided she was too unaware to notice a resonance, and he chanced a warming ward. He took a long pull at the steaming tea smelling of cloves. Setting it down with exaggerated care, he cleared his throat. "The *First Truth*," he began, "explains how to change matter to energy and back again."

"Like—when you use your source and tracings to make a cup?" Strell guessed.

"Um, yes." Lodesh looked cautiously at Strell, genuinely surprised at the piper's matter-of-fact attitude while discussing matters that, to him, were considered privileged information known only to Keepers and those who taught them.

"I told you," came Talo-Toecan's tired voice. "He knows too much already. He may as well know it all." Plucking a twig from a nearby bush, he began rearranging the coals. "Alissa has no sense of circumspection, none at all."

Shrugging, Lodesh continued. "Making a cup is the basic concept. It's a relatively simple task to draw from your source and bend it to your will to form matter. Any Keeper worth his source knows at least one something to make. "

Strell gestured to Alissa. "So this happens often?"

Busy with the fire, Talo-Toecan harrumphed, and Lodesh chuckled. "No," he said. "A set of tracings such as hers is begot from mankind only once every raku generation. Alissa has the ability to go beyond the simple shiftings of matter and energy. She can do it to herself." Expecting Strell to be impressed, Lodesh settled back on the bench and regarded him with raised eyebrows. "It sets her above Keeper status," he added.

"Herself?" Strell mumbled, his eyes vacant. "Why would that be any more difficult?"

"Well," Lodesh hesitated, "there's a problem. Transforming one's own substance to energy and back to mass again is an all-or-nothing affair. Once begun, there's nothing left to hold one's essence, one's soul if you will. It's only when possessing a highly intricate set of tracings that it's possible. Even then, I understand it's difficult." He glanced at Talo-Toecan with a knowing look. "You must have a very strong will to maintain your existence for even the breath of time it takes to fashion mass about yourself again, giving your spirit a place to reside."

"She will go mad," Talo-Toecan said to no one in particular.

Strell shifted, running an uneasy hand through his hair. "You do this, Talo-Toecan," he said, "and you don't go mad."

Lodesh snickered. "I know many who would argue with you over that, Strell."

The Master acknowledged Lodesh's comment with a long, slow look. "I was sired a raku," he explained. "My first shift was to a human form."

"I see." Strell sighed.

Realizing the bedraggled man hadn't a clue, Lodesh added, "It's only the first time that there's any danger. The slate is wiped clean and must be reconstructed. Talo-Toecan learned as a stripling. His first shift was from a young raku into a small child, and as you may know, there isn't much difference between a small child and a beast."

Talo-Toecan looked up in irritation, paused, then thoughtfully nodded his agreement. Taking a deep breath, he added, "She will be as a true beast, Strell, with only the barest recollections of her past. We must remind her of her humanity and force her to destroy what she has awoken, thereby ensuring it never gains control again. The sooner the better, for the longer she remains such, the less likely she will remember at all."

"How long?" Strell breathed, his face lined in torment.

"If she flies under starlight, the lure will be too strong. They never come back from that," Talo-Toecan said stoically. In the silence, the songbird trilled and was, in turn, answered.

Lodesh watched Strell stiffen, gaining control over his fear with a slight tremor, burying it deep as Lodesh had done himself so many times in the past.

"May I sit with her?" the plainsman asked in a whisper.

Talo-Toecan stirred. "Yes. But as soon as she begins to shift, I want you over there."

Strell's eyes followed Talo-Toecan's pointing finger. "There?" he questioned. "What can I do way over there?"

"She will be a great deal bigger, Piper," Talo-Toecan grumbled. "You want to be closer? Fine. Just be sure you don't back up any farther than that when she tries to eat you."

Strell swallowed. He went to kneel beside Alissa, brushing a wisp of hair from her cheek with a tenderness so obvious, it was painful. Lodesh steeled his features into impassivity. Rising, he beckoned Talo-Toecan out of earshot with a subtle gesture.

"It was nice of you to give him hope," Talo-Toecan muttered as soon as there was enough distance between them and the piper, "but it might have been kinder to have told him the truth."

Lodesh went straight to the crux of the matter. "How many successful first transitions have you heard of without using the holden?"

"From young raku to human? Uncountable. We use the holden more from tradition than need. A wild, human six-year-old is no match for even one Master. Fear alone keeps it from running, and sentience is quickly returned. But a first shift from adult human to adult raku? None."

"But," Lodesh continued brightly, "in theory it can be done. You only need to keep the beast grounded until you can return them to memory."

A wave of pain washed over Talo-Toecan. "Keeping a feral raku grounded is impossible. I tried to save Connen-Neute. I wasn't enough then, and I was younger."

"You were alone but for me and Redal-Stan. The sun was setting," Lodesh reminded him gently. "There was no way to save him."

"That's what I'm saying!" Talo-Toecan said bitterly. "Don't you understand! I—am—alone. I have no idea what I am doing. Keribdis won the lottery to oversee such an event, with all the combined skills and strengths of the Hold at her disposal. I know I have made mistakes in Alissa's schooling, but, blood and ash, Lodesh, I can't even say what they were!" He looked to the sky. "I'm an architect," he whispered, "not a nursemaid."

Lodesh was unconcerned. "If you can ground her, I can help keep her there."

"How?" Talo-Toecan barked, looking at Strell crouched mournfully over Alissa.

"She won't get past me, old friend, if you can ground her."

Grimacing, the raku seemed to accept this on faith. "We need at least three to have even a chance," he said dismally.

"Don't discard the piper so quickly," Lodesh warned softly.

"Be reasonable," Talo-Toecan cajoled, his eyes never

leaving Strell. The piper was whispering something, his shoulders hunched. "She will snap him in two," he predicted wearily.

"I think not."

The hint of warning in Lodesh's voice seemed to finally catch Talo-Toecan's attention. The Master looked sharply at Lodesh and then back at Strell. For the first time, Talo-Toecan appeared to see Strell's distress and what his presence might portend. "Is their bond already so deep then?" He frowned. "I had hoped to prevent it from forming at all."

"I deem that it is. It may be strong enough to bring her back."

Talo-Toecan shifted uneasily. "I don't like this. If by some miracle her awareness returns, she will be a student and Master of the Hold. I mean no offense, but she cannot be allowed to chain herself to him. If he were a Keeper, perhaps, considering the lack of suitable suitors and her background, but there isn't a breath of cohesion to Strell's neural net. He is a commoner, Lodesh. A commoner from an erratic line half the Hold has been surreptitiously trying to wipe out because it doesn't beget the traits their books and charts predict."

Lodesh's pulse leapt, and he struggled to keep his face neutral, but his heart nearly sang. Talo-Toecan would allow a match between a Master and Keeper! And Strell was neither. Steadying his thoughts, he calmly asked, "Would you rather she turn feral?"

"No, of course not." Talo-Toecan's gaze was riveted upon the two young people. "But she will far outlive her chosen partner. Once given fully, a raku's fancy is unwavering."

"I don't think they will care," Lodesh said.

Talo-Toecan sighed heavily. "No. Not at first. But the years stretch intolerably when you're alone—with only your memories to sustain you."

Silently they watched Strell sit helplessly over Alissa. "So what do we do?" Lodesh asked quietly.

"We wait."

"How long?"

"Not long."

Lodesh arched his eyebrows. "How can you know? The last such as her was before even your time."

"I'm her teacher. She is a precocious little thing. It won't be long."

The songbirds filled the garden with the joy of their certain future. A chill breeze slipped through the bare branches, bringing with it the scent of damp earth and growing things. It would have been pleasant if not for the terrible ordeal to come.

"Ah," Talo-Toecan murmured as he slowly moved to sit. "I'm too old for this."

31

Slouched at the firepit, Lodesh lazily opened one eye. He had settled himself in the sun to doze, knowing Talo-Toecan would warn them when Alissa was close to waking. To his left was Strell, slumped helplessly over Alissa, apparently not noticing the dampness of his knees or the cold turning the rims of his ears a bright pink. The Master, Lodesh harrumphed, didn't look much better, having arranged and rearranged the fire until his fussing had nearly put it out.

There was a small sigh, and Strell rose. "Isn't there anything we can do?" the piper whispered as he settled himself beside Lodesh. Strell's eyes went to his mud-covered knees, and he covered them with his hands.

Talo-Toecan looked up from his fire. "No. It's too late. It was the moment she opened my cursed book, and matters were made tenfold worse when it gave her that bit of nail."

"Nail?" Strell's eyebrows rose. "What nail?"

Lodesh chuckled. "The one hidden in the book, of course." Ignoring Talo-Toecan's sharp look at having said even that little, Lodesh sat straighter. The piper deserved to know. Perhaps a distraction was in order. "What I don't understand," he asked, "is how your nail and that book managed to become so dangerously close together."

Talo-Toecan tugged his coat straight. "It wasn't my fault," he fumbled. "I gave it to her father, a token to him before I left on my last sabbatical. I didn't know he was going to put it in the book, and besides, Meson's line wasn't being groomed to produce such as her. It shouldn't have mattered they were together. Apparently there wasn't enough research into her mother's genetic history—or someone made a mistake. And after I realized Alissa's potential, I was under constraints and couldn't recover it. Besides," he muttered, "the book attracts the tools it needs to accomplish its ends. If it hadn't been my nail, it would have been someone else's lost baby tooth fallen between the cracks of the floorboards."

"And this nail of yours is doing what to her?"

The Master harrumphed at the accusation in Strell's voice. "My nail is doing nothing. It's a catalyst. She bound it into her being, and now she is awakening a second, dormant code that lies buried deep within her. The information inherent in my nail will supplement hers, repairing any defects or gaps that may exist."

Wincing, Strell rubbed at his eyes.

Lodesh felt the corners of his mouth quirk. Talo-Toecan was being most generous with his information today, but he ought to at least try to make it understandable. "What he means is Alissa is polishing up the guide she will use to create her mass when she shifts. It will be a hybrid, a fairly equal mix if you will, of her own latent instructions and Talo-Toecan's, but only because it's his instructions she's using. Any Master's would do."

There was a soft grunt as Strell accepted that. A profound quiet settled, broken only by the birds, oblivious to the trials of men and raku alike. Into the hush, Lodesh began to chuckle. Talo-Toecan turned, his eyebrows arched in question. "I see nothing funny, Warden," he said.

Lodesh grinned. "Congratulations, Talo-Toecan. You have a daughter!"

"Very amusing, Lodesh," Talo-Toecan said darkly.

Strell turned to the Master. "So she can become anything?"

"No," Lodesh interrupted. "In theory she could, but anything but a raku or man would lack a complex enough set of tracings with which to shift back. She would be stuck as whatever she was."

Talo-Toecan tilted his head at Lodesh with a questioning surprise. "You seem very informed for a Keeper."

"And Bailic knew this would happen?" Strell interrupted in an obvious attempt to keep to the topic at hand.

Talo-Toecan shook his head. "No," he said firmly. "No one but a Master would know, and now you."

"But, Lodesh . . ." Strell stammered.

"Ah—Lodesh is a Warden of Ese' Nawoer," the Master said. "Many Keepers have read the *First Truth*, but only the Wardens are told of its real purpose. Unless the book claims and speaks to you, it's page after page of hard-to-decipher equations and untestable theories."

Strell's eyes grew wary. "So why tell the Wardens?"

"It's a courtesy, Strell," Lodesh said solemnly. "A show of respect, and we guard the wisdom jealously." The arrangement had begun long before Lodesh agreed to its stipulations. The knowledge had only one purpose: putting the leaders of the frail, short-lived humans on a more equal footing with the Masters.

Nodding slowly, Strell glanced to Alissa, his worry obvious. "You said we will have to keep her on the ground. With a ward?"

Lodesh shook his head. "That would be a mistake. Although a beast, she will still have her tracings. She won't recall them upon her own, and to remind her of them will give her another weapon with which to escape. She will be hard enough to catch without giving her the arsenal of tricks she has been exposed to already. No, the beast must be destroyed using only our cunning and physical strength."

"Are you sure?" Strell pressed.

"It was tried," came Talo-Toecan's tired voice, "long ago when it was realized a shift from human to raku was possible. The resulting chaos was said to be so horrific, it precipitated the loss of almost all concerned." Talo-Toecan shuddered, trying to disguise it by leaning to shift the fire. "Without the holden and the luxury of time it provided, I don't see how we can prevent her loss." His twig was abandoned to the flames where it caught and began to burn.

Lodesh leaned back and stretched in the sun, enjoying its warmth pressing down upon him. His medallion glinted, sending flashes of light to be lost in the muddy garden. Slyly, his eyes closed. "Why ever did you destroy the holden anyway, Talo-Toecan?"

It was a seemingly idle question, but upon hearing it, Talo-Toecan shifted noisily upon the bench. "I—um—lost my temper," he mumbled.

Lodesh opened one eye. "You lost your temper?" he said in a carefully contrived voice that practically oozed astonishment.

Talo-Toecan refused to look up. "You eat vermin and drink nothing but condensation for over a decade and see if you handle your sudden freedom any better."

"Bailic's dungeon?" Strell cried. "That's the holden? You tore the gate off!"

From beneath his half-lidded eyes, Lodesh watched Talo-Toecan, who, oblivious to Strell's growing anger, shrugged. "It wasn't meant to hold a Master after sanity was restored," Talo-Toecan said. "But it was deadly effective. I've had enough trouble from one-way doors."

Lodesh silently watched and waited. His simple and idle questions had been neither. He had successfully administered to a city of thousands. It was seldom his words were as thoughtless as they seemed. Knowing Strell had voluntarily taken the entirety of the blame of Alissa's fate, Lodesh acted to even it out. Talo-Toecan must take his share of the fault, and Strell should be the one to force him to do so. The question was, Lodesh thought, if the piper had the courage to call the imposing Master on his mistake. If he didn't, then Alissa was lost. For if Strell couldn't face Talo-Toecan's wrath, he couldn't hope to survive an encounter with the beast Alissa would soon become.

"How could you!" shouted Strell, rising from his seat. "You've practically condemned her by your lack of—of—restraint!"

Both of Lodesh's eyes opened wide. This was better

than he could have hoped for. The piper had enough bravery for two men. Either that, or he was extremely stupid.

Talo-Toecan's head came up, his eyes going from surprised, to irate, and finally choleric. "You *dare* question my actions?"

Although he turned several shades paler, Strell held firm, his jaw clenched.

Stiff and angry, Talo-Toecan rose. His imposing height bested Strell's by only a few finger widths. "I," he accused, "was not the one who fell asleep."

"Well, I wasn't the one who destroyed the one thing that would have ensured her sanity in a fit of temper!" Strell shouted back.

"I didn't know her potential at the time!"

"Even so!"

Talo-Toecan nearly choked on his outrage.

Sensing they would soon come to blows, Lodesh cleared his throat. An all-out war wasn't what he had intended. The piper would lose, badly, and he had to be alive to be of any help. Still, the exchange needed to take place or the resentment of blame would fester in their memories, forever coloring their futures. Now it could be forgotten. "Excuse me," he murmured into the tense air, "but if you two are going to bicker over who is more at fault, I'm going to leave."

Neither heard him, and Lodesh was the only one who noticed Alissa had disappeared in a swirl of pearly white. "She's shifting!" he shouted, and Strell and Talo-Toecan spun, their anger dissolving into dismay. In a breath, Talo-Toecan leapt from the pit and shifted as well.

"Quick! Move around, Piper," Lodesh warned, but it was too late. In a breath, Alissa's form swirled, grew, and solidified. Lunging across the pit, Lodesh grabbed Strell and roughly pulled him to safety. The two men stared up in awe at the shimmering vision of supple grace before them.

The beast, for in no way was it Alissa, swiveled her head to look at them. Lodesh could see no awareness in her gray eyes, and he felt Strell shudder, undoubtedly recognizing it as well. Though Lodesh knew it was impossible, he had hoped that Talo-Toecan would have been wrong, that Alissa would awaken as herself, but he couldn't find a glimmer of recognition in her eyes. They were Alissa's, but lost, overwhelmed by the beast she now was. Delicately she cocked her head and looked to the sky.

Talo-Toecan began a low, warning growl. The vibrations could be felt clearly as they shifted the fresh, clean air. Ignoring the larger raku, she stretched like a cat, her muscles sliding smoothly under her shimmering, golden hide. Wings unfurled, she shook them slightly as if testing the air.

"Hounds," Lodesh whispered. "She's a formidable beast."

Markedly smaller than Talo-Toecan by almost a third, she was no less imposing, the size of a small hut. Where Talo-Toecan's hide was creased and tough, hers was smooth and supple. Maturity hadn't yet filled out her frame; she was lithe and trim. The power and grace at her command were obvious. Talo-Toecan seemed clumsy next to her.

Shaking off his wonder, Lodesh steeled himself to edge left. They had to surround her, or she would simply fly away. With luck, they'd catch her before she ever left the ground.

At his first motion, her head whipped about to fix a fierce glare upon him. Lodesh froze, and Talo-Toecan's rumble turned into an aggressive hiss. Head lowered, he promised violence. It was an unmistakable threat even the beast could understand. Caught between them, the two men shrank down, trying to stay out of the way. Their argument had robbed them of the precious moments of warning before she shifted.

The smaller raku looked longingly to the sky, roaring her frustration. Talo-Toecan answered, his voice drowning hers out. Slowly, her wings furled, bowing to his larger size, lowering herself submissively.

Talo-Toecan seemed to relax, and Lodesh breathed easier. She was pinned between them and the wall of the Hold. Perhaps it was enough. Relieved, Lodesh followed Strell's eyes to the tip of her long tail. It twitched once, twice, three times.

"No!" Strell shouted. "Alissa, no!" but it was too late. Her carefully contrived posture vanished, and with a cry of victory, she launched herself into the sky, her eyes wild in her longing to be free from the heavy restraints of the earth. With a gust of wind that nearly knocked Lodesh over, she was away. Talo-Toecan followed a heartbeat behind. Her deception had worked just long enough. Now she would fly.

Strell watched, a mix of fear and wonder on his face, as the two golden forms rose and dwindled. All too soon they were lost in the absolute blue of the sky, and he slumped, turning to Lodesh. "She's gone," he whispered miserably.

His eyes still tracking what the piper's couldn't, Lodesh nodded. "She is absolutely magnificent," he breathed in wonder. "I had all but forgotten."

"She's gone!" Strell cried, roughly grabbing Lodesh by the shoulder and spinning him about.

Jolted out of his thoughts, Lodesh cleared his throat and dropped his eyes. "Yes, well, Talo-Toecan will bring her back. He's a clever beast himself and won't be tricked again so easily." With a last look at the empty sky, Lodesh began to head down the path to the kitchen.

"What—" Strell called. "Where are you going?"

"We should fetch your new pipe." Lodesh grinned. "You may need it to charm your savage beast." Clearly surprised, Strell hastily stumbled into motion behind him. "Besides," Lodesh said. "It's been centuries since I have heard anything played upon mirth wood. You finished it, didn't you?"

"You know I made a pipe out of Alissa's staff?" blurted Strell.

"Of course. That's why I made sure you would be the only one able to cut it. That staff of hers was far too long."

Strell matched step for step Lodesh's confident stride to the kitchen. Their booted feet were all but silent upon the wet, soggy ground. "It's not done, but it's playable. Music from a pipe of mirth wood will bring her down?" Strell asked as they passed into the Hold.

"I doubt it," Lodesh admitted as his voice echoed against the walls of the kitchen. "Despite its rarity, it's only wood, but it may distract or draw her in. It's rumored that when young, rakus are markedly enthralled by music—you may have already noticed that?—and Talo-Toecan will need all the help he can get. She's quite a handful, that one."

"Aye," Strell sighed, "she is."

32

*F*reedom. . . . The word seemed to come from the wind humming over her. No longer chained to the earth, she was a creature of wind and mist. Finding glory in her strength, she ascended, eager to test her limits. So far she had found none. Her wings responded to her slightest whim, reading the air slipping over her and acting instinctively. So enthralled was she with the day, she all but forgot her unwelcome companion, always beneath her, always a wing's length away.

He's old, she thought. He couldn't catch her.

Almost contemptuously, she ceased her climb, allowing the old one to come level with her. *Does he want to play?* she thought, dropping into a steep dive, eager for a game of chase. She fell like a stone, drawing her wings close to keep them from damage. The air, once a force to move easily through, became a roaring wall of sound and feeling, exhilarating her. The ground, once distant, rushed to greet her. Unable to see if her rival still accompanied her, she adjusted her path so she skimmed over the ground at a breakneck pace, her impossible speed the result of her own strength supplemented by her fall.

She tucked her head beneath her wing to see her aged companion still with her. It was pleasing. Perhaps the morning would be fun. She shifted her balance and began to rise. Never hesitating, the old one followed.

How high could she go, she wondered, and could he follow her there? With a single-minded purpose, she climbed. Muscle and sinew, bone and membrane, all focused together. Uncaring of the old one's limits, she rose until the air was so cold it burned. Her lungs heaved, and her wings grew heavy with the furious beats needed to keep her position in the thin air. The sky was almost purple and bitterly chill. It sank into her uncomfortably. The sun, she thought in confusion, looked no closer, and this was puzzling for she had clearly come a great distance.

Pulse pounding, she turned her attention from the riddle and looked down. Beneath her spread the earth, the hint of a curve on the misty horizon. Her rival was gone. Perhaps her day would lack amusement after all. Regretfully, she angled to begin a slow spiral downward. Her muscles were tiring, and she wanted a warm patch of rock on which to bask.

There was a small snort of mirth above her, and she started in surprise. The old one had gone higher than she! *Could he do this?* she thought, her eyes smoldering.

Once more she angled into a steep drop, her wings clenched tightly to her body. If they opened now, they would shiver like thin ice. It was a dangerous game that would become deadlier the longer it continued. The speed of her passage warmed her as the very air itself protested at her sudden arrival and departure. And still the old one followed, his task made easier by riding in her wake.

The air grew thick again, and her pulse slowed. Irate that he was still with her, she adjusted her fall and consumed her speed in a huge, elegant turn. The old one matched her, always a wing's length away, always above her. Vexed now, she wished him to be gone. Slowly, she angled away, signaling her desire to be alone. But he refused to leave, dropping lower to force her to the ground.

He didn't want to play, she thought fiercely. He wanted to ground her! Slipping into a level glide, she allowed the old one to drift within reach. She wouldn't be grounded, she thought vehemently, by him or anyone else.

Simultaneously, she broke into a dive and lashed out. Her tail met his wing where tendon joined bone just above the shoulder with a resounding crack. The old one grunted in pain as he fell away, his wing temporally paralyzed. She had struck carefully. He would recover before the earth met him.

She left without a backwards glance, streaking to the setting sun, to the sea, unaware and uncaring of what she left behind.

33

Talo-Toecan fell. Preoccupied with the task of survival, it wasn't until his wing responded again that he was able to ascertain what had happened. He cast wildly about for Alissa's golden form, angrily berating himself. How, he fumed, could he have been so ignorant? It was a game to her. Once she was finished, he was expected to leave. That blow could have easily been fatal. It was a warning, one he wouldn't—couldn't—heed.

He climbed in search of her, ignoring the dull pain that came with each wing stroke. He had fallen for only a moment, but she was so small and quick, it was hard to know where to look. His eyes narrowed at a faint glimmer on the horizon. It was farther than she could have possibly gotten, but he knew it was her, heading west over the mountains to the coast.

A quiet resolve grew within him. This one, he vowed with thoughts of Connen-Neute swirling through his mind, he would not lose, even if he need mortally wound her. But of course he couldn't. He was at a great disadvantage. He had to hold. She was free to rend.

He rapidly closed the distance between them. Even so, they were over the open sea by the time she flew beneath him, completely unaware that he was there. A shudder shook him at the sight of so much water, and with a last thought of the foolishness of old rakus, he dropped.

There was a flurry of wings and claws as he slammed into her, knocking her into an uncontrolled fall. Down they plunged as she struggled to regain control and strike him at the same time. Hissing wildly, she swung her tail in what would have been a deathblow had it landed.

He darted away, the sting from her talons cutting deep in the salty air. She caught the wind beneath her before hitting the sea. Redoubling her speed, she headed for the distant horizon.

Talo-Toecan knew his endurance was less than hers; he was over eight hundred years old. He was stronger, though, especially in the short term, and his breath came fast and in time with his wing strokes as he strove to overtake her and turn her back to the coast. There he had at least a hope of grounding her. If she continued out to sea, he would lose her and probably himself, too.

Slowly he pulled ahead in a great arc, swinging her to the east. She howled her frustration but had little choice. Soon the ground was again beneath them. Back to the Hold they sped. She dropped lower to hug the ground, darting over rocks and around treetops in a bid for freedom. Talo-Toecan followed, becoming angry. This, he seethed, had gone far enough.

Taking a higher path, he waited for the chance to reach out and physically catch her. He had more mass, he reasoned. He could drag her back if necessary. They shot over a clearing, and free from encumbrances, he put on a burst of speed and lunged. She must have sensed him, for she shifted, leaving him to grasp only air.

Her wing tip smacked into the ground as she overcompensated. Calling out at the sudden pain, she darted ahead. Talo-Toecan followed like a wraith intent on prey. The next mistake might be his last, but he would catch her. His games with Talon, he realized, were paying off handsomely. If not for them, he would have been outmaneuvered long ago.

Swerving through a narrow pass, they unexpectedly sped over a long coastal lake, its far shore growing close frighteningly fast. Talo-Toecan couldn't help a wicked smile as he reached out a clawed foot. She dropped, and in sudden horror, he realized she was going under!

His tail cracked the surface smartly as he pulled up at

the last moment. The raku that was once Alissa, didn't. With hardly a splash, she dove cleanly into the cold waters.

Talo-Toecan braked in a huge clap of noise, back winging to hover over the spot. He enjoyed water only in tame amounts he could easily consume and had never heard of such a thing. The disturbed water settled until even the ripples disappeared, showing only his image circling in worry. She wouldn't kill herself to escape him, he asserted firmly, but as the moments accumulated, he began to wonder.

Dropping lower, he skimmed over the spot she went down, peering into the blackness. There was nothing to see, especially when small waves began to disturb his vision. Ripples, he mused, his eyes narrowing. She couldn't have swum under the water, could she? He raised his gaze in disbelief and caught sight of the tip of her tail, vanishing between the far shore and scrub.

With a roar of frustration, he was after her, her squeal of protest as she took flight only adding to his fervor. She almost tricked him again. Enraged, he sped after her, determined to bring her down.

At the sight of the Hold, the beast surged ahead. Talo-Toecan dropped back, thinking she might be seeking refuge, then cursed himself as she flew over it and beyond. She was not running to it. She was running from it. Snarling, he reached out a clawed foot and grabbed the first thing he could get. It was her impossibly long tail and probably the worst thing he could have done.

She pivoted on a wing tip with a short cry of outrage, slamming her feet into him with enough force to knock them both from the sky. His breath hissed out in pain and surprise, and he found himself tumbling end over end as, in her rage, she refused to let go.

Talo-Toecan struggled to halt their fall and fend off her attack. He, too, refused to let go, and he suffered hard blows. *"Cease!"* he ordered, forgetting she wouldn't understand. It only made matters worse. Her kicking shifted to slashing, and her claws raked him painfully as they slowly lost altitude. He thought he was finally beginning to get the upper hand when she changed tactics and went limp.

Her sudden deadweight caused his grip to slip, and she fell away. She was too close to the ground to recover and smashed into it with enough force to shiver the nearby trees. Clearly dazed, she staggered to a stand in the clearing she had fallen into.

Talo-Toecan was unsatisfied with her state of confusion and barreled in behind her. He swung his tail with enough strength to shatter a lesser being's skull. There was a dull thud as it met the back of her head, flinging her face into the ground to plow a lengthy furrow. Pivoting in a tight arc, he landed gracefully before the bewildered raku. Lungs heaving, he lowered his head and hissed. *Hurry, Lodesh,* he thought, breathing hard. He couldn't keep her here alone for long. Already her confused look was being replaced by a virulent hatred. Her breathing, though fast, was slowing. Soon she would be away again, and this time, she would be harder to catch. He opened his wings and roared in a hopeless attempt to cow her.

"Play, Piper. Play!" he heard distantly, and then the gentle notes of a lullaby. The beast heard it as well, and pausing, she cocked her head to listen to the slow rise and fall of the music as Strell and Lodesh appeared from under the trees.

34

She watched, totally unconcerned, as the two small figures came into view. The noise of their rustling approach had been obvious, and despite her earlier state of confusion, she was prepared to leave. But now there was music. She couldn't help but pause.

"Easy," the first advised. "I'll stay here. You move to the other side so she is surrounded. I suggest you not cease your playing until we're all in position." His green eyes never left her as he spoke. He seemed overly confident.

This pale one—as she named him—couldn't keep her grounded. Neither could the old one. He had brought her down, though it cost him several long scores that oozed a bright red. She could slip from him easily, and the last one that made the lovely music was no threat at all. She would allow them to circle her like wolves.

Fascinated by the music, she watched the maker of music move between her and the old one. She could smell the fear in him as he stepped carefully between the old one's feet, too frightened to come any closer to her. It was pleasing, and she showed him her teeth. The music faltered as he balked at the sight. Annoyed at the lapse, the tip of her tail twitched. She would fly the instant the wonderful sounds ceased.

"Strell?" the pale one called. "Perhaps if you tried stopping for a moment?"

The player of music went ashen at the foolish suggestion.

"You can't play forever," the pale one complained. "Music won't bring her back. You must talk to her."

Never ceasing his playing, the musician fervently shook his head, and she agreed, her tail moving back and forth in agitation.

"What if you slipped out of it gently?" the pale one pressed. "Try slowing down."

She liked this not at all, but despite her warning look and low growl, the pace of the enrapturing sounds began to ease. As the last note drifted away and died, she extended her wings and looked longingly at the open sky.

The old one rose up to thunder a challenge that echoed off the nearby peaks. She reacted instinctively, having forgotten he was even there. Lowering her head, she hissed, thrashing her tail at the two small figures behind her. It was time to go. But first she had to back away from the old one to find the room to clear the trees.

The two men nimbly dodged her, but they didn't move enough to allow her escape. Aiming for the music maker, she whipped her tail in a sharp arc to knock him out cold. At the last moment, she changed her mind, and it went hissing harmlessly over his head. She didn't need to kill him, she rationalized, only scare him away. Sending her weapon in another direction, she struck it against a nearby rock buried half into the wet earth. It fractured into uncountable fragments. That, she thought, should be enough to frighten him.

But the musician stood firm. He was playing again, but it made no difference. She wanted out. She couldn't force her way past the old one. One of the men would die. She had warned them. It was their fault if they ignored her. With a savage growl, she raised her foot to crush the maker of music. He was clearly the weakest.

"Alissa! No!" he cried, taking a faltering step back as his instincts finally overpowered his sensibilities. It was the first time he had spoken, and she halted in confusion. She knew that voice. It was from her dreams. He stood beneath her upraised foot, trembling from his fear, but he wouldn't move. "Please, Alissa. Come back to me," he whispered.

She drew away with a start. His words had started an

uncomfortable feeling of disconnection. Avoiding it, she turned to the pale one instead. This, she reasoned, was a better choice. If she spared the musician, someday she might hear those wonderful sounds again.

Snarling fiercely now that her confusion was gone, she prepared to dispatch the pale one. The longer she remained on the ground, the more uncertain she became. But as she turned to him, he changed. His clear eyes grew thick and dusky, and he extruded a threatening stillness that sent a shock through her. This was not just a man. This one carried death!

"Come," the pale one invited sweetly, "I dare you."

She backed away, snorting in fear. The old one, too, could see the change and was staring in surprise. He wasn't afraid though, and that gave her courage. Frustrated, she howled and swung her tail in an arc to smash him like the rock.

"That's right," the pale one murmured seductively. "Strike me. I've become as Death's brother; she has loaned her talents to me. Pass me or strike me down, and I'll take you to her. Death has marked you. She'll allow me to claim you in her name. Come. . . . I dare you." The man who was Death's brother beckoned gently, his eyes glinting with a black sheen.

Rearing awkwardly, she backed up. Somewhere inside her, his invitation struck a response, and she knew his words were true. She was marked for death. Almost, she could remember how. In an absolute panic, she smacked her tail to the ground between them as a firm refusal. She wouldn't touch or try to pass him.

The man who carried her death ceased his advance to stand patiently. Death could afford to be generous; she always won.

She turned to the other man. No, she thought wildly, she couldn't hurt him, but why she couldn't was beyond her. Desperate to be away she looked at the old one again. He growled fiercely, thrashing his tail in quick thumps against the ground to make it tremble. She needed more room to slip past him. The maker of music would die for her freedom.

Must fly, she thought. *Must be free.* Head weaving, she lunged at the insignificant figure. He gasped, wide-eyed as she landed a hand's breath away, hissing her anger. His pipe slipped from his fingers, and trembling, he reached out to touch her.

"Please, Alissa," he pleaded. "I want this to end."

At his gentle caress, she drew back as if stung.

"That's it, Piper," Death's brother encouraged. He was standing casually, as if confident she wouldn't try his strength again. "Remind her of her past," he advised. "She knows you better than anyone."

"I have known her for six months," the man said raggedly.

"She has known me for two days," the pale one answered.

The musician took a shaky breath. "Alissa, please. You must come back. Do you—do you remember your swim? When we were traveling through the mountains?"

She paused, drawing her head back. Her impetus to flee was postponed by the strange visions his words invoked. Dreams of cold water and gliding forms, and a strange fascination with the warmth of a fire. Her whirling eyes slowed as she considered what it might mean.

Seeing her reaction, the man straightened. "The water was so cold," he said softly. "Your lips were blue when you came back. I put extra wood on the fire, knowing you would like it."

She had never been cold, she thought. Her swim was to escape. There was no fire. But another part of her was puzzled. She had once dreamed of a still lake, purple with the setting sun. Snorting, she shook her head to free herself from the conflict.

"And the gully where we met," he continued, his voice soft with emotion. "You were cold then, too. Your feet were like ice when I felt to see if your ankle was broken. You passed out, so you wouldn't know how I hoisted you from the ravine and carried you to your campsite."

Freedom, she breathed, looking to the sky. *Yes. Free to fly from the cold prison.* Her wings trembled with her desire to flee from his confusion.

His face went white with her reaction, and the man rushed to capture her attention again. "And Talon?" he cried. "She tore my hat to shreds that night."

Talon, she mused, her vision distant. *Talon flies.* She remembered now. . . . *Talon flies, too!* Finally finding common ground between her conflicting thoughts, she stretched her wings.

The old one growled softly, and Death's brother stood ready to make good his promise. "Piper," he warned nervously, "your choice of topics is getting dangerous."

"Alissa! Listen to me," the musician shouted. "She attacked me because we were arguing over whose homeland had the better crafting skills!"

She paused. She cared for nothing beyond an open sky, warm sun, and moonless nights with star-filled skies. This man was spouting absurdities, but slowly her wings drooped.

"You were right, Alissa," he said, his eyes turning from anxious to relieved. "Your people possess talents plainsmen can only envy."

That's right, she thought suddenly. *Those ignorant dirt eaters were so impressed with status and show, they continually missed what was under their stuck-up noses.* Shifting uneasily, she wondered where her strange thoughts came from. If only, she lamented, she could fly. She knew she could outdistance the discomforting visions forever if she could lose herself to the sky.

"You even managed to fix my old hat," the man continued, shaking his head in disbelief. "I was so angry at the time, I could have tossed you back into that ravine. Remember? You laughed and gave me yours. It took weeks for you to mend my old one. I knew you wanted to trade back but were afraid to ask." The musician took on a tender look, frightening her. "I wouldn't trade your hat for the most precious object in all the world," he whispered.

No! she asserted, her panic returning full force at the

visions his words provoked, images of peaceful evenings spent before a fire with a presence she needed more than the air itself. *It couldn't be!* she demanded. She needed no fire other than the sun, no companion but the wind. She must flee. She must fly. To remain alive, she must escape!

"Quickly, Piper. Something else," Death's brother whispered.

"Alissa," he called desperately, "remember your home with your mother? The smoke from her burnt suppers darkened the ceiling, but her smile was as pure and as honest as the rain. I met her before I met you. You're as strong as your mother, Alissa."

Dreams, she moaned, weaving her head in a frantic arc. How did he know of her dreams?

Seeing her indecision, the supposedly weak link exclaimed, "I got my map to the Hold from her!"

"It's my map!" she cried in anguish.

The old one jumped, his eyes going wide. His posture suspiciously confident, he looked to Death's brother. "I heard her, too, old friend," the specter murmured in astonishment, and then louder, "It's working, Strell. Her thoughts are becoming coherent."

The insignificant-seeming man stepped closer. "And our argument over Talon's shelter?"

"It was a dream," she wailed, shutting her eyes in pain. There was a terrible feeling of double vision, but the absence of sight only made it worse.

"It had rained for three days," her tormentor continued gently, "and you let your boots get soaked. Talon found that overhang." He shook his head. "I'll never forget the look on your face when you sat down and refused to move. I was so angry, worried really, the rain would turn to snow. But you were right. We both needed the rest."

"Let me go," she begged. *"I will be lost to the skies if you don't stop!"* But either he didn't hear her, or he didn't care. Sending her tail in great sweeps, she cleared a large swath of scrub and saplings, and the sharp smell of their sap rose to fill the clearing. She was bound by his words, her need to know if it was true. The old one shifted un-

comfortably. He apparently could hear her pleading, but he remained firm and didn't let her pass.

"And the chair, Alissa," the man said, his eyes full of a past torment. "Remember my chair? I didn't move it from your hearth. I thought you had thrown it into my room to tell me to leave you alone."

"No!" she cried soulfully, lifting her eyes to the sun. *"I thought you had!"*

"Careful, Piper," Death's brother warned. "She balances on the edge."

Her persecutor stepped closer. "You must come back to me, Alissa," he said firmly. "Who will I snitch bread dough from if you leave me?"

"I can't. I am . . . I must be free!" It was a piteous cry, and the old one winced. Even Death looked uncomfortable.

"And our evenings?" the man continued mercilessly, smiling all the while. "I would practice my craft, and you would practice yours."

Gnashing her teeth, she swung her head in a great arc. *"I won't go back. You can't force me,"* she asserted, but she was unable to strike him.

"Please," the man pressed, obviously seeing his victory. "You must know it's been I who has gentled you back to slumber every night as you tossed in someone else's dreams of abandonment and search."

"I will not be forced," she cried, shaking her head frantically. *"I am . . ."* Lashing her tail, a twisted oak near the piper exploded, sending heavy slivers to stab at the air. *"I won't!"* she screamed silently to the sky.

Stunned at the show of strength, her tormentor ceased his onslaught. For a moment, all was still. A shudder rocked her, and her head bowed to the earth. He had chained her with doubt, nailed to the earth as if part of the ground itself. *"Please,"* she begged quietly, desperately, heard by all but her torturer. *"Make it stop. I must be free to be alive. I won't allow myself to be forced."* Her wings collapsed, and the brilliant gold of her hide dimmed to almost gray. She would die before being dominated.

A look of horror washed over the music maker. "By the Navigator's Wolves," he whispered. "What have I done?" He took a faltering step forward, then another, his hand raised. Gently he touched her shoulder, and a shudder ran through them both. "Alissa, I'm sorry," he said raggedly. Taking a breath that was almost a sob, he looked up at the uncaring sky. "Look what I've done to you!" he cried.

She slumped farther, her head nearly to the ground, willing herself to death.

"Listen," he pleaded. "Please. You belong to the Hold. I can see this more clearly than ever, but it must be your choice, not one forced upon you. I could never stand in your way, even though I can't live without . . ." His voice broke, and he roughly caught his breath. "No," he whispered to himself, "I can't say that. Your freedom is more important."

At the word "freedom," a violent shudder rocked her. The old one and Death's brother exchanged glances across the clearing. "Piper," the pale one warned, "what are you doing?"

"Can't you see she will die before being forced into something she doesn't choose herself?" he shouted.

The old one and the one who carried death looked at each other nervously. They could do nothing, completely at the music maker's uncertain mercy. If they moved, she would fly. The one who had seemed to be the weakest was the strongest, and it was no longer clear where his loyalties would be. She waited, a thin hope making her muscles tense.

He tenderly passed his hand over her dulling hide. "Alissa," he said, his voice thick with pain. "I would like nothing more than to keep you so you would always be beside me. Ever since we met in that ravine I have only been happy when you were near. But look at you!" he exclaimed. "You don't need me. You're the wind and mountain made real!"

"Piper!" Death's brother shouted. "What are you doing?"

She quivered, seeing her freedom within reach.

The man closed his eyes, torture etched deep into his face. "I have no right to lay a claim to you," he agonized. "No one has. I must . . ." he choked, his hands clenched and his breath coming in a haggard gasp. "Oh, Wolves," he whispered roughly. "Alissa, I loose you."

The old one's roar of denial thundered, drowning out the pale one's cry of despair. They were undone. There was nothing they could do. She tensed to leap, to be free, but her strength left her, pulled away by something stronger than her need to fly. *"No!"* she screamed, reaching for the sky, not knowing why. *"I must be rid of the beast!"*

Tears of loss and regret slipped unknowingly from Strell as he turned away, unable to hear her cry of desperation. "It's your choice," he whispered. "I won't force you to take a path you don't want. Just know that I love you. . . . I always have." Looking broken, he bent to retrieve his pipe and slowly walked away, his head bowed by what he had done.

"Strell!" she cried, her dreams shattering back into reality. *"Don't leave me. I love you!"*

His eyes round in astonishment, Strell whipped around to see her last, longing reach for the sky. For a moment she hung, vibrant and alive once more, poised for flight, wings outstretched, her eyes to the sun, a shimmering vision of grace and beauty, and then, with a soulful cry, she collapsed into a crumpled mass of golden wing and hide.

35

Lodesh watched Talo-Toecan shift in a swirl of gray from an agitated raku to an angry, tired-looking man. "By my Master's Wolves!" Talo-Toecan shouted. "What did you think you were doing, Piper!" Ignoring Alissa's somnolent form, he strode to Strell, glaring as if it was only curiosity that kept him from tearing the hapless plainsman apart right then and there.

A relieved ambivalence coursed through Lodesh. Thanks to the piper, Alissa was safe. He had known Strell would be the means to bring her sentience back, but that didn't mean he needed to like it. Allowing himself a heavy sigh, Lodesh buried his feelings deep. Time was on his side. Strell would live out his span in a matter of decades. Alissa was now destined to live ten times that. Thanks to his curse, Lodesh could remain with her until he absolved his guilt. He had only to wait until Strell was gone. Or she remembered him.

But it would be hard. In order to help Alissa, he would have to continue furthering Strell's position. Knowing Talo-Toecan would never let the piper pursue her was a small consolation. And besides, he thought ruefully as he pasted a pleased expression on his face, he liked the plainsman who had been known to sing lullabies to restless kestrels.

"That wasn't so hard now, was it?" he called cheerily as he came from around Alissa's bulk. Her tail was bent in what was obviously an abnormal position, and he paused to shift it, straining at its weight. Nodding sharply at the result, he trod gingerly over the splinters of wood and stone to join Strell and Talo-Toecan.

So dazed and bewildered was Strell, he hadn't seemed to notice Talo-Toecan's outburst. "I heard her—in my head," Strell murmured. "She—she loves me."

"Aye," Lodesh said in bittersweet agreement. "I heard her, too." Seeing a wing pinned, he carefully shifted the unwieldy mass of bone and hide until it was folded against her properly.

The Master stood stock-still before Strell, his exhaustion barely hidden by his wrath. "Why," he seethed, "did you risk freeing the beast before Alissa had conquered it?"

Strell visibly shook off his wonder, starting at Talo-Toecan's anger. His own eyes narrowed, and he drew himself up, clutching his mirth wood pipe as if it would give him strength. "She was dying," he shouted. "How many times do I have to make the same mistake?"

"What mistake is that, Piper?" Talo-Toecan all but spat.

Slumping, Strell looked to his feet. "Alissa will seldom be forced into anything," he said. "Even if it's something she wants to do." He shifted a shard of stone with the toe of his boot. "Unless given a choice, she will always balk and do what is most contrary."

Lodesh shrugged. As long as Alissa was intact, he would be content. Making a *tsk, tsk* sound, he surveyed the unmoving raku and began to arrange her to be more comfortable.

Talo-Toecan pointed a stiff finger at Strell. "We're talking of the difference between insanity and a sound mind," he all but hissed, "not whether or not to have cookies with tea today. There was no choice to make."

"There is in her mind." Strell flushed. "I saw her in flight." He shot an uneasy glance at her. "She was vicious, savage, wild, and free. She may have been a beast, but she wasn't insane."

Lodesh smiled quietly as Talo-Toecan's shoulders relaxed. Spying a twisted foot, Lodesh braced himself and pushed, feeling himself turn red. It settled into its new position with a small thunk. Giving her a reassuring pat, he leaned up against her shoulder to catch his breath.

"We," Strell said angrily, "no, it was I alone, tried to force her to choose the Hold and all that went with it." He looked up, his dark eyes smoldering. "She remembered, and she refused to return because she had no choice. I took that away. She would die first." Strell looked at the wreckage of the clearing, his face reflecting its destruction. "And I did it to her," he whispered.

Done with Alissa, Lodesh returned, brushing his clothes smooth. It hadn't been easy, but he managed to keep them unwrinkled through the entire ordeal. "You recognized it, Strell. Even I didn't see. I thought you had betrayed us and Alissa both." Taking on an air of formality, he stood squarely before Strell. "I was wrong," he stated, "and I ask your forgiveness, Strell Hirdune." Lodesh executed an elegant bow, but he was smiling impishly when he finished.

"Uh—yes, of course," Strell stammered, awkwardly tucking his pipe away. "She wanted to remember but refused until given a choice. I thought her awareness might return if I freed her." He gestured helplessly. "I guess—I lost."

"Lost!" exploded Talo-Toecan.

"You didn't lose." Lodesh grinned, clapping the confused man across the shoulders. "You won!"

Strell's mouth fell open. For a moment nothing came out. "But—she's a raku," he finally managed. "I thought . . ."

Talo-Toecan chuckled. "You thought she would return to her original form as if a matter of course?" Smiling at Alissa, he harrumphed. "No, not yet, but she's Alissa. She named you in her last cry. She's returned to us, thanks to you."

Lodesh frowned at the old raku. It was his turn to apologize, and under Lodesh's watchful eye, Talo-Toecan would do it correctly. There were forms to be observed when one saved the sanity of another's student. The Master grimaced. He cleared his throat and shifted, sending a dark look to Lodesh. "Your decision to free her," Talo-Toecan began, "was correct. In hindsight, I can see there was no other way, and I ask your forgiveness for my harsh words."

"'S all right," Strell said as he rubbed the stubble on his face, clearly ignoring how hard it was for the Master to admit he might have been wrong. "Who could have guessed it would be her ability to choose that would allow her awareness to return?"

"Indeed," Talo-Toecan said dryly. "I've never heard of such a thing."

Strell's smile went soft. "And she loves me." Abruptly his face went ashen, and he glanced at Talo-Toecan who was, in turn, scowling. "Wolves," Strell swore. "I never meant to tell her. It just slipped out! I know I can't stay."

"That's correct," Talo-Toecan said. "You can't."

"Talo-Toecan?" Lodesh interrupted. He held his face in a careful balance of neutrality, hating himself for having to strengthen Strell's position. "He heard her."

"Only Keepers are suffered to live in the Hold," Talo-Toecan continued, lecturing the hapless musician as he looked miserably at the ground, clearly aware of how badly he had complicated his life with those three words, no matter how true they might be.

"Talo-Toecan, he heard her," Lodesh repeated patiently.

"Keepers and students, and Masters, of course, whenever they're under obligation or the mood strikes them," Talo-Toecan said. "Anyone else wouldn't last a week, what with all the touchy tempers and lethal wards lying about. Just get on one Keeper's bad side, and poof! No more minstrel!" His eyes were distant, lost in the pleasures of imparting doom and gloom.

Lodesh gritted his teeth. "Talo!" he shouted. The insult of his name being shortened broke through Talo-Toecan's fascination of his tragic predictions, and he looked up in annoyance. "The piper heard her. We all did," Lodesh said into the sudden quiet.

Talo-Toecan waited with arched eyebrows, not making the connection.

Lodesh shot an apologetic look to Strell. "He has no proper tracings? And I? I've never heard a Master of the

Hold before. No Keeper I can recall ever has." Finished, he glanced at Strell, and together they faced Talo-Toecan.

"Ah . . . M-m-m." The figure of an old man winced under their combined scrutiny. "I don't know," he finally admitted. "Keribdis would have. Perhaps because of Alissa's upbringing she will be able to converse freely to Keeper and Master alike. Lodesh hearing her I might understand. But you, Strell?" Talo-Toecan turned an appraising eye upon him. "How she can get through to you is beyond me."

"She loves him," Lodesh said softly, biting back a wash of jealousy as bitter and sharp as last year's fallen leaves. "Love shifts impossibilities into maybes."

"So you say," Talo-Toecan said sourly as he cast about the demolished clearing. "I must sit," he whispered, searching for a spot that wasn't covered in chips of stone or splinters of wood. Finally, in what must have been utter exhaustion, he consigned himself to the bare ground, not even bothering to make a cushion.

Lodesh joined him, looking up at the pine boughs rocking in the breeze. "Their bond is strong," he warned. "It saved her. You or I couldn't have brought her awareness back like that."

"I can see that," Talo-Toecan replied dourly, his eyes shut in the sun's glare.

Strell sank down uneasily between them. His gaze never left Alissa.

Pulling his sight from the heavens, Lodesh brushed at an immaculate sleeve. "You may lose her anyway," he said softly.

"She may turn wild again?" Strell gasped. Eyes wide, he began to stand but hesitated at Lodesh's reassuring smile. Even Talo-Toecan opened his eyes and raised a restraining hand. Clearly relieved, Strell sank back down.

"No, she's forever Alissa," came Talo-Toecan's reply. "She merely sleeps."

"When will she wake?" Strell asked.

"Before sunset."

"How long," he continued wistfully, "until she shifts back?"

Lodesh smiled in understanding. Talo-Toecan, however, frowned. "So eager are you?" he grumbled. "It depends." He regarded Strell as if trying to decide how much he should divulge. Then he grimaced. "Unless Alissa has a bit of her old form about to joggle her memory, it can take some time. With young rakus, there's a shed tooth or shard of nail set aside before the first transformation for just this reason. We could have done something similar with Alissa, but we weren't prepared. She will have to wait until her system calms down and she can recall her primary cellular pattern."

"You mean her tracings?" Strell guessed.

Talo-Toecan roused and looked from Strell to Alissa. "No," he said with a sigh. "Her neural pattern is entirely unchanged. I meant the form she was born into."

Strell was silent for a long moment. Frowning, he asked. "How long?"

"Not long. Maybe a decade," was Talo-Toecan's answer. "Give or take a few years," he finished apologetically as Strell went pale.

"Uh-huh." Strell winced. It seemed all he was capable of at the moment.

Lodesh's smile at Strell's confusion faded. A stirring in him as faint and compelling as a hidden child's sob prompted motion. His city needed him. Not yet, but soon. "I must go," he said, rising to his feet to rock restlessly on his heels.

Talo-Toecan slowly rose. Strell hastily followed suit. "Already?" the Master asked. "I would have thought you would enjoy watching Alissa realize her new position."

Lodesh arched his eyebrows knowingly, but then quite somberly said, "No, I must return to my city. It's a long walk."

"You must walk?" Strell stared at him in astonishment.

"I know what you're thinking," Lodesh said ruefully, "Don't ask. I'm still learning the rules of being a revenant myself. It's not much different than being alive. I get cold.

I must eat. All the drawbacks of life," he grinned, showing his teeth, "and possibly all of the blessings."

Talo-Toecan raised a circumspect eyebrow as he assessed this newest bit of information.

"But you showed up so quickly," the confused man said.

"Ah." Lodesh wisely set a finger to the side of his nose. "I knew when to leave."

"His timing has always been impeccable," Talo-Toecan said. "It's practically legendary."

Lodesh's hand went to his pendent, fingering the worked silver. As he did, he felt his posture droop, and his manner become grave. Feeling like the overburdened Warden of the prosperous and difficult population that he had been, he sighed. Somber and tired, he knew he appeared not only capable, but exceptionally so, despite his apparent youth.

"Bailic is in my city," he explained. "I don't like it. He has the *First Truth*. It's Alissa's now, regardless of what you may wish to believe, old friend, and it can be considered a token of Bailic's authority to act in her stead, to claim due allegiance."

Talo-Toecan nodded uneasily. He glanced from Alissa to Strell. The piper had turned to the young raku as well, an almost hungry look in his eyes. "If time permits," Talo-Toecan asked Lodesh pointedly, "I would have a small word with you?"

Lodesh inclined his head graciously, and together they moved a short distance away. Strell took advantage of their absence to examine Alissa closer—now that he wasn't in danger of being bitten or crushed. He picked a tentative path around her, his hands safely behind his back.

Watching his hesitant inspection, Talo-Toecan scowled. "I would ask a favor of you," he began.

"Of course." Lodesh, too, was watching the piper, but his thoughts were of patient understanding, laced with more than a touch of envy.

"You're wiser than I in the foibles of men," Talo-Toecan said. "I haven't studied them as diligently as you."

Inclining his head again, Lodesh acknowledged the compliment. "It's my second craft," he modestly admitted.

"M-m-m." The old Master arched his shoulders painfully. "Ashes, I'm tired. I haven't flown like that since Keribdis and I—in some time."

Lodesh smiled. "Just wait. Tomorrow you will be sore."

A smile flashed over Talo-Toecan. Then he sighed, his attention going back to Strell. "I'm fairly confident if the piper leaves, this infatuation will fade and free Alissa to find a more suitable match, especially now that she is caught in her raku form. Unfortunately, you may also be correct in that Alissa might abandon her new standing to follow him. Her will is even more obstinate than mine. It may be," he confessed slowly, "in everyone's best interests to make an exception of Strell so as to keep a watch upon her."

"By the light of the Navigator!" Lodesh exclaimed in mock surprise. "Break your rules?"

"Please," Talo-Toecan said, obviously pained, "if it ever got out—well, there's no one left to bring me to task, is there." He paused, his eyes lost in memory. "But before I open my Hold to any not of the Keeper's persuasion, I must know the makeup of his character."

Lodesh felt the corners of his mouth quirk. "Talo-Toecan! You take your parental duties seriously."

"Lodesh," The Master rebuffed gruffly. "She is my student. I'm only concerned. She's young, and if you're correct, her affections may be in danger of being gifted to a man who will live a fraction of her time."

Lodesh didn't like this at all. "You wish for me to pry?"

"No. I wish for you to evaluate." Talo-Toecan turned and watched Strell shudder as he ran his fingers lightly over one of Alissa's clawed talons. "Talk to him," he said, his eyes unwavering from Strell as a slight rumble of warning escaped him. "You're a better judge of the character of men then I am. I'd do it myself, but he is understandably wary of me."

Lodesh ran a hand behind his neck. "I know already he is worthy of her," he said shortly.

"Yes, it's unmistakable," Talo-Toecan admitted, and Lodesh eased. "I want to know if he can endure the rigors of acting as a Keeper without a functioning set of tracings, without a Keeper's skills to protect him." Talo-Toecan's eyes went distant in recollection. "It's a rough existence," he said, "tagging along behind a raku. One is likely to get into the most interesting of scrapes and acquire the oddest of scars and ailments."

With a nod of understanding, Lodesh looked to Alissa slumbering in the sun. "You're worried about her losing her temper and accidentally burning him, and you want to know if he has the fortitude to stand up to her regardless, knowing the fatalistic tendencies of such actions?"

"That's about it."

"No problem, old friend," he said. "I will find out if the lad is courageous enough to court your daughter." Terribly pleased with his jest, he laughed.

"Lodesh," Talo-Toecan grumbled.

Giving a last guffaw, Lodesh strode across the shattered clearing. "Strell!" he called, his voice ringing with a companionable sound. "Come with me. We have an unfinished task."

Strell straightened from beside Alissa, his face awash with surprise. "But . . ." He gestured, apparently unwilling to leave.

"These two oversized lizards need their rest," Lodesh quipped saucily.

"But Alissa—" This time he got a bit further.

"Will be fine," Lodesh finished. Turning, he asked, "Talo-Toecan, will you catch us up when she wakes?"

"Aye," he replied heavily. "But it may take a while. She will need to learn how to fly."

Astonishment flooded Lodesh, and Talo-Toecan laughed. The rich sound of it filled the clearing, seeming to wash away the last ugly remembrances of the afternoon. Even Strell smiled. "Ha!" Talo-Toecan said. "You don't know everything yet, do you?"

Lodesh scowled, then brightened. "I never claimed that," he upheld firmly.

Strell picked his way to Lodesh. "She flew," he said, catching himself as he slipped on a loose stone. "I saw her."

Placing his long fingertips together, Talo-Toecan took on the air of an instructor. "That was instinctive, as a beast," he lectured. "With awareness comes a healthy dose of fear. Alissa will have to overcome it. At the very least it will take some time for her to adjust to her new mass-to-size ratio. She will be lighter than she expects as most of her bones are nearly hollow. It may take a while," he finished regretfully.

Strell winced and asked the inevitable, "How long?"

"I don't know," Talo-Toecan said sourly. "I've never done this."

"You have no idea at all?" Strell pressed.

The Master hid his long hands in his sleeves. "It took me—and don't repeat this, Lodesh, or I will hunt you down and butcher you like a sheep—an entire summer. But I was a stripling, barely big enough to reach—ah—never mind. Needless to say, I wasn't very coordinated."

"Talo-Toecan," Lodesh exclaimed. "You were never young."

Shooting him an exasperated look, Talo-Toecan continued. "I'm sure Alissa will pick it up quickly. She already has the coordination and strength, and she obviously knows how." Stretching his back and shoulders painfully, he frowned. "She only needs the confidence."

"That," Lodesh asserted, "is something she doesn't lack," and Strell grunted his agreement. "So it's settled then," Lodesh said loudly, unconcerned he might wake Alissa. "Strell will accompany me, and the two winged dreamers will join us at their convenience. Just don't take too long," he advised darkly. "We may not leave anything for you."

"Bailic will be there?" Strell asked, his face grim and determined.

"Yes," was Lodesh's soft reply.

"Then I'll go."

"I thought you would."

Strell turned towards Ese' Nawoer, then back to Alissa. "She'll be all right?"

In answer, Talo-Toecan shifted to his raku form to stretch and settle in the sun. His tail curled over his nose, the blunt tip of it resting upon one of Alissa's arms. Even if he slept, which he probably would, he'd know the instant she awoke.

Apparently satisfied, Strell gave Alissa a heartfelt look. She was shimmering and golden as life itself. "Good-bye, my love," he whispered so quietly as to be unheard by all but Lodesh. "I will see you soon, I hope." Then with a sharp nod, he turned. Together he and Lodesh headed east. At the edge of the clearing they stopped, and from the shade of the hemlocks they both paused for a last look.

The spring sun pooled warmly, filling the glade with the scents of wet earth and running sap. In sharp contrast were the splintered stumps of trees, their shattered remains littering the once pristine clearing. Rock chips were strewn to look like splotches of dappled sun. The birds had reclaimed the open space already—the presence of the men disturbed them, the rakus didn't—and their thin, piping voices could be heard, discussing the exciting events of the morning. At the center of it were the rakus themselves, one old, one young, both golden, both asleep, a sight equally unreal and natural seeming.

"No one," Strell whispered, "will believe me."

Lodesh smiled. "That's why such tales are told as stories to amuse children." He clapped Strell across the shoulders, effectively beginning their journey again. "You really found her at the bottom of a ravine? What, under the open skies, was she doing down there?"

36

Oh, her head, she moaned silently, her eyes clamped shut lest they roll out of their sockets. This monstrosity of existence was unreal. Alissa held her breath, lest even that make it worse. But breathe she must, and ever so slowly, she let it out.

Aw, Hounds, she thought, as now it seemed someone small and without mercy was stabbing glowing needles into the backs of her eyes. She had been right; breathing made it worse. Alissa tremulously looked with her mind's eye to find all her tracings were clear. The headache was from some unknown cause and would have to disappear on its own. She whimpered at the thought of her unending agony, and to her surprise she heard Useless soft in her thoughts.

"What is it, young one?"

"My head hurts," she whined into his mind, sounding like a petulant brat even to herself, but her skull felt like it was in a vise, and she couldn't help it. For a moment she wondered why they were talking wordlessly, but then she guessed Useless must be in his raku guise. She didn't care. Actually she preferred it that way as she didn't have to breathe to answer him.

"Here," Useless thought, and her tracings began to resonate. It was a far-flung, horribly complicated pattern. Alissa stared at it hopelessly, trying to memorize it but not doing very well. Her head hurt that bad. Hoping it was something to make the pain go away, she set up the first circuit to try it.

"You found a resonance?" Useless asked in surprise,

then, *"No, don't try it. Used improperly, the ward does more damage than good. Best you wait until I have time to explain."*

His field settled about her, as warm as a puddle of brown, sun-warmed water. The rich sensation swirled and eddied through her, fading to leave a faint tingle where there was once pain. Its absence was a blessing, and as she felt her muscles loosen, she practically melted into the ground. *"Ah,"* she sighed gratefully into his thoughts. *"Thanks, Useless. What was that?"*

"That was a ward of healing. Couldn't you tell?"

"Course," she mumbled, almost falling asleep again. For what seemed like the first time in months she was comfortable, and content, and *warm.* But something was nagging at her. She couldn't set her finger on it, or perhaps she should say, her nose. Simply put, she could smell everything. There was the tacky scent of pine sap, the dry bite of cracked rock, and the bitter taste thawing earth. The breeze sifting over her was cool, carrying the hint of rain tomorrow. She could sense fresh herbs and grasses beginning to green up, and over it all was the unmistakable odor of—carrion.

Talon! she thought, and her eyes flew open. Sure enough, a few paces before her was the mangled, sad little body of a field mouse, its neck newly broken. Alissa cautiously looked for the great hunter herself, being careful to not move for fear of a return of that headache.

She was outside, which was puzzling, although she couldn't remember why. It was late afternoon; her entire morning was gone. For some reason she was between her instructor's forearms, because there they were, one nastily clawed hand to the right, one to the left.

That headache must have affected her vision because she was having a terrible time focusing. Anything closer than an arm's length was a blurry mess. Beyond that it was crystal clear. Colors appeared deeper, more vivid somehow, and it seemed as if there were more of them. The sky beyond the shifting pine boughs wasn't just blue, it was hundreds of shades of blue, the tints and hues drifting like fog.

Her hearing was off as well. Higher sounds were muted and dull as though heard through a pillow. Lower sounds she couldn't even recognize were loud and obvious. Alissa blinked in surprise as she realized the muffled melody she was trying to place was a chickadee. *"Useless?"* she thought. *"I had the strangest dream."*

"Do tell," he prompted silently.

"I dreamed I was a raku. I could see the wind, hear the mountain groan, and smell the rain before it fell."

"You couldn't do these things before?"

"Before?" Startled, she sat up with a great rustling of sound. *"Useless!"* she shrieked. She wasn't sitting between his arms. Those wicked-looking things were hers. She was a raku!

"Hush, you're fine, child," came his reassuring thought. Panic stricken, Alissa turned to see him curled up in the sun watching her, an amused smile in his eyes.

"What! How . . . It wasn't a dream!" she shrieked aloud, but all that came out was a strangled-sounding gurgle. Embarrassed, she clapped her hands to her—Oh, Ashes! It wasn't her mouth, it was a snout—and she had nearly put out her eye with an impossibly long, thin finger.

"Speak with your thoughts, Alissa, that's why the Master of us all gave them to you," Useless rebuffed. *"Your vocal cords are all but—useless."*

In mounting panic, she swiveled her head on what she thought was an absurdly long neck to see what she could. She looked exactly like Useless, wings and all. Well, not entirely. She was smaller, a great deal thinner, smoother of skin, or hide rather, and her tail . . . *Oh! How terrible,* she thought. It was twice as long as his, tapering endlessly down to nothing instead of the blunted end he had. *"Useless!"* she wailed. *"What did you do to me?"*

"Me?" he said around a yawn. *"I did nothing. You are what you see."*

"But—what happened?" Alissa looked over her shoul-

der and tentatively shifted her wings, needing to reassure herself they would respond.

Useless pillowed his head on his folded arms and appeared to go to sleep. *"What do you remember?"*

"I remember—the dirt under my nails," she mused, bringing them close to her eyes, then pulling them away as they got fuzzy. There was a film of red under them that smelled of blood, and she winced at how long and savage they looked. *"And the scent of mint."*

"That's all?" Useless prodded, opening one eye.

She thought back. Her breath caught. *"Strell fell asleep, and I didn't notice!"* she shouted. *"Where is he?"*

"He's with Lodesh. We will join them shortly."

Alissa relaxed. If he was with Lodesh, he would be all right. Then she realized—Strell was with Lodesh—and she became worried. As she gazed about, she became more so.

They were situated in a tiny clearing. In the nearby distance, the Hold's tower stood above the trees, that is, above the trees that weren't demolished. Their shattered leavings were everywhere. It looked like a violent summer storm had gone through. *What, by the Navigator's Wolves, had happened?*

And with a sudden implosion of memory, she remembered. Reeling from the shock, Alissa put out what was once her hand. Useless rose to steady her as if he had expected it. *"I read my book of* First Truth," she mumbled soundlessly.

"Yes, your book." Useless heaved a sigh.

"And I changed my mass to energy and back again," Alissa said.

"That you did, young one."

"And I flew . . ." Her eyes alight, she gazed hungrily up at the skies.

"And," prompted Useless.

"You brought me down," she accused.

Useless said nothing as he released her shoulder. Alissa stumbled as she caught her balance. *"You three pinned me down!"* it was almost a shout, *"and made me remember!"*

"What of it—student?" was his cold reply.

"You had no right! I was happy. I was free."

"Are you unhappy now?" Useless asked. *"Are there chains on your wings?"*

"No." Sitting back on her—she guessed they were her haunches—Alissa stared sullenly up at the sky. But it was hard to stay angry while watching the shifting streams of air. They were so inviting, it made her want to leap up and ride them again, just for the sheer enjoyment.

"Please," Alissa heard plaintively in her thoughts. *"You promised we would fly. . . ."*

Alissa shook her head with a snort. Useless eyed her closely, but it wasn't he who had spoken. It was *her,* but a part of her she hadn't known existed, buried and hidden under a lifetime of civilization and society. *"Who are you?"* Alissa whispered into her darkest thoughts. Talking to yourself isn't insane, unless you find something answering back.

"You forgot already? I'm your beast," came a soft answer, and Alissa stiffened in a wave of panic. Wolves! It was real! She had gone mad! *"Don't tell,"* the thought frantically warned, *"or the old one will make you destroy me, and you—you promised you wouldn't? Remember?"*

Her heart beat wildly, and she blinked several times as if trying to replace herself. She thought it had been a dream. She had become feral, and that new state had evolved its own identity to suppress her true self. She had made a pact with it in order to regain control.

Alissa's eyes widened, and she froze, afraid to move. What had she done! She had given her word to a beast! How could she trust it not to take over again? It could be lying!

"A beast can't lie," came a confused thought into hers. *"I would have ripped out your throat already if I could. You let me live because I have something you don't."*

Alissa gulped. *"And what's that?"*

"The memory of your first flight."

She felt herself slump in understanding, and her pulse began to slow. The beast was right. Alissa would allow her feral incarnation to exist as a silent observer. In turn, she

would be able to relive, if just for a moment, the insur-
mountable feeling of absolute freedom. If Alissa had destroyed her feral side, the memory of her first, wild flight
would be lost. She would be less.

"That's why you won't destroy me," whispered her
beast into her thoughts, sounding relieved.

Nervous, Alissa glanced at Useless.

"He can't hear. We speak too deep," the beast murmured, and Alissa felt it settle so deep into her unconscious
as to almost disappear. *"Don't worry,"* the beast said
around a yawn. *"I won't overstep my bounds. We have a
pact, and that comes before all."*

"Love comes before all things," Alissa said timidly.

"Love?" It was a sleepy hint of a question.

"Yes." Alissa began to smile, remembering Strell's last
words. Then she warmed in embarrassment. Strell had said
he loved her. In front of everyone! And she had done the
same.

Useless stirred, settling deeper into the sunbeam. *"Did
you say something?"*

"No, nothing at all," Alissa replied lightly, terribly relieved her beast appeared to have vanished. Perhaps it was
gone for good. With a grimace, she noticed her entire color
had shifted two shades to pink. She was blushing. *"Oh,
Hounds,"* she groaned. *"Doesn't this form have any advantages?"* But then she noticed something that completely overwhelmed her current state of embarrassment.
"Useless!" she cried, taking on an almost red tint. *"Where
are my clothes!"*

Shaking in silent laughter, Useless stood and stretched
like a cat. There were long, painful-looking scratches
across his belly and forearms. Alissa felt a stab of chagrin.
It was his blood under her nails. *"Now that,"* he chuckled,
"would look silly. A raku in a skirt and hat."

"No, it wouldn't," she thought, crouching to curl her
tail over her face.

Useless surveyed the sky. *"You'll become used to it,"*
came his light thought, *"but to answer your question, you
broke them, and everything else on your person, down to*

their constituent atoms, using them to add to your considerably increased bulk."

Obviously he didn't care one whit about her discomfort, and Alissa slipped her head above her tail, not understanding what a consituent atom was, but very sure she was now lacking even the smallest stitch of clothing. "*Where did the rest of my mass come from?*" she asked, thinking of all those long mornings of sewing wasted. Ashes, even her brand-new hat was gone.

"*Your source,*" he answered simply. "*It acts like a sponge, absorbing and releasing mass or energy as needed.*"

Alissa was going to ask him to explain further, but there was a fluttering, and she turned to see Talon land on the top of a nearby hemlock. "Talon!" she cried aloud, but what came out was a low rumble. Alissa drew back in surprise, but Talon recognized it, or her, and abandoned the bobbing perch. The tiny bird hovered, scolding all the while, until Alissa extended a single digit for her.

"*She appeared a few moments after Strell and the Warden left,*" Useless told her as Alissa gingerly scratched the top of the bird's head. "*She knew right off it was you. I thought it would take her all day to get out of the snare I set her in.*" His eyes narrowed in response to Alissa's cooing rumbles. "*But apparently, she is as clever as her mistress sometimes appears to be.*"

"*What a lovely little mouse,*" Alissa praised her, ignoring his exasperated look. "*Go ahead and take it. I'm not hungry.*" Actually, she was starving. That sweet roll was ages ago. "*And how clever of you to know it was I,*" she added warmly, tossing the dead thing into the air. Talon couldn't possibly hear her, but her actions were familiar, and the bird seemed to know Alissa had acknowledged and refused her offering. With a quick snatch, Talon had it and was on the stubby remains of a tree to consume her meal.

Alissa swallowed hard at her bird's rip and tear. The smell of dead mouse caught at her. Feeling ill, she turned away. "*How do I turn back?*" she asked weakly.

"*We weren't prepared, child,*" Useless thought gently.

"It will take nearly a decade for you to remember your first form unless you have a tooth or nail from it to induce your memory."

"Useless?" She winced, holding a hand to her middle as she took in that splendid bit of news. *"I don't feel so good."*

His eyes widened. *"Take a deep breath, Alissa. You're looking gray."*

Alissa fixed her eyes upon the ground. She could still smell Talon's dinner, and it only made things worse. Her bird's dietary habits had always been hard for Alissa to take, but now, with her increased sensitivity to smells, it seemed almost unbearable. *"Oh, no!"* she exclaimed, feeling herself go ashen. *"Useless, I'm gonna—"*

The rest of her thought went unvoiced as she was overtaken by the dry heaves—as if things weren't bad enough. Useless patiently waited, trying not to look too obvious about it, until she regained control of herself again. Near to tears, she huddled in a large lump of misery *"Useless?"* she whispered into his mind. *"I want to go home."*

She had never asked for this, any of it, and she wanted her old life back. Even her mother's rock-hard biscuits would be welcome. Maybe, she thought wretchedly, she could even eat one now. With all her sharp, new teeth, it might be possible.

"You are home," Useless murmured. *"Listen to the wind, Alissa. Hear it call?"*

Alissa looked up, only to be stunned at his silhouette against the dusky heavens. He was gazing deeply into the early evening sky, evaluating it, as she now guessed, for a particular tint that indicated an updraft. But what shocked her was his longing, his need to be in it. Useless, the most reserved, sedate soul she knew, had the lonely spirit of a wanderer, a poet, a warrior.

Sitting straighter, Alissa focused on the pristine heavens as well, losing herself in their unfathomable depths. As she did, a curious sensation slipped over her. It was a relaxed tautness, instilling a curious feeling of a want, and she shifted restlessly.

Useless pulled his gaze from the deepening blue to her. *"Yes. You do hear."* Then he harrumphed, and his usual grumpy demeanor slipped back over him. But she had seen his yearning, and recognizing the same want in herself, she realized she could never go back to the life she had before. Ever. The thought was both comforting and frightening, and she trembled.

"You aren't going to vomit again, are you?" Useless growled into her thoughts.

"Ah—no."

"Good." He snorted. *"We need to go to Ese' Nawoer."*

Alissa rose eagerly to her full height as thoughts of Strell filled her. She hesitated in surprise. The ground was quite a bit farther away now. *"Strell is there?"*

"Yes, and Lodesh, and—Bailic."

"Bailic." The word escaped her in a snarl, and she balked at the savage sound of it.

Useless turned to her, his brow raised in question. *"Your dislike runs so deep already?"*

"He has been nothing but an—irritation—for almost the better part of a year," she thought.

Useless shifted his hide, giving the impression of a shrug.

"He has my book of First Truth?*"* she asked pointedly.

Useless nodded slowly, evenly, calmly.

"He strives to claim the citizens of Ese' Nawoer?" she continued, her pulse increasing.

Again a slow nod.

"He bothers them with demands of battle?" Her long fingers, despite her efforts, began to twitch.

"I would be astounded if he weren't," was his placid answer.

"Then," she concluded, *"I would be done with him."*

"Why?" came his calming thought.

Alissa relaxed in sudden confusion. *"So he doesn't dominate the plains and foothills in a tyranny of cruelty and terror, that's why."*

Shaking his head, Useless sighed. *"Your background, young one, is showing."*

"Don't you care?" she shouted into his mind.

"Of course I care." He fixed a sharp eye to hers. *"But he will only last a few decades longer, and everything will return to normal. He's a passing thing. I wish to put an end to him as well."* Useless lost his outward calm, and his eyes glinted malevolently as he turned to the east. *"But let's be certain it's for a reason that's worth the risk."*

"Risk?" she asked.

"We can't go about ridding the world of evil forces as if we were pulling weeds."

Puzzled, Alissa sat on her haunches and waited.

"You have gardened?" he asked needlessly.

Slowly she blinked her answer.

"Then you know how if you care for a patch of favorites it becomes dependent upon you. First you must weed, then water, then even remove the very insects from the leaves. Slowly over the years, the plants multiply. The flowers become more numerous and larger, responding to your care by putting forth an overabundance of flower and fruit. Soon, though, you find yourself propping up stems gone soft from your attentive care. Even the rain, once a life-giving force, poses a serious threat as it weighs down the foliage. Once sturdy and strong, it's now thin and weak, all its energy put to beauty and delight.

"Eventually, a storm comes up while you're away, and you return to find your beloved garden devastated, destroyed by your own hand. Its neighbors, left untended and uncared for, are less colorful, less promising, but still standing, the neglect and poor conditions having made them strong." Useless turned away, but not before she saw the deep regret in his eyes.

"I understand," Alissa thought meekly, knowing he was speaking of Ese' Nawoer, not his garden. *"But must all the weeds go unpulled?"*

Turning back to her, Useless smiled with his eyes. *"No. The trick is to know which ones to pull, and why—and when."*

"Then we are going to kill him!" she shouted, and her wings, she was embarrassed to admit, nearly flew open.

Useless shook his head in patient understanding. *"Let's say we were going to do away with him. How would you do it?"*

"Enclose him in an impervious field," was her prompt answer.

"He would break it," Useless thought dryly. *"Bailic is wickedly quick with his wards and fields. He doesn't have as much strength to draw upon or as large a scope of abilities as I, but what he does know, he has explored to its utmost. And he is a fast learner."*

"Oh." Her knees suddenly weak, she sat back down.

"And if you have to take this much time to come up with a plan, he will undoubtedly kill you," he said gently. *"Bailic won't sit idly by as you think up a plan of action."*

"Can't I drop a big rock on him?" she suggested.

"He'd throw it back at you." Useless chuckled. *"That is, assuming you could even lift it."*

Depressed, Alissa lowered herself, propping her jaw up on her tail. *"So I can't kill him because I'm inexperienced,"* she complained.

"That's right," Useless asserted. *"And I expect you to stay in the background and mind your manners, girl, or you will stay here and miss all the excitement."*

Worried, Alissa sat back up. Talon flew from her perch to land upon Alissa's head. *"You wouldn't."*

"I most assuredly would—student." He glowered at Talon. *"Go away. You look ridiculous up there,"* he snapped, his thoughts stinging Alissa with his impatience.

Talon squawked and raised her feathers in an unusual display of temper as Useless waved at her. Alissa was forced to pluck her off and sit the bird on her hand as her shoulder was now too steep for Talon to perch upon.

Useless scowled at the two of them. *"I'll never hear the end of this,"* he muttered. *"A gray-eyed Master with a pet bird!"*

Alissa froze in absolute misery. Her eyes had always been a source of ridicule and distrust, setting her apart from plains and hills people alike. Now it seemed she couldn't make a proper raku, either.

"Come on," Useless thought gruffly. *"Let's go."*

"I don't want to." Alissa looked at the ground, horribly depressed. Talon alternately crooned encouragingly to her and glared viciously at Useless, somehow knowing he was the reason for her unhappiness.

"Oh, for scattered tea leaves!" Useless sighed as she grew even more upset. She felt a tear form and slip down to make an audible splash at her feet. *"Please, Alissa,"* he said contritely. *"I am sorry. You make an absolute first-rate raku."*

She looked up, desperately wanting to believe. *"Really?"*

"Yes, really." He shifted awkwardly.

"But my eyes . . ."

"True, they're not golden as are most," he admitted. *"But neither were my teacher's, and he was a well-respected raku."*

Alissa sniffed, interested despite herself. *"What color were his?"*

"Brown," was his quick response.

Brown, she mused. It wasn't gray, or even blue, but it wasn't gold, either. *"The color of your eyes,"* whispered her beast smugly, startling Alissa, *"matters little when you can outfly every last winged being that dares to share the sky with you."* Alissa couldn't help but smile, and Useless rolled his eyes, unaware that she could see him from the corner of her sight.

"Would you care to try a quick flight to test your wings?" Useless offered.

"Now?" her beast whispered eagerly.

With a practiced flip, Alissa launched Talon and watched as she rose, riding the visible air currents. *"Now,"* she agreed. With a controlled leap, Alissa was in the air and circling above the Hold before Useless had wiped the astonishment from his features.

Alissa couldn't fly. She would have been scared out of her wits if Beast, as Alissa now referred to her, hadn't taken control of their actions. It was as if glory swept through Alissa as she easily rode the air, the wind marking her passage in a cool, silky sensation, seeming to hum like Strell's clay on the single miraculous occasion she centered it. It was a simple thing really, she thought, and Alissa wasn't sure if it was her or Beast who had thought it.

Talon chattered wildly and flew circles around her, glad, Alissa supposed, to have her mistress in the air where the bird thought Alissa ought to be. The kestrel made a mock dive, and Alissa eagerly gave chase, Beast taking complete control of the situation. Darting erratically, her kestrel kept maddeningly out of reach. Spotting a moist, earth-scented updraft rising from an open field, Alissa rose high to drop upon her.

"Gotcha!" she cried in delight as her absurdly long-fingered hand closed upon empty air. Snorting in surprise, Alissa flipped head over tail to see where the bird had gone. With a burst of speed she caught up. Talon spun to the right and plunged once more. Consumed by the need to catch her, Alissa pirouetted on wing tip to follow. She was about to close the gap when Useless dived out of the sky to snatch Talon.

There was a startled squawk as Talon protested.

"Never forget your z-axis," Alissa heard him say as he released her.

Grousing as only she could, Talon landed on Alissa's head. *"Oh, no you don't,"* Alissa vowed vehemently, doing barrel rolls until Talon left. A beast of burden she wasn't. Talon could do her own flying.

"This way, Alissa," Useless said, a wary tone in his voice. *"We must join Strell and the Warden."*

Wondering what she had done now, Alissa meekly followed his lead to Ese' Nawoer. Its buildings and surrounding walls were visible in the distance, glowing red in the setting sun. What was once a morning's walk was now a moment's consideration.

"Where did you learn to fly like that?" Useless asked tightly as she drifted up alongside.

"Like what?" she thought, worried that perhaps she wasn't supposed to know how to fly if her feral side had been destroyed. After all, Beast was the one who was flying, not her.

Useless reached out a wing tip and stole a small part of Alissa's wind. Instinctively she compensated, losing very little momentum. *"Oh, that!"* Alissa flushed. *"From watching Talon—I suppose."*

"M-m-m-m," he said suspiciously. *"Look at me,"* he commanded, and his head swiveled close, his golden eyes seeming to glow.

As casually as she could, Alissa turned, praying he would only see a civilized, well-mannered farm girl mirrored in her eyes. For a long moment Useless searched her face. She wondered if he was going to ask to search her thoughts as well, but he turned away with a satisfied harrumph, willing to accept her answer as there could logically be no other. In hindsight, it must be true, for Beast was her, and she had no prior experience. The knowledge was always there, but unusable until now.

"And what marvelous ways that wisdom can be used," Beast whispered, causing Alissa to smile in understanding. Even this short jaunt was absolutely splendid, and she had to fight the urge to dive screaming down into Ese' Nawoer. Instead, she sedately followed Useless as he circled in the warm, dry air above the city, trying to find Strell and Lodesh.

The city spread below them in an elegant pattern of well-ordered streets and buildings. Large swaths of weeds and trees dotted the cityscape, providing relief from the stone. It was obvious that its construction had been meticulously planned out, and it saddened her that such an effort lay forgotten in the mountains. The sense of an impending something was thick in the cooling air, and Alissa shivered, causing her altitude to slip. Slightly abashed, she looked to see if Useless noticed.

Talon caught up and passed them. Straight as an arrow, the bird dropped to the center of the long-abandoned city, down to the bare glade of mirth trees, Useless and Alissa in tow. Gliding under the trees, Talon disappeared. Alissa heard Strell's surprised grunt followed by Bailic's displeased snarl.

"Remember," Useless directed as they circled above the

trees. *"You're here on sufferance, to observe and hopefully learn something. And please, no matter how tempting it is, don't antagonize him."*

"Strell?" Alissa blinked in surprise, and Useless frowned.

"No. Bailic," he growled, then dropped. Slowing to almost a stall, he slipped expertly under the bare branches to the high, open, roomlike area she remembered. Gulping, Alissa followed, hoping she would be a help rather than a hindrance in what was to come.

37

Alissa alighted next to her teacher's comforting bulk. Much to her dismay, he shifted to his smaller form and stood with his arms crossed, silently taking in the situation. A sharp, almost metallic smell hung in the air, and she kept her breathing shallow to avoid it. The sun hung between the horizon and the lowest limbs of the mirth trees, lighting everything with an uncomfortable, reddish glow.

Bailic stood within shouting distance. He looked at her without recognition, his astonishment at seeing another raku almost overpowering his rage. Alissa could feel him watching her, not knowing who she was and what her presence might mean. Her open book was in his arms.

Strell shifted to stand beside her, vainly trying to soothe Talon. He barely seemed to notice the bird's claws piercing his hand. Next to him was Lodesh. With his feet firmly planted upon the moss, he appeared surprisingly severe and determined, but upon catching Alissa's eye, his manner shifted like a fickle spring wind. Much to her embarrassment, he performed an extravagant, graceful bow, completely turning his back upon Bailic.

"Oh, milady," he said formally, his eyes dancing in amusement. "I can't begin to say how pleased I am that you were so disposed to honor my fair city with your presence this evening."

"Good evening, Lodesh," she murmured into his thoughts alone, and her eyes dropped. Having heard only Lodesh, Useless gave a rude snort, Bailic stared, and Strell began to glower.

"May I take this opportunity," Lodesh continued, clearly relishing the reaction of all present, "to tell you your flight today was the most breathtaking display of raku expertise I can recall seeing in my entire lifetime. As I have told your most worthy companion, you're simply the most stupendous rendition of raku flesh to grace these mountain skies in nearly a generation, and assuredly," he arched his eyebrows, "a credit to your new standing."

Nearly crimson, she stammered, *"Thank you."* Her eyes flicked to Strell. He was smoothing Talon's feathers, his eyes shifting uneasily between her and Lodesh.

"Yes, Lodesh," Useless said. "We're all present now, all who would witness the end, or mayhap it's a beginning." He slowly backed up, undoubtedly putting a raku length between himself and Bailic to keep his wards a secret for as long as possible. With a tug upon her awareness so rapid she barely recognized it, Useless drew a sphere of raw energy from his source and physically flung it at Bailic. It sped across the twenty-five paces to slam into him. Bailic brought up his own field and ward to intersect it.

There was a thunderous boom as Bailic turned the energy into sound. The backwash smashed into them, nearly knocking Strell, Lodesh, and even Useless down. Talon darted away to be lost in the deepening gloom. Alissa watched her go, thankful she was out of harm's way.

"Hm-m-m," Useless mused as Bailic rose from his instinctive crouch. The rumble of the blast's echo returned from the surrounding buildings with the sound of distant thunder.

"I tried that already," Lodesh said. "He seems to be able to counter everything."

"Is anyone tied to him?" Useless asked, his long fingers drumming together.

Lodesh glanced sidelong at Strell. "No. I removed it."

"Good," Useless said with a frown. Turning, he called, "Bailic? Leave now, and I promise—"

"Promise me what, insufferable lizard?" Bailic haughtily adjusted his coat. "I thought you wouldn't bargain with me anymore."

"I set no bargain before you—student." His voice smooth and confident, Useless's words slipped easily across the small space. "I promise if you cease now, I will make your end quick. "But not," he added, tilting his head to view the empty branches, "necessarily painless."

Bailic grew livid. "You can't stop me, Talo," he raged. "I'll admit I don't know what the book is for yet, but I've already woken the city, and—"

"No, wait!" Lodesh shouted as Useless savagely threw a second ward after his first. This time the powerful forces met with a crackle of black and gold sparks that burst into existence to light the grove for several heartbeats. Everyone, Useless included, cowered as the pinpoints died to leave the tangy taste of spent energy. It was the same smell as when she first entered the glade.

"I tried that, too," Lodesh said, eyeing the falling sun. "I think it's Alissa's book."

Useless went still. A long-fingered hand crept up to touch his chin. "Oh," he murmured. "I was afraid of that."

Slowly, they all turned to him. Strell's face was laden with a questioning accusation, but it was Lodesh who found his voice first. "You—er—knew this might happen?"

Wincing, Useless nodded. "The book is vulnerable when open and will unwittingly protect anyone who's touching it."

Strell scrubbed his forehead and turned away.

"Then why didn't you kill him when he was in the tower?" Lodesh accused.

Useless shrank into himself. "I wasn't sure, and I didn't want to risk soiling my room."

There was a small bark of hopeless laughter from Strell.

"You saw my room," Useless shouted. "It's a big enough mess as it is!"

"Oh!" Lodesh said, his hands pinned to his hips. "I see. But it's all right to sully my grove with his foul remains, eh?"

"Are you finished yet?" Bailic shouted from across the clearing.

Scowling in annoyance, Useless flung another ball of energy. Alissa thought it was just to get Bailic to shut up.

The resulting boom shivered the trees and made the ground tremble. But Bailic's protection was absolute, and he straightened with a defiant smile. Useless glanced at him and then away. "As long as he has possession of that book, he can turn anything we throw at him to his advantage. Our very actions make his protection stronger."

As he spoke, an odd feeling of detachment slipped over Alissa, and she shook her head, trying to rid herself of it.

"He may not be able to do much against us . . ." Useless paused to give her a sharp look. She was unable to speak; her thoughts had grown quite foggy. In fact, she couldn't recall what was bothering her in the first place, so she contentedly stared at him. "But neither can we overpower him," Useless finished. He frowned, deep in thought, and Alissa turned to Bailic, unable to take her gaze from his bitter smile. For the life of her, she couldn't remember how to catch her balance. She watched, fascinated, as the trees began to lean.

"Talo-Toecan?" Strell said, sounding worried.

"Just a moment, Piper," came his terse reply.

"Talo-Toecan . . ." he tried again as she began to stiffen.

"What is it?" Useless turned, his face creased with irritation.

"Look out! She's going down!" Lodesh cried as he leapt back.

Alissa's jaw hit the dirt with a sharp crack. The metallic tang of blood ran under her tongue, but she couldn't swallow or cry out at the sudden pain.

"Wolves!" swore Lodesh. "What did you do to her?"

Dazed, but not unconscious, Alissa watched Bailic take a confident step closer. She could sense Strell's helpless anger building, and she wondered at his courage. He hadn't the barest of skills to protect himself, yet there he stood. Concentrating intently, she remembered how to roll her head until she had a view of him, then lost all desire to move at all.

Lodesh knelt on the other side of her head with Useless, desperately trying to break the ward she was under. Bailic must have made it earlier and held it in readiness, thereby avoiding the telltale resonance that accompanied its creation. Recalling the skill he had shown at holding multiple fields when sculpting dust, Alissa realized there was a practical use to his art. But why waste that much effort on a ward that only befuddled?

Bailic chuckled. "Your new companion, Talo-Toecan?" he drawled into the frantic quiet. "She is very young—even for you."

Lodesh looked toward Bailic, his eyes smoldering. "Release her."

"I don't recognize her," Bailic continued. "Perhaps you have had her secreted away all this time—keeping her for yourself as it were?"

Ignoring his insinuations, Useless continued to search for the way to free her. Lodesh got to his feet. "I said, 'Release her,'" he said, anger beginning to show in his ever-calm demeanor.

"Oh?" Bailic's voice oozed a mock surprise. "Really now, Warden. Surely you haven't set your sights so high as to pursue raku flesh?"

Coloring, Lodesh's face took on a shocking look of hatred. His next words went unvoiced as Useless gave a silent shout of success. But as Useless sundered the ward from her, she realized there wasn't one, but two wards, the first overlaying and effectively hiding the second. It would burn both their neural nets to less than ash.

"Trap!" Alissa shrieked into his mind as soon as her thoughts responded. With a snap that shook her frame, Useless formed a field to envelop both their thoughts, cocooning their tracings in an insulating layer of soft gray. The grove of mirth trees was gone with a frightening suddenness; his field precluded all else. There was a sensation of warmth as Bailic's second ward burned violently. Then the gray stuff broke away, its protective qualities spent, and the grove was back with all its unpleasantness.

Useless sent a whispered, "Thank you, Alissa," which she returned wholeheartedly, as it had been his field that saved them both. The ward had been simple in its design.

Burn until nothing was left. She was furious that Bailic would use her as part of his strategies.

Alissa picked herself up, briefly meeting Strell's relieved eyes. They were both more of a liability than an asset, but she wouldn't leave, and she knew Strell wouldn't, either, if only to see for himself the end of Bailic. Lodesh took what was once her chin in his hand and turned her gaze from Strell's to his. "Are you whole?" he asked, his brow pinched with worry. Alissa nodded, wondering how she could have two such men concerned for her.

"Curse you, Bailic," Useless seethed. "You've been a tear in my wing long enough."

Bailic returned his scowl, clearly disgusted for his snare having been discovered before it had a chance to melt her and Useless's tracings to slag. Then he shrugged and began to chuckle as if privy to some private joke, all the while slowly putting space between them.

Lodesh and Useless exchanged an anxious look. "It goes too fast," Lodesh muttered, glancing to the west. Alissa's eyes followed his to where the sun was dipping closer to the horizon, glowing an almost unreal red.

A high-pitched laugh burst from Bailic. "That's right. It goes too fast!" he cackled, filling the grove with his dementia. Her eyes narrowed as she watched him nearly dance in delight. The only thing that prevented his imminent demise was her book clutched to him. *Hers,* she thought fiercely. *It had no idea what it was doing.*

"Can't stop me now!" Bailic boasted between half-crazed outbursts. "You're too late. Too late! I've already won!"

That was Alissa's limit, and she turned a contemptuous look upon him. *"How?"* she said so that everyone, Bailic included, could hear her in their minds.

Bailic's laugh broke in a strangled gurgle. A profound silence fell as everyone turned. Although clearly startled she had broken her silence, Lodesh nodded. Apparently he knew where her thoughts lay and approved of her plan. Useless, though, frowned in consternation. Strell waited, showing no emotion as Bailic's laughter turned to astonishment.

"How?" Bailic said with a gasp. "No raku, no Master of the Hold, can speak wordlessly to a Keeper."

Alissa drew herself up to her full, imposing height, clenching her wings to herself to keep them from quivering. The setting sun struck her, turning her from gold to bloodred. *"I,"* she said, hoping her thoughts wouldn't give away how scared she was, *"am a Master of the Hold and a student of the same. I do as I wish."*

Beside her, her protectors silently waited.

Bailic's eyes narrowed as he assessed the possibilities.

Her pulse raced as she moved from her sheltered position to sit before Bailic. The pale man watched in undisguised fascination as she curled her tail not once but twice about herself. *"There was a time,"* she murmured as she examined a wicked talon in an attempt to at least look confident, *"when you asked me to join you, to act as your eyes. Is the offer still open?"*

Comprehension filled Bailic, and he took a step back. "You are—Alissa," he breathed. "That's the book's purpose. I can't believe such a thing is possible!" He licked his lips eagerly. "Can—can anyone work this wisdom?"

Alissa could feel her teacher's eyes bore into her. He didn't want her to answer, but Bailic already knew most of it. *"No,"* she said, feeling ill. Her stomach hurt. If she vomited on his boots, Bailic would know she was only after her book.

Bailic's gaze flicked behind her, undoubtedly reading the truth of her words in Useless's posture. "Pity. Still, given enough time, all things are possible. Perhaps with a little help I might be able to see the way?" He smiled invitingly.

In her thoughts, Useless whispered, *"This is too dangerous,"* then aloud he shouted, "No, Alissa!"

Bailic jumped as if struck. "Stay out of this," he hissed, clutching her book to himself. "Your student and I have something to discuss." Tugging his stolen Master's vest straight, he dropped the book and put his foot on the open pages. "Do forgive me for that ward a moment ago. Had I known it was you—" He shrugged. "Well, you're fine, and it's in the past."

She forced her eyes from her book, her heart pounding. *"You haven't changed at all, Bailic,"* she said boldly.

Useless took a step forward. "Leave off, Bailic."

"I think not." Bailic beckoned her closer, willing to chance her nearness only because it bothered Useless. Her breath came shallow as she stepped over her tail and moved to within his arms' reach, sitting so she could see Strell out of the corner of her eye. Lodesh was gripping his shoulder, holding him back from what would be a suicidal attack against Bailic.

"Easy, Piper," Lodesh admonished so quietly as to go unheard but for her new hearing. "She must be free to choose, remember? Trust her. I do, with my and all my peoples' souls."

With a last pang for Strell's frustration, Alissa focused on Bailic, hazarding a glance at the *First Truth.* His foot had slipped from it, and its pages fluttered in the harsh, red light. Her breath caught. No field protected it now. It knew she was close and had dropped it. Unfortunately, Useless couldn't act, lest the book create a new field around her and Bailic, making her a hostage in the extreme.

"Stop," Useless hissed into her thoughts. *"He knows you're only after the book."*

"I can get it, Useless. I know I can," she pleaded, and then to everyone, *"Tell me your plan before I choose sides."* She shifted herself a touch nearer to her book, sealing her fear away.

Bailic chuckled, elegant despite his mud-splattered hem and the stocking down about a pale ankle. "Really. I think I could get to like you after all." Stomach churning, she smiled back with all her sharp, new teeth as Strell groaned and shook off Lodesh's restraint. "Very well," Bailic decided. "It matters little if you know. This useless, empty relic we stand in was once the renowned city of Ese' Nawoer."

She felt Lodesh stiffen at Bailic's tactless description.

Insulted as well, her eyes narrowed, and she leaned close. *"It still is Ese' Nawoer,"* she grated, her teeth a breath from his face.

Bailic waved a careless hand, knowing he was safe. "The entire population that hid behind its walls wasted their lives trying to assuage their guilt for what they thought was a heinous crime. Pathetic, isn't it?" he said with a sneer. "But it wasn't enough, and so when they died, they remained. It's only guilt that traps them. They could rest if they weren't so—conscientious." Bailic practically spat the last word.

"You say that like it's an insult," Useless interrupted.

Bailic glanced at him, and she shifted closer. Frowning, Bailic turned to the sun. The savage red glow imparted an almost healthy appearance to his otherwise pasty complexion. "I was attempting to wake them," he said, "with some success, when I was interrupted."

"I see no signs of your army," she pointed out, and then to Useless, *"Just a little more . . ."*

Bailic gestured belligerently to the men behind her. "That vain peacock restraining your piper wears the city's flower. He is the eminent Lodesh Stryska, the Warden of Ese' Nawoer, the one whom all the blame and responsibility falls upon. He walks the earth. He's awake. He appeared as I entered the city's green field and demanded his presence."

Alissa swiveled her head to gaze questioningly at Lodesh. She couldn't believe he would appear at Bailic's command. Ever so lightly she heard him chuckle into her thoughts, *"A good bit of timing, milady. Rules are rules, but I'm not his yet."*

"True," Bailic continued, clearly having not heard this, "the Warden has striven to keep me from waking the rest, but I will bring him to heel. Where he leads, the rest follow. The people of Ese' Nawoer were said to have been loyal to a fault to their Wardens, especially the charismatic Lodesh."

Bailic paused, and his face went slack. "But you already know him," he whispered. "Why else would he have

greeted you like that? How is it, Alissa, that you already
know the Warden?"

Alissa's eyes went wide, and she and Bailic turned their
attention to Lodesh.

"Ah—oops!" Lodesh shrank back and grinned apologetically.

"Oops?" Useless raged. "Your mooning about finally
catches up with you, and all you can say is oops?"

"I'm sorry, Talo-Toecan," Lodesh apologized, making
frantic motions at her. "I see a pretty face, and I can't help
myself."

Her book! she realized, and using Lodesh's distraction,
she lunged. Her outrageously long fingers stretched out
and actually touched its silken pages when Bailic's booted
foot smashed down upon their thin frailty. Bones snapped
as he maliciously ground his heel. Agony flamed, and an
involuntary scream escaped her as she pulled away. Alissa
lashed her tail, but he ducked, and it slammed into a mirth
tree with a dull thunk and an accompanying wash of pain.
But it wasn't the tree that shattered, it was her.

"Alissa!" Useless and Strell simultaneously cried. But
she heard nothing else as an impervious field cracked into
existence around her. Suddenly her crushed hand and tail
were the last thing on her mind, as she found herself struggling to breathe.

"Out!" she screamed in the thick darkness of her mind.
"I must get out!" Panic ruled her, and she would have been
lost if Beast hadn't laughingly reminded Alissa she could
hold her breath for longer than the short time it would
probably take to break Bailic's field.

Appearing to go unconscious, Alissa relaxed, mentally
kicking herself for having shown an impervious field to
Bailic. She had forgotten all about him when she so inno-
cently bound that small, gray, whatever-it-was this morning. Could it really have been only this morning? she
wondered as she ran her awareness over Bailic's field to
find it perfect. Well, it won't be perfect for long, she
thought.

With the utmost of care, Alissa made a point of her

awareness as sharp as she could imagine it. She strengthened it with her resolve, then sent it furiously into Bailic's field. It made only the tiniest hole as it shot through, but it was enough. His field shattered, its cohesion broken. Sitting up, she cradled her injured hand and took a gulping lungful of the cool, damp air as she tried to figure out what had happened.

"*Strell!*" she shrieked and sprang, wings outstretched, to where he lay unmoving.

Lodesh was crouched beside him. "Stunned only," he said tightly as she landed. "Talo-Toecan miraculously managed to get ahead of him and deflected the worst of it. He will recover, but I imagine his head will hurt for a while."

"*What happened?*" she asked, her thoughts harsh with worry and guilt.

Twin explosions in quick succession shifted the air. Gasping, Alissa whipped about to see Useless thrown across the clearing. She half rose to help him, but he picked himself up and limped to stand before them.

"Cursed book," he swore, dabbing at a bleeding lip. "It always was touchy, but this is totally unreasonable." He glanced back at a wide-eyed Bailic, then half knelt by Strell. "Will he mend?" he asked quietly, watching Strell's slow breaths.

Together, Lodesh and Alissa nodded.

"Good." Useless stood. His eyes hardened as he faced Bailic. Lodesh also stood, and together they watched Bailic slink backwards, looking like the twisted shadow he was in the fading light. They could do nothing to stop him. They were powerless before the book.

Bailic put his back against a fallen tree, its trunk wider than he was tall. "You stupid, foolish girl," he spat, his eyes darting erratically. "You've made your last mistake. You all have!" Looking up towards the yet unseen stars, Bailic clutched her book of *First Truth* to him with one hand. With the other he gestured wildly in the air. "Lost souls of Ese' Nawoer!" he screamed into the red twilight, "I call you awake. I, Bailic Caldera, once Keeper of the

Hold, now claimant of the book of *First Truth*, summon you from your unrest to serve me!"

The sun, a swollen ball of red, touched the rim of the earth and began to sink. There was a trembling in the air, and it grew close and oppressive. Although they stood alone under the open trees, it felt as if they were surrounded by untold thousands, and perhaps they were. Alissa became more afraid. She felt her skin tighten and her color gray.

Beside her, Lodesh shuddered. Her wings trembled as his face went somber and careworn. He looked no older, but he exuded a feeling of patient suffering far beyond his appearance. "Alissa," he said, his green eyes intent. "Don't forget us. I *know* you can remember. It will be by you that we will all be saved or damned." There was not a whisper of his usual flirtations in his voice or eyes, and she felt a stab of fright. "Remember," he said, and turned to Useless. "Talo-Toecan?" he said wearily, "Forgive me, I have no choice in this." Appearing as an unwilling but capable leader of men, he slowly moved from them.

"Useless?" Alissa said, afraid. *"What's Lodesh doing? Bailic can't command the city."*

Useless sighed and straightened resolutely. "Apparently he can. Whether Bailic knows it or not, it seems your book can be considered a token for him to act in your stead. Burn it to ash. I was afraid of this."

"Alissa?" Strell mumbled, his eyes struggling to open.

"I'm here, Strell," she cried, bending close. His hands rose and touched what was once her face. They dropped in astonishment, and his eyes flew open.

Useless hauled Strell stumbling to his feet. "Come on, Piper. It's not over yet."

Gulping, Alissa turned her attention to back to the grove. Useless's final strike had wrapped Bailic in a field so strong it was visible as a faint black shimmer laced with streaks of gold. It was produced solely by her book and was absolutely impenetrable by all but the most subtle of forces. It wasn't impervious—Bailic did have to breathe— but any show of strength or threat would only make it stronger. Seeing them standing silently before him, he began to laugh wildly. He knew they had lost.

"*I'm sorry, Useless,*" she whispered miserably. "*I thought I could get it.*"

"*I know,*" his thought came to calm and reassure her. "*Bailic was aware you were after it. We will all heal—if we last the night. Together we'll salvage what we can.*" His eyes glinted regretfully in what was left of the light as the sun inexorably disappeared.

Bailic's howl of victory broke over them. "You see!" he crowed as Lodesh stopped before him. "They're mine! Sixteen thousand souls. You, Lodesh Stryska," Bailic stabbed a thin finger at his unbowed figure, "The wise—the just—*the foolish.* I have need of a great force of people, your people, to serve my ends."

Bowing his head in grief, Lodesh sighed. "What would you have us do?"

"I will lord over the plains," Bailic cried, "the coast, and the mountains. You will serve as my minions, driving the plains and hills to set upon each other in a savage rage," he raved.

Lodesh stirred. "You ask that we set the hills and plains against each other?"

"I don't ask this," Bailic shouted, his face twisting, "I demand it!"

Bowing under Bailic's wrath, Lodesh cringed. Then he straightened. "You ask us to destroy what we vowed to protect," he protested with a soft persistence. "We made this mistake once. We don't wish to do so again."

"You will!" Bailic howled, nearly delirious with his fervor.

"We are as you see us," Lodesh said, "because we turned from those who deserved our compassion. It's a mistake to ask us to bring this upon the people we once abandoned."

Bailic stamped his foot in impatience. "I do!" he shrieked, his eyes growing frenzied.

The sun was nearly gone, and by its fading light, Alissa watched helplessly as Lodesh bowed his head and looked to the moss, soft and green under his feet. "We exist to serve," he said softly, "until our penance for our failure is done. We have no choice."

"Yes! I know!" Bailic's triumphant laugh rang out, filling their ears with the deranged sound of his pride. "I command you," he shouted, "you and all your people, to rise and annihilate all who work against me." He began to laugh maniacally, pointing a shaky finger at Strell, Useless, and Alissa. "Start with them," he added breathlessly, nearly doubling over in hilarity.

"Wolves," Strell whispered, and he and Alissa shrank back. Her pulse pounded.

Lodesh slowly raised his head, tilting it with a familiar sly, self-assured air. Alissa's breath caught. "Ah," he seemed to sigh in satisfaction. "There's no ambiguity now. Thank you."

Bailic's laughter cut off sharply.

"We serve the one who wakes us," the Warden said into the absolute silence.

"I—I . . ." Bailic stammered, suddenly uncertain. "I woke you." In the hush, the sun slipped away. The ghastly red glow was replaced by a soothing gray. Bailic, Alissa knew, would be effectively blind. "I woke you!" he exploded.

"You did not," Lodesh asserted mildly.

"No," Bailic whispered.

"The one I serve woke us gently from our grievous slumber with a vision of peace and tranquillity. She wouldn't ask this of us. You may carry her book as her token, but by your request to destroy her, it's clear your claim to act in her stead is false." He smiled, a tired but true smile. "I won't destroy her. I can't."

"No," Bailic cried, head slowly moving in denial. His voice was ragged, seeing his prize torn away even as he reached for it. He had damned himself by his own request.

The twilight seemed to be drawn to Lodesh, darkening him into an indistinct shadow. The faint scent of apples and pine disappeared, completely overwhelmed by the throat-choking stench of decay. *"It's Death,"* the beast within

Alissa wailed. For a moment Alissa struggled to maintain control of herself as Lodesh took up the mantle of skills he had fashioned while abiding with death for three centuries. Much to Alissa's relief, Useless's form swirled and shifted until two rakus and a lone piper watched.

"My lady would stop you from bringing death to the plains and hills," Lodesh said calmly as he stepped closer to Bailic. "As she is unable, my people and I will take this small but unpleasant task upon ourselves."

"No!" Bailic demanded.

"What you ask is an outrage against the dead as well as the living." Drifting closer, Lodesh whispered his next words, but it was so still, even Strell could hear. "The dead," the Warden murmured, "you can do no harm to, and so you will join them. You, Bailic Caldera, fallen Keeper of the Hold and wrongful claimant of the book of *First Truth*, have lost."

"No!" Bailic screamed as Lodesh stepped easily through Bailic's barrier of ward and field. It denied strong, violent forces, but apparently Death wasn't considered a threat, and so Death could enter with impunity. It could enter, and of course, leave.

38

As Lodesh joined Bailic behind the field, a great rushing of unseen motion swirled about them. She swung her head wildly, seeming to catch sight of something out of the corner of her eye, but upon turning, it would vanish in a blur of shadow. The smell of decay rose thicker, clogging her senses in a muzzy blanket of anguish. All around, the mutterings of a multitude of angry voices built to a great unrest. Frightened, she backed up until Useless's comforting bulk stopped her.

The souls of Ese' Nawoer were decidedly awake. They surged and eddied about Bailic in a half-sensed maelstrom of frustration and rage. The torment Bailic wanted them to bring to the plains and hills would be so horrific, the single act of destroying him would wipe the guilt from the lost souls of Ese' Nawoer. The way to avenge themselves had been made clear by their Warden.

"By the Maker of us all," whispered Strell in horror as Bailic's form grew indistinct.

"No-o-o!" Bailic screamed in what had to be utter terror as he sought escape. The high-pitched sound cut off with a terrible suddenness, and Alissa hid her face against Useless, unable to watch. His wings opened to shield them, but she could still hear the horrific sound of sixteen thousand beings rending Bailic's soul. The noise mounted and clamored, filling the glade with memories of regret and misery. Their aching need for this release, to assuage their guilt in a tangible and indisputable way, surged through her unchecked. This was what they had been waiting almost four hundred years for. They would not be deterred.

As the great wind of mental force buffeted them, Useless stood as firm as the mountain itself, keeping them intact, protecting them from the worst of the terror. Still the tumult soared and multiplied. Bailic couldn't possibly exist any longer, but the good people of Ese' Nawoer, too far in their destructive release, didn't know it. They were out of control.

"Now, Alissa," Useless demanded tightly in her thoughts. *"Set them free."*

Turning a tearstained face up to his old, craggy one, she half sobbed, *"How?"*

"The glade," he snapped. *"Lodesh said you must remember. Make it as you saw in your vision that awakened them. Before it's too late! They have mislaid themselves and need to be reminded of their home."*

"Home," she sobbed. Her home was so far from her now. She knew how they felt, lost and alone with nothing to claim as familiar.

"I can't do it. You must," Useless demanded. *"Now! Or they will spread their madness, and Bailic will have his victory even from his grave."*

"I—I'll try." Roughly catching her tears, she focused her attention from the tremendous outpouring of dark emotions hammering upon her. *"It begins with a flower,"* she said grievously, and she recalled the pure perfection of her mirth blossom. Taking a ragged breath, she imagined she could smell the spicy fragrance of apples and pine under the stench of chaos. Her tension eased as she exhaled, and the swirling bombardment of hate, although it grew no less, seemed to pause and take notice. *"The sky,"* she said woefully, *"would be clear and star-filled,"* and so, in her imagination, it was. With a final hiccup, she immersed herself completely in her illusion, closing her eyes. Around her, she felt Ese' Nawoer falter and slow.

"A soft, warm breeze from the west," Alissa whispered, *"slips through the dark branches, no longer empty of leaf or bud, but shimmering with a light paler than the moon. It takes the fear and heartache away as easily as it bears the scent of the flowering trees."* As she spoke, she felt the

wind come from her thoughts to glide like a gray, mist-covered stream about them. Easily now, Ese' Nawoer remembered, and at long last, began to forget.

"Gentle voices," she murmured, and the tension melted.

"Soft music," she breathed, and from somewhere in the distance of time, she could hear the pipes and drums.

"And the full moon," she said with a sigh, *"rises above the distant mountains as the petals drift down, seeming to be peace and happiness made real."*

Content and warm, she opened her eyes and gasped, staring in amazement. The full moon had risen just as in her dream, spilling between the trees in a silken mist to outline their black branches in a faint glow. But the trees were no longer bare. They were covered in a layer of white. The trees were in bloom! It was her imaginings come to life—with one exception. The space under the trees was filled with more than the moon's glow. Uncountable figures were within it, helping to light the night with their own incandescence. They danced, or played music, or rested on the moss. Oblivious to anything else, they enacted a long-ago evening of tranquillity and contentment. Slowly, they began to fade, and the clearing grew dark.

Finally, there was only the lone figure of a young woman. She held a small basket in one hand, a blanket in the other. Casting anxiously about, she suddenly knelt and dropped her bundles. Smiling, she flung her arms wide to embrace a small boy who sprang from behind a tree. He was so young as to still be unsteady as he rushed to her, and the sound of his giggles danced away to play hide-and-seek among the drifting flowers.

She rose with him in her arms. The child pointed urgently to the ground, his feet thumping rhythmically against her. With a silent laugh, the woman bent gracefully to retrieve her basket. She soundly kissed his forehead and turned away. Slowly they moved through the fragrant, white rain. The child looking over her shoulder smiled at Alissa and waved good-bye, his chubby fingers shyly opening and closing. And then, without fanfare or notice, they were gone; the city of Ese' Nawoer was empty.

For a moment they remained still, reluctant to break the spell of contentment hanging heavy in the air. It was Strell who moved first, going to where Bailic had last stood. He stared down for a moment, then reached for Alissa's quiescent book. Blowing a petal from it, he whispered, "What happened?"

Useless shifted in a swirl of gray to his human shape. "The people of Ese' Nawoer took him in sixteen thousand pieces," he said softly. "Bailic's soul is rent so thoroughly, it will never coalesce again."

A heavy sigh broke the stillness, and Alissa swiveled her head to see Lodesh sitting at the base of a mirth tree. His long legs were outstretched; he had a very satisfied air about him.

"Lodesh!" Strell exclaimed. Setting the book down beside her, he strode across the short distance to grip the man's arm and pull him to his feet.

The Warden wearily made his way through the swirling flowers to stand before her. "My trees . . ." He gestured. "They bloom again. Thank you. It has been long since they remembered how to do so." He breathed deeply of their scent, and his eyes closed in a long blink. When they opened, he was almost his old self, and her last knot of worry began to ease.

Useless gaped at him. "You remain?" he blurted. "Was that not enough?"

Lodesh smiled softly. "Aye," he nodded, "in a manner of speaking. Bailic would have caused more misery than we inflicted with our walls and refusals to help. Preventing him was enough to exonerate all of my people, or singly I. My people are innocents compared to me. They were my walls. They were my decisions." With a short, rueful chuckle, he shrugged. "The choice was easy. I, old friend, will never rest. My guilt is forever."

Saddened that he was barred from journeying with his kin, Alissa bowed her head. A single tear came unbidden to splash upon the ground.

"Here now," Lodesh admonished. "I'm not worth raku tears." He tilted her head to force her to look at him. Gazing into his clear, green eyes, she read the peace in his heart, but under it was a longing and regret he couldn't hide from her. *"I am content,"* he murmured for her thoughts alone. *"To serve such a* beast *as you will be a pleasant task."*

Alissa caught her breath as he had given the word *beast* an unusual amount of importance.

"It's a dangerous pact you have made with yourself," he continued silently, confirming her anxious thoughts.

"You know of Beast!" she blurted into his mind, and he nodded, his face deadly serious.

Glancing at Useless, who was frowning up at the night sky, Lodesh continued. *"I spent many hours with Keribdis,"* he explained silently. *"I learned much of rarities such as yourself. She did so take her responsibilities seriously, and they were never far from her thoughts. You're lucky she isn't here. She would spot Beast in an instant and force you to destroy her."*

"She is part of me," Alissa argued weakly. *"Losing her would make me less and serve no purpose."*

"Yes. Well. I can keep a secret," Lodesh said aloud as he straightened. "I just feel bad for Keribdis." Lodesh grinned wickedly as Strell approached, his arms full of wood.

"Keribdis?" Useless murmured. He looked darkly at Strell's wood, and Alissa guessed what his frown meant. She knew Useless would want to return to the Hold immediately, and she didn't relish the conflict that was brewing.

Lodesh beamed. "As I was telling Alissa . . ." He winked at her. "Keribdis would be most unhappy to find all her studies and preparations were for naught." He chuckled. "Imagine, spending hundreds of years preparing for an event and then skipping out at the last moment, leaving it for your—"

"That will do, Lodesh," Useless interrupted sharply. "They're gone. It's impolite to speak of them."

Shrugging, Lodesh crouched to arrange the precious mirth wood for a slow-burning fire.

Alissa's hand began to throb dully. She had forgotten about it, but now it was clamoring for attention, just besting the complaints from her tail. Holding her hand close, she ignored it for a little longer and tried to help Lodesh. Useless took on a disapproving stance, his slippered feet planted firmly on the moss. Alissa sighed heavily. He wanted to go. She, however, couldn't bear the thought of leaving. She was staying, at least for the night.

Useless grimaced. "Let's go back to the Hold. Even walking, we can be there in time for a late supper."

Without a word, Alissa wound her battered tail about herself and curled up, placing her head on her unhurt hand. She set the wood to burning with a quiet thought. Ignoring Useless, she gazed into its glowing existence. A weary sigh escaped her, nearly putting out the fire.

Strell shook his head at Useless. Sitting cross-legged next to Alissa's head, he slipped his new mirth wood pipe from his coat and began inspecting it for damage.

Lodesh was on her other side. He stretched his feet to the bright flames, his breath leaving him in a puff of weariness. "What a day," he mumbled. Sitting up, he unlaced his boots, pausing as Alissa raised an eye ridge and rumbled questioningly. With a small grunt, he reconsidered and left them on. There was, after all, a lady present.

The three of them ignored Useless as he stood, his hands upon his hips, watching them settle in for the night. "I suppose," he said dryly, "it would be useless to protest?"

"I'm staying with Alissa," Strell said. Apparently satisfied that his pipe had survived intact, he began a soft tune. Alissa felt a tear threaten as he played with his old proficiency, every note true and sure upon his new mirth wood pipe.

Useless turned to Lodesh. "Warden?" he asked.

Lodesh settled back on the mossy ground and turned his eyes to the flowers drifting down. "Do you really think I will leave when my trees are in bloom?" he asked, and then louder, "I, too, choose to stay with Alissa. Besides, you won't be sleeping in your bed tonight." He arched his eyebrows. "Slivers . . ." he said mysteriously.

"Oh, very well," Useless grumbled. There was a tug on Alissa's thoughts as several thick blankets appeared along with a dull, lumpy cushion. Useless commandeered the latter, and still out of sorts, he sat down across from her with very little grace.

"Now isn't this cozy?" Lodesh quipped as he reached for one of the blankets. "I have always said a raku makes the best of traveling companions."

Strell paused in his playing to rub the back of his head. "I would beg to differ," he said.

A familiar chitter drew Alissa's eyes upward to see Talon. She hovered and fussed until Useless held up a long-fingered hand for her to alight upon. "You fly at night?" he murmured, stroking her gently to settle her. "Why not?" he said as he set her to perch on the firewood.

Everyone was accounted for, and Alissa was absolutely and utterly exhausted. The mirth wood burned, sending the smell of autumn apples to drift upon the cold, early spring air. The fire was unique and would probably never be repeated. Mirth wood was too precious to burn, but it had lain for decades and was good for little else. Strell continued to play, lulling her to sleep as he often did when he wanted to avoid a reading lesson. Tonight, she expected he simply wanted her to rest. Too exhausted to ask Useless about her hand, she blinked sleepily and shut her eyes. Her last sight was of Useless, his fingers steepled, gazing deeply into the fire.

"Did you know," he muttered uneasily, "that she eats nothing with feet?"

Lodesh laughed, and with that pleasant sound drifting in her ears, Alissa succumbed to a restful and unbroken sleep.

39

White, she thought. *Everything is white.* Blinking in the late-morning sun, Alissa raised her head and looked around. Mirth flowers slipped from her in a soft hush to pool about her folded arms. Their spicy aroma filled her nostrils, and she breathed deeply, enjoying the chill air.

Falling blossoms had covered everything in a gentle blanket of fragrance during the night, yet the branches above seemed full, barely diminished by what had already fallen. Her injured hand had been expertly wrapped in a bandage of black silk. It looked like it had originally been one of Useless's sashes. The binding was so tight, she could only manage the smallest of twitches. It didn't hurt at all, and her tail was only a dull throb. Alissa smiled. Useless must have healed her as she slept.

Their camp was deserted, the blankets stacked neatly on Useless's cushion. Even Talon was absent. The ground where the flowers had been recently disturbed was green with the fresh color of new moss, but it was disappearing fast as the petals continued to rain down in a lazy, sedate shower. It was simply breathtaking.

She looked to find Useless in his raku guise, sitting at the edge of the grove in the rising sun. He, too, sported a thick layer of white and must have been unmoving nearly half the night to have acquired such a heavy covering. Alissa stretched, sending the last of her flowers to join those on the ground. *"Good morning, Useless,"* she greeted him softly with her thoughts from across the distance. *"Thank you for mending my hand and tail."*

With a gentle rumble, Useless turned, causing his blanket of white to slip away and reveal his true color. His scratches were gone, and he looked as he always did. *"Good morning, Alissa,"* he murmured silently. *"Don't thank me for your hand, though. It's still broken. I've only deadened the pain. And your tail was only bruised."*

"Broken?" She froze, almost afraid to move. *"I thought you used a ward of healing again."*

Sensing her distress, he sent a comforting thought. *"Your hand will heal without permanent impairment. I set the bones last night as you slept. What you feel is only a deadening of pain. I couldn't safely give you a second healing ward before your body had time to replenish its reserves. Three days, at the very least. Everything has its limits."*

"Oh," Alissa thought. *"So that's why you didn't heal your scratches yesterday. You wanted to wait until after—"* She stopped, not wanting to say his name.

Useless slowly blinked. *"Yes,"* he said slowly. *"I was waiting until after Bailic."* Unperturbed, he returned his attention to the sky. *"How does the day find you?"* he asked, somehow managing to look regal despite the flower now perched rakishly above his left eye ridge.

Alissa flexed her wings, and with one downward thrust, she made the short hop to where he stood. Petals whirled up, obscuring everything in an explosion of white. She landed lightly and smiled in intense satisfaction as the fragrant blossoms swirled and danced, creating a singular sight. *"I'm hungry,"* she thought brightly, enjoying the novel sensation of falling flowers upon her back. She held her injured hand tightly to her. It didn't feel broken.

"Yes . . ." Useless drawled as the self-made storm subsided. *"What will you eat?"*

Alissa turned a hopeful expression to him. *"Fish?"*

His eyes pinched dubiously. *"I know where you can find a wild sheep, or even a—"*

"Fish," she affirmed, trying not to shudder.

"Fish." Useless drew back in dismay. *"I suppose you can catch one?"*

"I'll have to. I'm not suited for pancakes anymore." Suddenly suspicious at his less-than-enthusiastic response, she eyed him closely. The last thing she wanted was to appear odd again. Her eyes set her apart enough. *"Why?"* she asked warily. *"Is there a problem with eating fish?"*

Useless snorted in alarm, quickly turning from the sky to her. *"No!"* he shouted. *"Eat what you want. It's just— all that water."* And he actually quivered.

Alissa was going to ask him if an aversion to water was endemic to all rakus or just him, when a soft scuffing came to them. It was Strell, still at the far end of the grove. Even from there she could tell the night's rest had done him good. No longer sporting that ghastly shadow of a beard, he looked as she recalled him from their weeks of travel: relaxed and sure of himself. Bailic was gone. He could be himself again. Somewhere he had found a new set of clothes, exquisitely tailored in that shade of dark green that suited him so well. He looked absolutely wonderful to Alissa's love-struck eyes, and she caught her breath as he strode confidently through the drifting, white flowers and waved his distant greeting.

Seeing her reaction, Useless frowned. *"You didn't listen to me."*

"Your warning came too late," she said softly, her gaze fixed firmly upon Strell, the beginning of a smile in her eyes.

"I can see no further good coming from this unfortunate tie," Useless continued.

"I don't care," she whispered. His words of doom fell on deaf ears as Alissa tentatively waved back with her good hand.

Maneuvering his massive bulk gracefully, Useless tried to block her view. *"He will grow old, while you will appear to age but a few years."*

Alissa tore her eyes from Strell. *"I don't care,"* she wailed. *"Is there no way?"*

"I cannot break the laws of nature, child," he said gently.

"But you can bend them," she pleaded.

Useless started slightly. *"Odd,"* he mused. *"That's exactly what Strell said last night."*

"You talked of us last night?" she thought in alarm. The idea of how that conversation probably went filled her with a thick sense of foreboding.

"Of course. We all did." Useless chuckled. *"There was little else of interest to discuss."* Then he turned to Strell, leaving her alone with her troubled thoughts.

"Good day, Talo-Toecan." Strell greeted her teacher first as was proper, but his eyes never left hers. "Good morning, Alissa," he said, lowering his voice and gazing intently at her.

Alissa caught her breath and dropped her eyes. It was as she feared. Somehow, in less than a single day, Strell had picked up some of Lodesh's mannerisms. His words weren't as flamboyant, but his look was just as inviting, just as warm, and said what his speech couldn't.

"Hello," she murmured shyly into his thoughts.

He jumped, startled at the sensation, and Useless chuckled. Still laughing, he shifted to his man form so he could speak with Strell. "It takes getting used to, doesn't it?" Useless said as he coalesced back into existence, referring to the wordless speech she was forced to use now.

"Yes," Strell muttered. Brightening, he turned and favored her with one of his largest grins. "I'm just glad we can talk at all. I don't care how we manage it."

Her instructor's smile vanished. Alissa knew he wasn't enthusiastic about her and Strell's new mutual understanding, but at least he could try to accept it. It wasn't as if anything had really changed. Stuck as she was as a raku, there wasn't much chance their relationship would develop any further. She grimaced, and Useless harrumphed in understanding. Alissa had a suspicion he was glad she couldn't shift back. It made his task of keeping her respectable a lot easier.

Useless looked Strell up and down. "You," he said, his eyebrows raised, "look like an entirely different person."

Strell ran a finger between his neck and the collar of his shirt. "Lodesh showed me his family's holdings this morning. Did you know there's a well for every ten houses?" he said, his eyes wide in astonishment. "And the spent water runs in great covered ditches under the street to irrigate the field we're now standing in! Can you believe it?"

"Really?" she said quietly so as not to startle him, pitching her thoughts so both Strell and Useless could hear her.

"And Lodesh found me something to wear," he continued, fingering the fine cloth.

"You look just like him with that emblem on your shoulder," she pointed out.

Strell shifted nervously and peered down at the ornate needlework. "Ah—yes."

Useless bent close and sniffed in consideration. "I'm surprised," he said, his eyebrows jumping in agitation. "Only the Wardens and their immediate family are allowed to wear the image of the mirth flower."

Strell became even more uneasy, his eyes going everywhere but to Alissa's. "Ah," he stammered. "Lodesh seems to believe—well—he thinks we're related."

"Really?" she exclaimed as Useless snorted his disbelief and looked at the sky.

"Through his youngest sister." Strell winced. "The one who ran off with my supposed great, ever so great ancestor."

His eyes on the updrafts, Useless rumbled his opinion.

"That would make him your great, ever so great uncle?" Alissa guessed, not sure if she liked the idea.

Laughing now, Strell shook his head. "It's sand in the wind, if you ask me."

Useless turned to Strell with a hint of amusement in his eyes. "Can't you trace your lineage back that far?" he asked, clearly jesting. After all, it was almost four hundred years.

"Well, yes," Strell admitted to Alissa's surprise. "But to tell you the truth, I'm afraid to."

With a guffaw, Useless nodded. "I understand," and he looked at Strell appraisingly.

"Understand what?" Lodesh stepped from behind a

tree. Still waiting for a response, he went to stand by Strell. Alissa raised an eye ridge as she looked at them, then Useless. *"Well?"* she privately asked her teacher.

Not saying a word, he simply shook his head. Seeing them standing next to each other, the similarities were unmistakable. True, Lodesh's hair was blond where Strell's was brown, but it curled in the same fashion. Their eyes, too, were unalike, but they both glinted mischievously when they thought they had gotten the best of a situation. Being nearly the identical size and build, they looked like dissimilar brothers from the same family. They even stood the same way, confidently poised, wondering why Useless and Alissa were staring at them.

"I can't imagine why you would have to chart your family line, Strell," Useless said around a dry chuckle. "Just look at you two."

Taken aback, the two men eyed each other. Then Lodesh grinned as Strell grimaced, and the effect was spoilt. "No," Strell asserted with a slight shiver. "It must have been some other Hirdune."

"Harrumph," Useless grumped, seeming to not care one way or another.

Slowly, an uncomfortable silence descended. Alissa wanted to talk with Strell, but not with Useless and Lodesh lurking about. She hadn't a chance to speak with him since yesterday and didn't quite know how to gracefully excuse herself. Eyes pleading, she looked to Lodesh. Strell, too, seemed uncomfortable, and he cleared his throat as he shifted from foot to foot.

Lodesh glanced from Strell to Alissa and back again. A slight smile hovered about him. "Talo-Toecan," he said overly loud. "I'd have a word with you concerning that question of yours?"

"Can it wait?" Useless asked irately, obviously reluctant to leave them alone.

"M-m-m . . . no."

Frowning, Useless turned to the grinning Warden. "Oh, very well," he agreed. "Let's go see if there are still any fish in that puny ditch of yours you so elegantly name a spring."

"Fish?" Lodesh cried as they moved away. "Of course there're fish. It wouldn't be a spring without fish."

Alissa laughed silently for a moment, then slumped.

"Oh, Alissa," Strell said ruefully. "We've got ourselves in a nasty tangle." Collapsing where he was, he lay back to look dejectedly up at the branches thick with flowers.

Curling up, Alissa rested her head on her tail. Her eyes were nearly level with Strell's now, and she could almost forget she was stuck in this leathery excuse for a body. *"Useless warned me,"* she thought wearily, *"but I don't care."*

"Me neither." Pulling his gaze from the heavens, he met her eyes. "Talo-Toecan says it will be years before I see your face as I recall it."

"I know." Heavy-hearted, Alissa puffed at a flower as it fell, and it went whirling away to lose itself with the rest.

"I'll wait," Strell assured her quickly, almost desperately. "You know I will." His eyes shone defiantly as if expecting her to deny his claim.

"I know." She sighed again as she felt tears threaten. It just wasn't fair. Strell had done so much. She would have remained feral if not for him.

"But I can't stay," he said. "Talo-Toecan won't allow it. It's not safe."

"Talo-Toecan," she thought fiercely, her frustration spilling into anger. *"Talo-Toecan! I'm sick of what he says!"*

"He is the architect of the Hold," Strell said gently. "He has a right to make the rules."

Alissa's head rose in protest. *You spent all winter!* She desperately grasped at any excuse, but she knew it was a losing battle. Strell wasn't even trying. He had already resigned himself to leaving.

Shaking his head, he placed his now small-looking hand upon hers. "Yes, and see what happened? Since I've met you, I have nearly lost my life—what—nearly half a dozen times?"

Alissa drew her head back in surprise. *"It hasn't been that bad."*

Strell began ticking off his fingers. "Let's see. I was attacked by a raku . . ."

"No," she objected, her eyes wide.

Smiling faintly, he nodded. "Yesterday, by you."

"Oh." Crestfallen, she dropped her head back down.

"Nearly fell to my death freeing Talo-Toecan, suffered a concussion when you blew the wards off your window."

"Sorry," she quietly apologized.

"Broke my ankle, lost my finger, burned my hand—"

"I can fix that now," she interrupted, forcing herself to sound cheery. *"Or will soon,"* she added, remembering that Useless hadn't actually given her permission to try the difficult ward yet.

Seeming to ignore her, Strell continued. "Suffered Bailic's wards—completely at his mercy." Pursing his lips, Strell frowned. Blinking, he came back to the present. "We all could have died last night."

"He's gone now," she said in a small thought as Talon arrived in her usual suddenness. Alissa had heard the wind slipping under her wings, but Strell jumped.

"Oh, yes," he added, "and attacked by your feathered defender here." For a moment they fussed over Talon's catch, a fine little shrew.

"Talon would never hurt you now," she crooned as she tossed Talon's breakfast to her. Snatching it, the kestrel flew only a short distance before tearing into it with gusto.

"I'm not complaining, mind you," Strell said, picking up his earlier thought, "but you get the idea. The rules are strict for a good reason. It was only because there were no Keepers that I lasted as long as I did. Talo-Toecan says a new, raw batch of students will begin to show up now that Bailic is gone. He says they will be all fire and temper, and he thinks I won't survive more than a week once they begin to experiment with their newfound skills."

"It's not that dangerous," she muttered petulantly.

Shrugging, Strell met her gaze. "You're right, but try convincing him of that. I spent all night and got absolutely nowhere." He turned to where Useless and Lodesh were strenuously arguing in the distance.

Positively miserable, Alissa looked down. She couldn't bear the thought of him leaving. Not now. Not ever. *"How long can you stay?"* she found herself asking, her throat tight with grief.

Strell pushed the petals aside with the toe of his boot. "A few days. The lower passes have been open for weeks. Maybe come fall, I could show up and get conveniently snowbound."

The thought cheered her somewhat, and she returned her sorrowful eyes to Strell.

"I don't care if you have little white feet, or large clawed ones, Alissa," Strell pleaded. "I just want to be with you. In ten years or so, perhaps . . ." He stopped and looked at the ground.

Ten years, she thought, her sight beginning to swim. It was a long time.

"Oh, here," Strell said awkwardly as he began to search his pockets as if looking for a distraction. "Lodesh thought I should give this to you." Digging deep, he pulled out a fold of yellow cloth and opened it to reveal a round bit of gold lace. He placed it in her hand. "I don't really need it," he explained. "He thought you might like to have it."

Looking at it so small and frail in her hand, she frowned. *"It's a love charm,"* she said, her thoughts full of wonder that such an exquisite thing existed. *"You made this?"*

Strell dropped his gaze to his feet, his ears reddening. "Yes, well, I had some extra, and well—you know."

"Extra?" she asked with a stirring of hope. *"Extra hair?"*

Strell smiled faintly. "Remember your luck charm? In order to be most effective, you need to craft a charm from a lock of hair."

"Whose?" she breathed.

"Well, yours of course!" Strell began to look worried.

"It's mine!" Alissa exclaimed as her hand went up to her nonexistent hair and she stood in a flurry of petals.

Strell's eyes widened in alarm. "I'm sorry," he apologized as he rose as well. "I didn't think—" The rest of his thought went unvoiced as he watched, openmouthed, as the small bit of gold winked out of existence.

"No! Wait!" Useless shouted in exasperation from across the clearing.

"What!" Strell cried, backing up as she winked out of existence in a swirl of pearly white. "What did I do?"

Excess mass reverted easily back to energy and flowed to her source as she accessed her original cellular pattern, her memory of it triggered by Strell's love charm, never to be forgotten again. Strell was ill prepared when she coalesced back into reality and beaming, threw herself into his arms. Her old clothes were gone, replaced by a too-large, gold-colored robe, tied loosely about her with a black sash. It was so big, she was lost among its folds, but at least it covered her. She didn't care where it had come from. She only knew she was back, and Strell was here, and he could hold her.

"Oh, Strell," she sobbed into his shoulder. She wasn't sure if they were tears of joy or sadness. He still had to leave, only now it was a hundred times worse. Clearly bewildered, Strell held her tightly as she cried. In the distance, Alissa could hear Lodesh and Useless approach.

"Come on, Talo-Toecan," Lodesh cajoled. "I know you aren't cold blooded. Show me your heart isn't, either. Just look at that pitiful display. You can't say no now. Let the piper stay."

Her head buried against Strell's shoulder, Alissa caught her breath in hope. The sudden throbbing of her broken hand was all but unnoticed. Strell, too, was still, and together they waited as first Useless grimaced and then finally sighed. "I cannot hope to prevail when you begin to scheme against me, Warden," he said dryly. "The piper may stay."

Overjoyed, Alissa turned a tear-wet face to Strell's and smiled expansively up at him. "You can stay. . . ." she breathed, absolutely elated.

"Provided," Useless continued sharply, "he agrees to

several stipulations, which I will come up with in the very near future."

"Anything," Strell whispered, and he held her close.

Useless's eyes narrowed. "Tell me, Lodesh. What was it he gave her?"

"A love knot, of course." Lodesh chuckled, drawing her teacher unwillingly away.

"Made from her hair?" Useless asked, craning his head back over his shoulder at Strell and Alissa.

"What else?" The Warden of Ese' Nawoer took Useless's elbow firmly and led him off through the slowly drifting blossoms. "I must admit," Lodesh said slyly, "the robe was rather thoughtful of you. A little big for her though, isn't it?"

"I only know one size," came his voice, beginning to go faint with the distance. "I will not have my student wandering about naked to the wind. I'm just glad you got us back before she completed her shift."

Losing herself in Strell's embrace, Alissa barely heard Lodesh's merry laugh. "That," he cried, "was the easy part. It was, after all, only a matter of timing, old friend. Only a matter of timing."